Gift-Wrapped Love

Have these ladies unwrapped more than they
bargained for this Christmas?

Three passionate novels!

In November 2006 Mills & Boon bring
back two of their classic collections,
each featuring three favourite
romances by our bestselling authors…

GIFT-WRAPPED LOVE

Christmas Knight by Meredith Webber
Christmas in Paris by Margaret Barker
Home by Christmas by Jennifer Taylor

BLACKMAILED BRIDES

The Blackmailed Bride
by Kim Lawrence
Bride by Blackmail by Carole Mortimer
Blackmailed by the Boss
by Kathryn Ross

Gift-Wrapped Love

CHRISTMAS KNIGHT
by
Meredith Webber

CHRISTMAS IN PARIS
by
Margaret Barker

HOME BY CHRISTMAS
by
Jennifer Taylor

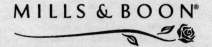
MILLS & BOON®

*MILLS & BOON and MILLS & BOON with the Rose Device
are registered trademarks of the publisher.
Harlequin Mills & Boon Limited,
Eton House, 18-24 Paradise Road, Richmond, Surrey, TW9 1SR*

GIFT-WRAPPED LOVE
© by Harlequin Enterprises II B.V., 2006

Christmas Knight, Christmas in Paris and Home by Christmas
were first published in Great Britain by Harlequin Mills & Boon
Limited in separate, single volumes.

Christmas Knight © Meredith Webber 2002
Christmas in Paris © Margaret Barker 2002
Home by Christmas © Jennifer Taylor 2002

ISBN 10: 0 263 84973 2
ISBN 13: 978 0 263 84973 8

05-1106

*Printed and bound in Spain
by Litografia Rosés S.A., Barcelona*

CHRISTMAS KNIGHT

by

Meredith Webber

Meredith Webber says of herself, 'Some ten years ago, I read an article which suggested that Mills & Boon® were looking for new medical authors. I had one of those "I can do that" moments, and gave it a try. What began as a challenge has become an obsession, though I do temper the 'butt on seat' career of writing with dirty but healthy outdoor pursuits, fossicking through the Australian outback in search of gold or opals. Having had some success in all of these endeavours, I now consider I've found the perfect lifestyle.'

CHAPTER ONE

TROUBLE rode into Testament on a hot sultry summer afternoon. The storm clouds hanging low above the lone motorcycle rider were nearly as black as the full suit of leathers he wore.

The shiny black and chrome bike tooled slowly up the main street, then turned and came back down.

'Here's trouble,' Mrs Ellis, on the stoop outside the newsagent's, said to no one in particular.

'Trouble if there's more than one of them,' Dick Harris, the local police sergeant, muttered to his constable.

'Trouble looking for somewhere to stop!' old man Carey, who was propping up the table by the window of the pub, told his mate Digger, though Digger showed little interest, continuing to sniff at a greasy spot on the pub floor as if it might offer a new taste sensation.

The bike slowed outside the pub, and a helmeted head turned towards the building, as if the rider might be tempted to try a cold one, then the motor revved, and the rider continued. Down the street, past the school, then left towards the northern end of town.

Another tourist passing through.

Those inhabitants of Testament who'd seen him pass forgot about him, though perhaps with an unidentified sense of regret, as if a little excitement might have brightened up their lives.

In the big house next door to the hospital, Kate Fenton knew nothing of this. She was in her bedroom, peering down into a crib and giving the little alien who'd so disrupted her life what for!

'The trouble with you is,' she said, to the now sleeping

5

baby, 'you've got no sense of timing. No understanding of the simple words, Wait just a minute. If we could sort this out, we might get somewhere, but, no, you're just like your father—demanding instant gratification.'

She heard her own words, cursed loudly, then added apologetically, 'I'm sorry for that last remark. I swore I'd never use that ''just like your father'' phrase. After all, I'm the one who decided to have you, so I can hardly blame him for anything, can I? Particularly not when he's washed his hands of both of us.'

The baby moved milk-rimmed lips and slept on, while Kate studied the tiny face, the dark eyelashes like feathery caterpillars against the still crumpled skin, the miniature fingers clenched into fists as if the little scrap was ready to take on the world.

'Damn, but you're useless!' she muttered, swearing for the second time in as many minutes. If she didn't stop this habit right now, the 'damn' word would be the first the baby said.

And that thought made her say it again, though she did promise herself it would be the last—the very last—time! 'Jeez Louise', her favourite expression of despair back when she was a student, still living at home, might work. Though it would mean dicing Louise from the 'perhapses' for a name.

A rumbling outside made her glance towards the French doors, open to catch the slightest hint of breeze. The storm must be closer than she'd thought. Though the next sound, footsteps across the front veranda followed by a pounding on the front door, suggested the rumbling noise might have been something else.

She cast one final and now worried glance at the baby, then walked, soft-footed, to the bedroom door, closing it behind her. Her stomach cramped with the anxiety that had been such a totally unexpected consequence of giving birth, she doubted she'd ever get used to it.

Given the heat, the front door was also wide open, so, as she stepped into the hall, she saw the tall, dark-clad figure looming in the square of light, and beyond it, on the drive, a hulking black and silver monster of a motorbike. Her anxiety turned to panic.

'Can I help you?' she said, moving quickly as if speed might somehow lessen any risk to the baby.

'Dr Fenton?'

There was so much doubt and disbelief in the deep male voice that Kate found herself checking her body to make sure she was dressed. These days, if there'd been no morning surgery, she was just as likely to be in her night-attire at midday.

But today she was OK—her post-pregnancy tummy squashed into old jeans, and a reasonably milk-free cropped top ending somewhere near her midriff.

'Yes,' she said, stepping more cautiously towards him now.

'Katie Fenton, the bank manager's daughter?'

The 'd' word reverberated in her head again, but she managed to keep it internal, while peering at the leather-clad colossus leaning negligently on her doorjamb.

Was she supposed to know him? Was it someone with whom she'd been at school?

'You're supposed to be pregnant!' he said, in such accusing tones she almost apologised, but by now she could see his face more clearly, and a vague stirring of memory, more sensory than mental, was shifting her emotions to a new level of disquiet.

'Pregnancies aren't permanent, you know,' she told him, telling herself it couldn't possibly be Grant Bell. The Bells had all left town when the bank had foreclosed on their property—her father's bank, in fact. She herself had heard Grant say no one would ever see him in Testament again— words which, at the time, had broken her heart...

'You mean you've already had the baby? When? Where

is it? You *did* keep it, I assume. And how the hell have you been handling the practice, childbirth and a new baby all on your own?'

He sounded cross, but not nearly as cross as she was becoming, standing here in her own hall, being berated by a stranger—whether he was Grant Bell or not.

'With a great deal of difficulty, if you must know,' she told him, hoping the ice she'd managed to inject into her voice might stop him asking personal questions. 'Now, if you want to see me professionally, the surgery, which is through the side entrance to the yard, will open at six.' Then she remembered it was Sunday. 'No, it won't, but you can go to the hospital and if they need me they'll call.'

She moved forward, intending to shut the door, then realised he was leaning against the hinged side of it.

He must have guessed her intentions for he stepped backwards, but put up a hand.

'It's too darned hot to shut it. Anyway, I'm coming in.'

He began to strip off his leather jacket as he spoke, peeling it away like a second skin, to reveal a lurid Hawaiian shirt, printed with unlikely flowers in shades of red, green and purple. Then, as the leather jacket was slung on a chair near the door, he started on the trousers, unzipping them, then easing them down over blue board shorts and long, solid legs with a sheen of dark hair slicked to them by the leather.

Kate dragged her eyes away from the legs for long enough to recall his final sentence.

'There's no surgery today but the hospital is just next door,' she repeated, because 'no, you can't come in' would have sounded rude to a stranger. Certainly to a stranger bigger and stronger than she was.

He glanced up from reefing his boots off his feet, and as he grinned at her, she realised it might, indeed, be Grant Bell.

'I've not come as a patient, but as your knight in shining

armour.' He straightened and spread his arms wide as if presenting himself for inspection. 'Do you still read fantasy romances, Katie Fenton?'

'Kate, not Katie,' she said in her most professional tones, then she realised her name wasn't the point—his was! 'Who *are* you?'

Her visitor grinned, his blue eyes gleaming in his sun-tanned face.

'You don't go for the knight in shining armour? How about a knight in dusty leathers?' Again he held out his arms. 'Don't you know me, Katie? Don't you remember the boy who—?'

Kate felt embarrassment start way down in her toes and wash upward through her body, so her thighs and breasts and cheeks all burned with it.

'Grant? Grant Bell?' Her voice was so faint—forget the voice, *she* was so faint—it was a wonder he heard it.

'Aha, you do remember!' he said, and she had a feeling his delight stemmed more from the hectic colour in her cheeks than from her muttered delivery of his name.

'So! Shall I come in?'

'No!'

Kate wasn't sure why she'd said it so firmly, but Grant Bell had been trouble all his life, and there was no way she was inviting him into her house. Particularly now, when she had the baby to consider.

And more particularly now, when bits of her she'd thought would lie dormant for ever were reacting, if not to his presence then to the almost forgotten memories he'd conjured up.

'No!' she said again, frowning at him to reinforce the word, while he was studying her, if not with a frown then with a definitely puzzled look in his eyes.

'But—' he began.

'No!' she said again, then, right on cue, a thin wail rose above the distant rumble—this time it *was* thunder—and

Kate knew it was only a matter of seconds before the wail
became a demand and, seconds past that stage, a furious
complaint.

'The baby's crying.' Grant stated the obvious while Kate
hesitated, wanting to shut the door, to shut him out, but
knowing every other door onto the veranda was open so
shutting this one was no guarantee of keeping him out.
'How old is it? Was it premmie, or did you have your dates
wrong?'

He grinned as he asked the last question, and once again
hot flushes of embarrassment flooded her body, as more
memories returned to mortify her.

'I've got to go,' she gabbled at him, and now she did
shut the door.

As the noise had reached demand stage, she went straight
to the bedroom, lifted the red-faced mite from the bassinet
and held the tiny form against her shoulder, patting her
gently on the back and murmuring soothing nothings to her.

The baby obliged by burping sickly-sweet-smelling milk
onto Kate's shoulder, so she felt the dampness seep through
her cotton top to her skin—skin which was still hot with
memories of Grant Bell, explaining the facts of life to her,
though using cattle as examples so her knowledge of sex,
at twelve, was badly skewed.

A mistake not sorted out in spite of sex education classes,
until she was sixteen, when he'd demonstrated how it
worked with humans, down by the creek, one hot and hu-
mid summer afternoon, two days before her father had foreclosed on Grant's parents' property and a month before the
family had left the district for ever.

'Didn't you know I was coming? Didn't Aunt Vi tell
you?'

The cause of her embarrassment walked through the
French doors.

'The baby looks as if it's gone back to sleep. Is it a girl
or a boy? What did you call it?'

He'd never waited for an answer to his questions, Kate remembered, as she set aside the last series to concentrate on the first.

'Tell me what?' she demanded. 'What was Vi supposed to tell me?'

Once again, Grant spread his arms wide.

'That I was coming,' he said, so obviously pleased with himself Kate wanted to throw something.

But all she had to hand was the baby, so that wasn't a good idea.

She settled the little one back into the bassinet, then, knowing for sure that Grant Bell on her veranda was better than Grant Bell in her house, she walked towards him, put one hand on his chest and pushed him back out the door.

Well, she pushed and he backed up. Had he not wanted to move she doubted whether he'd have gone anywhere.

'What's with you?' he complained, grasping her by the shoulders to stop her pushing him any further. 'Why the antagonism? If anyone should be feeling leftover anger, it's me, Angel-Face. After all, it was your father who tossed my family off the property.'

'It was the bank that foreclosed. My father was just the instrument they used. He hated doing it,' Kate told him, then she added, a little late and with far too little venom, 'And don't call me Angel-Face.'

Broad shoulders lifted in a shrug and a cheeky smile that had, if anything, improved with the years stretched his lips.

'Sorry, Katie,' he said softly, and she had to step away from him before she could reply.

'And don't call me that either! Katie's a kid's name and, in case you hadn't noticed, I'm all grown up now.'

Eyes as blue as summer skies skimmed across her body, scorching where they touched.

'Oh, I'd noticed,' he murmured, and the way he said it made her conscious of her untoned stomach, overly large breasts and the damp, smelly milk stain. 'So, what do I call you? Katherine? Dr Fenton?'

'You don't have to call me anything, because you won't be seeing any more of me. It would have been great to catch up, and I hope you enjoy your visit to Vi, but right now I'm flat out, what with the baby and the practice and all, so we might as well say goodbye and you can get on your bike and ride off into the sunset.'

It was a pretty good speech, she thought, then her brain, which hadn't been working well for months and seemed to have lost even more usable cells since she'd given birth, prompted her to add, 'My friends call me Kate.'

His smile finally faded, which made looking at him slightly easier, though now she could see past its attraction to the little lines fanned out from his eyes, the faint furrows in his forehead, the fine creases that smile had pressed into his cheeks.

Grant Bell—all grown up!

All grown up into a ruggedly handsome man.

'Katie,' he said, speaking slowly as if he realised her brain cells were dying by the million, 'I'm here to stay. I'm your locum. Didn't Vi explain? The woman who was to come took up a permanent position, and the agency was scrabbling to find someone. Vi knew I was at a loose end for a couple of months, so she got in touch and here I am.'

He did the hands-outstretched thing again, as if offering himself to her as the answer not only to her problems but to all the troubles of the universe. Just so had he held his arms when, as a sexy, hormonally charged teenager, he'd offered himself to most of the girls in high school. Back then the gesture had meant 'Hey, take me, I'm yours.' And most of them probably had!

Right now, Kate didn't know what it meant, though she did know she shouldn't even think about it.

Grant Bell was trouble. He'd been trouble back then, and he was still trouble now. Just the way her body warmed to his gaze, and reacted to his grin, told her that. And now she was a mother, with an infant daughter to consider, someone like Grant Bell gave a whole new dimension to the 't' word.

She frowned at him, set aside, with difficulty, the 'trouble' thing and considered the words that had accompanied his gesture.

'You're here because my locum couldn't make it?' she said. She'd obviously lost far more brain cells than she'd realised. 'But I need a doctor, not a—' her eyes took in the lurid shirt and board shorts '—beach bum!'

He managed to look hurt, but he'd been able to do that since she'd first met him when he'd pulled one of her ringletty curls in church, then had denied being the culprit when she'd turned to glare at him.

'Beach bum?' he echoed, with such incredulity it *had* to be false. 'I'll have you know I was on holiday when Aunt Vi's summons came, and I left the waves at Byron Bay to come racing to your rescue.' He grinned again. 'The knight thing, you know.'

'I think I'd better sit down,' Kate muttered, while telling herself giving birth couldn't possibly have killed *all* her brain cells.

Ever the gentleman, Grant used his foot to hook a chair towards her, then, as she sank gratefully into it, he propped himself against the railing, folded his arms and gave the impression of a man willing to wait for ever, if she needed that long.

But wait for what?

The locum who wasn't coming?

An explanation of why Vi had contacted Grant and, more to the point, why he'd come?

Kate stared up at him, hoping the horror dawning in her mind wasn't visible on her face.

'Did you— No, you couldn't have— Surely not—'

'Are you going to finish any of those questions or is it

a new guessing game that hasn't reached the wilds of Byron Bay?' he asked.

'Why are you here?' she asked, though reasonably sure she'd asked it before and the answer hadn't helped.

Grant did the arms-outstretched thing again and she managed, with difficulty, not to think about sex.

'I'm your locum.'

'You're a doctor?'

On a scale of one to ten, her disbelief would have ricocheted off the chart at about one hundred and seventy-five.

'Y-you can't b-be!' she stuttered, answering her own demand because he was doing the hurt look again. 'You were always more interested in animals than people. Why be a doctor?'

'Well, there was a time when you were going to be a missionary and save the heathen, until I pointed out to you that most of the so-called heathen had perfectly good religions of their own and wouldn't want you.' He grinned, again, and added, 'And as you're obviously not a missionary, why shouldn't I be a doctor?'

Kate couldn't find an answer to that question. He'd been bright enough, though his extra-curricular activities of chasing either cattle or girls had meant his high school grades had never been excellent.

But the question of whether or not he was a doctor wasn't the issue—him being here was. She'd intended for her locum to live in—the house was certainly big enough for two people and a very small, almost minute baby—but having Grant Bell move in was asking for—well, the only word for it, though certainly not strong enough, was trouble.

She had to say no—to stop this before it went any further.

'I wanted a woman—Vi knew that. I put flowered sheets on the bed.'

Even before she'd finished speaking she knew it had been the wrong thing to say.

Grant didn't smile but she suspected laughter was lurking in his eyes when he said, very gently, 'I don't see flowered sheets as an assault on my masculinity.'

'But we'll be sharing the house,' Kate protested.

'Worried about what people will think?'

She looked blankly at him.

'If I was worried about what people think, I wouldn't have come back here single and pregnant,' she snapped. 'I'm worried—'

She stopped dead. Telling Grant Bell the truth—that she was bothered by the thought he'd see her, tired, rumpled, milk-smelling and at her most unattractive as she ambled round the house in the early hours of the morning, grouching and grumbling as she tried to get with it enough to organise her day—just wasn't an option.

'You're worried?' he prompted.

'About sharing the house—sharing the kitchen and the bathroom. These old houses only ever had one, you know, and the baby cries, you'll be disturbed.'

'More disturbed than a woman by a baby crying? What happened to sexual equality? Or doesn't it apply to crying babies?'

The storm rumbled closer and a loud clap of thunder, followed by a vivid flash of jagged lightning, sent Kate scurrying back to the bedroom, certain the baby would be woken.

'Storms always come from the west, so I'll shut the doors on that side of the veranda,' Grant called after her.

Perhaps if he showed how useful he was it would make up for him not being a woman.

Though she *was* worried. He had seen it in the stiff set of her shoulders, the way her arms had wrapped protectively around her body, but her concern only made him more determined to stay—to help Katie Fenton, who, according to Aunt Vi, needed quite a bit of support right now.

He followed the veranda around to the front of the house and went into the hall, turning first into the lounge room to shut the two sets of French doors in there, then the dining room, thinking all the while of Katie.

He'd looked into her huge green eyes with the dusty gold lashes and seen the strain repeated there. Was it he who bothered her, or would any man have generated the same response?

And why?

Because whoever had fathered the baby had let her down?

That must be it. The bastard had turned her off men for good.

So if he neutralised himself in some way...

'What about your bike?' Kate called, and he cursed as he dashed back outside through raindrops as big as peanuts. Seeing Katie Fenton again must have rattled him more than he'd thought it would, as he'd forgotten to put the bike away.

He wheeled it into the garage where it fitted nicely beside the dark green Subaru she must drive.

A sensible, neutral kind of car, saying nothing much about the owner.

Neutral!

Neutralise. Perhaps he could do something to minimise whatever danger he represented to her.

He could pretend he was gay, but suspected Katie wouldn't fall for a sudden change in his sexual persuasion.

Still thinking, he grabbed his bags out of the luggage compartments and dashed back through the now thundering rain to the house. His shirt was sodden, clinging to him like an—

Over-friendly woman!

That was the answer. He might be a man, but a man attached to a woman was safe—neutralised!

He walked through to the kitchen, knowing from the rattling noises out there he'd find Katie—Kate.

'I must phone Chlorinda,' he said. 'Getting this lovely shirt wet reminded me.'

'Chlorinda!' Kate repeated, in such disbelieving tones he knew he'd made a huge mistake, but for reasons beyond his understanding the name had just popped out.

'My fiancée,' he explained.

The disbelief in her voice was equally apparent in Katie's beautiful eyes.

'No one's called Chlorinda these days,' she snorted, and, anxious to retrieve the situation, he tried again.

'Actually—' big shame-faced grin '—her name's Linda, but I can't help playing with names and somehow Linda, Chlorinda, you know how it happens. Like K-K-K-Katie, swallowed the ha'penny. Remember?'

'Of course I remember! You teased me with that stupid rhyme often enough.'

Fierce eyes flashed green fire, but he guessed the neutralising thing had worked.

He held up his bags.

'The bedroom? Where have you put me—or put the flowered sheets?'

She didn't answer, and the distracted way she pushed at her hair, at the heavy, dark blonde mass of riotous curls, suggested Vi had been right. Katie Fenton was just about at the end of her tether.

'You could stay with Vi,' she said, but there was no force in the suggestion, and before he'd had time to object she contradicted herself. 'But that's stupid. I wanted the locum here so I didn't have to change the phone around—so she could take the night and weekend calls.'

She glared at Grant.

'It's not a full-time position—you know that, don't you?

The woman who was coming was studying for another degree so didn't mind it being part time, job-sharing. Although there should be two doctors here. I tried to get the Health Department to agree to pay some of the locum's wages so it would be full time but that wretched Paul Newberry hasn't resigned. Apparently he's on stress leave...'

The distraction—almost panic—was in her voice now as well, and Grant found it hurt him to see Katie Fenton, who'd always been willing to take on the world—and any stupid dare her schoolmates had ever dreamed up—so uncertain.

'Look, why don't we sit down and have a cup of tea? In fact, you sit and I'll make it. It will show you how useful I am, and anyway, you've probably been doing far too much straight after the birth of the baby.'

She gave a funny little smile that held a hint of the Katie he remembered.

'Didn't you once tell me that in some countries women gave birth in the fields, wrapped the baby in a sling across their backs and kept working? I've been reminding myself of those stoical souls for the last ten days!'

'I was probably exaggerating—or the book I read it in wasn't telling the entire truth. And anyway, that's not you, so sit. I'll find the tea—or would you prefer coffee—no, you shouldn't have coffee, we don't want the baby addicted to caffeine from birth, now, do we?'

'Ten minutes in the house and already you're giving orders?' Kate said, but she sank down into the chair, certain she'd be better able to handle the situation while seated. She'd been tempted to say she wanted coffee, but she'd managed to wean herself of the caffeine habit while pregnant, and now, while the smell of coffee still pleased her, drinking it made her feel queasy.

She sank lower in the chair, and watched Grant Bell opening and shutting cupboard doors, the situation so bizarre it was easier to believe she was dreaming. In fact, she was tired enough for it to be a dream.

Then, because watching him was disturbing in ways she couldn't begin to understand, and bringing back not only the happy memories but the anguish she'd felt when he and his family had left town so many years ago, she leaned forward, folded her arms on the table and rested her head on them.

Just for a moment, she told herself, as her eyes slid shut.

Surprised to find she'd given in so easily, Grant turned to ask about milk and sugar, and found his companion sound asleep.

She *must* be exhausted, he thought, while the mix of pity and anger he felt made him wonder if the 'knight in shining armour' concept was as good as it had seemed back on the beach at Byron Bay, where the waves had been practically non-existent and he'd been bored by the holiday that had barely begun.

But whatever he felt, it was obvious Aunt Vi had been right. Katie Fenton needed help.

And he'd been available.

He made himself a cup of tea, and found a couple of cracker biscuits he could eat with it. If she had cheese—

A thin wail stopped his explorations of the refrigerator, and, certain Katie would wake if the baby continued to cry, he shot through to the bedroom, hesitating momentarily before bending to lift the tiny form from the crib. He actually hadn't thought about the baby part when launching into his knight act, but now he was here he'd just have to cope. After all, it was just another anonymous baby, like the hundreds he'd handled at the hospital over the last year.

'I didn't even ask your name,' he said, holding it close against his chest. 'And now you're making my shirt even wetter. But I can fix that. I'll change you. Would that be nice?'

Talking, rocking, moving all the time, he looked around

the room. There was a pile of folded nappies on the dressing-table, and various boxes and bottles of lotions and potions squashed alongside them.

'I'll check out the system Katie's using as I undress you,' he said, placing the little one on the bed then unwrapping a loose cotton cover from around it. 'Do the blue flowers on your singlet mean you're a boy? We'll soon find out, won't we? Though you're not as new as I thought you must be!'

He touched the still red navel, surprised to find the remnants of the umbilical cord already gone, then undid the nappy, discovering the new arrival was a girl. The system obviously decreed a blue nappy liner inside the nappy. Well, that was easy—they were in the box.

'Little Katie!' he murmured, leaving the outer covering flat on the bed while he gave in to temptation and marvelled at the miniature limbs and digits—the tiny, perfect finger- and toenails. His heart tightened, memories crowding in, but he couldn't help but tell her, 'You're beautiful, did you know that? Does your mummy tell you all the time?'

He fastened the nappy with deft, remembered actions, found a clean cotton sheet and rewrapped his charge, but the idea that Katie Fenton was the mummy in question was causing him as much internal confusion as the baby.

'She was always trouble,' he told the infant as he returned her to the crib. 'I was always getting her out of it.'

He rocked the crib until the little eyelids dropped and dark lashes fanned out over rose-petal cheeks.

'Or getting her into it,' honesty forced him to add.

CHAPTER TWO

THE ringing noise startled Kate awake, but she'd been so deeply asleep it took a moment to realise where she was. Asleep at the kitchen table?

And dreaming of Grant Bell, of all people!

By the time she'd set the dream aside, wiped what felt suspiciously like drool from her cheek and stood up, the ringing had stopped, but there was another noise—more unusual, frightening even. A man's voice!

As she walked, slowly and cautiously, towards the living room she realised Grant Bell hadn't been a dream. He was here—right in front of her, now she was in the doorway—and apparently intending to stay.

Her locum!

'Yes, Mrs Barrett, it's great to be back. No, I haven't seen Vi yet, but if George's in pain, shouldn't we be talking about him?'

He paused and Kate imagined the torrent of words pouring through the receiver from Mrs Barrett.

'She'd talk under water,' Grant said, smiling happily at Kate as he hung up. 'George has had a back spasm. Has it happened since you've been here? Any advice or should I just go out there and help the poor chap onto his bed and order him to stay there until it gets better?'

'I haven't seen him as a patient since I've been here,' Kate said, then honesty forced her to continue, 'Haven't seen a lot of the older men. Going to a woman doctor is evidently a worse admission of weakness than going to one of the males of the species. If they were desperate, they went to the hospital to see Paul—when he was here!'

She'd barely finished speaking when another thought struck her.

'Actually, that's a good reason for me to go, rather than you. It's a great way to break the ice and maybe prove something to the man. The Barretts' place is Kintower, isn't it? Out on the western road. I'll get the baby.'

'Get the baby?' Grant's voice was charged with disbelief. 'I've just changed her and put her back to sleep and you're going to wake her and take her out there? In a storm?'

Damn— Jeez Louise! What the hell was she thinking?

If Grant hadn't been there, she'd have thumped her forehead with the heel of her hand.

'I'll call Tara to come over and watch the baby,' Kate muttered, moving determinedly towards the phone although her reluctance to leave Tara in charge when she was farther away than next door at the hospital made her head ache. She knew Tara was good, but the girl did tend to lose herself in whatever she was reading…

Though Grant was here…

Right here! Grabbing her shoulders, giving her a little shake.

'Get with it, Katie,' he said, almost roughly. 'You've got a locum so you don't have to go out on calls. The locum goes, and that's me. Now's not the time to be proving yourself to George Barrett or any of the other dinosaurs in town. Now's the time to be thinking of your own well-being, and if you can't manage that, at least put the baby first.'

He was so close Kate could see the dark shadow of beard beneath the tanned skin on his chin—see individual follicles, and the outline of his lips…

You have a baby and he has a fiancée, an inner voice reminded her.

'Though I will take your car, if that's OK. You've a bag in it?'

The lips were moving but the words weren't making

much sense as she struggled to come to terms with feelings that *had* to be a hangover from the past.

'Keys?'

Keys? Car keys, presumably.

'In the kitchen, hanging over the cupboard near the back door.' She answered automatically and he moved away. Then, as if released from a spell, her heartbeat settled and her mind began working again. She hurried after him.

'Have you had any experience as a GP? Are you qualified to be doing this?'

He turned and grinned at her.

'Rather late to be asking those questions, isn't it, Katie? What do you think? I'm really a criminal on the run and Aunt Vi is helping me hide with this locum thing? Actually, if you go into your spare bedroom and open the briefcase in there, you'll see a file with all my qualifications and experience in it.'

He lifted the keys from the hook, and repeated his question.

'You've a medical bag in the car?'

She nodded.

'In the back,' she said, and was about to add more when he smiled again.

'Of course, papers can be forged,' he reminded her, and dashed out into the rain.

I shouldn't have said that, Grant admitted to himself as he drove out along the once-familiar road to the Barretts' property. He was here to help her, not to make things worse. But Katie Fenton had always responded so well to his teasing that the impulse had been irresistible.

He peered ahead through the slashing rain, looking for the gateposts that marked the entrance to Kintower. For her to have even considered bringing the baby out in the storm showed how rattled she must be. No wonder Vi had sent the SOS.

But why had he answered the call? The question had

nagged at him on the five-hundred-kilometre ride north-west, and, though he had plenty of glib replies—the surf was poor, he was bored with holidaying, Katie had been a friend, seeing Testament again so he could finally shut the door on the past—none of them seemed particularly satisfactory.

Particularly not when you considered the baby as part of the equation—although when Vi had phoned, the baby had, supposedly, been many weeks from the due date.

Or Vi had deliberately not mentioned its arrival…

The gateposts appeared and he swung cautiously off the road, aware that the red soil shoulders turned to treacherously slippery slush with a bit of rain. Thank heavens the Barretts' drive was sealed. After the long ride, he was glad he didn't have to handle a slick mud surface, though the neat Subaru, with constant four-wheel-drive, should have performed OK.

Mrs Barrett was on her front veranda, waving to him as if he might, by some mischance, miss the house. It was the only visible building though he knew there were sheds behind the grove of trees at the back of the house. He leaned over to grab the bag, noting with approval the properly secured capsule harness in the back seat, then dashed through the rain to the Barretts' front veranda.

'He's in the tractor shed. I left him there. He called me a stupid woman and pushed me away, so I left him there.'

Mrs Barrett seemed quite pleased by this decision, but Grant, soaked to the skin again, felt she could have told him this on the phone, or at least pointed to the area behind the house, rather than waving.

He refused her—surely inappropriate—offer of a cup of tea and raced back to the car. Backed up, and turned towards the sheds, pleased, as he approached, to see space where he could drive in and so save himself another wetting.

George Barrett was at one end, his body dwarfed by a

huge tractor. He was bent over, as if peering at the wheel studs, but Grant guessed from his pale complexion he was that way because any alternative was sheer agony.

Grant walked towards him, reading surprise and something like relief in the man's face.

'I don't know who you are,' George said, 'but can you give me a hand? There's a camp bed in the room out the back. If you can get me onto it, I can stay there until the damned thing stops paining.'

The thundering rain on the roof meant he'd had to shout to be heard.

'I can do better than that,' Grant shouted back, pulling the bag out of the back of the vehicle. 'I'm Grant Bell, Doug's son. I ended up studying medicine and I'm here helping Dr Fenton for a few weeks.'

He reached George's side, and rested his hand on the man's shoulder.

'Bad, is it?'

'Too right it's bad!' George muttered, the words almost inaudible given the background noise. 'Think I'd be here counting the cracks in the tractor tyre if it weren't?'

'How's the rest of your health? Any other problems? Allergies? Kidneys OK? Are you on any regular medication for your heart, blood pressure, arthritis?'

He raised his voice loudly enough to be heard, and at the same time opened the bag and searched through the neatly maintained compartments until he found the vial he wanted.

'Could we discuss this when I'm lying down?' George demanded, and Grant hid a grin.

'As long as I know you're not going to keel over on me from a drug interaction, I can give you a shot of morphine that will make getting from where you are to a bed a whole lot easier.'

He drew the liquid into the syringe and set it aside while he found a sterile swab.

'I don't take anything,' George finally admitted. 'I'm supposed to take things for my back but they don't make a scrap of difference, so why bother?'

'Have you had spasms like this before?' Grant asked, pushing up the man's sleeve and swabbing the skin above the biceps.

'No! It gets crook from time to time, and then I take the tablets and when it gets better I stop.'

'Fair enough,' Grant told him. 'Now, here goes. Hang on a bit and it should ease.'

He slid the needle into the muscle and injected the fluid. Relief wouldn't be instantaneous, but before long he should be able to help George to the bed. He filled the waiting time by cautiously examining his patient, but very little could be felt, and George's assertion that all he'd done had been to bend over to check the tyre pressure on the tractor tyre suggested a muscle spasm probably associated with deterioration in the spine.

The rain was still rattling down on the tin roof above them, so putting George to bed for a week in the shed wasn't all that good an option.

'I'll put you in the car and drive you back to the house,' Grant told him, as George began, tentatively, to straighten up.

But he could only go so far and, obviously in too much pain to argue, he allowed Grant to lead him to the car and settle him in the front seat.

'Sitting's going to hurt far worse than standing,' the older man said, the words coming out through pain-whitened lips.

'It won't be for long, and it will save Mrs Barrett having to come back and forth to feed you. You need bed rest for a week,' he added, though he knew he might just as well tell the rain to stop. Farmers worked when they had to, whether they were in pain or not.

Though the rain might keep George indoors for longer than he would normally stay.

'I know you won't take any notice of me,' Grant continued, pulling up at the bottom of the steps but not moving. If they waited, the rain might lessen and the drug would have more time to work. 'But try to rest it as long as you can. And no rubbish about lying on the floor because a hard surface is good for backs—that's not right and you'll do more damage getting up and down to go to the toilet than you would lying on the softest of beds. I'll check out your bed, and show you how to lie.'

'You're really Doug's boy? I heard your dad passed away. I'm sorry, he was a good man.'

George was obviously feeling less pain if he'd been able to think of something else. It was as good a time as any to tell him he'd need an X-ray.

'You'll do it or the woman?' George asked, the suspicion in his voice confirming what Katie had said about the older men's reaction to her position as the local GP.

'Actually, whoever is the technician at the hospital will do it, but Dr Fenton and I will read it. After all, she is your doctor. I'm just temporary.'

George muttered something Grant took to be disgust at a world so changed a man had to be treated by a woman doctor, but before Grant could ask for him to repeat it, Mrs Barrett appeared, a large umbrella held above her head.

'I'm already wet so I'll come around and help you out,' he told George. 'Sit tight for a moment.'

He met Mrs Barrett at the car door and opened it, then leaned in to take George's legs.

'I'll swing them out then help you stand,' he told his patient, who was grumbling under his breath, but more, Grant realised, with disgust at himself than with pain.

Together, he and Mrs Barrett got the man onto his bed.

'You can lie on either side with your hips and legs flexed, or on your back but propped up and with pillows under your knees. I'll leave some tablets here to keep you going over the weekend and a script for more, should you need them, for next week.'

Grant turned to Mrs Barrett.

'He'll probably be more comfortable in pyjamas. Do you want some help undressing him?'

She laughed.

'Me need help to undress him? Get away with you, young Grant! I've been undressing the useless hulk for years. Every Friday night it used to be, until drink-driving meant he couldn't drink at the pub till closing time. But I haven't forgotten how,' she added.

'It wasn't that I couldn't do it myself, young fella,' George put in. 'Just she was always desperate to get at my body!'

Grant found himself chuckling at the ribald exchange, though the depth of affection behind it reminded him of his parents' conversations, and the love they'd shared.

And, just as his enforced holiday at Byron Bay had seemed curiously flat once he'd settled in and relaxed, now he wondered if it wasn't perhaps his entire life that was lacking something.

Surely not because he needed someone with whom to share a joke—someone to tease and be teased by?

Though there was no guarantee marriage would provide the answer—he'd already learnt that lesson.

'I want some X-rays to check on what's happening in that lumbar region,' he told Mrs Barrett. 'But wait until he's well enough to travel. In the meantime, if you can keep him in bed, well and good. If you can't then walking—just gentle upright movement—is better than sitting.'

George began growling again, and Mrs Barrett, after telling him to hush, led Grant out of the bedroom.

'Four-hourly for the tablets?' she asked, as Grant dug through the bag again to find some analgesics.

'Yes, but once the effects of the injection wear off, these

mightn't be enough. I'll leave a couple of Valium as well, which will relax the muscles and sedate him slightly. He can take one tonight and another in the morning. If the pain hasn't eased by tomorrow evening, call me again and I'll come out.'

Bursitis was another possibility, he was thinking, as he said goodbye to Mrs Barrett and again ran through the rain. Then, as he settled behind the wheel in the unfamiliar vehicle, he grinned to himself.

It was like riding a bicycle, the way it all came back. Though he wouldn't tell Katie how long it was since he'd done any general medical work. She'd only worry.

Katie!

He drove back thinking about her, replacing the mental picture he'd carried with him for so long—of a skinny, restless teenager—with one of the tall, well-built woman she'd become. Though the wild untamed hair was still the same, and the eyes, if anything, were larger and more luminous, so expressive he'd once believed he could read every thought she ever had. Her skin was pale, but that was understandable, given she was probably exhausted, and everyone was aware these days of the damage sun could do. Though the young Katie had laughed off such warnings and had tanned to a golden glow every summer.

Then he remembered how the baby—Katie's baby—had felt in his hands, and his mood darkened. Had he been foolish to say yes to Aunt Vi's pleas and persuasion?

He was happy to help out—more than happy, given how boring he'd found his 'holiday' and how much he'd wanted to return to Testament, in spite of his teenage vows. He was even happy at the thought of helping Katie, who'd been a close childhood friend, at first thrown at him by his father— 'Be nice to the kid. I'll need all the help I can get from her dad if we're to survive' —but later as a friend in her own right.

More than a friend for a brief few weeks of summer heat and raging teenage testosterone...

His body stirred at the ancient memory and he wondered if he wasn't better thinking of the baby.

As long as he didn't get fond of it...

Though that was unlikely, given Katie's protective attitude and the fact he'd only be here a few weeks, six or seven at the most.

The rain had eased by the time he drove back into the town. He passed the pub and considered stopping for a beer, then remembered he was, more or less, on duty and resisted the impulse. Turned towards the hospital and was surprised to feel a slight anticipatory thrill—actually, more a nudge than a thrill. To do with being back at work, he was sure, not with seeing Katie.

The back door was open, making the dash from garage to house less hazardous, though now the rain had settled into a reasonable kind of splatter, and he was damp, not soaked, when he came through the door.

'Chlorinda's shirt's been more wet than dry this afternoon,' Katie greeted him, and he very nearly blew his neat idea by asking, Who's Chlorinda?

'I'll take it off—have a shower if that's OK with you. I gave George a shot of morphine, got him from the shed to bed, and left Mrs B. ravishing his body.'

Katie's eyebrows rose, but she must have decided not to go there, asking instead, 'Did you leave medication? Ask him to come in for further investigation?' The green eyes darkened with worry. 'I'm not sure about this locum stuff. I mean, do you resent me asking how you've treated someone? Even though the person will still be my patient later, so I'll have to know? In a group practice, notes are written on the patient cards, but it always seemed to me, although they said what the patient had come in for and how the doctor had treated it, a lot of personal but helpful stuff could be missing.'

Grant moved towards her, aware of how attractive she looked, freshly showered, and clad in a long skirt of some clingy, shiny material and a plain green T-shirt hanging out over it. Her hair, which she'd tried to tame by ramming combs into it to hold it somewhere near the top of her head, was escaping in long corkscrew curls.

'You never did have that cup of tea,' he said, 'and though Mrs Barrett offered sustenance, I refused. Let's sit and talk about it, shall we? I can shower later. I certainly don't mind you asking what I did, or how I treated someone—asking anything, in fact. Believe me, I'll be asking heaps of questions myself. It's a long time since I've done a locum, though three years in A and E has prepared me well for the kind of thing you'd get called out for.'

'Prepared you well for anything,' Kate said, concealing a shudder as she remembered some of the bizarre cases she'd experienced in a far shorter stint in Accident and Emergency, as part of her training. 'You sit, I'll make the tea. I've made some scones as well. I'm not good at scones, but if you've reasonable digestion, they're a bit of solid nourishment to carry you through to dinner-time.'

'You made scones?' The words shot across the room, propelled by such incredulity she might have said she'd won the lottery.

'You don't have to sound so surprised!' Kate fired right back at him. 'After all, you don't know me. People do grow up, you know. Now, do you want tea and scones or don't you?'

He nodded and dropped into a chair by the table, in the easy, loose-limbed way she remembered from the past.

Turning resolutely away from loose-limbed movement and memories of the past, she made a pot of tea and plonked it on the table, unhooked two mugs from their wooden holder and put them beside the pot, then lifted the tea-towel off the scones and tried to tell herself she'd meant to make them small.

But when they made clunking noises as she put them on the plate, she sighed.

'You'll need good teeth as well as good digestion,' she admitted, looking into familiar blue eyes that held an even more familiar understanding.

Which prompted her to confess, 'You were right to be surprised—I'm still no cook. You know, Grant, I actually thought skills like making scones might come along with motherhood but, from the look and taste of these, it's another of those myths, like instant bonding.'

A puzzled expression swept away the understanding.

'Instant bonding?'

'With the baby,' she explained, pleased to have someone other than herself with whom to debate this strange occurrence. 'I thought, because I'd given birth to her, I'd have some instant affinity for the wee thing. Go all warm and protective and filled with overwhelming love.'

He still looked puzzled but his easy grin was longing to appear—she could tell by the little twitches at the corner of his mouth.

'Didn't happen, huh?'

Kate shook her head, the movement causing more bits of hair to come floating free, which added frustration with her looks to her gloomy mood.

'She couldn't have been more alien. I mean, I didn't hate her or hold her responsible for anything that's happened, and I still want her and love her to bits, but in the beginning it was like having a stranger come into my life.'

She paused, then added, 'For ever!' in such tragic tones, Grant lost his battle with his amusement and not only grinned but laughed out loud.

'I've often wondered about the bonding thing,' he finally admitted, accepting the mug of tea she pushed in his direction and picking up one of the scones. 'Nature usually gets it right, and maybe it makes human infants so totally dependent to give the parents time to bond. I mean, most newborn animals can almost fend for themselves at birth. Admittedly, mammals need milk but they get up and go find it.'

He cut the scone, with difficulty, and reached for the jam.

'Use plenty. It softens them and masks the taste,' Katie said, and he laughed again, assuring her the scones couldn't be that bad.

'They are,' she told him, and when he took a bite, he had to agree.

'But it doesn't matter,' he told her. 'Setting yourself motherhood goals like instant bonding and scone-making is setting yourself up for failure, Katie. My mother couldn't make scones and she was a country wife of whom it was expected, and a great mother—still is, in fact. And my bond with her, though it may have been dependence-based originally, is now one of loving friendship—of respect, which I hope, from time to time, is mutual.'

'Kate.' She corrected her name, though absent-mindedly, continuing with her main train of thought when she said, 'Your mother's different. She was never a scone sort of mother.'

She looked wistfully at Grant.

'Perhaps I should use her as a role model rather than mine, who sent the scone recipe, along with various others—including of all things, a sponge cake—within a week of my shifting back to Testament.'

Grant grinned at her.

'As if you were expected to start the transformation to Katie—sorry, Kate—the perfect countrywoman, as soon as you started breathing country air.'

His words prompted another thought—why wasn't her mother here, supporting her at this time? But she was looking less distressed and he didn't want to chase that mood away just yet.

He bit into the jam-loaded scone and chewed carefully.

'You know, the Americans call scones biscuits, and if

you call it a biscuit, it's perfect, just the right amount of chew and hardness.'

That won a smile, of sorts, but he could see the sadness lurking in her eyes and wondered what had happened to his brave, confident, daring, laughing Katie to turn her into this uncertain woman.

Not wanting to ask, he told her about his visit to the Barretts'—what he'd done, prescribed and suggested.

'If we have time each day to talk over the patients, we shouldn't have any trouble keeping track of what's going on.'

She nodded. 'That's one of the reasons I wanted the locum to live in.'

The doubt in her voice told him she no longer considered it quite as good an idea.

'Very sensible arrangement all round,' he said, hoping a firm confirmation might banish some of her doubts. 'And though I'm not a woman, I'm quite capable of watching over a small baby when you're working or want to go out.'

That drew a smile.

'Out on the town, you mean?' Katie—Kate—teased. 'Hitting the high spots of Testament?'

He answered with his own smile, then added, 'You still need time for yourself. Even perfect mothers need that.'

She nodded as if she knew it was true, but her eyes told him she didn't—well, not entirely—believe it.

'I think perfect is way beyond my reach,' she admitted. 'Right now, I'd settle for adequate.'

She leaned back in her chair, put her hands behind her head and stretched, then sighed.

'Almost adequate?'

Unable to believe she could have had so much stuffing knocked out of her—it had to be the man, the father, who'd so undermined her confidence—Grant was about to go into confidence-building speak when a faint cry alerted both of them to the fact the baby was once again awake.

'I'll get her, you stay there and rest,' Grant said, leaping to his feet so quickly he knocked over the chair.

But Katie was up just as quickly, taking advantage of him having to right the chair, so she beat him to the door, where she turned to say, 'Nonsense! Even almost adequate mothers can do the changing-feeding thing. There's no reason why you should be chasing after her.'

He followed anyway, and saw colour return to the pale cheeks as Katie leaned over the crib, murmuring quietly as she lifted the wrapped bundle out and snuggled her momentarily against her shoulder.

Fascinated by this maternal and obviously baby-doting Katie—he'd be damned if he'd call her Kate—he settled on the far side of the big queen-sized bed and watched as she lowered the baby onto the bed, then turned to sort through the paraphernalia he'd investigated earlier.

'We haven't been properly introduced, your daughter and I,' he said, making conversation while he watched her hands fumble through the still unfamiliar task of removing the wet nappy. He leaned forward and inserted his forefinger into one tiny hand, knowing the little fingers would grip his larger one. Wanting to feel that grip again. 'I'm Grant Bell,' he said formally. 'And you're…'

He glanced up at Katie, expecting an answer, and found her frowning ferociously at him.

'Don't ask!' she warned.

'You haven't named her?' he guessed, then wished he'd managed to sound a little less disbelieving.

Kate pushed her fingers through her now riotous hair and knew she'd have to at least try to explain.

'It was like the bonding thing—you know, instant motherhood? I thought when she was born I'd take one look and say, Hello Annabel, or Rachel, or Sophie or whatever it was she looked like. Or he'd look like if she'd been a he. I thought I'd *know*!'

'But you had nine months to think about names. Didn't

you have a few you rather fancied all ready for hers and hims? Don't most people make a list?'

'Don't talk to me about lists!' she said, injecting the words with enough venom to stop even someone as insensitive as Grant Bell had apparently become. 'If one more person suggests lists, makes a list or sends me a list, I won't be answerable for the consequences.'

Then, aware she'd raised her voice, causing what looked like wariness in her daughter's large blue eyes, she completed the nappy change, lifted the infant and said, more quietly, 'I'm going to feed her now.'

Grant made no attempt to leave the room. In fact, if anything, he looked as if he was settling himself more comfortably on the bed.

Her bed.

'In here,' she added, because it seemed kind of prissy to be asking him outright to leave the room.

'That's OK,' he told her in a genial voice she recognised from their schooldays. It meant he understood but didn't necessarily agree.

This reading of his vocal nuances was confirmed when he added, 'I love watching babies nurse. There's something so wholeheartedly selfish about it. They tug and pummel away at their poor mothers' breasts, with no thought for anything but the acute physical satisfaction of being replete.'

'Well, this poor mother would prefer to have her breast tugged and pummelled in private,' Kate told him.

'You mean you haven't fed her in front of anyone yet? What about in hospital? Or at work? Vi said you were planning on taking her to the surgery and whoever was there would mind her between feeds. Hasn't that happened yet? Or do you let them do the dirty work of changing nappies and burping but don't let them have the satisfaction of watching her feed?'

'You make it sound like a rare treat for all concerned,'

Kate said crossly. 'I'll have you know a lot of people are still offended by seeing women breastfeed in public, and though I'd defend to my dying breath their right to do it, it isn't my thing. Not yet, anyway.'

She gave him a glare that should put him back in his place—though she wasn't entirely certain where that was—and added, in case he hadn't got the message, 'So go! Unpack. Check out the surgery. Do something, anything, just not here.'

CHAPTER THREE

GRANT walked back to the kitchen, and wondered what to do next. A shower was the obvious answer, but Katie's behaviour—the vulnerability he sensed beneath her usual confident manner, made him wonder about the baby's father—and about how much she might be hurting inside.

Vi might know something, but asking Vi seemed like a betrayal—as if he'd be going behind his old friend's back. He put off the shower, mooching through the house instead, not exactly searching but seeking some hint as to the identity of this man.

Not that it was any of his business, he told himself, when the only photos sitting on her study desk proved to be of her parents.

Which made him wonder again where they were and why her mother wasn't helping out with the new baby.

His heart clenched with concern for his old friend and, realising that wasn't a good way to be feeling, given that his stay in Testament was definitely short term, he sought about for a diversion. Maybe he should have that shower!

Though it was still raining outside, so perhaps he should check out the surgery first. Providing he could find the keys…

They were in the kitchen, labelled, should anyone break in looking for them, SURGERY. The set-up was as he remembered—a consulting room and opposite it a small treatment room were set behind the main reception and waiting areas. A small locked room must hold medical supplies while the other store cupboards held such an accumulation of junk that he wondered if any of the doctors who'd served the town had ever thrown anything out. Sorting through it was a bit like going to a medical museum, and he was so caught up in the treasures it wasn't until it became too dark to see that he realised how long he'd been there. He packed everything back in, but not before promising himself he'd sort it out properly one day.

One day? You're only temporary, he reminded himself, so it's none of your business.

By the time Grant returned to the house, the storm had passed, and a glance at his watch told him it was after six, while his stomach reminded him it was a long time since he'd eaten, if you didn't count a biscuit scone. Presumably the woman locum would have shared responsibility for meal preparation. Well, that was OK. He could rustle up a meal for the two of them.

He opened the refrigerator and peered inside.

There wasn't a lot to see. The remains of a dubious-looking casserole someone must have left for Katie, cosied up to two wrinkled apples and a loaf of bread. She did, however, have four litres of milk and a couple of small feeding bottles of what he assumed was expressed breast milk.

He tried the freezer next and winced at the neat stack of frozen meals. Pushed them aside, and continued searching. There had to be real food here somewhere.

There wasn't.

Forgetting his decision to present a professional demeanour, he stalked back to the bedroom where, noticing the baby had dropped off to sleep in her arms, he delivered his tirade in a loud whisper.

Kate heard the words—nothing to eat, bad nutrition, looking after herself, thinking about the baby—and the kindly thoughts she'd been thinking about Grant Bell dried up.

'It wasn't my fault the baby came early,' she told him, standing up so she could fight him toe to toe. 'She was supposed to come in a fortnight, on the Friday, last Friday, and I'd intended shopping before that. Then I'd have had the weekend in hospital to rest, and with the locum here, she could have started on the Monday, tomorrow, and I could have worked part time during the week. But the baby was early and the locum wasn't here, and the shopping wasn't done...'

She stopped, aware she was repeating herself and, even worse, sounding self-pitying. Better to attack.

'And for your information, those frozen meals are very well balanced, nutritionally.'

'Ho!' Grant scoffed. 'Don't tell me you believe what's written on the packet.'

She was about to tell him about labelling laws when she realised they'd got way off the subject. And though she hated to admit it, the meals left her feeling unsatisfied, so they'd never do for Grant for his dinner.

Checking the time on the bedside clock, she realised the store would be closed and she had no time to retrieve the situation.

'We can have Chinese take-aways tonight, and I'll shop tomorrow,' she suggested, settling the baby in the crib and leading the way out of the bedroom so if, or when, they argued again, they wouldn't wake the little one. 'Though I don't know what good that will do,' she added honestly. 'I'm not much better at meal-cooking than I am at scones. I can grill chops or steak or sausages, steam vegetables and mash potatoes, but nothing fancy.'

Grant smiled.

'I can do the fancy stuff,' he told her. 'We'll take turns, shall we? And we'll both shop tomorrow. That way we can get what we need and the baby can have an outing.'

'Both shop? Together?'

Kate knew it made sense, but the idea bothered her.

'Worried what people might think?' Grant asked.

'No,' she said, too quickly. If she'd thought about it, a

yes would have been better, then he wouldn't persist, as he surely would.

'Why, then?'

He came in right on cue, but she could only shrug as if her worries were inexplicable. Which, to some extent, they were. She could hardly tell him that it seemed too like a family for the three of them to be shopping together. If she came out with something so fatuous within hours of their unexpected reunion, he'd realise just how many brain cells she'd lost.

He didn't ask again, merely picking up the restaurant menu she had stuck on the fridge door and studying the offerings.

'Do you have any particular fancy? Any favourites? I should probably let you choose as you'd know what's good.'

Kate found herself smiling.

'You're asking me? I think frozen meals are good,' she reminded him. 'But I do like the crispy duck. It's loaded with cholesterol-raising fat, but it's so-o-o delicious. I usually have a vegetable dish as well. As a nod to dietary propriety. And lots of rice—that's carbohydrate so, all in all, it's a balanced meal.'

He crossed to the phone and, watching him dial, hearing his deep masculine voice as he ordered, Kate felt a sense of loneliness, as if having Grant here—perhaps anyone here—brought home to her just how alone she'd been these past six months.

'That's set. Now I really will have that shower I've been talking about since I arrived. Then we'll sit down and relax with a long cool drink and tell each other lies about how successful we've become.' He flashed a smile that made her heart falter for a moment. 'Isn't that what medicos usually do when they see each other?'

Kate returned his smile, though she knew hers was more restrained. The faltering-heart thing had shocked her with its intensity. And she wasn't going anywhere near that final question, although it was exactly how Mark had always behaved when he'd met up with fellow doctors.

However, they would have to talk about a lot of other things—work hours, payment, shared expenses for food. She was searching through the bottom of her handbag in the hope of finding enough spare change to pay for the meal when this thought struck her. Generally locums took over while the doctor was away, so the question of expenses didn't arise. Why were there no rules for the little things in life?

So many little things—like bathroom etiquette in a shared house.

'I've been thinking about names,' Grant announced, reappearing far too quickly for her peace of mind and looking, in another flower-festooned shirt and red board shorts this time, incredibly laidback and devastatingly handsome. 'We could think of a few—a few isn't a list—then try them out on her. Use one one week and another the next to see which fits best.'

She ignored her physical reactions to the devastatingly handsome bit, and should have told him the baby's name was none of his business, but the idea of changing names on a weekly basis was so far out, she went for that instead.

'Couldn't it do her irreparable harm, to call her Sophie one week then Louise the next? And I can't have Louise, which I quite like, because I've decided to use "Jeez Louise" as an expletive so she doesn't say "Damn" as her first utterance.'

Grant seemed to understand this reasoning, which, when she actually said it, sounded weird to Kate, but when he spoke she realised he'd probably ignored most of what she'd said.

'You mentioned Sophie before—do you like it? Is she starting to look like a Sophie?'

Kate sighed.

'That's just the problem,' she said. 'I can see a grown-up Sophie—even a teenage Sophie—but as a name for a little tiny baby? It sounds too mature somehow.'

She spoke so earnestly Grant knew he had to hide the smile that was his reaction to her statement.

'I can see your point. Like Jack—one of my nephews. I always thought it a great name for a grown man, but a little harsh for a newborn.' He looked across the table to where Katie, for all her dislike of lists, appeared to be making one. 'But you do get used to it. It's my experience that babies grow into their names.'

Kate glanced up at him, the green eyes sweeping across his face as if trying to read messages on it.

'Are you humouring me?'

He shook his head.

'Now, why would I do that?'

'Because I'm disorganised and possibly neurotic and haven't any food in the house?' she suggested. 'I also haven't any cash to pay for the meal, and I have no idea how to organise your pay or our shared expenses or who uses the bathroom first, so you could add disorganised to my failings.'

She gave a huge sigh, blinked back all but one escaping tear, swiped at it, then sniffed.

'You know, Grant, people talk about the baby blues. I've even said to weepy post-partum mothers, "Don't worry, dear, it happens to most new mums." But I never for a minute thought I'd go to pieces like this.'

He walked around the table and pulled a chair close so he could put his arm around her shoulder.

'From what I've seen and heard, you have every right to go to pieces. Sophie arrived before you were ready for her, you've had to manage the whole pregnancy on your own and juggle work commitments at the same time. And being Katie Fenton, I bet if anyone offered help, you refused it.'

She gave him a watery smile.

'Vi brought a casserole. I accepted that,' she said.

She hesitated, then added, 'Actually, a lot of people have been very nice to me. But they don't run any antenatal classes here because most of the women go to Craigtown for their babies. Paul Newberry—he was the hospital doctor when I arrived—preferred not to deliver babies, claiming it was too risky without a specialist in town, and while he didn't actually refuse to do obstetrics work, his attitude was enough to put most women off.'

'You mentioned his name earlier—I gather he's now the ex-hospital doctor.'

'He left six weeks ago. His wife left first—not long after I arrived. Apparently she couldn't stand the country. Then he suddenly disappeared without a word to the board, or me, or anyone, as far as I know.'

'So who did you see for your pregnancy check-ups?'

'Paul!' A defiant glint in her eyes suggested it hadn't been easy to get him to agree to this arrangement, but before Grant could comment she added, 'And, no, I don't think the imminent arrival of my baby was what forced him out of town, although to hear some of the nursing staff talk, you'd wonder. Anyway, although he wasn't happy doing the checks, he did them until he left, though he never talked about what to expect—the tiredness all the time, this weepy business. To be fair to him, I guess he thought I knew it all.'

'And being an independent spirit, you did nothing to disabuse him of this notion,' Grant muttered as the true extent of Katie's isolation struck home.

She sighed, then shook her head.

'You know, I came back here because I remembered being so happy and secure here. When things changed and I needed somewhere to establish myself and the baby—somewhere I could make a safe, stable, happy life for the two of us and at the same time give something back to the community—by chance the practice was for sale. Serendipity,

I thought. But breaking back into a country town isn't easy.'

'Give the locals time,' Grant said, withdrawing his arm because holding her was making him think things he shouldn't think—suggesting perhaps he could kiss away her despair. 'Country folk take a while to make up their minds, but once they accept you, you've friends for life. And you have to remember your position sets you a little apart. Most people feel doctors are entitled to respect.'

'Respect? When the entire town remembers me as the girl who danced naked on top of the water tower? I'd actually forgotten that until I came back and the first patient I saw mentioned it.'

She shifted back in her chair, the better to glare at him.

'And no one seems to remember it was your fault, anyway. You dared me to do it—well, maybe not to dance, but to climb up to the top and take my clothes off.'

'I didn't think you'd do it,' Grant protested, remembering the skinny eleven-year-old who'd not only taken the dare but had capered naked about the top of the tower until her father had appeared on the street below and ordered her down.

'How is your father, by the way? And your mother? Both parents well?' he asked, as thinking of her parents reminded him of the lack of support for Katie. Illness might have prevented them coming out to be with her at this time.

'Conversational switch, but I can see why you thought of my father,' she acknowledged. 'They're both well. Though, with my usual lack of judgement, I managed to have a baby right in the middle of my father's long-service leave. They'd planned a trip around the world—talked about it for years—and finally had it all booked and paid for when I discovered I was pregnant. They wanted to cancel it, but I couldn't let them do that.'

The words were clipped, and suggested something else was bothering her as far as her parents were concerned.

He raised his eyebrows, and waited.

'Mum wanted me to have an abortion and couldn't understand why not, especially as Mark wanted to marry me.'

Mark? She'd been involved with someone called Mark? Terrible name.

Then Grant put aside his strange reaction to hearing Sophie's father's name and followed another puzzle.

'Why did she want you to have an abortion if Mark wanted to marry you?'

Katie's green eyes met his and a flicker of what must have been remembered temper flared briefly.

'Mark wanted it, too. He had a list,' she said flatly, as if she'd ironed all the emotion out of the subject long ago. 'First abortion, second engagement, third decide what specialty I should pursue, and finally, if I behaved myself and toed the line—or should that be followed the instructions— we'd get married.'

Grant frowned and shook his head.

'I must have missed something. He wanted you to have an abortion when you were getting married anyway?'

'So it didn't look as if we'd had to get married. In fact, on the list, babies came way down—ninth or tenth if I remember rightly.'

Her voice was so husky he suspected not quite all the emotion had been ironed out, particularly where babies were concerned. But another item on the list puzzled him as well.

'And what about number three? Choose your specialty? Did you want to specialise? And was it any of his business, even if you did get married, what you chose?'

The eyes flashed sparks again.

'Exactly!' Katie said, straightening in her chair and looking more like the fighter he'd known in the past. Then she chuckled. 'Actually, I can see his side of things. I must have driven him nuts, doing dribs of this and drabs of that. When I actually sat down and thought about it, although

I'd always said I was doing the short courses—you know, the ones in Obs and Gyn, anaesthesia, surgery—to try them out before specialising, I realised I was preparing myself for something entirely different—for general practice and country general practice at that.'

She looked across at Grant and smiled so warmly he felt a jolt like an electrical current run through his body, causing a muscle spasm in his heart.

'Remember Dr Darling? When we lived in Testament, even though there was always a hospital doctor, Dr Darling did everything for his patients—delivered the babies, diagnosed problems, whipped out the odd appendix, the lot. I realised that's what I wanted to be, not just a token doctor but someone people could rely on—an old-fashioned kind of doctor with the welfare of the community and each individual at heart.'

He heard the commitment in her voice, and saw it shining in her eyes, and for a moment envied the passion she had for this dream she was pursuing. And though he had commitment by the bucketload, he hadn't felt the fire of passion since he'd given up his dream of buying back the farm.

'So you saw yourself as another Dr Darling?' he teased, when he realised it was his turn in the conversation. But as he said the words, warning bells clanged furiously in his head.

Watch yourself, linking words like that, his common sense warned.

'Was that Sophie?' he asked, because Katie was looking at him as if the words had startled her as well and he wanted to divert her attention. 'I thought I heard a cry.'

'Her name's not Sophie, you know,' she said—showing the diversion had worked. 'You can't just walk in here, pull a name out of a hat and give it to my baby.'

'I didn't pull it out of a hat,' Grant protested. 'You mentioned it twice yourself. I'm happy for you to choose something else, even on a temporary basis, but we can't keep calling her ''hey, you'' or ''the baby''.'

A mulish expression, familiar from their shared youth, settled on Katie's features.

'I don't see why not!' Kate said crisply, determined to put Grant Bell in his place, then a knock on the front door put paid to this plan. She'd have to borrow money to pay for the meal, which was a little awkward if one had just been rude to the only available funding source.

'I'll get it. We'll work out the financial ramifications later,' Grant said, and walked away before she could object. Then the phone rang.

'Single vehicle accident out on the highway,' Narelle Speares, the nurse covering A and E at the hospital, said. 'One person, the driver, in the vehicle. The ambulance is on the way out, with an ETA back at the hospital of an hour. I'll give you a call when I get a definite time, but I thought you might like the extra warning to organise the baby.'

'Thanks, Narelle. I appreciate that. I'll call Tara now.'

She was still standing by the phone, uncertainty nibbling at her confidence, when Grant returned with a plastic bag trailing the tantalising whiff of delicious food.

'Called out just as dinner hits the table?' he asked, and she realised he'd have heard the phone.

'No, I've time for dinner.' She explained briefly but still hovered by the phone.

'I'll take the accident case when it comes in,' Grant said. 'After all, it's right up my alley. Three years in A and E, remember.'

He'd found plates and set them on the table and was now opening the plastic containers, releasing more saliva-producing aromas, but Kate still hesitated.

'Come and eat,' Grant urged. 'I'm starving and I can't start without you.'

'I'm coming,' Kate assured him, then she lifted the receiver and dialled Tara's number.

'Hi, Tara, it's Kate. Dr Fenton. Could you pop over in an hour and watch the baby for me?'

She accepted Tara's assurances she'd be there, if not with relief then with less concern than usual, and sat down opposite Grant.

'And Tara is?' he asked.

'A year-twelve student who babysits. She's very obliging, comes in at night or weekends, stays over if she needs to and doesn't charge the earth.'

'And why are you so uncertain about this paragon?'

'I am not!' Kate retorted, but knew from his snort of disbelief she hadn't said it firmly enough. 'She's easily distracted,' she admitted. 'Wants to study medicine, and will start a science degree as a preliminary next year. She loves to read and the problem is, once she's stuck into a book—even something as boring as *Principles of Medicine*—she loses track of time and place.'

'So you sometimes wonder if she loses track of a baby crying as well?'

Kate nodded.

'Though she's very good with the baby. She calls her "little scrap". I really should do something about a name, or the poor thing *will* get confused.'

Grant saw Katie's forehead furrow with worry and wanted to reach out to smooth the pale skin, then he remembered why he was here, ate some more food and asked the question he should have asked before getting sidetracked onto Tara.

'If I'm going over to meet the ambulance, why are you organising a sitter for Sophie?'

He knew by the swift frown that Katie was about to argue the 'Sophie' thing, but then a more important matter apparently took over and she smiled.

'I thought we could both go. Or that I'd make arrangements so we'd both be available if needed. It's such a great opportunity, Grant, to prove that country hospitals can do far more than stabilising patients and sending them on to a regional centre, which is all Paul Newberry ever felt obliged to do. I honestly believe that's happening too much and it's detrimental to patient welfare, as well as being inconvenient and often downright disruptive to the family. With you here, if the patient has injuries a simple operation can fix, we can do it, with one of us acting as anaesthetist and the other as surgeon.'

'We're not talking major stuff here, are we?' Grant asked, pleased to see Katie so enthusiastic but dubious about tackling too big a job with the limited facilities of a small country hospital at their disposal.

'No!' she snapped, so crossly he guessed she'd argued this before. 'I'm talking about suturing or setting simple fractures, things a small hospital should be able to manage. I read back through old hospital files when I first came here, and a young man, injured in a fall from a horse on a Picnic Race day, died on the way to hospital, when a burr hole might have saved him.'

'Burr holes I can do,' Grant assured her, 'though let's hope this patient doesn't need one. Eat up. I see your point. We're getting back to Dr Darling, aren't we? To doctors in those days doing far more varied work within their practice and the hospital.'

Kate forked up some food, savoured the taste for a moment, then leapt back into the conversation.

'Exactly! Even in Dr Darling's time, Testament used to have a series of young doctors at the hospital for a year, or in some cases less than that, so people relied on him far more than they would otherwise. Then, when Dr Darling retired, and the practice became vacant, I suppose the hospital doctor became too busy to do much more than stabilise people and send them on. I guess it was inevitable the hospital became a kind of rehab centre for patients after they'd been treated elsewhere.'

'So how does all this affect your grand plan?' he asked, amused by the enthusiasm lighting her eyes and deepening her voice.

'To be the world's best single mother and country doctor?' She grinned at him. 'Disastrously, that's how. At the moment, the first ambition seems like an impossible dream—even adequate's a battle—and as for doctoring... Once Paul left, and even before the baby arrived, I was flat out keeping up with the extra responsibilities at the hospital on top of my own work, so I haven't had a moment to think about, let alone organise, things like well-patient clinics and all the other ancillary things I think a country GP could do.'

Kate paused, savouring the taste of the food, while her mind whirled with the ideas she'd been unable to share.

Until now.

'If we can get some stability into the hospital position, then I know I can convince the board and nursing staff it's worthwhile to do more here. Obstetrics would be a start. And most of the nurses would be happy to have more challenging work than they're currently doing. Several have expressed interest in doing further training, especially in anaesthesia.'

'Most of the nurses?' Grant echoed, and watched her wide, full lips twist into a grimace.

'Remember Sister Clarke who did the sex-education lectures when we were at school? The ones that made me even more confused than your lecture on how cattle did it?'

Grant chuckled, but felt his body respond to the question, remembering more the demonstration than the lecture.

'Well, she's still here and more than happy with the status quo. She's one year off retirement and doesn't want any hassles. In fact, the fewer really sick people she has in the hospital, the happier she is. A couple of weeks ago she wanted to send old Ma Chisholm to Craigtown because of a simple case of pneumonia, which cleared up in a few days when treated with IV antibiotics. Poor old Ma cried when Sister Clarke suggested it, and I had a no doubt much-talked-about argument with Sister before insisting Ma stay.'

'Did you yell?' Grant asked, remembering how Kate's voice had always got louder and louder as she'd argued.

'Just a bit!' she admitted, smiling at him across the table. 'I was having labour pains at the time, so I wasn't at my most conciliatory. Though I did try being nice to start off with.'

'I can imagine,' Grant said, smiling as he pictured the confrontation between the pregnant woman and the formidable old nursing sister. 'But I can understand what you're saying. It's better, especially for the sake of the patient's family, for people to be treated close to home, though the clustering of specialist services in larger hospitals has reduced the opportunity for that to happen.'

'I think we're getting over-specialised,' Katie said, her ready enthusiasm firing colour into her cheeks. 'Look at orthopaedics, where you have knee, hip, hand and probably even finger sub-specialties. And are patients getting better service? I don't think so.'

Grant, determinedly ignoring the attractiveness of pink cheeks, was about to point out that in some cases they probably were, but the phone rang and someone tapped on the front door, then footsteps in the hall suggested Tara felt enough at home to come straight in.

'The ambulance should be there in ten minutes.' Katie put down the receiver and turned to welcome Tara with a smile and a hug.

'This is Grant Bell—your parents would remember his family. He's gone from being the town bad boy to a respectable doctor, or so he tells me, and he'll be taking most of my calls.'

'So you won't need me to mind the little scrap as often?' Tara said, in such tragic tones that Katie laughed.

'You can come and read my books any time,' she offered, and Grant saw the affection in her eyes as she looked at the young student. 'Admit it—they're the attraction, not a boring baby. Speaking of which, there's milk for her in the refrigerator, and we'll just be at the hospital. We mightn't be long, depending on what we find.'

'Katie mightn't be long—I'm supposed to be the one on call,' Grant added, but Tara was already moving off towards the study.

'She seems keen,' he said, as Katie led the way out the back door where a concrete path crossed to the back of the hospital.

'And starved for reading material,' Kate told him. 'As soon as she heard I was pregnant she offered her services, free, as a babysitter, which was comforting as I'd been trying, without much success, to find someone who'd be willing to come in on a daily basis once the baby arrived.'

'But if she's at school, she can't do that,' Grant said, trying to make sense of the arrangement.

'I *know* that!' Katie told him, coming to a halt at the back of the hospital. 'I had this weird idea that finding someone to look after a small baby would be easy.' She grinned at him. 'Easy-peasy, in fact,' she said, using the phrase she'd always used in her childhood. 'But, boy, was I wrong. I'm quite convinced that some people, if they can't be brain surgeons or super IT company bosses, don't want to work at all. So, at the moment, the baby comes to the surgery with me during the day. Vi and Sally, the clerk, mind her there while I'm working, then evenings and weekends I've got Tara.'

'Who might or might not hear the baby cry, depending on how engrossed she is in the alimentary system or whatever else she's reading up on.'

'Exactly,' Katie said, then, as the approaching siren grew

louder, she walked up the ramp and in through the rear entrance of the hospital.

'It smells the same as it did when I broke my leg when I was twelve, and was in traction for four weeks of the summer holidays.'

Katie nodded.

'I thought the same the minute I walked into the place, and at first assumed it was just a hospital smell, but then I realised it's hospital mixed with oleanders—the line of shrubs on the other boundary. Though why anyone would plant something as potentially deadly as oleanders in hospital grounds is a mystery to me.'

Grant sniffed again, not able to distinguish anything except familiarity.

Kate looked at him, standing there in the brightly lit doorway, sniffing the air with the same intensity he'd always done most things.

Familiarity! That's all that's unsettling you, she told herself, though other bits of her knew it was more to do with the way his body had matured, and the twinkle in his blue eyes when he smiled at her, as if she was somehow special.

But they'd twinkled the same way at Tara, and without much effort she could recall the name of several high school girls who'd thought that twinkle had been just for them.

'Come and meet people,' she said, aware the sirens had stopped and their patient had arrived. Then she remembered it had been Narelle who'd phoned.

Boy, were Grant's eyes about to twinkle when he saw the tall brunette.

For a moment, Kate regretted bringing him across, though that was stupid. If two doctors could offer better service to the patient, then why not use both of them?

CHAPTER FOUR

KATE watched closely, but though Narelle had the expected effect on Grant, who twinkled away at her, it was Narelle who overdid things, positively gushing with delight to meet the new man in town, though rumour had it she was all but engaged to the recently arrived area agricultural advisor.

And given that Grant was also engaged, shouldn't he be twinkling less?

'Actually, I might have got you here under false pretences,' Narelle said, speaking to Kate but smiling at Grant. 'The lad's car was a write-off but he wasn't badly injured. Concussion and a watching brief, I'd say. Dr Bell could see to him while you go back to the baby.'

It was a blatant dismissal and Kate hesitated, uncertain how to handle it, but when Grant said, 'Don't you trust me, Katie?' she knew she had to go. She could hardly stay and appear to be overseeing his examination of the patient.

Though until a new doctor was appointed, the patients in the hospital were her responsibility, so whether or not Grant—or Narelle—liked it, she would stay.

'As Tara's already minding the baby, I'll just check the patient with you then go through to the office. Catch up on a bit of paperwork,' she said, and led the two of them towards the admitting area.

The patient was, as Narelle had said, not much the worse for wear. Contusions on his face and one arm, and bruises coming out on his skin, but sitting up on the gurney and chatting to the ambulance bearers.

'Gareth Crowe! I might have known!' Kate said as soon as she saw him. 'Well, maybe this is good luck. You can meet the man people are always talking about and comparing you to. Gareth, this is Grant Bell.'

'You're *that* Grant Bell?' Narelle said, eyeing Grant even more lasciviously.

'Hey, are you really?' Gareth asked, putting out his hand then wincing as pain caught him with it half-extended. 'I thought you might have been made up—you know, like the bogeyman. People have been saying "You're just another Grant Bell" to me for so long, I'd started to think you were one of those things they have in books—a myth.'

He studied Grant, taking in the flowered shirt and board shorts, long bare legs and sneakers without socks.

'Did you turn out as bad as people predicted? Are you a beach bum? Did Dr Fenton bring you in to show me how I might end up?'

He grinned at Grant.

'I'm actually a doctor,' Grant told him, and Kate guessed he'd been taken aback by Gareth's questions. 'I was holidaying at Byron Bay when I heard Katie—Dr Fenton—needed a locum, so all I had with me were beach clothes.'

'You're a d-doctor?' Gareth stuttered. 'Like Dr Fenton? Like Tara wants to be?'

Kate chuckled at his astonishment.

'Ordinary people, like Grant and me and Tara—though she's far brighter than Grant and I were at school, so not so ordinary—and even you, do become doctors, you know. It takes a bit of work and study, but most people can make it if they decide it's what they really want to do.'

'Which is a better reason for going into something like medicine than for the money you can make.'

Grant's statement was so un-Grant-like that Kate was temporarily shocked, then she remembered it had been many years since she'd seen him and, however much they might have seemed familiar to each other, she had no idea what kind of man the teenage Grant had grown into.

Neither had she checked he really was a doctor, but as

Vi had brought him back to Testament, and she trusted Vi, who'd run the doctor's surgery since Dr Darling's days, Kate had to assume it was OK.

'I'll leave you to judge what kind of doctor he became,' she said to Gareth, then, determined not to make a fool of herself by hanging around, she walked through to the office where there was a genuine pile of paperwork awaiting her attention.

She had just settled behind her desk and was considering where to start when Narelle appeared.

'Grant says can you come,' she said, and Kate knew from her voice something had gone very wrong.

'Maybe you should have crossed your fingers when you mentioned burr holes,' Grant said, as he helped a wardsman wheel the gurney towards the theatre. They weren't running, or in any other way indicating panic, but they moved with swift purpose. 'Gareth complained briefly of a bad headache then lapsed into unconsciousness again, his systolic pressure's shot up and heartbeat's slowed.'

'Dilated pupil?' Kate asked, knowing a period of unconsciousness followed by a lucid period then a lapse back into coma was usually a sign of an acute epidural haemorrhage.

'Right side. We were about to X-ray his skull for fractures when he deteriorated.'

Grant kept speaking as they moved, and Kate took in what had already been given to the young man. Her mind raced ahead, working out drugs and dosages—always dicey in the case of brain-injured patients.

Though once they'd drilled a hole and released the leaking blood which was causing pressure on Gareth's brain, he should make a full recovery.

If they were quick enough…

'You've done it before?' she asked Grant, and saw his quick nod.

'Then I'll do the anaesthetic and Narelle can assist you.'

She went ahead, entering Theatre through the dressing rooms and hurriedly donning theatre pyjamas over her clothes, exchanging her own sandals for the floppy paper slippers, pulling a cap over her unruly hair and grabbing a mask.

In the theatre itself, she set up the monitor and found the drugs, catheters and tubing she'd need. Narelle came in with a sealed bundle.

'I've seen this burr-hole bundle,' she said as she unwrapped it to expose the instruments and swabs Grant would need, 'but never thought I'd see it used here.'

'Did you check the date on it?' Kate asked, knowing the paper wrappings on the sterile bundle of instruments and swabs could deteriorate, allowing contamination into the bundle.

'It's current,' Narelle assured her. 'All the bundles were changed when Paul arrived—it was one thing he did do.'

Kate wasn't surprised by the remark, as she had yet to hear many positive comments about Paul Newberry. Though, now she considered the urgency, the use-by date on the bundle was irrelevant.

The patient was lifted onto the operating table, and while Narelle and Grant scrubbed Kate readied him for the operation, positioning him on the table with the injured side uppermost, propping his right shoulder on a towel so his head was rotated with the dilated pupil uppermost, draping his body with sterile sheeting and covering all but a small portion of his skull with the green, papery material. She checked the airway Grant must have inserted and made sure its connection to the oxygen supply was clear but out of the way, and that the leads to the monitor were also connected but not about to impair access to the site of the operation.

Working with deft fingers, she inserted a catheter and taped it to the back of Gareth's left hand, then glanced at her watch. It had seemed like ages, but only five minutes earlier he had been talking to them.

She chose an anaesthetising agent which could be easily reversed. Though Gareth was unconscious now, it wouldn't do to have him coming to as the pressure was released during the operation.

Grant and Narelle came in, Narelle taking up her position beside the trolley where the instruments were displayed.

'At least we don't have to shave his head,' Grant remarked. 'No way would we have been allowed at school with shaven heads.'

He was talking as he measured and marked the place where he'd cut, his fingers moving swiftly into position above the lad's temporal area, above the zygomatic arch and behind the ear. With skilful movements for a man not used to surgery, he sliced through the skin, separated the muscle away from the bone, drilled through the skull to the inner surface and changed the drill for a softer burr.

There was no chit-chat, no jokes, all of them aware, without the need for words, that Gareth lived or died depending on the speed and success of what they were doing.

'I'll scoop out a little more soft material then syringe out the blood,' Grant said, and Kate found herself admiring Narelle's efficiency and the smooth way she and Grant worked together.

And wondering why the observation made her feel more grouchy than pleased.

'Suction?'

Kate watched and waited, and even through the loose-fitting theatre garb saw Grant's shoulders relax.

'It's thick, coagulating, nothing fresh and red, so hopefully the little bleeder's shut itself off and we don't have to look any further.'

Kate felt her relief like a physical lightening of weight, though she knew this end stage of the operation was up to her. While Grant patched and stitched the hole he'd made, she had to bring Gareth slowly back to a level just below consciousness, then find a satisfactory means of keeping him sedated enough to make the journey to Craigtown comfortably and with a minimum of distress. Once there, the decision would be made as to whether to keep him in an induced coma for a few days while any swelling in his brain subsided.

'I'll take it from here,' she told Grant. 'He'll have to go to Craigtown for scans and observation so I'll get him ready to transport. His parents are probably here by now, so maybe if you could talk to them? Explain…?'

He'd pulled off his mask as he walked away from the operating table and he turned to smile at Kate.

'You want me to do the dirty work?'

'I do not!' she said indignantly, though the smile had sent a quiver across her skin. 'Anyway, I'd have thought you'd be pleased to see Helen Crowe.' She paused for a beat then, straight-faced, added, 'She was Helen Jones—Miss Jones to you and all the rest of the senior maths class.'

'Our Miss J-Jones?' Grant stuttered, moving his hands in the air to indicate an exaggeratedly hourglass figure.

'The very same,' Kate assured him, smiling at the expression of horror on his face. 'She's Gareth's stepmother.'

'I'll do the reversal,' he offered. 'Take over from you. After all, you're the local doctor, you should talk to them.'

Kate chuckled.

'You're what, nearly thirty-one, and still afraid of your old maths teacher?'

'You may laugh,' Grant said grimly. 'But there wasn't a boy in high school who didn't lust after that woman, but she could cut off your legs and shrivel your—well, you know what she could shrivel, with one glance. Then she'd complete the annihilation by doubling the maths homework.'

He paused then added, 'Actually, it's a wonder we didn't all end up sexually impaired for life.'

'One assumes you didn't?' Narelle said cheekily, returning to the theatre in time to catch the tail end of the conversation. 'Helen and Peter Crowe are outside and would like to see you, Grant.'

Kate watched him go—watched them go—and once again felt a totally inappropriate niggle of what could only be described as pique.

'Watch yourself,' she warned, as she concentrated on Gareth and getting him ready for the two-hour trip to Craigtown.

'Are your weekends always this busy?' Grant asked, when, with Gareth despatched to the bigger town, they walked back to the house. 'We've barely had time to say hello, let alone go through your working hours and discuss what you want me to do.'

Katie failed to answer and, sensing her distraction, he turned to study her more closely as they walked under the light at the boundary between the house and the hospital.

'Why the frown?'

She heard him that time, spinning towards him with a hint of panic in her lovely eyes.

'Was I frowning? Did you ask something? I'm sorry.'

She pushed her hair around a bit on her head, obviously trying to remove the bits that fell forward over her face but not succeeding.

'Honestly, Grant,' she admitted, 'this motherhood thing is so weird. It's as if the body takes over from the mind in the decision-making process.'

'Not only in motherhood situations,' Grant interrupted, thinking of times, even between the two of them, when that had happened.

'I'm not talking about sex,' she snapped. 'I'm talking about everyday life, here. I mean, I should have been thinking about Gareth or whatever you were asking me but, no, my breasts are aching and I'm hoping Tara hasn't fed the baby because my body obviously thinks it's time to feed her, and I'm trying to remember when I last fed her, and if a feed's due. It's pathetic! My life is dominated by my mammary glands.'

'Not so pathetic if you think of the number of young men who failed maths as they went through Testament High, because their brains were reduced to mush by Helen Crowe's bounteous breasts. Perhaps, while you're in this situation, we could do a paper on it—the correlation between breasts and brain function from both male and female perspectives.'

They'd reached the kitchen and walked in to find Tara sitting, feet up on a chair, a book propped in front of her, while the baby slept peacefully in her arms.

'She's been fed!' Katie said, in such tragic tones Grant had to laugh.

'No, actually, she hasn't,' Tara responded. 'She had a little cry so I picked her up, changed her and carried her out to heat the milk, and by the time I got here she was asleep again.' She grinned at the pair of them and added, 'Let sleeping babies lie—isn't that the rule?'

'Most definitely,' Katie agreed, but Grant saw the way her eyes went to the sleeping infant, scanning, checking, emitting uncertainty and love in equal measure.

Not unlike what he was feeling towards Katie herself, though the love was certainly a nostalgic emotion—like an emotional hangover—inextricably linked to childhood and adolescence.

Then, because his mind seemed inclined to debate this issue, he focussed on the baby.

'Do you like Sophie as a name for her?' he asked Tara, and was pleased to see the studious young woman put down her book and earnestly consider the small face.

'Nah! She's way too pretty for a Sophie. Sophies are elegant—attractive, rather than pretty. And I reckon, though she's just about perfect now, the little scrap'll probably end up with that wild, untamed sort of look Kate has—too elemental for a Sophie.'

The statement drew protest from Katie, but Grant found himself considering it.

Elemental! That was the word he'd been looking for when he'd been thinking of Katie's fire and passion. Katie's beauty burned from within—

'I don't know where you two get off with naming my baby!'

Her protest cut into his thoughts.

'Well, you're not doing much about it,' Grant reminded her.

'I am so!' she snorted, but far too quickly for him to believe it.

'OK, tell us what you're thinking. Share a little.'

Kate saw the challenge—and amusement—in Grant's eyes, and though she longed to reel off any number of suitable names, for some reason the only female name that came immediately to mind was Hortense, and neither Grant nor Tara would believe she was seriously considering it.

She leaned over to pick up the baby, willing her to wake and demand her supper, but, of course, lacking any sense of timing—a failing she'd already lectured the baby on today—the wee thing slept on.

'My grandmother's name was Rose so I thought that might fit in somewhere,' she said, when she realised the silence in the kitchen had been caused by her failure to reply. 'Rose, Lily, Ruby, Sapphire—they're all coming back into fashion at the moment.'

Grant's expression of disbelief was so comical, she'd probably have laughed if she hadn't been feeling so confused about so many things—him being here now taking over from baby names in the prime position of concern.

'You can't call a baby any of those names,' he protested. 'Not if she's going to live in the country where people still think names like Linda are New Age. I bet Tara's mother felt very brave choosing Tara and I'm sure when Gareth's mother named him Gareth, the entire town blamed the fact that she was an in-comer—a city girl with city ways. Who was she, by the way, and what happened to her?'

'She was another teacher, and you're right about the city ways. She hated the country and left her husband with Gareth when he was only young.' Tara supplied the information then frowned at Grant.

'Why did you think of Gareth?' she demanded. 'Do you know him?'

Kate saw the flush on the girl's cheeks and remembered Gareth mentioning Tara's name. Was a romance budding between the high school's best achiever and the local bad boy?

Again?

She set aside the thought, wondering how much she could tell Tara about the accident, but before she could decide, Grant had taken over. He'd slipped into a chair opposite Tara and was explaining the accident, and when he grabbed the whiteboard Kate kept to jot down messages to herself, and began to draw a skull, Kate realised Tara was just as interested in the mechanics of the operation as she was in Gareth's well-being.

'I'll feed Hortense,' she murmured, but neither of them heard, and, as she walked through to her bedroom, she wondered if she'd have been the same—back then. Though she'd been two years behind Grant at school, and medicine hadn't always been her goal.

But the young Kate—or Katie as she had been then—and the teenage Grant accompanied her, like friendly ghosts, to the bedroom, and, as the baby began to suckle and her stomach muscles tightened in response, she couldn't help but think of that other summer.

'Coming swimming, Katie?' he'd asked, and his voice, so familiar though he'd only started phoning her regularly since the holidays had begun, had made her stomach cramp and tighten, while her heart had flip-flopped in her chest like a just-landed fish.

'I'll have to ask Mum,' she'd said, knowing she'd tell her mother it was Sally on the phone. Her mother wouldn't have stopped her seeing Grant—it was just that the shift in their relationship had been too new, too delicate and fragile, to be shared.

'It's OK. I'll ride out,' she'd said, returning to the phone once the lie had been accepted and permission given.

'See you soon,' he'd said, and she'd known he'd ride to meet her, then they'd turn off near the boundary to his parents' property, seeking a secluded stretch of the river where the banks were steep so the cattle rarely strayed.

'It wasn't that the cattle were a problem,' Kate told the baby. 'Only the people who might be looking for them and inadvertently find us.'

Not that they'd planned to go beyond the kissing—not that day, or really any other day in the near future.

'The kissing was mind-blowing enough,' Kate said, burping the baby before shifting her to the other side. 'The shift from friends to more than friends was really weird. It just happened those holidays and, boy, did it happen. Talk about passion!'

The memory brought a warmth she hadn't felt for ages, but the baby had fallen asleep and needed to be changed again before she was settled for the night—or whatever part of it she might happen to sleep.

'It must have been the heat—or only having swimsuits on,' she told the sleeping infant, while her body, so long dormant, now rippled with sensations that had nothing to do with breastfeeding.

A tap on the door made her look up, feeling so guilty about her thoughts she could feel her cheeks awash with heated colour.

'Tara's just gone. I walked her home, but I didn't pay her. Should I have done?'

'No!' Kate said, then realised the word had sounded far too abrupt when Grant put up his hands as if to ward off an attack.

'Hey, I was only asking about paying the babysitter, not if I could mount an assault on your virtue.'

Kate shook her head, then she gave a quiet laugh.

'Actually,' she admitted, 'that's more or less what I was saying no to. I was thinking about that last summer—about the day you rang to ask me to go swimming.'

Grant was startled by the admission, but the funny little smile lingering around Katie's lips, and the softness in her voice, suggested the memories were happy ones.

'We did enjoy it, didn't we?' she said, busying herself with changing the baby's nappy so he could no longer see her face. 'I mean, it *was* fun, wasn't it? Not just a rose-coloured-glasses view of the past.'

Uncertain how to respond, but aware of a need to step with the greatest delicacy, Grant walked closer, then, as she finished wrapping the baby in the snug cotton sheet, he lifted the little bundle and held her to his shoulder.

'It was the best summer of my life,' he said simply. 'Not just because I discovered sex, but because I discovered it with you.'

This time Katie's look was of blank astonishment.

'You discovered sex with me? But you'd had… Everyone said… You made out…'

The run of unfinished sentences ended abruptly and she came closer, peering up into his face.

'Are you telling me, Grant Bell, that you knew no more about it than I did? That we were both virgins?'

He nodded, though not sure it was the correct thing to do right now.

'Well, of all the cheek!' she stormed. Remembering the baby, Katie seized her from Grant's arms, tucked her back into the crib, then all but shoved him out of the room, shutting the door behind them, no doubt so she could yell without waking the baby.

'You let me believe you knew all about it. You even told me the proper names for bits of my anatomy I'd barely realised existed, and gave me a lecture on what happens during orgasm. Were you making it all up?'

Grant hustled her towards the kitchen.

'I'd read it out of a book Mum had at home,' he admitted. 'She'd bought it for my sisters to read.'

'But you had condoms!' Kate reminded him.

'Everyone had condoms—well, all males of teenage years had them, and I wouldn't be surprised if some of the girls didn't carry them as well!' Grant replied. 'Talk about hopeful! I'd actually had a supply of them since I was twelve. Every time we went to Craigtown, I'd get a packet at the supermarket. And don't look so shocked—it was better than buying them at Patterson's Pharmacy here in Testament. Mrs P. would have been on the phone to Mum before I was out the door.'

Kate shook her head, though somewhere, deep inside, was a little bubble of warmth she suspected might have been generated by pleasure at Grant's revelations.

Though he needn't know that.

Definitely needn't know that...

'I can't believe you made out—' she began, but he interrupted with his wide-eyed, innocent 'who, me?' look, followed by a smile of sheer devilment.

'Actually,' he said softly, 'we both "made out"—remember?'

She was twenty-eight years of age, a doctor and a mother, and she was *not* going to blush!

But just in case, she turned away.

'That isn't what I meant, and you know it,' she muttered, heading back to the kitchen for a cup of tea before going to bed. 'I can't believe you pretended to know it all! Or pretended to know, in the biblical sense, most of the girls in town.'

'Would it have made any difference?'

She had to turn again, to face him, and when she realised he was serious, she had to think about it.

'I would probably have been far more tentative and uncertain, but I was such a show-off that thinking *you* knew it all made me anxious not to appear a complete amateur.'

She shook her head, remembering.

'Gosh, we were intense, weren't we? I don't think I've ever felt that level of intensity in a relationship since then. It was probably a hormonal thing, like risk-taking among teenagers. Once the hormones settle down, you don't get that terrible rush of heat and longing.'

She spoke with clinical detachment, as if it was something that had happened to two other people. So why, Grant wondered, did his body feel a faint quickening of interest?

Because whatever he'd had with Katie was unfinished?

Because 'that terrible rush of heat and longing' described those feelings so well, and he, too, had never experienced them again.

'What *are* you thinking about?' she demanded. 'Do you want a cup of tea is one of those "answer yes or no" type questions. It doesn't require frowns, or even a great deal of brain power to reply.'

He looked into the green eyes and told himself it was dangerous to think of anything apart from the job. Excessively dangerous to go wallowing into the murky waters of the past. Worse than diving into unexplored parts of the creek—near where they'd…

'Sorry, didn't hear you. Yes, please.'

'I've shop biscuits. They may be a bit old, but I've a wonderful assortment of jam, pickles and chutneys to spread on them to disguise the oldness. I think everyone in town has brought me a bottle of homemade something since I've been here. They've been good that way. There are the hard scones as well.'

She was bustling around the kitchen, filling the electric kettle and setting it to boil, finding mugs, tea bags, talking.

Talking?

Grant smiled to himself.

Katie had always talked too much when she was nervous. Maybe the nostalgic memories had quickened *her* body, too.

So he needn't feel so bad, and he could put the small incident behind him, back in the furthest pigeonholes of his mind where those happy teenage memories belonged.

'There!' She set a mug on the table in front of him, with the air of someone who'd just split the atom using only a blunt kitchen knife. 'I've sugar somewhere if you want it, and litres and litres of milk. You want milk?'

Grant picked up the string of the tea bag and jiggled it furiously, hoping to darken the watery brew.

'No milk, no sugar. Working in A and E makes shopping erratic so, rather than hating the taste of tea with no milk when it went sour or with no sugar when I ran out, I learned to live without both.'

'Why A and E?' she asked, dropping into a chair opposite him, removing her tea bag and placing it on a saucer.

Grant hesitated, then decided there was nothing to be gained by not telling the truth.

'Money,' he said simply, then he grinned at the astonishment in her eyes.

'Hey, I had my reasons,' he said, hoping to banish the disbelief which had followed the astonishment. For some unknown reason, he didn't want Katie thinking badly of him. 'When we had to leave the property—and I know it wasn't your father's fault, no matter how I acted at the time—we shifted to Sydney where Mum's family were. But the country was still in my blood and I vowed I'd get the place back one day. Well, maybe not that property but *a* property. Somewhere I could run a few cattle—I didn't want the hassle of sheep or even crops.'

He shrugged, then smiled as he admitted, 'I guess it was that teenage intensity you were talking about earlier. Anyway, you'd always talked about becoming a doctor, and I knew a lot of doctors made a lot of money so, once I'd accepted I wasn't going to be raising cattle in the immediate future, I thought I'd be a doctor, earn heaps and buy back the farm.'

'Easy-peasy!' Katie teased.

'Exactly,' Grant agreed, though the silly phrase jolted his complacency about having the past tucked securely back in the pigeonholes. 'Once I qualified, I stayed in hospitals, working the weekend and night shifts in A and E whenever possible, often moonlighting as well in private twenty-four-hour clinics or on-call services.'

'And when did you realise you'd kill yourself with work before you ever had enough money to buy a cattle property around here?'

Her lips flickered into a smile, her eyes were alight with a teasing laughter and he found himself grinning happily back at her, feeling dangerously at home in Katie's house—in Katie's life!

More than at home...

'Pretty soon after I'd started,' he admitted, banishing all other thoughts. 'I decided I could settle for somewhere less expensive, fewer cattle, maybe a hobby farm. Though, by the time I figured it out, I was hooked on the A and E department. Talk about an adrenalin junkie! I'd have fitted right into one of those manic scenes in televised medical dramas.'

'So you stayed three years?'

He nodded, but realised just how close he'd come to talking about other things.

'Well, it's been a long day. I might head for bed. OK if I use the bathroom?'

Kate nodded, and watched him leave the room. They hadn't discussed work tomorrow, or wages, or shared housekeeping, or any of the things which should have been discussed, but when she'd asked about the length of his stay in A and E, a dark shadow had clouded Grant's blue eyes and drawn lines of strain down his cheeks, and she'd known he needed to get away.

Right then!

Before he told her more?

What kind of more?

She shivered in the warm night air, sensing a darkness in the heart and soul of her old childhood companion— some kind of wound that hadn't healed. And her heart, which she'd been sure was armour-plated against all emotion, ached for Grant.

CHAPTER FIVE

GRANT BELL was the last person on her mind as Kate stumbled into the kitchen in the light of early dawn. The baby—today, much later today, she'd decide on a name—had woken every two hours, and though she'd gone happily back to sleep after each feed, for a new mother hoping to get four or even six hours' straight sleep, the two-hourly demands had been a nightmare.

Kate poured milk into a mug and, clutching it in one hand and a slice of bread in the other, was making her way back to bed, fuzzily working out that if she went straight to sleep now, and could stay asleep until eight, she'd have—five from eight leaves three—three hours' sleep before starting work at eight-fifteen. Surely she could shower and dress in ten—

'Go back to bed and stay there!' The gruff order interrupted her muddled mathematical calculations. 'I'll take the morning surgery—it's why I'm here after all. If I need any help Vi can't give or information she can't supply, I'll phone you.'

Kate stared blankly at the man who'd emerged from the spare bedroom. She'd known he was there—had been aware, all through the night, of another presence in the house. But seeing him, recognising him as Grant, standing and talking to him—she in a faded old shirt she wore to bed, and he in boxer shorts that seemed, to her sleep-deprived eyes, to have big red lips all over them—was too way out to believe.

'I thought I might have dreamt you,' she admitted, then added ruefully, 'Though I guess I'd have to have been asleep to dream, wouldn't I?'

72

'Bad night?'

'Just interrupted,' Kate said quickly, remembering she'd promised herself she wouldn't be one of those mothers who complained all the time about the demands of any aspect of motherhood.

'Though they've every right to complain about two-hourly night feeds!' she grumbled to herself.

Then she glanced guiltily at Grant, hoping he hadn't heard. But if he had, he gave no sign of it, merely studying her with an intent kind of interest, as if he, too, was slightly bemused to find the two of them meeting like this in a passageway.

'Bed!' he repeated, making a command of the word, and Kate's mind, fuzzy with tiredness, wondered how it would sound as an invitation.

'And don't smile at me like that!' he added, sounding quite cross now, so she didn't dare to ask, Like what? 'I'll do morning surgery, you rest. We can talk over lunch, decide on a rough programme, then shop before afternoon surgery.'

'That sounds suspiciously like a list,' Kate told him.

'It's not a list, it's a plan. Now go back to bed, Katie, before Fiona wakes again.'

'Fiona? I thought you'd decided on Sophie—for this week at least.'

'I'm flexible,' Grant said with a grin, then he put his hand on her shoulder, turned her around and steered her into her bedroom.

Which was when Kate realised just how great a danger to her peace of mind Grant Bell represented.

It wasn't so much the touch, which had started the shivery-skin phenomenon again, as the rightness of the touch—and *that* was a really scary thought!

She glanced over to where he was studying the sleeping baby, trying out the name Fiona, if Kate's reading of his lips was correct. Tall, lean and hard, though she doubted he did much physical work these days, there was a familiarity about Grant as if the very cells that made up her body recognised a match in his.

Nonsensical meanderings of an overtired mind, Kate chided herself, but her eyes continued to watch him, and her body cells to recognise his.

Well, she hoped that's all it was—the recognition thing—because there was no way she could possibly be feeling sexy. Not two weeks after giving birth—it just wasn't possible. And Grant Bell was passing through Testament, then going back to his Linda, while she was setting up a life for herself and the baby—a life and a career.

'I think Fiona would suit her.'

The statement startled Kate, bringing her abruptly out of her straying thoughts, but not swiftly enough to deny his words.

'I'll think about it,' she said, 'when I've had some sleep and my brain starts functioning again.'

She smiled at Grant, because he was there, and being kind, and it certainly wasn't his fault her body was behaving the way it was.

'I'm glad you're here,' she admitted.

He'd been doing all right until she'd smiled, Grant realised as he left the room, shutting the door firmly on the woman and sleeping baby. Or had it been the 'I'm glad you're here' that had thrown him?

Whatever—but the two, taken in conjunction, had caused a tremor that could only be anxiety. And given his decision to remain preferably single and definitely childless, getting tremors of any kind in a bedroom with a sensual woman and tiny sleeping baby was not good.

But she had looked so incredibly sexy, in her big, loose shirt, her hair tousled into a tangle so seductively sensual it was all he could do to keep his hands out of it. Maybe it was because she was feeding the baby, and positively oozing maternal hormones, that his body found her disturbingly attractive. It was all to do with primal urges, and procreation, with a bit of a protection thing thrown in. Though he, of all people, knew protection didn't extend far—knew the futility of thinking anyone could keep another human being safe.

He went through to the kitchen, his arms aching again in a way they hadn't ached for eighteen months, and, as he slumped into a chair and stared out the window at the pale relentless blue of an early summer morning sky, he wondered why he'd come to Testament.

And why he hadn't realised his coming would peel away the scabs of healing wounds and expose him to pain he'd thought he'd conquered.

'You came because Vi said Katie needed help, and helping anyone was better than hanging around a beach that lacked enough swell to make a ripple, let alone a wave, feeling sorry for yourself,' he reminded himself. 'And speaking of Vi, it's time you got dressed and went over to investigate the surgery. No! Bakery first. Some fresh bread. Maybe Katie would like a pastry or two when she wakes later.'

Which was being practical, not protective.

Thus assured his motives were OK, he was out the door and almost at the back lane when he realised he was wearing the 'hot lips' boxer shorts and nothing else. Shirtless might just pass in Testament at six in the morning, but boxer shorts?

He doubted it!

Back inside he pulled board shorts over the boxers and a flowered shirt over his chest. Looking at the flowers reminded him of the fictitious Chlorinda. He'd invented her on the spur of the moment, to make it easier for Katie to accept him, then hadn't followed up on the idea. Should he let that story drop completely, keep her in reserve, or bring her to the fore of his conversation—use her like a shield to

deflect the emotional weakness he was in danger of expos-
ing if he became too involved in Katie's and Fiona's lives?

It was a dilemma he would normally have considered as
he walked briskly down the road towards the shops, but a
carolling magpie peering, bright-eyed, down at him from
the branch of a she-oak, raucously chattering galahs flying
like a pink cloud overhead, the scent of eucalypts in the
air, the sun flirting with the leaves, turning them from green
to silver, all combined to banish thought from his mind. He
moved along, barely conscious of the physical effort as his
body revelled in a sense of homecoming so strong he
wanted to shout out loud and spread his arms wide enough
to embrace the world.

'Embrace the bloody world? You've gone bonkers, you
have!' he muttered, then he nodded good morning to a startled dog walker who'd caught him talking to himself.

He concentrated on practical matters—food first, then
check out the appointment book in the surgery and have a
quick look at the patient files so he wouldn't be completely
at a loss when the patients came in. Too late now to phone
Vi to assure her he'd arrived safely but, given the efficiency
of country-town grapevines, she'd probably know anyway.

'Grant Bell! Heard you were back in town but didn't
believe it.'

The greeting, as he walked into the bakery, redolent with
the smell of new-baked bread, suggested the grapevine still
worked, but though the face which uttered it was familiar
it took a while to dredge up a name.

'Codger? Codger Williams? But your father was the
postmaster, not the baker.'

Codger—whose real name, Grant remembered now, had
been Bill, William Williams of all things—shoved out a
hand the size of a baseball glove.

'Never fancied eating letters,' he said. 'Did my appren-
ticeship here under old Harry Smart and took over when
he retired. Not that he properly retired—the old fellow still

comes in each day to tell me what I've done wrong with the pies or coffee rolls.'

Grant shook the offered hand and, suspecting Codger was about to embark on a lengthy game of 'do you remember', gave his order.

'I'll be back to have a chat as soon as I'm settled,' he said. 'But since arriving yesterday I've been on the run so I haven't had time to check out the surgery.'

'Fancy you becoming a doctor,' Codger said, using tongs to lift pastries into a white paper bag. 'Katie Fenton—well, we all knew she'd go that way. Bloody brilliant, she was. But bad boy Bell? That's a different story. Saw the light, did you? Decided there was more money to be made in the medical profession than swiping chocolates off the display in the newsagent's?'

'Ben Whiting swiped the chocolates, I just got the blame,' Grant protested, though his mind was scooting backwards, wondering if everyone in town—including all the patients he was about to see—would have a 'bad boy Bell' tale to tell.

'Yeah?' Codger said, making the word so disbelieving Grant knew it would be a waste of breath to argue.

He handed over a note, and took the change and his purchases, leaving the shop with a promise to return to talk over old times.

Not in this lifetime! he added to himself as he walked back towards the house. As if I don't have enough embarrassing memories of my own without people like Codger digging up more.

The walk back to the house was undertaken with a marked diminution of enthusiasm. So much so, the thought of the wave-less beach seemed positively enticing. He tried reminding himself it was nearly Christmas, but it was so long since he'd felt anything approaching a festive spirit at this time of the year that the thought was more dampening than uplifting.

But when he moved quietly through to the bedrooms, opening Katie's door and peering in, the sight of her, sleeping deeply, as if confident he'd take care of everything, reminded him that it was good to be needed sometimes.

He glanced towards the crib and saw the baby stirring, then, before he could decide if picking her up would be a good idea, she gave a funny snuffle, made a little grunting noise and waved her arms as if expecting company. Telling himself it was just this once, and picking her up didn't mean getting involved, he crossed the room in two long strides and lifted her, turning to snag a couple of everything from the piles of baby necessities by the bed.

He saw the sling, hooked over the doorknob, as he was leaving the room, and grabbed that as well.

'I know there's expressed milk in the fridge, but as it doesn't come with a use-by date, I have no idea if it's fresh. No idea how long it stays fresh, now I come to think of it. Debbie used formula. But as I also know you were fed only an hour ago, I think we'll give it a miss.'

The huge blue eyes studied him, as if taking in every word he said, remaining fixed on his face as he set her down on the couch and proceeded with nappy changing.

'I'm quite adept at this,' he told her. 'Which is good for you, as I might be doing a bit of it over the next few weeks. Your mother needs to rest. You understand that, don't you?'

The sling took longer to work out than he'd expected, but eventually he had the baby tied securely, if not neatly, to the front of his chest.

'Damn! Should have had the cup of tea first so I don't run the risk of slopping scalding liquid over your downy head.'

He peered down at the downy head in question, and added, 'Though now you appear to have gone back to sleep, that's less likely to happen.'

Moving cautiously as he adjusted to the difference in his

body shape, he set out the pastries on a plate and covered them with plastic film so Katie would see them when she came into the kitchen. Made himself toast, and decided to risk the tea, though he did add cold water so, should an accident occur, it would be warm and not scalding liquid splashing everywhere, concentrating all the time on the practical, so he didn't have to think about the warm bundle pressed against his chest.

'Good heavens, look at Dr Dad!'

He swung from the sink where he was rinsing off his plate to see Aunt Vi come through the door. He moved towards her, leaning carefully forward far enough to plant a big kiss on his favourite relative's cheek.

'Katie's sleeping and Fiona didn't need feeding, so I thought I'd keep her occupied for a while,' he explained.

'Fiona? Kate's finally named her, then?'

Vi seemed so pleased Grant hated to disabuse her of the notion, but honesty compelled him to explain.

'You can't try out names on babies!' his relative protested.

'Why not?' he demanded. 'It seems eminently sensible to me. Anyway, I should be over at the surgery learning what's where, not arguing with you about a name for a baby that doesn't belong to either of us.'

Vi cast him a funny look.

'Bringing too much back, is it? I did wonder when I asked you to come, but after that wretched Paul left town, then the locum woman let Kate down so badly, I had to find someone.'

'I was happy to come,' Grant assured her. He couldn't bring himself to deny the 'bringing too much back' comment, so he let it slide. 'Now, did you want something from here, or were you just checking there was a doctor available to start work?'

'I was just checking,' Vi said, 'but now I've checked, are you really coming to work like that?'

Grant peered downward.

'I thought I'd take the baby off before I start. Katie said you'd been minding her at work.'

'I wasn't talking about the baby, but the shirt,' Vi told him. 'And the shorts.'

'It's all I have. No, I lie! I have one pair of long, cotton, draw-string trousers—cargo pants really—but it's far too hot for long pants out here. They were for going out. I've been in Byron Bay, remember.'

'Yes!' Vi said faintly, then she squared her shoulders as if readying herself for battle. 'Well, if a single, pregnant Katie Fenton arriving in town as the new doctor shocked a bit of life into the place, I can't wait to see what you in your lurid beach gear is going to do!'

'Liven the locals up a little more,' Grant said, smiling and moving closer to give his aunt a hug.

She responded with a quick kiss on his cheek.

'It's about time you came home,' she said.

Home?

Now, that was a scary—no, forget scary, that was a positively terrifying thought.

An impossible thought.

'I've only come to help Katie out,' he reminded Vi. 'And seeing how isolated she is, I'm glad I was available. You know that hospital doctor did nothing more than the basic checks during her pregnancy, and there are no antenatal classes. The poor woman's been at her wit's end.'

'She told you all of that?' Vi demanded.

Grant peered at his aunt, puzzled by the disbelief in her voice.

'Why shouldn't she?'

'Why shouldn't she?' Vi repeated. 'There's no earthly reason why she shouldn't except that, since the moment she arrived in town, she's been Miss Independent. Miss I-can-manage-on-my-own. Offers of help were met with polite smiles and thanks but, no, thanks. I was surprised when

I took a casserole around and she didn't give it straight back to me.'

The picture Vi was painting was disturbing, and as his aunt pulled patient files from the shelves, and he unwound Fiona from his chest, he said, speaking more to himself than to Vi, 'I wonder why? I wonder what made her so unwilling to accept favours from people? Even to the extent of assuring her parents she didn't need them here for the baby's birth?'

'From what I can gather, both the baby's father and her own mother suggested an abortion,' Vi said, closing the cupboard door and turning to take the baby from his arms. 'So perhaps she feels, having decided to go it alone, she doesn't deserve help, particularly from strangers—which is what we are to her after all these years.'

'That's why her parents should be here—or at least her mother. Katie says they'd planned their overseas trip for years, but I wonder if there's more to it. If there's been a family feud over her keeping the baby.'

Vi led the way to the reception area, then turned towards him.

'She was always a bit of a snob, Mrs Fenton,' she mused. 'And since he became State Manager of the bank, I imagine she's got worse. Kate's choice of single motherhood mightn't have sat well with her. But Kate was always a loyal young thing—she certainly wouldn't say if there'd been serious trouble.'

'You're right about the loyalty, but there can't be an irreparable feud. She sent Katie recipes.'

'Which the poor girl needed like a hole in the head,' Vi fumed. 'Overseas trip or not, Mrs Fenton should have come herself. She should be cooking not only all the meals but stocking up the freezer for when she leaves, and babysitting while Kate works, and taking her granddaughter for walks, and generally supporting her daughter, not sending flaming recipes.'

Grant smiled at Vi's vehemence.

'If the scones were an example of the way Katie cooks, they probably will be flaming,' he said. 'But enough of Katie for now. Let's see the patient list. Who do I know?'

'Just about everyone, though they've all aged a bit.' Vi set the baby down in a little basket positioned on a wide table at the back of the reception area. Beside it, neatly stacked, were piles of baby gear, similar to the ones in Katie's bedroom.

'Does no one use cupboards and little chests of drawers any more?' he asked, forgetting they were supposed to be in work-mode.

'That's another thing her mother should have seen to,' Vi said darkly. 'The poor girl has no baby furniture and changing that baby on the bed instead of on a high table or baby-changing thingy will wreck her back.'

Grant tucked the words 'baby furniture' into the back of his mind, though he could see it all—the chest of drawers with duckling decals on it, the changing table with little pockets everywhere for the odds and ends a baby needed, the bag that hung from the ceiling and held folded nappies.

'You'd better remind me who people are,' he said to Vi, shoving the mental image back into the furthermost corner of his mind. 'You know, the old "you remember Mrs Woulfe" trick.'

'I'll try,' Vi told him, 'though there are sure to be some slip-ups. It's twelve years since you were in town, and we have had some newcomers in that time.'

'A new bank manager for a start,' Grant said, reading through the names in the appointment book and trying to put faces to them. 'How long ago did the Fentons leave?'

'When Katie was in her final year of high school. They actually left mid-year and she stayed on with the Williams family so she didn't have to move schools.'

'Codger Williams's family?'

'That's right,' Vi replied, totally unconcerned by this

revelation that was causing Grant considerable dismay, though why he wasn't sure. Actually, he was sure! The thought of the teenage Katie and the libidinous Codger sharing a bathroom was enough to make anyone uneasy, no matter how far in the past it was.

He concentrated on the names.

'Mrs Russell—that's not old Mrs Russell, is it? She was over a hundred before we left town.'

'She was eighty-eight when you left town and turned a hundred earlier this year. Her kidneys are giving up and the specialist down in Brisbane recommended she go on this Eprex. It means weekly injections. Kate got a lot of information about it, and has to order in the injections through the specialist. I'll get the file.'

She passed a thick file to Grant, who opened it and found the information leaflets explaining the drug Mrs Russell would be getting. Eprex was a trade name for erythropoietin, a hormone synthesised in the kidneys and released into the blood to stimulate the production of red blood cells.

In people with chronic renal disease, the kidneys failed to produce the hormone, leading to a drop in the red blood cells. Because these cells carried oxygen throughout the body, the patient suffered from breathlessness and the general debility a lack of oxygen would cause. But athletes, needing an increased oxygen-carrying capacity to give them an added edge, would find the hormone invaluable. No doubt it was on the banned list, which explained why only specialists could prescribe it.

He read through the rest of the information, then the most recent pages of Mrs Russell's file. Though he'd seen cases of acute renal failure during his years in A and E, he'd usually slated such patients for admission and passed the problem on to people better trained to deal with the disease.

Vi tapped on the door and helped Mrs Russell manoeuvre her wheelie-walker into the room.

'You remember Mrs Russell,' Vi said, following orders but totally unnecessarily in this case. 'Granny, this is Grant Bell. My nephew. He's doing Kate's job for a while.'

'So bad boy Bell's come back, has he?' Granny Russell cackled, and Grant, who'd been thinking country GP work might be more interesting than he'd thought, groaned inwardly and wondered how long it would be before the locals dropped the 'bad boy' tag.

Speaking slowly and carefully, he led Granny through a recital of her general health—bowel and bladder habits, fluid intake and appetite—while taking her blood pressure, a surprisingly reasonable one hundred and sixty over seventy, pulse and checking her lungs for any sign of congestion.

'I'm good as I was at eighty,' she told him. 'Maybe even better, since Kate sent me to Brisbane to get my kidneys checked and we started on these injections. You know, some of the lads in the high school football team'd kill to have some of the stuff I get.'

'You're right there, Granny,' Grant told her, surprised to find the old woman knew so much about the drug—and obviously had no trouble remembering what she'd been told about it. 'Nothing much wrong with your memory, is there?' he said, wondering why some people retained all their mental faculties while others began losing theirs so early.

'Nothing wrong with most of me—just my kidneys,' Granny said. 'The specialist said I was too old for a transplant, though I bet they've given them to people who didn't appreciate a second chance as much as I would.'

She was so definite that Grant was startled into questioning the remark.

'What would you do with a second chance, Granny?'

She looked up at him, the rheumy blue eyes as alert as those of the magpie he'd passed earlier.

'Live a little, love a little,' she sang, so off-key both she and Grant started laughing, though when she started coughing she sobered up and said, 'We all deserve a second chance, don't you think?'

'I do,' Grant agreed, though he wasn't so sure it covered both the suggestions she'd made. 'And that being the case, how about you start with me? Spread the word I'm a nice guy—no longer bad boy Bell.'

Granny laughed again, then told him to get away with him.

'You were never really bad, just into everything,' she said. 'The name kind of suited you.'

She eyed his clothes as he unwrapped the syringe.

'I should get a shirt like that,' she said.

'I'm glad you like it,' Grant said. 'Aunt Vi was horrified, but I *was* on holiday at the beach when she phoned and asked me to come. Now, where do you want this? Upper arm, thigh, stomach? Any preference?'

'Kate did the right thigh last time, so let's go for upper arm. My left one, as I've got a lot of cooking to do this afternoon.'

She studied Grant for a minute.

'If I gave you some cookies you'd take them, wouldn't you?'

He nodded, and she smiled and bared her arm, ready for him to swab it then inject the drug just under the skin.

He was seeing his elderly patient out when the phone rang. Knowing it was likely to be Katie, waking to find her baby had been stolen, he hovered by the reception desk so he could hear at least one end of the conversation.

'No, she's fine. She's sleeping. I'll bring her over when she wakes. In the meantime, as Grant hasn't killed his first patient, why don't you relax and enjoy a morning off?'

Grant smiled as he imagined Katie's reaction, but Vi would have none of it.

'Don't you come near this surgery!' she ordered. 'I've already told you I'll bring Fiona over when she wakes.'

Grant could hear Katie's protests from four feet away.

'Oh, sorry!' Vi said. 'It must be the excitement of seeing him again. I was sure he said you'd decided.'

There was a pause then Vi added, 'Sophie yesterday? Well, I like Sophie. Mind you, I like Fiona, too.'

The look of shock on Vi's face suggested Katie had slammed the receiver down in her ear.

Suspecting she'd come barrelling over to give him a piece of her mind, he grabbed the next file, checked the name, looked enquiringly at Vi who shook her head just enough to tell him he didn't know the patient, then he called Mr Ridley in.

'Brian Ridley,' the man said, when Grant had closed the door and introduced himself. 'I'm the bank manager, though I didn't take over from Dr Fenton's father. There were three or four in between him and me.'

The man seemed nervous but, then, patients often were. With reason, considering some of the things they were expected to tell their doctors.

'How can I help you?' Grant asked, and Brian looked around the room, his eyes darting desperately from one poster to the next, as if seeking some solution to whatever ailed him.

They settled on a warning that immunisation didn't last for ever, the thrust of it being one should have regular boosters, especially for tetanus.

'I haven't had a t-tetanus needle f-for a while,' Brian stammered, and Grant, wise in the way of patient denial, wondered just how serious the real problem was.

'Are you planning some digging in the garden? Or are you around horses a lot?'

The man looked startled.

'No. Why? Are regular tetanus shots only recommended for people who will be in contact with horses? Can't ordinary people get them as a precautionary measure? Doesn't tetanus lead to lockjaw? That would be a terrible thing to get.'

Especially for a bank manager, Grant thought but didn't say.

'I'm only filling in here,' he said aloud, 'so I'm not certain what's kept on the premises. I'll check with Vi if we've tetanus vaccine available. If not, I'll write you a script, you can pick it up at the chemist and come back for the shot.'

'Are you doing all the surgery sessions?' he asked, and Grant, thinking maybe Brian would be able to pluck up the courage to talk about what really was wrong, said reassuringly, 'Yes! Just for a week or so until Katie gets back on her feet.'

'She doesn't like being called Katie,' Brian said earnestly, but it was the pink that washed into his ears at the same time that gave him away.

'Yes, unfortunately,' Vi said later, when Grant, after inoculating Brian against tetanus and sending him on his way, relayed his suspicions to her. 'The poor man is hopelessly, besottedly, helplessly in love with Kate and she's the only person in town who doesn't know it. She says he's being nice to her because she's part of the bank family. Honestly, he moons around the place, mows her lawn on Saturdays, comes in for appointments on the flimsiest of pretences, rushes out to serve her when she goes into the bank, and she all but pats him on the head, like you would a favoured pet.'

'I hope he isn't married—making an idiot of himself like that!' Grant muttered, failing to see the amusement that was shaking Vi's frame.

'No, he's a bachelor. It makes it even funnier because he's been in town three years now, and every unwed woman within kilometres—and a few married ones as well, no doubt—have made a play for him. We'd all begun to think he was gay when Kate arrives in town and, bang, Brian falls for her in a big way!'

Grant frowned at his still chortling aunt.

'Isn't that baby awake? Shouldn't you be taking her back to her mother?'

He grabbed the next file, read out the name, and it wasn't until he was heading back to the consulting room, the patient, Mrs Milward, on his heels, that he realised here was someone else he knew.

He swung around.

'Mrs Milward who taught me in Grade Two?'

The woman beamed at him.

'Fancy you remembering that! Though you always were a clever boy.'

'But you left town,' he said, remembering the big party at the school when he'd been a few years older.

'I came back,' she said simply. 'When you find a place as nice as Testament, you know you have to come back.'

Yeah, well! Grant thought, then he shoved the words way back in his mind, with the nursery furniture and second chances. Right now he had to concentrate on work.

CHAPTER SIX

KATE, feeling alive and well after the extra sleep and a long, hot shower, where she'd had time to wash her hair, met Vi halfway between the house and the surgery and took the baby from her, peering down into her daughter's face as if to check she had the right child.

'I don't think she looks much like a Fiona, do you?' she said, inviting Vi to join her in her scrutiny.

'You can't tell at that age,' Vi said firmly. 'But you can't call her Fiona Fenton anyway. Too many "f"s".'

'You're right. Will you tell Grant or should I?' She heard the stupidity of the question and immediately repudiated it. 'No, that's nonsense. So's this name-practising he's carrying on with. I'll just ignore him.'

And on that eminently sensible note she headed for the house, where, as the baby—she wondered if Sophie would do—looked as if she might sleep for ever, Kate put her back in her crib and did some housework, finding pleasure in simple household tasks she rarely found time to do.

Once dusting, vacuuming and dishwashing were finished, she went back into the garden and picked some long strands of gaudy pink and white bougainvillaea, bringing them inside and filling three vases with the bright blooms. The house looked like a home again.

'Which is what we need, sweet thing,' she told the baby, who finally woke and demanded feeding now—immediately! 'A home. Our home. Yours and mine.'

'It must have been the sleep,' she explained to Grant a little later, when he'd walked back to the house after surgery to find a salad lunch and crisp rolls awaiting him. 'I woke up

89

so full of energy I not only cleaned the house but, after the baby was fed, we shopped as well. I know you wanted to be part of that expedition, so I left the butcher for you.'

Grant seemed puzzled—well, he seemed more stunned but as she hadn't done anything to actually stun him, after all everyone shopped—she went with puzzled.

'Mick Gazecki works there,' she explained, thinking maybe it was the butcher part puzzling him. 'He was in my year, but you'd probably remember him. Worst flirt in the world. He's married now with about five little Gazeckis and even when I was hugely pregnant and ugly as sin with it, he carried on with the kind of winks and comments that made me want to hit him with his meat cleaver.'

'Do you still have these murderous urges or was it part of being pregnant? Like cravings?'

Kate considered the question for a moment. 'I don't think it was a pregnancy thing—I didn't get cravings either.' She grinned at him. 'So you'll just have to take your chances, won't you? But I don't have a meat cleaver, only a very blunt knife.'

'That's reassuring,' Grant said, though in truth he was less reassured—less assured as well—than he made out. He'd wandered back over to the house filled with a kind of low-key anticipation commensurate with sharing work talk with a colleague.

Then he'd seen the colleague and been struck dumb. The transformation was surely more than a few hours' sleep could have achieved. There had to be a fairy godmother, complete with magic wand, lurking in the background.

Katie shone! From the top of her freshly washed head, ablaze with golden curls, to the tips of her freshly painted toenails, she gleamed with such radiant well-being he felt dull and lifeless just looking at her.

Though there was little dull or lifeless about his physical reaction. No, sir!

However, with the discussion centring on meat cleavers,

now wasn't the time to be admitting to any physical reactions.

'You were supposed to be sleeping, not tidying the house or shopping.'

He was aware he sounded cross, but couldn't help it. Not that it affected her at all. She simply beamed at him and held out her arms as if for inspection.

'I did sleep,' she said, 'then I washed my hair and shaved my legs...' she raised a ridiculously long, tanned leg for him to inspect '...and cleaned the house and picked flowers and fed the baby and still had time to shop.'

'In those shorts?' The words were out before he could stop them, and Katie's startled look, followed by a slight narrowing of emerald green eyes, told him exactly what she thought of the question.

'And who are you to question what I wear? The fashion police?' She pointed derisively at his shirt. 'The final arbiter in suitable man-about-the-country attire?'

Seething with the injustice of her words, and with her ingratitude and attitude and attractive legs, Grant scowled at her.

'I was thinking it's no wonder the local butcher leers at you!' he said, then he saw her lower lip and remembered how Katie had always hidden any uncertainty or pain behind a show of bravado—the showier the better.

'Oh, Katie, don't cry. I didn't mean it.' Two strides took him around the table so he could put his arm around her and draw her lush softness close to his body.

She blinked away the tears, and the smile this time was soft and very genuine.

'I really don't want to cry,' she said. 'I mean, I'm not unhappy. I think there might be a link between milk ducts and tear ducts which would explain why nursing women become weepy at the slightest provocation.'

She wriggled out of his embrace, which, given his body's

reaction and her attitude to Mick Gazecki and meat cleavers, was a good idea.

'Let's eat,' she suggested. 'And you can tell me all about your morning. Did Granny Russell come in? And who remembered you?'

Grant returned to the opposite side of the table and sat down.

'Everyone remembered me—well, not so much remembered me as remembered bad boy Bell. If I'd heard those words once more, I swear I'd have belted whoever said them.'

'You might have to borrow Mick's meat cleaver!' she teased, as Grant tackled his salad with enthusiasm. Sublimating one hunger with another? 'Though I'm sure they think of bad boy Bell with affection, whereas their Katie Fenton memories are recalled with shock and much tut-tutting. I imagine my return, pregnant and unmarried, led to a spate of "I told you she'd come to no good!" comments among the locals.'

'But you'd have known that before you came—you'd lived in country towns long enough to know how they operate.'

She had her head down, slicing soft pink ham and pushing it onto her fork, so he couldn't see her face as she replied, 'Yes, I did know that, but Testament still felt like a place where I could make a home for myself and the baby. The town's big enough for there to be good schools, yet small enough for most people to know each other. As a single mother, I thought that was important—that the baby, as she grew, would know the names of the people in the street, and they'd know her and look out for her. I knew once the original tutting stopped, the locals would gradually come to accept me—and they'd know the baby from her birth, so she'd be a local. What I did miscalculate—'

She stopped and Grant wondered what had happened.

Had to know.

'What?' he demanded.

She shrugged and a rueful glimmer of the radiant smile he'd seen earlier lit her eyes.

'Well, down in the city I was always hearing about the unemployment crisis in the country and I assumed, when I got here, it would be easy, finding a nanny for the baby. I didn't want a professionally trained person, just a nice grandmotherly type who'd had kids of her own and knew which end did what. I'd employ her during my working hours and have a couple of high school girls on standby for weekends and after hours, and all would be well.'

'Didn't happen, huh?'

Kate shook her head, the glimmer gone, leaving her eyes more sad than sober.

'One woman came in response to my ad, and she'd have minded the baby, but wouldn't do washing or even the lightest of housework. I didn't want her washing down the walls, just throwing a few nappies into the machine. I mean, with a baby this size who sleeps all the time, what was she going to do all day? *And* she wanted more money than trained nurses make at the hospital.'

'And no one else applied?'

Kate shook her head.

'Vi's got feelers out, but so far she hasn't come up with any solution. I just hope there's not some kind of embargo in place, because I turned down the first applicant.'

Grant shook his head, puzzled by the reaction as he, too, knew of the unemployment problems in regional areas. More than puzzled by the scrunching feeling around his heart as he'd listened to the doubt and hesitation in Kate's words.

It was probably pity. Pity for an old friend was acceptable—almost obligatory in fact. Though with an old friend like Katie, it was probably best she didn't see it—pity would be the last thing she'd accept. Visions of the meat cleaver rose obligingly in his head.

'So what are you going to do if Vi doesn't come up with someone?' he asked. There was more to this knight business than he'd originally thought.

'While she's little I can manage. Take her to the surgery or on calls when it's not too hot to have her in the car. Tara's available after school and at weekends and once school finishes next week, she'll come when I need her through the eight weeks of the Christmas holidays.'

'And then?'

Katie shrugged but the smile reappeared, sparkling in her eyes and seeming to shine in her skin.

'I'll have to get a city girl up here, and won't that stir the locals? As well as an unemployment problem here, there's a woman shortage. I'll have every young bachelor in town and out of it hanging around—like when a new clutch of female schoolteachers arrives. I could possibly set up as a marriage agency as a sideline—bringing young women to town on a regular basis, checking their household and baby-minding skills, then marrying them off with a good reference.'

'Not very good for Rose, all those changes in her life.'

'Rose?' Katie shrieked. 'I thought we'd ruled out flowers, days of the week, months of the year, seasons and anything that sounds like a mood or emotion.'

'You suggested Rose,' Grant retorted. 'Anyway, there are some nice names included in that sweeping embargo. And I thought you hated lists, and here you are, listing all the no-nos to me.'

'That wasn't a list—it was a statement. Lists presuppose an order—a first, second, third.'

Grant chuckled.

'I can't believe this! Was there ever a time we didn't argue?'

She shook her head, so the bright sunlight streaming into the kitchen made glints of gold dance through the curly tresses of hair. An almost overwhelming urge to run his fingers through it—to feel the warmth where the sun was touching—made him wonder, yet again, if the knight thing had been such a good idea.

He reminded himself of why he was here and began to ask questions about the hospital, eventually wondering what it had been like from a patient's point of view.

'Don't ask,' Katie muttered, when he asked the question aloud. 'Though to be fair, I didn't get much chance to test things out.'

She sighed, then, with the honesty he'd always admired in her, added, 'When Paul left, I intended going to Craigtown when the time came, then the baby was early, and to give Sister Clarke her due, she's a wonderful midwife, but I discharged myself as soon as possible. It was driving me nuts—all their "plural" stuff. We should do this and we should do that and how are we feeling today. I know I was still the size of two normal people, but there was only one of me, and a not very happy one at that.'

Grant found himself laughing, imagining Katie's ire at such behaviour.

'But admit it, Katie, you've probably done it yourself. We've all been guilty of it at some stage of our careers.'

'Not me!' she retorted. 'Not once—never!'

And Grant laughed again, but this time with the sheer pleasure of being with her again, with the old Katie who'd stood up for herself—and all her friends—and who'd been willing to take on the world, if necessary, to defend what she saw as right.

'I guess you told them what you thought of it as well,' he said, when his laughter had died down sufficiently for him to speak.

'Well, yes, I did. I wasn't feeling particularly well. You don't, you know, after a long labour during which the entire support staff have done the "we" thing. So when someone came in before dawn next morning and said it was time for us to have a nice sponge bath I told her what I thought of people who couldn't use a patient's name, and that individual patients were singular not plural, then I told her where to stick her sponge, picked up the baby and came home.'

'And you wonder why no one wants to work for you?'

He'd meant it as a joke, which he regretted as soon as he saw the stricken look on her face.

'I'm sorry,' he said, hoping to make amends, 'but you must admit, you probably didn't leave them with the impression you'd be a cheerful, happy, easy-to-get-on-with employer.'

'You're right,' she admitted, 'though I'd forgotten all about that little tantrum until now.' She gave a little laugh. 'When I think about it, I must have looked a right sight. Because the baby had come early I hadn't taken a bag to the hospital, so I was wearing a hospital-issue gown, one of those that comes together on one shoulder and down one side with Velcro, and it was flapping open, the baby was ready for a feed and screaming, and I couldn't find where they'd put my shoes so went barefoot, then foolishly left the path and stepped on every pebble in the backyard so I was hopping about like a madwoman.'

'Then, no doubt, you had to go back and face them all to reclaim your clothes.'

She nodded, cheeks becoming pink at the recollection.

'Had to go back to see a patient, in fact, though I did get dressed and put on sandals before I went. Sister Clarke did her ''really, Dr Fenton'' thing and told me the nurse I'd yelled at was so upset she'd had to go home, and that had mucked up the nursing schedule until two thousand and ten.'

'Sister Clarke obviously hasn't improved,' Grant said, with such empathy in his voice Kate felt something, probably left over from her youth or perhaps to do with the loneliness she'd been feeling, tug at her heart.

But whatever it was, she had to ignore it. Grant was an

old friend, and it would be good to have him—or anyone—here for a while, to help with the work while she adapted to life with the baby and the Health Department appointed a new hospital doctor. But he'd be going away again, so getting too dependent on his friendship would be a *bad thing*, and feeling heart-tugs for someone who had a Linda-Chlorinda stashed away back in the city was *an even worse* thing.

Thinking about Grant's fiancée made her stomach tighten, but she couldn't help but wonder…

No! Wondering about anything connected with Grant's personal life was definitely off-limits. Think of something else. Anything!

Baby names?

'I might make a list,' she said, startling Grant with his fork midway to his lips. 'Of baby names I quite like,' she explained. 'That way, if you persist in addressing her by name, I won't be constantly appalled.'

'Good move,' he said, but the lips, still awaiting the fork-load of food, twisted upward at the corners and seemed to quiver as if holding back a smile might soon prove too much.

The teenage Grant Bell had had killer lips, but these full-grown features were even better. Full, but not too full, beautifully shaped and clearly delineated by a neat, pale rim, so in a lip contest he'd have to be a frontrunner. And they were ultra-mobile as well—ready to smile, or open in a shout of laughter.

'Yo, Katie? You still with me here? We were going to make a list.'

His words brought her abruptly out of her contemplation of lip structure, though not completely.

'Have you been in touch with Linda? What does she do? Is she a doctor? Does she live in Sydney?'

His startled look told her she'd asked far too many questions—showed way too much interest. While the sensible

Kate who resided in her head was scoffing at her lack of moral fibre, allowing killer lips to distract her.

'I thought we were discussing baby names,' he reminded her. 'I've a pencil and a paper. I'm ready.'

He managed to sound hurt, an act she didn't believe for a moment, but as he obviously wasn't going to answer her questions about the woman in his life, she might as well go with the baby-naming option.

'I quite like Sophie.'

'I've already got that down. Come on, there must be more than one—though if there isn't then Sophie she'll have to be.'

'No, it's not quite right. What other girls' names are there? You must have been out with dozens of women—what were their names? Apart from Linda, because I'd always think of the Chlorinda thing, and I must add I find it very strange, considering you used to tell me about all the girls at school with whom you were passionately in love—before you and me…you know—that you're being so close-lipped about her.'

The 'lip' word made her look at his again, and this time she shivered, remembering, just before those lips had touched hers the first time, him saying he'd only talked about the other girls to make her jealous.

She'd wanted to believe it then, but didn't need to now.

'I once took out a Rachel—do you want it on the list?'

'Rachel? Rache? Would that morph to Roach so the poor thing would be known as either a cockroach or an iffy cigarette?'

Grant crossed out 'Rachel'.

'Let's go alphabetically. Anna, Annabel, Alison, Archimedes?'

'You're being silly now,' Kate said crossly. 'I told you I didn't like lists—and this is why. I know I suggested it, but I'm no good at it.'

'Don't you have a book with baby names in it?'

She looked at him with wide-eyed surprise.

'And where would I get one of those? At the local news-agent so everyone in town would know I didn't have a name picked out for the baby?'

'They all know by now, anyway,' Grant said gently. 'Every patient I saw this morning asked if you'd decided yet.'

Katie shrugged as if the whole conversation was aggravating her, then got up and began to clear the table.

'Megan. I'll call her Megan. Or will that clash with Fenton? Megan Fenton? Isn't there a rule about having a different number of syllables in each part of the name, though you've got one and one and it suits you.'

Grant stood up and carried his plate to the sink. He set it down, put his hands on Katie's shoulders and turned her so he could look directly at her.

'Don't panic about this, Katie. There's no rush and there are no rules. She's your baby, and you can call her what you like and take as long as you like deciding, though she'll hate you if you're still calling her "the baby" or, even worse, just "baby" when she goes to school.'

He received a wobbly smile for his efforts.

'I tell you, Grant, this motherhood caper is for the birds. I seem to be managing my learnt skills like doctoring just fine, but as far as everyday living goes?' She shook her head. 'Whatever neurones I possessed have closed down, and my body seems to have reverted to automatic responses that come from primitive instinct, before *Homo sapiens* developed the skill to reason.'

'Sometimes it might be best not to reason,' he said softly, then, because she was so goldenly beautiful, so soft to the touch, and so very, very familiar, he leaned forward and kissed her on the lips.

Beneath his fingers, he felt her shoulders stiffen, then an almost imperceptible relaxation of the muscles as her lips moved against his, not exactly responding but definitely not drawing away.

Sanity returned in time for him to do the drawing away.

'You taste the same, Katie Fenton,' he said, hoping lightness might carry the day, while his head berated him for his folly and reminded him he had no excuse, like recent childbirth, to explain why he'd given way to primitive instinct.

'You say that as if people taste different,' she said grouchily. 'All skin's made up of the same chemical and molecular composition, so there shouldn't be a difference.'

'There is if someone's been eating a lot of garlic. Don't tell me you can't taste it in the sweat,' he argued out of habit, and because it saved him thinking about his body's reaction to kissing Katie.

'I haven't ever licked the sweat off a garlic-eater so I wouldn't know,' she said, with sufficient huffiness for him to wonder if she, too, had been disturbed by the kiss.

Physically disturbed?

'And shouldn't you be heading off to the butcher's? The baby will wake any minute, expecting to be fed, so I can't come with you, but remember, my cooking skills are restricted to throwing something under a grill, or into a frying-pan, or on a barbecue. Words like "braising" bring on heart palpitations.'

'I told you I'll do the fancy stuff,' Grant promised, realising it was a good idea to get away from her while he worked out why he'd given in to the urge to kiss her—and how he could prevent it happening again.

He was out the back door when she called him back.

'Wait. I didn't give you money. And we haven't talked about pay or board or the patients you saw or any of the things we should have talked about at lunchtime. You diverted me with baby names and now look where we are!'

He grinned at her.

'Calm down—we have all afternoon to talk. It's Monday

and, according to Vi, you don't have afternoon surgery on a Monday—just an evening session, six to eight.'

'Oh!' Kate said, because there didn't seem to be anything else to say. Then she remembered the money again but it was too late. He was already crossing the paddock at the back of the hospital, taking the short cut everyone used to reach the shops.

She pushed her hands through the thick mass of her hair, and for the thousandth time since summer had begun she considered getting it cut. But growing her hair long again had been the first of her post-Mark rebellions. He'd always insisted she keep it short— 'I mean to say, Kate, a mop like that just won't fit into a theatre cap, now, will it?'

No, she wouldn't cut her hair, but she'd have to do something about the brain-drain she was experiencing. Perhaps it was the heat, as well as the after-baby problem, that was causing her neurones so much trouble.

Though she doubted she could blame the weather for her reaction to Grant's kiss, for the sizzle it had caused deep in her abdomen, and the fiery rush of longing that had triggered a trembling in her limbs and a pit-a-pat of uncertainty in her heartbeats. Maybe the heat and longing she remembered from the long-ago relationship hadn't been anything to do with their age...

Maybe it was to do with some special chemical balance between the two of them...

But Grant's presence was temporary, *and* he was engaged to another woman, and even if he'd been available, there was the baby to consider...

With confusion raging in her head, Kate pressed her hand to her chest. Perhaps if she could regulate the still uneven thumping of her heart she'd be able to think more clearly.

It didn't help so, because her knees remained unreliable, she sat down.

That didn't help either.

Distraction—she needed distraction!

Maybe she *should* get into lists. She could start with one
of things to do—discuss wages with Grant, discuss board
with Grant, discuss division of labour with Grant, ditto patients, ditto kissing. No, no more kissing, and definitely no
discussion of it.

Grant was here as a friend, doing a favour for his aunt.
Temporarily here. And Grant had a Linda he didn't want
to discuss, so even if Kate wanted a man, which she didn't,
Grant wasn't the one, which was just as well as he'd already admitted he was in medicine for the money he could
make, and she could never marry someone who saw the
career she loved as nothing more than a means to an end.

Although if the end was buying back the family property,
or replacing it with another one, surely that was allowable,
if not admirable…

She frowned out into the garden. Was making money
with a reason behind it better than making money for the
sake of it? Mark was in medicine for the money, as were
a lot of his friends. Money had been the reason Mark had
wanted her to specialise. But Grant?

Recalling the 'making money to buy back the farm' conversation they'd had, she remembered it had shifted focus.
She'd sensed Grant's initial aim was no longer relevant, or
that his career now had another goal—something he hadn't
wanted to discuss.

Something to do with the sadness she caught glimpses
of behind the twinkle in his eyes?

Or maybe Linda didn't like cattle.

The baby's cry roused her from the pointless speculation,
and by the time she'd changed and fed the wee darling and
popped her, sleepily digesting her tucker, back to bed, the
subject of her musings had returned and she went out to
have the talk they should have had earlier.

Was it because she'd been studying his lips earlier that she
found it so hard to concentrate? OK, so they'd settled on a

reasonable recompense for him, and on who'd do which surgery sessions. She'd, reluctantly, agreed he could mind the baby while she worked a couple of sessions a week, though she'd insisted Vi would manage if he wanted to get out of the house, perhaps have a look around the place, explore old haunts.

She'd even managed to retain most of what he'd told her about the patients he'd seen that morning, but throughout it all a separate part of her mind had been cataloguing his features, checking out the strong, straight nose, with enough of a flare to the nostrils to make it distinctively attractive. And the eyebrows—thick but nicely shaped, arching neatly over those incredible blue eyes.

So far, she'd managed to avoid too close a study of the eyes, though she suspected she'd get there eventually.

And find them shuttered against her?

'Are you listening?'

'Y-yes, yes, of course I was,' she stammered, more flustered than she cared to admit. 'You were talking about Mrs Milward, your old Grade Two teacher. She was gone before I came to Testament, though I'd already done Grade Two by then.'

The lips she'd given an A-plus to earlier twisted into a funny kind of smile.

'Mrs Milward was three patients ago. I thought you'd zoned out on me. Go and have a sleep, Katie. I picked up a baby-name book at the newsagent, and I'll go through it and write down names you might like.'

She should have said, Don't bother, and reminded him the baby's name had nothing to do with him, and probably suggested he go out somewhere—look up old friends—but somehow the concept of Grant buying her a baby-name book, together with the A-plus lips, had sent what useful bits of brain she retained into a spin, and having a sleep seemed like an excellent idea.

Grant watched her go and sighed with a release of tension he hadn't been aware he'd been feeling. This rescue scenario wasn't playing out the way he'd expected. The kiss had been bad enough but, OK, that was a mistake he could live with, but after he'd made his escape, and cooled down on his walk across the back paddock—cooled down metaphorically, not physically as it was hotter than Hades out there—he'd been thrown back into chaos at the butcher's.

His murderous feelings towards Mick Gazecki, who'd winked at him and made lewd suggestions about how sexy new mothers usually felt, had made him realise Katie's impulse to brain the butcher with his own meat cleaver had some merit.

He'd even gone so far as to eye the implement in question.

The heat must be getting to him. He needed something to do.

He'd put away the meat earlier, dividing it into portions and freezing most of it, though he'd decided to use the mince tonight. He could do that now. Make a pasta sauce and shove it in the fridge until the evening surgery finished. He could reheat it while he cooked the pasta. He assumed she did have pasta.

He checked the pantry, and there among the basics found an open packet of little pasta bows that had possibly been there since Dr Darling's time.

Not that pasta suffered much with keeping. The corner store where he shopped when home probably had older stuff on its shelves.

But while his mind tried to stay focussed on the merits of aged pasta and the construction of a suitable sauce to accompany it at dinner-time, another part of it was recalling the softness of Katie's lips, the luminous quality of her skin, the way her eyes caught and held his, the brash confidence in them undermined by an apprehension he guessed only he could see.

He was standing in the pantry, pasta packet in hand, when she came, soft-footed, back into the kitchen.

'I'm just getting a drink of water,' she explained, but now there was more apprehension than confidence in those fascinating eyes, and he waited, knowing she'd eventually get to what she'd come to say.

'I drink a lot—it's something I vaguely remember from the early Obs and Gyn lectures, about nursing mothers needing to keep the fluids up. I don't think we should kiss any more.'

And with that she was gone, leaving him wondering if she'd really tacked that embargo on the end of a statement about the fluid intake of nursing mothers.

He made to follow her, then realised it would be a mistake. But standing in the pantry with a packet of pasta in his hand wasn't much use either. He returned the packet to the shelf, checked on the other ingredients he'd need, then walked through to the bedroom with the floral sheets.

He had plenty of time before he needed to start cooking. He'd get his leathers and take the bike out—tool around the country, visit old haunts as Katie had suggested. Ride past the old property and see how it looked.

Banish a few ghosts.

He pulled on his leather pants, then boots, and lastly shrugged into the jacket. It was too hot for full leathers, but experience told him only speed would do at times like this and he wasn't stupid enough to risk it without some protection.

But a new ghost rode right along with him. The friend of his childhood, the Katie he'd first known—laughing, joking, daring and being dared. The slim, vibrant Katie who'd suddenly, that long-ago Christmas holidays, grown breasts and hips and had made his loins ache just being near her. Who'd become more than a friend, firing his blood to madness with her kisses, entering passionately into their first explorations of their sexuality.

The real Katie, today's Katie, was different. For a start, she had a lush, full, womanly body, and it was, once again, having an unfortunate effect on his loins.

But she also had a baby, he reminded himself as he passed beyond the limits of the town and opened the throttle on the bike, hoping speed might banish his uncertainties and blow away the memories.

Though he knew he couldn't outrace all of them. Hadn't he tried it before? He eased back before the bike reached top speed and rode more cautiously, enjoying the rush of fresh-scented air, the sight of wide paddocks stretching out on either side of the road, white-faced cattle resting beneath shady trees, lifting their heads to watch him pass.

CHAPTER SEVEN

LIFE settled into a routine. Baby names were added and crossed off the list that wasn't really a list, and Katie began not only to feel human but to fret about not doing more.

Especially when Grant had free time, because being with him, whether in the house talking over the day, or out of it walking the baby or going for drives to places they'd frequented as children, was making her think things she shouldn't think. Being with him was giving her an idea of family that was dangerous in the extreme as Grant would be gone within weeks and she'd be more alone than ever.

'I've found a phone number for an agency in Brisbane,' she announced, when he came back from surgery to join her for lunch on the fourth Monday of his stay.

'Looking for another locum? What did I do wrong?'

His teasing smile caused heart problems which were another reason she should be doing more. It was having so little to do that had her mind thinking things it shouldn't think, while Grant's constant presence had her body behaving in ways that the new mother in her found shockingly irresponsible.

'I need a nanny, not another locum. Vi's come up with one or two possibilities, but one lass is engaged to a young man in Craigtown and will be moving away as soon as they're married, and the other is just the kind of woman I want but she's planning a three-month trip overseas early in the new year. And also, I don't know if a live-in mightn't be better—for call-outs.'

'Vi was talking about Mrs Carter, the woman who's going overseas. I don't know about her. One of my younger sisters was at school with a Carter and I'm sure Sue said Mrs Carter used to beat her kids.'

'Mary Carter? That can't possibly be right.'

'OK, not beat them but wave a wooden spoon at them,' Grant conceded, though why he felt obliged to throw a spanner in the 'nanny' works, he wasn't sure. Looked at sensibly, having someone else in the house, if only during the day, was a good idea. It would provide a kind of buffer zone between himself and Katie, so maybe his body would stop reacting to her presence and his mind stop thinking things it shouldn't think.

'All our mothers waved wooden spoons at us as kids— it was the ultimate threat. Mum's actually connected with the back of my legs from time to time, and I don't think it's done me any irreparable damage.' She paused, then half smiled as she added, rather sadly, 'Though maybe Mum thinks it has. Or maybe she's thinking she didn't do it often enough.'

'What's happened between you?'

Grant hadn't realised he was going to ask the question, but there'd been so much pain in Katie's words, he'd blurted it out.

She hesitated, sighed, then said softly, 'She's old-fashioned, I guess. And me coming back to Testament made things worse. You know what Mum was like. Underneath, she'd do anything for anyone, but she did tend to lord it over people. She always had a huge sense of her own importance. If I'd taken off for Craigtown, pregnant and unwed, she'd probably have reacted better, but coming here...'

'But she will come? They'll come? When they come home from their trip?'

Katie nodded.

'Of course. After all, it's likely to be their only grand-child, but, well... It's my fault, too,' she said, her voice thick with the emotion she was trying hard to hide. 'We argued, Mum and I—back in the beginning—and I said things I shouldn't have said, things about her marriage.'

She looked up at him, then admitted, 'You know me— act first and think later.'

Grant, who'd been about to question the 'only grandchild' statement, found he was more intrigued by the final admission and set the other remark aside for consideration later.

'What kind of things?'

He saw a smile flicker on her lips, although the sadness in her eyes remained.

'Stuff that must have been stewing for a long time, but was probably quite wrong—like wanting more than she and Dad had had from marriage. More than mutual affection and respect, which was all I had for Mark. In fact, as our relationship continued I didn't even have the respect part, and though I probably would have married him to give the baby a father, and made a go of it, the way Mum and Dad had, I'm sure I'd have always felt something was missing.'

This time her smile was warmer, and cheekier, and it did things to his intestines he didn't want to think about.

'All in all, it was probably a good thing he made having an abortion a condition of us getting married, then was so adamant about not having anything to do with the baby if I went ahead with the pregnancy. It got Mark out of my life, though it did cause problems between me and Mum.'

There was a silence as he ate the sandwich she'd prepared, while she cut hers into little pieces then rearranged them on the plate, as if by shifting them she'd fool him into thinking she was eating.

'You'll sort it out,' he said, speaking gently—wanting to make things right for her.

She nodded.

'I know. After all, as I keep telling myself, we're both adults.' Then, with typical Katie-bravado she added, 'Though getting Mum to agree with that isn't easy.'

She ate a minute piece of sandwich then looked up at Grant.

'Do you think I'll be the same? Is mothering a hereditary trait? Will I be able to accept the baby's old enough to make her own decisions when she's, what? Fourteen? Eighteen? Twenty-six?'

'Never, if you're still calling her ''the baby'',' Grant told her. 'And I think decision-making is something that you learn as you grow and develop. Take a six-month-old tasting solids for the first time—if he decides he doesn't like them, splat, they're spat right back at you. Two-year-olds can probably decide whether they want jam or peanut butter on their toast, four-year-olds know if they play with the hose and get all their clothes wet, they'll be in trouble, so have to decide if the fun is worth it.'

Kate heard the words, but underlying them was something she didn't understand. Though one thing was certain—Grant wasn't winging this conversation. He'd thought it through, considered it, worried about decisions and responsibilities himself.

'Does Linda have a child?'

She didn't know why she'd asked, but as soon as the words were spoken, she knew they'd have been better left unsaid. Grant's expression changed from a momentary perplexity to understanding to pain. He shook his head, added 'No' in case she didn't understand head shakes, then he pushed back his chair, stood up, muttered something about a note he'd forgotten to write at the surgery and walked out.

You're here to help Katie, not add to her burdens by dumping your baggage on her, he told himself fiercely, striding across to the surgery and unlocking the door. What he had to do was find someone to take care of the baby, so Katie could ease back into work, then, once she was happy with the arrangement, he could get out of town.

If the young woman who was getting married later next

year could work until Mrs Carter came back from over-seas…

Or would a trained nanny from the city be better? Some-one who'd been to nanny school and knew all the right things to do?

He thought back to couples he knew who'd employed these paragons, and remembered a discussion he'd had with one of the employers. Phoned the house.

'A city nanny would have to live in,' he said to Kate, then smiled to himself as he imagined her mental adjust-ment. 'And from what I've heard, they need their own space, a kind of bed-sitting room and *en suite*. Definitely their own bathroom. Have you thought of that?'

'They need an *en suite*?' she repeated, in tones of such disbelief he had to smile. 'But I haven't got an *en suite*!'

The expletive she wasn't going to use again was quickly followed by, 'Jeez Louise! I hadn't even thought of bath-rooms. I mean, a live-in is good from the point of view of having someone here if I'm called out, but if they have to have a bathroom…'

There was a pause, then she asked, 'Why are we talking on the phone? Have you a lot of paperwork to do? I said I'd do all of that. I'm bored rigid doing nothing, and the house is so clean it's starting to feel like one of those dis-play places.'

Another pause.

'Only they usually have two bathrooms, don't they?'

And on that note she hung up.

Grant knew he should stay away, even take off on the bike, but he was drawn back to the house by the same irresistible attraction that led moths to a light.

Kate was in the third bedroom. She had pinned her hair up so it was doing its 'falling down all over' thing again, and in the loose curls behind her ear he could see the end of a pencil. In one hand she held a tape measure and in the other a piece of paper.

'You'd think they'd make measuring tapes longer than a metre,' she complained, as she scratched a mark on the carpet then moved the tape along.

'They do,' Grant told her. 'You buy them at hardware shops, though the idea that you'd own such a thing as a tape measure intrigues me no end. One usually associates such things with button bottles and sewing baskets, and I remember you loathed sewing as much as you hated cooking when you were younger and had to do it at school.'

'But I did have a sewing basket,' she told him primly, moving the tape again then searching for her pencil to write something down. 'Still have it, though I doubt I've used it from that day to this. Can you see my pencil?'

'It's in your hair, but there's an easier way to do this, unless you want the measurements exact to the last centimetre.'

She straightened so she was squatting on her heels, pulling the short shorts very tight across firm buttocks.

'I'll step it out,' Grant said, desperate to distract his mind from that part of Katie's anatomy—any part of Katie's anatomy. 'I assume we're doing this to see if we can fit another bathroom in here. There, it's three metres by about three and a half, not big enough for a decent bedroom and an *en suite*. And though a second bathroom is an excellent idea, are you sure you want someone living in?'

She reached out a hand and he pulled her up, though that was a mistake as any time she was within arm's length he had a terrible urge to kiss her.

An urge not much diminished by the frown she was directing his way.

'Why shouldn't I?' she said. 'Have you heard horror stories of people with live-in help? Are there implications I should know about?'

Grant hesitated, mainly because the remark had been instinctive. *He* wouldn't want anyone living in—not in a house this size where someone else would be…

Would be what? he asked himself. A barrier between you and Katie? A curb on your lustful thoughts?

Get real here, mate. A live-in help is just what Katie needs.

And you won't be here, remember?

But no amount of talking convinced him, deep down in his gut, that it was the right move.

'Well, while I'm here the nanny thing isn't a problem, so you don't have to decide immediately. But a spare bathroom's good. Let's walk right through the house and see if we can't figure out the best place for it.'

'I thought I already had,' Kate muttered to herself, but she went along with him, mainly because she was puzzled by his failure to answer her live-in nanny questions, and was more concerned with figuring out why than with asserting her authority over where the bathroom should go in *her* house.

Apart from the fact a city girl might hate the country and the baby might have to put up with a few of them before one eventually stuck, having live-in help seemed a great idea.

The baby!

She really should choose a name—now she wasn't so sleep-deprived and her body had settled into the routine of feeding.

'What was the name you suggested yesterday?'

They were in Grant's bedroom now, and Kate realised she hadn't been in here since he'd arrived. She looked around, seeing how tidy he kept it, smelling the air, which was definitely different—decidedly male.

'We're talking about bathrooms, not names at the moment,' he reminded her. 'And as this is the largest of the bedrooms, it would probably be most suitable to convert into a kind of bed-sitting room. See, you could take part of that wall out and put a small *en suite* in there, plus a dressing room. You'd lose that small bedroom, but you'd still have three. One for you, one for the baby—Caroline was yesterday's name—and one for the nanny or for visitors.'

'So I couldn't have both at once,' Kate said, though she was thinking more of how strange it felt to be in a male's bedroom—in Grant's bedroom, as it was right now. 'The nanny and visitors.'

But her eyes were drawn to Grant's bed, and she was imagining him lying there.

Naked...

'Shortened to Carrie, or Cassie, or even Caz, and all of them are OK.'

She blinked away an image of a naked Grant and peered suspiciously at him.

'Weren't we talking about bathrooms?'

His grin suggested they'd moved on from that conversation some time ago.

'Yes, we were, but you'd lost that particular plot so I assumed you were thinking of the other conversation we were kind of conducting. Baby names? Caroline? Not bad when shortened?'

'Is it wrong for me to want to go to bed with you?'

The question came so completely out of the blue, Grant could only stare at her.

'Well, not especially with you, but with anyone. Shouldn't my sexuality be in abeyance when I've just given birth and am feeding a very young infant? Do you know anything at all about it? Perhaps I should look it up? Would I find it in a medical book, or would it be under psychology?'

And whether to suit action to the words, or to go off on some equally bizarre quest, Grant couldn't tell, but she left the room without waiting for an answer to any of her questions, which was just as well, for it could be a day or two before he recovered sufficiently to even gabble out a reply.

'The problem is,' Kate told the baby as she bathed the little body, 'I was so used, when I was growing up, to talking about anything and everything with Grant. Arriving in town in the summer holidays, and Dad having meetings with his father, he was about the first kid I met. From that time, he kind of took care of me, making out I was a nuisance but looking out for me anyway. Especially when I started high school, and was too big for my boots and always getting into trouble.'

The baby kicked at the water as if to agree with what had been said, but didn't offer much else in the way of an opinion.

'And the other problem is,' she added, while silently marvelling at the perfection of miniature toes and toenails, 'that when I considered our future, yours and mine, building a life together here in the country, I never considered for an instant that I might ever feel sexy again. I mean I hadn't—with Mark—not for a long time, and I thought it was probably age or that women didn't feel an urge for sex the way men did, especially as they got older. So this attraction thing is just so totally unexpected—and definitely unacceptable, given all the circumstances.'

The baby offered no opinion on female sexuality so Kate sighed and resolutely turned her thoughts to more practical stuff.

'Would you like to be called Caroline? While you're small, and the name's a bit grand, we could call you Cassie. Would you like that?'

A smile she knew wasn't really a smile hesitated on the tiny pink lips and, in the surge of excitement the almost-smile generated, Kate called for Grant to come.

'Look, she almost smiled. I called her Cassie—well, I suggested it to her—and she really did smile.'

'Is that why you yelled? I thought something terrible had happened.'

'I didn't yell, I called,' Kate argued. 'And I thought you might be interested.'

Though now he was here, splashing water on the baby—

yes, Caroline shortened to Cassie might work well—Kate remembered her previous conversation with the man, and regretted the yell—call.

'Aren't all smiles put down to wind until the baby's, what—six weeks old, is it?'

'How could she have wind when she hasn't been fed? And anyway, five weeks isn't so far off six weeks,' Kate muttered, though why she felt compelled to argue with him was a mystery.

However, Grant seemed unperturbed, by both the argument and, apparently, her previous idiotic questions. He was catching the tiny feet as they splashed, and getting very wet in the process, and if the baby—Cassie—wasn't smiling, then she had a whole lot of wind.

'She might be precocious. What do I have to do with a precocious child? Do you accelerate them? Put them into programmes so they get maximum stimulation?'

These new worries brought on the familiar sense of panic over the future which Kate experienced so regularly she sometimes wondered if she could survive motherhood, but Grant was laughing—at her this time, not the baby.

'I don't think they're issues you need to address right now. I could be wrong, but I doubt they have stimulation programmes for bright five-week-olds.'

'You're right,' Kate admitted, feeling some relief but a new concern over the effect of Grant's laughter—here in her bedroom. 'And bath-time's over.'

She grabbed a towel she'd set out on the bed and bent to lift the baby from the small tub, but something went wrong, and though the baby ended up in the right place, in her arms, the tub upended itself, splashing across the bed.

'You are so totally disorganised,' Grant told her, grabbing other towels to mop up the mess. 'Why you set a bath on something as unstable as a bed is beyond me! As you haven't bothered to get proper nursery furniture, why don't you bath her on the kitchen table?'

Kate clasped Cassie—yes, it suited her—to her chest and glared at her accuser.

'I did until you came, then I thought you might think it wasn't too hygienic so I changed to doing it on the bed, and I haven't got proper nursery furniture because it's not the sort of thing you can buy in Testament, and what with taking over a very neglected practice and working out how to do the paperwork associated with being a single-practice GP, and Paul Newberry leaving, I didn't have time to go to Craigtown. Vi gave me the crib and after that...'

She'd started out mad, telling him off, but her confidence had oozed away so by the time she finished the little speech she sounded so uncertain that Grant wanted to put his arms around her and promise her he'd take care of everything.

But he couldn't do that. He was only a temporary solution, and if they got too close, his departure would leave her life even more barren than it had been before he'd arrived.

And if they got too close, his departure would undoubtedly leave *his* life more barren than it had been.

Though until his return to Testament, he'd doubted whether that would be possible.

'I'll chuck the towels into the washing machine—your sheets, too. They're soaked.'

He spoke because he had to say something to explain a hurried departure from the room, but in his heart he knew it was already too late—the getting-too-close thing. Knew his life was going to be more barren than it had been, when he left Testament and Katie.

For a brief moment, as he measured laundry liquid into the machine, he contemplated not leaving. Fear, terror, helplessness and grief—emotions he'd thought he'd conquered long ago—rose up to engulf him. Katie worried about how she might cope with an exceptional child, and whether she'd be too dominating a mother.

She didn't know the half of things there were to worry

about—things that clutched at your heart and drove you to the edge of madness with the pain they caused.

He started the machine, then, by way of insurance, walked back to the bedroom and poked his head through the door.

She was sitting on the driest part of the bed, her back propped on pillows, shirt unbuttoned, and Cassie was sucking greedily on one finely blue-veined breast. The image was so serenely beautiful it stole his breath, and it took a moment before he could speak.

'Sorry!' he said, more abruptly than he'd intended. 'I know you don't like being interrupted but I wanted to tell you I'm just popping over to the surgery. I meant to phone Linda this morning, then didn't get a chance. I'd use my mobile but the battery's flat and it's on the charger. I'll pay for the call, of course.'

He walked away, hoping he'd sounded sufficiently impersonal to undo any closeness that might have been developing between them. The Linda thing had been a masterstroke—if only he didn't keep forgetting to use it. He had to bring her up more often. And though he'd invented her originally to reassure Katie he was harmless—as far as being a man was concerned, Linda could now act as a suit of armour for himself.

Kate watched the door close behind him, and told herself she should be pleased he had a Linda. She also reminded herself it had been her own choice to go the single-mother route.

But enough of her brain was working for her to not believe a word of it. Far from not wanting him with her while she fed the baby, she'd positively ached to ask him to come in, to sit with her and chat, while Cassie—yes, that was the name—had her afternoon tea.

This was dangerous ground, and having Grant here for another however many weeks—she kept forgetting to ask

Vi what arrangements she'd made with him—was asking for trouble.

She lifted the sleeping baby to her shoulder, patted her half-heartedly in the hope she might burp, reminded herself of something she'd once read that said burping was useless anyway and put the little one—Cassie—down.

On the way through to the kitchen she grabbed a phone book and the notepad and pen she kept by the phone. She put on the kettle for a cup of tea, set the notepad on the kitchen table with the pen beside it and made a new resolution, though it was still three weeks to New Year.

'I will become organised and if that means becoming a list-maker, then so be it.'

Said out loud, the resolution sounded pathetic, but as no one was around to hear it didn't matter. Once her tea was made, she settled at the table and opened the phone directory at the Yellow Pages.

Would there be a listing for bathrooms, or would she have to get separate people in—a carpenter and a plumber, and possibly an electrician because the nanny would probably want a power-point for her hair-dryer? She wrote these trades down on her list, one beneath the other, and marvelled at how neat it looked and how proud of herself she felt.

And she'd need a painter—added painter to the list—although perhaps she could do that part herself. Keep her busy and out of Grant's way when he was home.

Crossed the painter off.

She checked the index, found bathrooms and turned to the right page, but most of the so-called 'bathroom renovations our specialty' ads had addresses in the city, and bringing them all this way would be expensive.

Perhaps if she phoned the nanny agency and checked on the bathroom thing first.

Wrote 'Phone agency' on the list.

She'd sound like a twit but it might save some money.

Money! She'd spent her savings and practically mortgaged her soul to get the house and practice.

Phone bank manager.

Somehow the thought of asking Brian for a loan made her feel queasy. It wouldn't feel right—having to admit to a patient you had so little in the way of financial stability you had to borrow for a bathroom.

She drew a line through the last item, then leafed through the book in search of finance companies.

Unfortunately for that idea, she could remember her bank manager father explaining how families like the Bells, who'd been on the land for generations, had been consumed by financial difficulties because they'd overextended themselves and borrowed through finance companies to stay afloat.

'It only prolongs the inevitable,' her father had said, as he'd tried to stem her rage and despair by explaining the bank's decision was unavoidable—and not his sole responsibility!

She wrote 'Phone Brian' on the list, because banks knew how far you could extend yourself without getting into serious trouble.

'Don't tell me you're writing a list!'

Grant's voice made her turn towards the back door, where he was standing regarding her, a teasing smile playing around the lips which had become the focus of her nightly dreams.

'I'm getting my life in order,' she told him. 'Kettle's boiled if you want a cup of tea. And Cassie's just gone off to sleep so she should be all right for an hour. If you've got nothing you want to do, could I leave her with you while I pop over to see Vi?'

His blue eyes narrowed with what looked like suspicion.

'I want to ask her who might be able to do the bathroom,' she added, though she didn't really need to explain to Grant why she was going.

'Fair enough,' he said, then he grinned at her. 'Just tell me. Is Cassie it, or are we just trying it on for a week?'

She had to smile—impossible not to.

'I think it's it,' she told him, while telling herself that, of course, it was possible to not smile back. 'But I guess we'll have to wait and see.'

She fled past him, out the door, because every minute she was near him she was at the mercy of her unreliable hormones—the ones with a direct line to her even more unreliable mouth which was likely to come out with something outrageous like, Let's go to bed—should she remain in his vicinity.

Grant watched her departure, telling himself this was good, then he saw the list and realised, if she was getting serious about a spare bathroom, she must be equally serious about a live-in nanny.

The thought depressed him for reasons he didn't want to consider, and the last name on the list— 'Brian' —underneath 'Bank Manager', which she'd crossed out, obviously feeling it was too impersonal—well, that just made him angry.

Was she going there now? Was the Vi story just a ruse?

He peered out the window, but couldn't see her, though if she'd gone uptown, rather than to Vi's, she'd have walked across the back paddock.

Wouldn't she?

He threw the cup of tea he'd made down the sink and went into the living room to brood.

CHAPTER EIGHT

BROODING produced no answers—mainly because Grant wasn't sure of the questions. Not all of them.

Maybe he'd cook instead.

But that didn't help because, after only three weeks in the house, he felt at home in Katie's kitchen, and feeling at home there was a dangerous concept—something he didn't want to consider, let alone brood over.

He was stirring his simmering stock when she returned, accompanied by an elderly man who greeted him with great affection.

'You don't remember me, do you?' the stranger said, 'but you were the best little builder's labourer I've ever had. Back when you were about four—before you went to school—and I put in the new shearers' quarters for your dad.'

'Mr McConagle? I *do* remember. Well, I remember a very kind and patient man who let me think I was helping. I had a great time and for years after was certain I was going to be a builder.'

'More a handyman than a builder,' Mr McConagle said. 'That's what people need out here. Someone who can turn his hand to anything. I suppose doctors in the country are a bit the same.'

'Or should be,' Katie said darkly.

'Well, let's have a look at the job,' Mr McConagle suggested, and Katie, after a quick 'Is it OK if we go into your room?' to Grant, led the handyman through the house.

Grant fell in behind then realised it was nothing to do with him so went back to stirring his stock, which didn't need stirring. The task also lacked any degree of job satisfaction as he kept wanting to know what was happening and wondering why he was getting uptight about a live-in nanny for Cassie.

'Mr McConagle says he can do it before Christmas,' Katie announced, beaming with pleasure as she returned, alone, to the kitchen to impart her news.

Then some of the delight faded, and her eyes took on the concern which seemed to be an almost permanent fixture.

'Though it will mean you moving into the smaller bedroom next to mine, and there'll be sawdust and stuff around. Do you mind? Do you think the sawdust will harm the baby? Oh, dear! How can one small baby cause disruption that's way out of proportion for its size?'

You don't know the half of it, and I pray you never do, Grant thought, but as he couldn't say it, he concentrated on practical matters.

'It shouldn't harm her, if you keep the bedroom door shut. You can take her over to the surgery or out somewhere else while Mr McConagle is doing noisy things.'

He pretended the stock required his attention, though it needed only to be left simmering and later strained.

'You didn't answer about moving into the smaller bedroom.'

'Only because I was thinking it might be easier if I move to Vi's. After all, you're going to be wanting the small bedroom for the baby soon, and while Mr McConagle's working here, you could start decorating it.'

'Decorating it?'

'The baby's room—ready for the baby to move into.' She looked so stunned by this concept he found himself adding, 'I'll give you a hand if you like.'

But he doubted Katie had heard. She was still staring at him—well, in his direction—but a blankness in her eyes suggested she wasn't seeing him.

'Why hadn't I thought of that? I haven't even bought a

mobile. She's got fluffy toys patients brought as gifts, but she'll need colour, stimulation.'

Now the eyes which still had the power to mesmerise him regained focus—him—and she stepped towards him.

'Grant, what's wrong with me? Why am I making such a hash of all this mother-thing? Am I just not cut out for it? Will I always be this way? Will Cassie suffer because of it?'

She was literally shaking with the fears her imagination was feeding her, and instinct made it impossible for Grant not to step forward and take her in his arms.

'Will you stop upsetting yourself with such nonsense?' he said, drawing her soft, still trembly body close against his, hoping to warm as well as reassure her. 'You'd have got to decorating the baby's room in time—just as you'll sort out the nanny thing eventually. There's no hurry—not while I'm here. Right now, your main concern is getting to know young Cassie and allowing her time to get to know you. And staying calm. That's another big job you have to do, so she feels secure and gets plenty of tucker.'

The trembling had stopped, and her warmth fed into his until he found it hard to tell where her body stopped and his began—except that his was the one now feeling more than comfort and responding to hers in ways that went far beyond friendship.

But he couldn't draw away too abruptly and hurt her feelings, so he kind of edged away, far enough to take her chin in his hand and tilt her head up towards him.

'Feeling better?'

A slight nod answered his question, but the doubtful expression lingering in her green eyes suggested she was still worrying.

'So smile for me,' he ordered, knowing he had to move farther away—and soon.

The smile was his undoing. It trembled, as her body had earlier, and failed to remove the apprehension in her eyes, so it occurred to him he might have to kiss the worries away.

As in 'kiss it better'.

This final excuse flitted through his mind as his lips closed on hers, then his mind fogged over and his body, held in check for so long, took over.

Kate felt his fingers slide into her hair as his hands framed her face. She felt gentleness in the lips touching hers, and understood it was a gesture—kindness—but her body, so long given over to carrying, then bearing and feeding the baby, wanted more, so she forgot about all the consequences—forgot where kissing Grant had led before— and kissed him back.

A big mistake, as the kissing reminded her body of other things it had been missing, and it pressed closer to his, demanding some of the attention her lips were currently giving and receiving. As if in answer to her silent demands, Grant's hands caressed her back, tucked her buttocks closer to his body, then he slid a hand between their bodies and gently grazed his fingers across her breast.

Someone, she suspected it might have been her, moaned with a mix of need and sensual delight, and as Grant tipped her back across the kitchen table and began to unbutton her shirt, she wanted him so badly she began to shake again.

Then, as suddenly as the kiss had started, it stopped, Grant pulling them both upright, setting her gently away from him, steadying her with his hands on her shoulders.

'Noises off!' he said by way of explanation, then he added grimly, 'Which is just as well!'

As he stepped towards the stove to rescue a pot that had boiled over and sent stock spluttering onto the hot-plate, Kate became aware of both the phone ringing and the baby crying.

Guilt slammed into her, and she ignored the phone, knowing Grant would answer it, and hurried to the bedroom. She was changing Cassie when he poked his head around the bedroom door.

'Tractor accident out at Nevertire, the driver's pinned by the legs. I'm on my way. You're OK to do the evening surgery?'

She nodded, but he hesitated, and Kate wondered if he was going to mention the kiss, but in the end he shook his head then said, 'Katie, it's no wonder you didn't have time to get ready for the baby. This practice might have the occasional lull but, if the last few weeks are any indication, I'm surprised you've managed as well as you have since the hospital doctor took off.'

Thinking about the necessity for a second doctor in town was infinitely preferable to thinking about the kiss, but it wasn't a problem she could solve.

And the kiss, or her reaction to it, kept intruding so it was only with an enormous effort of will she stopped herself dreaming of things that couldn't be.

She'd contact the Health Department again—hospital appointments usually began in January so surely they'd have someone lined up by now.

Inevitably, she thought of Grant, but he had Linda stashed away in Sydney and some job awaiting him there. Quite what job, Kate hadn't yet managed to fathom, though from time to time she'd led the conversation close enough for him to say.

Which was strange, now she considered it. Grant had always talked about his plans and dreams. Growing grass that could withstand drought, turning around the rivers which wasted their water by flowing into the sea so they flowed inland to the thirsty land. They were ideas Australians had played with for generations, but still seductive enough for an enthusiastic teenager, always brimful of plans for the future.

Now, although she sensed a purpose in him—knew there was a deadline to his stay in Testament so there had to be a job of some kind waiting for him—he certainly wasn't talking about it.

Because it meant a lot to him?

She nodded to herself. Yes, that fitted. It was probably also why he rarely mentioned Linda.

She meant too much to him.

The idea was so depressing she sighed as she rocked Cassie's crib, though she had no right to be getting maudlin over Grant Bell's future career or personal relationships.

It was the kiss that had done it—made her think things she shouldn't think about the man who was helping her out of a very difficult situation. A man who'd given up his holidays to come to her rescue. And what did she know of relationships anyway? She'd made a mess of the only serious one she'd had, and hadn't she come out here determined to make a secure and happy life for herself and Cassie? Wasn't that her goal? Hadn't she committed herself to be the best single mother she possibly could be?

So why was she lusting over the first man who'd crossed her path? A man already engaged to someone else?

How responsible was that behaviour for a committed single mother?

She continued to scold herself even after Cassie dropped off to sleep, but as she wandered back to the kitchen she wondered if even committed single mothers might not be allowed a little daydream now and then...

Not if they involve Grant Bell, she answered herself firmly as she fixed a snack to eat before evening surgery.

When Grant still hadn't returned by the time she finished work, she had jam on toast for dinner, then went to bed, knowing he could be late and one of them should be getting some sleep.

But the question of what Grant planned to do after he left Testament lingered in her mind, so at breakfast next morning, when he'd filled her in on Kevin Cockburn's accident—crush fractures to both legs—and despatch to

Craigtown where he was then airlifted to Brisbane, she asked, 'I know you worked in A and E for three years. Was that leading somewhere? Are you going to specialise? Become an intensivist perhaps? Aren't they the newest "big thing"?'

He grinned at her but his eyes were shuttered, hiding whatever expression they might hold.

'They are, but it's not my career of choice.'

He continued eating his cereal as if he'd answered all her questions—not just the final one.

'Well?' she demanded.

This time he let her see his eyes, but there was something in the blueness she couldn't understand, though it did send a shivery sliver of ice along her veins.

'I'm going to specialise, yes. I start in the middle of January and, as I hadn't had a break for a few years, took a holiday rather than take a short contract somewhere. Which explains why I was at the beach and available for the summons from Aunt Vi.'

Which told Kate a lot she had known, some she hadn't and had avoided the main question quite neatly.

But she wasn't going to be put off.

'In what?' she demanded, pique at his evasion adding to her curiosity.

He sent her a puzzled look, so blatantly false she gritted her teeth so she wouldn't yell. 'What specialty?'

'Oncology. Paediatric oncology.'

He stood up as he said the first word, and crossed to the sink and was rinsing his cereal bowl as he added the further explanation.

Kate stared at him, aware of a shift in the balance between them, of a change in the atmosphere, more noticeable than a sudden drop in air temperature. Then Grant wiped his hands and walked out the back door, but whether he was heading for the hospital or the surgery, or even uptown, she had no idea.

The only thing she did know was that Grant was hurting. She'd seen that same stiffness in his shoulders, the blankness in his eyes, way back when he'd had to leave his beloved home. And he'd coped by refusing to talk about it. By going to some place deep inside him, where even she hadn't been able to reach or follow. The memories were as clear as the leaves on the eucalypt outside the kitchen window.

But then she'd known what had happened—known the extent of his loss. Now all she had to go on was whatever they'd been discussing when the change had occurred.

Specialties.

Oncology.

Paediatric oncology?

She remembered the way he handled Cassie—with care, experience, even love, if she needed burping or changing. But putting her down as soon as the task was complete—not cuddling her or talking to her for too long. Staying aloof—apart.

Kate had assumed that while he was aware of a baby's needs, he just wasn't too fond of very small humans, and from time to time she had felt a little peeved he didn't show more wonder at the perfection of her daughter.

But if he was deliberately distancing himself…

For protection from some memories…

'D— Jeez Louise! Surely not!'

'Talking to yourself? Bad sign, Katie! I just popped over to the surgery to phone Brisbane. They're operating on Kevin's legs later this morning.'

Grant's sudden reappearance in the kitchen might have startled her, but not enough to miss the message he was giving her. He was over whatever had upset him and the subject was closed. Possibly for ever.

He put the kettle on to boil and popped a couple of slices of bread into the toaster. Watching him moving about her kitchen with such ease, undertaking simple domestic tasks, made her feel happy and empty at the same time.

Which was ridiculous!

'I hope it goes well,' she said, to show him she'd got the message, both messages—the one about the patient and the silent one—though she wasn't as certain she'd take much notice of the latter.

However, Kate was aware that now wasn't the time to push further, though there *was* something she wanted to talk to Grant about.

'Mr McConagle. We never finished that conversation— worked out about the new bathroom and where you'd sleep.'

Then she remembered why they hadn't finished the conversation, and heat crept into her cheeks.

'Gosh, is that the time? We'll have to talk about it later as one of us should be heading for work. I was going to go over and do some paperwork, but maybe I'd better spend the time sorting out the nanny *en suite* thing.'

But Grant didn't take the hint. He remained where he was, leaning against the sink, sipping tea and eating his toast while watching her with a frowning kind of academic interest, as if trying to remember who she was.

Grant knew he had to move, but it was difficult. Though staring at Katie wasn't producing answers so he may as well be working.

He finished his breakfast and walked across to the surgery, his mind still puzzling over why the question of a live-in nanny was bothering him.

Because once Katie had this paragon in place, she'd no longer need him?

No, it couldn't be that. He was going anyway.

He had to go.

Cassie was one baby, but the work he'd chosen to do might eventually save the lives of hundreds of babies.

Though the position on the team had been hotly contested and one of any number of able men or women could be chosen to take his place.

No!

The word sounded so loudly in his head he glanced around in case he'd actually said it aloud. But the birds in the cassia seemed unfazed, and the young mother dragging her toddler up the path towards the surgery's front door hadn't even glanced his way.

Loving a baby was like having your heart held to ransom. No way could he go through that again.

The mother with the toddler was his first patient—she was also pregnant according to the test kit she'd bought at the chemist.

'I didn't want another baby quite so soon,' she told Grant, though the pleasure in her eyes belied her words. 'But seeing as it's coming, is there any way I can have it here? Now you're here, surely it would be OK.'

Grant must have looked as puzzled as he felt for, without waiting for a response from him, she went right on talking. 'Dr Newberry, before Kate came, said it wasn't possible to have little Brendan here because, as the only doctor, he mightn't be around when I went into labour, but Mum says Dr Darling delivered all the babies in Testament for years, and he wouldn't always have been around when the mothers went into labour. I mean, given how long labour takes, it shouldn't have been a risk, but now there are two doctors—'

'I'm only temporary.' Grant blurted out the words, determined to stop this misconception before it went any further—or he felt any guiltier. 'But once a new hospital doctor is appointed it should be OK. I know Katie—Dr Fenton—is interested in the local women having their babies here. She's done a short obstetrics course and is really very keen. If you ask Vi, she can make sure you see Katie on your next appointment.'

The young woman smiled so broadly Grant wondered if

he'd overstated the case. And was Katie's desire to do obstetric work dependent on the appointment of a hospital doctor or would she go ahead anyway?

He completed his examination of the woman, made notes on her card, then saw her out.

Vi came in with some drug-test results.

'So Katie's organising a live-in nanny,' she said, and looked at Grant, obviously expecting some reaction.

'It's the sensible thing,' he said, quelling his own reservations about the move.

'I guess,' Vi said, though her tone was glum. 'But such a pity when she's obviously enjoying parenting, and I think, deep down, she'll hate handing so much of it over to someone else.'

'It was her decision to go along the path of single motherhood,' Grant reminded his aunt, though the gruffness in his tone was more to do with the bad feeling in his guts than with Katie's difficult choice.

He picked up the papers from the pathology lab and pretended to study them so Vi would realise the subject was closed.

Not that Vi would take any notice of something as subtle as a hint.

'Maybe marrying Brian wouldn't be such a bad idea. She'd have security so she wouldn't have to work full time for financial reasons, and she could get someone to take over the practice, just do a few surgeries a week and start up some of the ancillary things she feels are missing in the town.'

Vi walked away. Though Grant had heard the rest of the conversation, it hadn't made a lot of sense as the words 'marrying Brian' had kept hammering away in his head.

They were still echoing there, in spite of the demands and conversation of nineteen more morning patients, when he returned to the house for lunch. Katie was there, dressed not in her usual uniform of short shorts and a cropped top but in a flirty skirt with blue and yellow flowers on it and a yellow T-shirt which gave her skin a special golden glow.

There was a similar glow in her eyes...

She must have been out, and though he wanted to ask where—and perhaps why—the noise in his head took precedence.

'I thought you'd got rid of Brian,' he said, and saw the glow fade from her eyes and puzzlement take its place.

'Got rid of? Brian? What are you talking about?'

'Brian who was doing your lawns. I told you I'd do them. I did them last Saturday.'

'Yes?'

She sounded confused but it could be a ploy.

'So what's Vi talking about?'

Katie shook her head, making her curls dance and jiggle in a way that told him she'd washed her hair as well.

'Vi?' she asked, still sounding confused. 'What did Vi say?'

'That you were going to marry Brian?'

'Marry Brian? Brian Ridley? Vi said that?'

Her disbelief penetrated the cloud of anger and, yes, he had to admit to some confusion.

'Well, she mightn't have said exactly that, but she gave that impression.'

Katie stared at him as if unable to make sense of what he was saying, then she shook her head so the curls bobbled about again and distracted him.

'Nonsense!' she said. 'You've got it wrong. Maybe you're working too hard. I should have taken morning surgery. You had a late and stressful night last night with Kevin, and—'

'I am not overtired or overstressed!' Grant told her, speaking slowly and just a trifle loudly to make sure she understood. 'I simply don't think you should consider marrying a man like that. You've Cassie to think of, and she'll need someone with strength and character as a father, not some chinless wimp of a bank manager.'

It was the way she straightened up that told Grant he'd gone too far. Straightened up and looked at him, green eyes narrowed in anger.

'Before you get that foot out of your mouth and insert the other one, might I remind you that my father was a bank manager. And furthermore, Brian Ridley happens to have a most attractive chin, which, I might add, doesn't jut out stubbornly when he's arguing. He also has a nose that doesn't keep poking itself into other people's business. And if you're not overtired, or overstressed, then I suggest you think of some other excuse for your behaviour, which is totally unacceptable.'

And on that note she spun on her heel—high, and part of a most attractive golden sandal—and stalked out of the room.

Grant leaned against the sink and stared out the window.

He did try to think of some excuse for his behaviour, but could come up with nothing—apart from temporary insanity. And if he pleaded that, Katie would ban him from seeing patients in case it happened in a doctor-patient situation.

And rightly so.

Though he didn't think it would. The insanity thing seemed to be solely connected to her.

He was still trying to think when she walked back into the kitchen, this time carrying a handbag that matched the cheeky sandals.

'Cassie's down the road at Tara's place, and I'll be back in time to feed her there before afternoon surgery. If you take any emergency calls that come in between now and then, I'll take the surgery, so you'll be free from two until tomorrow morning. I'll leave you the car.'

She was halfway out the kitchen door when he had to ask—just had to.

Though he tried hard to sound casual about it.

'Where are you off to—should I need you?'

He was congratulating himself on injecting just the right degree of nonchalance into the words when she turned, smiled brilliantly at him, then answered.

'I'm having lunch with Brian.'

CHAPTER NINE

HAVING lunch with Brian wasn't quite the 'date' Grant might have been imagining, but it served him right for butting in with remarks about her private life.

Having lunch with Brian, Kate realised, as she trudged uptown towards the bank, was about on a par in the excitement stakes with cleaning the fluff out from under the washing machine. And on top of that, now she was actually on her way, it renewed all the guilty feelings she had about the rift with her mother. Her parents would be only too happy to lend her the money for the renovations—in fact, her father would be hurt if, by chance, her application for a loan came to his attention.

Not that it should—state managers had better things to do than check out small personal loans made in remote country towns.

But if Brian had to get approval from a district manager—who happened to be one of her father's best friends...

Or if her father were to idly flick through a data bank on his computer...

By the time she reached the bank, she was so confused she wondered why she'd ever made the appointment.

'Kate—lovely to see you. And how beautiful you look. Motherhood does suit you. The baby's well?'

Brian always seemed to rush into speech as soon as they met, but today Kate appreciated the verbal outpourings as it gave her time to recover her nerve and steel herself for whatever lie she might have to tell as she persuaded him to keep her request to himself.

'We're both fine,' she replied, smiling at him to make

up for any lack of enthusiasm in her words. 'It's kind of you to make time for me like this.'

This mild appreciation prompted another flood of assurances, delight and confused half-sentences, making Kate wonder if he might be as nervous as she was over the meeting.

He ushered her into his office and shut the door, and, anxious to get the matter out in the open, she came straight to the point.

'I need a loan—a personal loan—for a second bathroom—for a nanny, you see, or visitors, or whatever—and I know you probably have to get approval, but I don't want my father thinking I'm not managing very well should it happen to come to his attention through someone who knows someone. He might also think I'm over-extending myself, and I wondered if there was any way I could get some money that only you know about.'

'Well, I know the bank would approve a small loan through the usual channels, or I could lend it to you myself if you'd like that better,' Brian said. 'We'd do it legally, with signed agreements and all, but I've quite a bit put by, and I'd be happy to do it, Kate. Only too happy. Any time. A private arrangement, no worries, and you needn't think I'd cheat you on interest. I could let you have it interest-free, say, for twelve months, then we could discuss it again.'

Kate felt an enormous weight lift off her shoulders. She could see the bathroom taking shape.

Of course, it would mean Grant shifting into the small bedroom, but he'd said he wouldn't mind, and the baby didn't need it yet. Though having Grant just through one wall instead of two—

'So what about it?'

She stared blankly at Brian. She'd been so lost in her plans for the immediate future she'd totally missed whatever he'd been saying.

'I'm sorry. I was thinking of the bathroom, and phoning Mr McConagle, and all the other things I need to do. Christmas decorations, too.'

Brian looked confused.

'What were you saying?' Kate prompted.

'You haven't said yes or no.'

He was smiling at her, and suddenly Grant's words about marrying Brian came rushing back to her. Had she been wrong thinking Brian's friendship had stemmed from his anxiety to be nice to the big boss's daughter?

And if it *was* more than that, then accepting his offer would almost certainly be wrong because it might give him the wrong idea.

But it *would* solve all her problems!

'I'm sorry.' She offered a smile of her own. 'I guess I didn't think it would be so easy. I need to think about it—about which way to go.'

She was stumbling over the words, anxious not to hurt him, wanting to avoid conflict with her father, but uncertain of the ramifications of borrowing privately, so when he spoke again she was still weighing up the pros and cons—or trying to ignore the cons.

'I wondered if you'd like to come to the bank's Christmas party on Saturday night,' he said. 'It's a dinner-dance at the Commercial Hotel, for the staff and their families and some of our larger accounts. That country and western band from Craigtown's doing the music.'

Pleased to have something easy to answer, Kate rushed in.

'That would be wonderful—I really need to get out and meet more people in the town—as people rather than patients—but I can't promise, of course. I had suggested to Grant that he take the weekend off, so I'd be on call.'

Brian looked so disappointed she rushed to reassure him.

'Not that I'd be likely to be called out.'

He beamed at her, told her he'd look forward to hearing

from her about the loan and would draw up two sets of papers ready for her signature so, whatever she decided, the loan wouldn't be delayed.

'And now the business is done, let's have lunch. I asked the Star Café to send in sandwiches. I hope that's OK.'

His nervousness prompted her to overreact again, assuring and reassuring while wondering how someone who always seemed so ill-at-ease could handle his responsible job, but as they ate he chatted on about the district, seemingly more relaxed when not in bank manager mode.

Kate glanced at her watch before she left the bank. Not enough time to buy Christmas decorations before collecting Cassie from Tara and getting to work.

She walked with long, swift strides, pleased the loan could be organised though not sure which way she'd go. A personal loan would solve so many problems—but would it lead to more? Probably! She'd think about other things— the alterations and the baby—think about anything that would take her mind off personal loans and, more particularly, off Grant Bell—off the feel of his lips on hers, off the hardness of his body as she'd pressed against it.

'Such a happy lunch with Brian you're still smiling?'

It was as if her thoughts had conjured him up, but when she recovered from the shock of Grant's sudden appearance and looked around, she realised he'd come out of the bakery.

'Yes! In fact, it was such a happy lunch I might be smiling for a couple of weeks,' she told him. 'Have you been reminiscing with Codger?'

'Trying his pies. They're not bad.'

Grant spoke lightly, but no smile accompanied the words. Kate glanced towards him and caught the faint markings of a frown lingering between his eyebrows.

'Not good either?' she asked, then added, 'Codger's pies,' when he looked confusedly at her.

'I don't know what you're talking about.' He spoke so

crossly Kate let the subject drop, though even walking with
Grant, his steps fitting hers, his body so close, was filling
her head with all the things it shouldn't think, and tantalising her nerve endings with a fuzzy kind of excitement
that was dangerous in the extreme.

Talking would be much better.

'Brian's willing to lend me the money for the renovations.' It was the first thing that popped into her head. 'So
I can phone Mr McConagle from work and let him know
to start.'

They'd reached Tara's house and she opened the gate
then turned back to Grant.

'Isn't it exciting?'

Definite frown this time.

'You mean the bank's lending you the money?' he
growled as Tara appeared, Cassie in her arms.

'I was just going to give her a bottle, but saw you walking down the street and thought she could wait. If you're
on your way to work, do you want to feed her here rather
than go home?'

'Thanks, Tara, it would certainly save a little time.'

Kate glanced towards Grant, who was still standing on
the footpath outside Tara's front gate.

Frowning.

'I'll see you later,' she said, aware she hadn't answered
his question and wondering about her reluctance to do so.

Because he'd put into words her own doubts or because
it was none of his business?

He nodded, but in such a way she knew he was aware
of the omission.

And, no doubt, intended to rectify it.

It was none of his damn business where she got her money,
Grant told himself as he walked back to the house.

Neither was being one room closer to her any different
from where he'd been, he assured himself as he packed his

extremely limited wardrobe and shifted into the smaller bedroom.

But whether it was proximity, or the nanny thing, or the thought of 'Brian' lending her money, not even a ride on his bike, a quiet ride past gum-shrouded waterholes and wide grassy plains stretching to the rugged mountains so familiar from his childhood, could lift the black mood that enveloped him.

Katie came home as he was stripping off his leathers.

'I hope you haven't been speeding. It's bad enough you ride one of those death machines, without taking risks by going too fast.'

He turned towards her. She was still glowing—he hoped it was the yellow top, not Brian, prompting the inner light—and Cassie rested easily in one arm. Which should have stopped, not increased the rush of physical attraction that tightened every sinew in his body.

'And what business is it of yours?' he growled, and felt a spurt of satisfaction when she started at his tone.

'I need a locum, that's what business it is of mine,' she snapped, recovering far too well. 'At least until I get a second bathroom and a nanny.'

'After which, as far as I'm concerned, I can kill myself on my bike?' He spoke without thinking, giving way to some of the venom poisoning his blood.

She went so white he thought she'd faint, and he reached out automatically to grab hold of her. But she shook him off, glared at him, then said, 'Don't you *ever* say things like that, Grant Bell. Don't you ever even *think* things like that!'

Then, clutching Cassie more tightly to her chest, she walked away, leaving Grant more shaken by her reaction—and his own reaction to her reaction—than by the words. Pulling his leathers back on and going for another ride wasn't an option, though it was the most appealing idea.

He decided it must have been a momentary shock, perhaps to do with the fact she'd had the baby in her arms when she'd looked as if she'd faint, that had made his heart squeeze so hard it had hurt him. It had been a protection reflex, that's all, and protection was a normal male reaction—to protect and procreate, weren't they the basic reasons for men's existence in the scheme of things?

He wouldn't think about the procreating now, though certain aspects of it were never far from his mind these days. And he'd accept that the protection thing was simply instinctive—nothing to do with the fact that it was Katie who'd turned so white.

Though he'd better check she was OK.

He walked into the house, still confused, and found her, whatever she might have felt apparently forgotten, smiling as she chatted with Mr McConagle on the phone.

Which reminded him of the loan—and the question she hadn't answered earlier.

Aware that it was none of his business, but needing to know nonetheless, he waited until she finished the call then tried a casual approach.

'So, you got a bank loan for the extensions. Well done. Would you like a drink to celebrate? A small glass of white wine shouldn't bother Cassie.'

He opened the fridge as he spoke, and pulled out the bottle of wine he'd bought earlier, then, aware of the silence descending on the room, turned to look at her.

At pinkness in her cheeks?

'What's wrong? What did you have to do? Have sex with him in the office?'

His voice, which had started as a low growl, grew harsher as imagination raised the level of his anger.

The pinkness turned to the red of rage and she stood up and stepped towards him, her arm lifting ready to swing towards his face.

He caught her wrist in time to stop the slap, but couldn't stop the flow of words.

'How dare you talk to me that way? How dare you even suggest such a thing? What's wrong with you, Grant? What's got you so screwed up your mind would even think of something like that?'

He heard the rage in her voice, but his own had gone way beyond the point of no return. Still holding her wrist gave him the power to draw her towards him.

With her face no more than six inches from his own, he answered.

'I'll tell you what's got into me, Katie Fenton. You have. You and your short shorts and long legs and your tangled, sexy-as-hell hair, and living in the same house, seeing you, smelling you, sensing your presence in the air. It's driving me to distraction—but it would only be sex, and I'd still be moving on, so in fairness to you I'm fighting it. Understand?'

Huge bewildered green eyes looked appealingly into his, and resolve, accompanied by good intentions, flew out the window.

'But I can only take so much!' he muttered, then he bent and claimed her softly parted lips, sealing whatever she might have been about to say with a kiss so hot and needy he felt her gasp before her body slumped against his and she slipped her wrist out of his grasp so she could reach for his shoulders to steady herself while she kissed him back.

He was aware of her softness, so different to the angular Katie he'd known, but the passion with which she responded was exactly how he remembered it, and the way it fed his own desire, like fierce winds fanning bush fires, reminded him of those wild encounters by the river.

When they stopped for air, and because he had to stop right then or carry her off to the bedroom to finish what he'd never intended starting, he had to steady her with his hands on her shoulders and ignore the silent appeal in those so expressive eyes.

Then she breathed deeply and put it into words.

'I could probably do with some sex. It's been a long time and it was never much fun with Mark.'

She spoke like someone in a dream, then shook her head and stepped away from him.

'Though I wouldn't ever do that to another woman—help her man to cheat. I couldn't do that to Linda.'

Grant was so busy assimilating Katie's bold confession about the sex that it took a while to work out who Linda was and why she'd entered the conversation. And by that time Katie was prattling on about Mr McConagle starting the following day and would Grant mind doing the morning session again as she had to sign Brian's loan papers at the bank?

A jolt, different from the one he'd felt earlier but just as strong, all but rattled his bones.

'Brian's loan? You mean the bank's loan.'

The pinkness that had started all of this returned to her cheeks, but this time it was accompanied by a defiant tilt of her slightly pointed chin.

'No, I mean Brian's loan. It's a personal arrangement.'

'But you can't borrow money from him,' Grant protested. 'It puts you under an obligation and, given the way he feels about you...'

Oops. Foot in mouth again—in fact, so far in it was probably lodged in his chest.

Katie's eyes glittered dangerously, but her voice, when she spoke, was very soft.

'And what business of yours is it? Whatever Brian does or doesn't feel about me has nothing whatsoever to do with you!'

She stalked away before he could find an answer, though she obviously wouldn't have listened even if he'd thought of something to say.

Damn it all! As she'd told him earlier, it was none of his business what she did and the sooner he got that into his thick skull, the sooner they could get things back onto a friendly footing.

Friendly footing? Hollow laughter sounded in his head. As if such a thing would be possible after that last kiss.

His body tightened at the memory then became more aroused as he remembered her admission that she wanted sex as much as he did.

Though she hadn't stipulated him as a partner...

And Brian was lending her money...

Desire ebbed away.

Kate's fury took her as far as the bedroom. She was aware she'd made things worse by pretending she'd already decided to accept Brian's offer—and needling Grant with the pretence—but she'd been so confused by the kiss...

Fury gave way to guilt, only this time it wasn't the guilt she'd felt when she'd realised how much she wanted to take Grant's kisses further—when she knew full well he was engaged to another woman—but guilt that she could bring her anger so close to her child.

'Sorry, little one,' she said, peering into the crib and feeling relief that the baby slept on, apparently unaware of the tension Kate assumed had been radiating from her body.

She slumped onto the bed and stared at the ceiling. It was her turn to cook dinner—steak and salad—and she should be in the kitchen, putting bits of lettuce in a salad bowl and chopping things to make the lettuce more interesting. But as her anger had eased, then been deliberately doused in the bedroom, an uncertainty had risen at the other end of her see-sawing emotions.

Was she wrong to borrow money from Brian? *Would* it put her under an obligation to him?

Yes, and yes, the stern internal killjoy said, in answer to these questions.

Maybe she shouldn't have agreed to go to the dinner-dance...

Though she *was* a bank customer, and if the bank was lending her money it should be OK.

Though the personal loan was still tempting...

No!

A light tap on the door startled her awake.

'Katie! Are you there? Dinner's ready.'

She leapt from the bed, horrified she'd been asleep, and raced to open the door.

'It was my turn,' she told Grant, who was hovering uncertainly in the hall. 'I'm sorry! I must have fallen asleep.'

His lips eased into the grin that made her bones melt, even though she'd now remembered she was furious with him.

'You probably needed it. And I had nothing to do, so it was no bother.'

He walked away, but not before she'd read confusion in his eyes.

Confused *and* uncertain?

Get real, Kate! She *had* to be imagining it.

But her own uncertainty had her hesitating now. She checked the baby, went through to the bathroom to drag a comb through her unruly hair and straighten the now crumpled skirt and top.

Perhaps she should change.

'Come on, Katie. The steaks will go from medium to well done to charcoal if you don't come now.'

Unable to dither any longer, she walked through to the kitchen where they ate all their meals. A spray of bougainvillaea rested in the centre of the table, place-mats were neatly aligned opposite each other and the presence of both wine and water glasses suggested there'd be another offer of a celebratory drink.

Was it an apology?

'I made a Caesar salad and a potato salad, so help yourself while I whack the steaks onto a serving dish.'

It sounded like an apology—of sorts!

Kate helped herself to healthy portions of each of the salads, then held out her plate for the steak he was offering. Once again he smiled, this time as he slid the piece of meat onto the plate, but the blue eyes when they looked at her were still clouded with some emotion she didn't understand.

Though lack of understanding didn't stop the rush of longing that flooded through her body, a longing she recognised not as lust but love—love and the pain it brought in its train when the loved one was hurting.

He has a fiancée, and a city career awaiting him, and has told you all he wants from you is sex, so forget it, Kate.

The stern admonition had so little effect she might as well have saved her brain cells for working out how to combat the implications of this new revelation.

'Eat!'

The order came so abruptly she glanced up, and once again the blue eyes were her undoing. Scrabbling around in her head for something to discuss before she blurted out how she was feeling, she remembered where the argument and kiss business had begun.

'I considered getting a loan from Brian and not the bank because I really didn't want it to get back to Dad. Although I know it's unlikely it would, stranger things have happened. They'll be coming for a visit as soon as they get home and I don't want Dad spending the whole time lecturing me on keeping within my means.'

The words came out in a rush, but didn't seem to appease her companion. Far from understanding, he looked even more annoyed than he had when she'd first mentioned Brian earlier.

'What about credit cards and overdraft facilities? As a bank manager he could have increased your limit on those without anyone else being any the wiser.'

Kate contemplated this statement, and felt the frown

puckering her brow. Although she'd nearly—well, almost certainly—decided not to get the loan from Brian, she still couldn't fathom Grant's interest.

Or his reaction.

'But credit-card rates are really high, and I've already got an overdraft—that's how I bought the house and practice. What's so wrong with borrowing from Brian?'

She didn't add, 'from your point of view', though that's what she meant, as she knew her own reservations.

Grant's frown looked far more ferocious than her own felt.

'Because it puts you under an obligation—it's not as if you know him well.'

'Of course I know him well. He's been a good friend to me since I came to Testament. He mows my lawn.'

'Mowed your lawn,' Grant corrected, still frowning. 'And I thought I was a friend as well. Why not borrow from me?'

Kate cut a piece of steak, lifted it to her mouth and chewed carefully. She had about forty easy answers to Grant's question. Why should I? I didn't think of it. What would Linda think? Those were only three of them, but she had a feeling that, while the loan might be the obvious topic of conversation, there were undercurrents to it she didn't understand.

But were they dangerous enough to sweep her away?

The idea was weird enough to ignore but the feeling too strong for her to banish completely, so she kept quiet about the second loan offer and pursued the matter—but trod carefully.

'I intended getting it from the bank, but when I mentioned doing it quietly, Brian came up with the offer. It's no big deal, Grant.'

It wasn't, of course. Grant knew that, though he couldn't bring himself to admit it to Katie.

Neither could he understand how screwed up it made him feel inside.

'Well, as long as you don't feel under any obligation,' he managed to reply, hoping his voice didn't sound quite as growly to Katie as it did in his own ears. Then, just as things might have settled back onto an even keel, some malign fate reminded him of the remark Katie had made earlier. 'I could do with some sex,' she'd said.

'In any way!' he added, not even attempting to hide the growl. 'And you know what I mean! You've admitted to having sexual needs, and he's been kind, and gratitude can be mistaken for other emotions and then you'll end up in a tangle.'

'You mean in his bed!' Katie said, icy disdain sharpening her voice to razor-like proportions. 'And you wanting to have sex with me while engaged to Linda isn't getting you into a tangle?' Kate's green eyes glittered with something he didn't quite understand. 'I'll admit I hadn't quite thought of Brian that way,' she continued, as cool as the ice in her voice, 'but, now you mention it, he does have a good body and, yes, I'm a woman and I do have sexual needs, so maybe Saturday night, after the dinner-dance—'

'You're going out with him? See, it's the obligation thing already. And having sex with a man because he has a good body is the most irresponsible thing I've ever heard of.' Grant was on his feet, leaning across the table, wanting to grab her shoulders and shake her to make her understand. But the eyes that met his were now easy to read—they glowed with an anger so hot he wondered it wasn't scorching his skin.

'Are you suggesting that me having sex with someone with a bad body would be more acceptable?'

Grant slumped back into his chair and pushed his half-finished dinner away.

'I'm not suggesting any such thing, Katie Fenton, and you bloody well know it.' He searched for something else to say—something to make things at least part-way right between them again. 'But you've Cassie to consider, and small-town gossip, and how that might affect her later on.'

'Are you saying I should keep myself pure but frustrated, so Cassie doesn't have kids whispering about her mother when she goes to school? For how long? Five years? Or eighteen, until she leaves home, when I can then have sex with every man in town?'

He could hear the quiver in her voice, and see the strength of her emotions in the trembling of her fingers. Devastated that he'd made such a total hash of things, he reached across the table and took her hand.

'I'm sorry, Katie. I was way out of line. But I want so much for you to be happy, and for you and Cassie to have a wonderful and fulfilling life. And if that means having a man in your life, I hope you find one who truly loves and appreciates you.' The words nearly choked him, but he got them said so he could add the rider. 'But take your time. Don't fall into bed with the first man who comes along. Guard your emotions so you don't get hurt again.'

Too late for that warning, Kate thought, but her hand felt so warm and right in Grant's she let it stay there.

And she found a smile to offer him in return for the comfort of those long, strong fingers.

'Isn't that a bit defeatist, Dr Bell? Especially coming from the lips of a prime risk-taker like yourself? And leaving Mark, when the time came, didn't hurt. In fact, it was the easiest of partings, because I knew it was right for me.'

His thumb was rubbing the back of her forefinger and, though she'd never considered that bit of skin as part of any erogenous zone, the movement was sending startlingly explicit messages through her body.

She should remove her hand.

Now!

But he probably didn't even realise he was doing it—

and certainly wouldn't in his wildest dreams have guessed what it was doing to her.

So to withdraw her hand might seem…unfriendly?

She turned her attention to his face, and found him smiling at her—with eyes as well as lips this time.

'I can't imagine you admitting if it had hurt, Katie,' he said gently. 'You might have railed against what you saw as injustice, or taken up a fight on behalf of someone else, but I never heard you complain about your own lot, or saw you cry over an injury.'

'Until the week you arrived, when all I seemed to do was weep. It's a wonder you didn't turn around and go straight back to Byron Bay.'

His grip tightened on her fingers, sending more tremors through her body.

'Maybe it would have been better if I had,' he said quietly, then he released her hand, stood up, tipped his dinner into the trash can and dumped the plate in the sink.

'I'm going out,' he said. 'Leave the dishes and I'll do them later.'

'Nonsense—I'll do them,' Kate told him, surprised she'd managed to form the words when she was breathless with fear for him. Then, much as she tried not to say it, she couldn't hold back the words. 'N-not on your bike? You won't ride your bike?'

Grant was at the back door as she stammered out the feeble pleas, and turned, frowning again.

'I'm only going over to Vi's,' he said. 'On foot!'

And though her panic eased on that count, another worry arose to confront her.

The 'maybe it would have been better if I had' statement he'd made before his precipitate departure.

CHAPTER TEN

IT WAS nonsense, Kate assured herself, but the sick feeling in her stomach and the dull ache in the region of her heart suggested it probably *would* have been better if Grant had gone straight back—or if he'd never come.

She thought back to the strange conversation that had preceded his departure—to her rage over his reaction to her innocent acceptance of Brian's invitation to the bank's Christmas party. She'd stood up for herself then, flinging stupid words at him as her temper had flared, but that's all they'd been—words. In truth, when she'd decided to go ahead with her pregnancy and had planned her life—hers and Cassie's—she'd never for a moment considered a relationship with another man somewhere further down the track. In her relief to be free of Mark and the emptiness of what they'd shared, the single state had seemed to offer everything she'd ever need.

Until Grant Bell had come back into her life, reawakening not only the heat and longing of desire with an intensity she'd thought she'd never feel again but, worse, reminding her of the ease with which she could talk to him, the special bond she'd always felt in his presence, the sense of completeness he'd brought to her life—so many years ago.

Yes, maybe it would have been better if he had, as he'd murmured, gone straight back to Byron Bay.

Though she certainly wouldn't have managed without him.

The sharp summons of the phone brought her out of the useless cogitation, and the emergency, a child who'd swallowed half a bottle of cranberry capsules because they'd looked pretty, had her on the phone to Tara, then hot-footing it across to the hospital.

'They probably won't do any harm,' she assured the pan-icking parents, 'but we'll try to get rid of them anyway.'

She was examining little Richie Webb as she spoke, talk-ing quietly to him, asking how he felt.

The four-year-old was alert—perhaps too alert, though he was always an active child, and his respiration and pulse were normal.

'Rather than intubating him to use a stomach pump, I'd rather try an emetic—something to make him sick,' she told Mrs Webb. 'It's less traumatic than the stomach pump.'

The anxious mother nodded, and Kate explained to Richie that he'd have to have a drink and it might make him sick.

'But being sick is good because it will get all those silly tablets out of your tummy.'

The little boy nodded, and Narelle, again on duty, hurried off to get a basin, while Kate measured out two teaspoons of syrup of ipecac for the little boy.

'Just drink this down, Richie, then I'll give you a glass of water.'

She glanced up at his parents.

'Be prepared for a fast reaction, though if it doesn't work within thirty minutes I can give him another dose.'

The second dose wasn't needed, and the fourteen tablets, still encased in their gel coating, were safely remitted.

Leaving Richie resting on a table in the emergency room, Kate took the empty bottle of cranberry tablets and hurried through to her office. As the capsules still looked intact, there was a chance none of the constituents had entered Richie's stomach, but she'd have to check the list of ingre-dients against known contraindications before giving him activated charcoal as a precautionary measure.

She explained this to Mr and Mrs Webb when she re-turned minutes later.

'So, just in case some bad stuff got out of the tablets and into your tummy, Richie,' she told the little boy, 'I want you to take this tablet. You know how Mummy's sponge picks up spills in the kitchen? Well, that's what this tablet will do in your tummy. It will pick up any bad stuff left and you'll be OK.'

'Will I have to be sick again?' he demanded, giving Kate a look that suggested he'd rather be poisoned.

'No, not this time,' she assured him.

'Then where will it go?'

His clear, pale blue eyes challenged her and, with his parents exchanging amused glances, Kate grabbed a diagram of the alimentary canal and proceeded to explain just how it worked, in simple enough terms for a four-year-old to understand.

Richie's main delight was in the end result.

'He's at an age when "bottom" is the funniest word he knows and anything to do with bodily functions is a cause of great interest,' Mr Webb explained.

Kate nodded, knowing children of friends who hooted with laughter over the same word, and whispered behind their hands about the less attractive features of the end product of their alimentary canals. Then, while Richie regaled Narelle with some of the things his friends said at preschool, Kate spoke to his parents about precautions they might take in future.

'I do know all that,' Mrs Webb said earnestly. 'We've a child-proof lock on the cupboard under the sink where I keep cleaning things, and Jeff has a lock on the garden shed. But my grandmother's staying with us, and she takes the cranberry, and heaven knows what else. Richie must have slipped into her bedroom while we were having dinner, and it wasn't until Grandma was going to bed that she realised the tablets were missing.'

'You can't be on guard all the time,' Kate assured her. 'And there's no harm done. A good night's sleep and he'll be back to normal. Although if he does seem unusually quiet or if you're worried about him in any way, don't hesitate to call me.'

Both parents thanked her, then Mr Webb lifted their son into his arms and carried him out to the car.

How long would she be able to lift Cassie? Kate wondered. Until she was five—six?

She scuffed her feet against the path as she walked home, concerned because the spectre of bringing up a child alone was once again a pressing concern on her shoulders.

Smiled to herself, because Grant had been so reassuring whenever she'd expressed the stupid fears that beset her so regularly. Then she remembered how they'd parted, and stopped smiling.

He was going, anyway, and she'd have to manage on her own—as she'd always intended.

But thoughts of Grant lingered in her mind, and after paying Tara and seeing her safely on her way home, she walked through the house, knowing he wasn't there but looking for him anyway. His bedroom door was open but the room was empty. Not only emptied of his possessions, but totally emptied. He must have shifted things while she'd been at work.

She walked to the next door—which was pulled close but not shut—and tapped before pushing it open. The bed with flowered sheets had been moved in and pushed against the other single to form a larger bed. She should have done that earlier, for someone as tall as Grant. The chest of drawers from the bigger bedroom was tucked behind the sliding doors of the built-in wardrobe where there was plenty of room, given Grant's lack of clothes.

Kate sniffed the air, already masculine though he'd barely used it, then she saw the briefcase on top of the dressing-table.

'My papers are in my briefcase in my room if you'd care to look.'

She recalled the words he'd said that first day, before going out to see George Barrett.

She'd never looked, and although, tonight, it seemed like an invasion of privacy, she assured herself it was a responsible thing to do. A little late, admittedly, but still responsible!

She carried the worn leather case to the bed, rubbing her fingers on the leather because she knew his fingers had touched it. Telling herself not to be pathetic but doing it anyway.

Opening the clasp, she leafed through the manilla folders it held. New appointment letter—she'd like to look at that but had no right. Personal. Nothing to do with her. Definitely nothing to do with her. Bills—well, that one she didn't want. CV. That was it.

She pulled it out and opened it, laying it flat on the bed. Read through his school results—Miss Jones's mammary glands couldn't have had all that damaging an effect, from the results he'd got in final year maths. Results Kate hadn't known because he'd been gone before they'd been published.

She flipped over pages, trying not to think of that summer, and came to the précis of his medical career. University of New South Wales, then North Shore Hospital, followed by A and E at St George for three years.

Making money to buy back the farm, until he'd become an adrenalin junkie and had decided he liked it. Recalling his words, she studied the time frame once again. Three years and two months. Not a contract, then, in that fourth year. Contracts were usually longer—three months minimum. It looked more as if something had happened.

She went on to the next line. GP training—big switch. Perhaps he'd been waiting for a training position in a general practice and had continued in A and E until one came up. She checked the dates but they didn't fit—there was a four-month gap between when he left A and E and when he took up his post at the practice. Perhaps he'd been overseas, though leafing through the folder gave no indication of any overseas experience or study.

'It was a holiday—after three years and two months in A and E he'd have needed one.'

She spoke out loud, hoping to convince herself, but the words didn't have any more effect when heard aloud than when she'd thought them.

Kate turned a page. Twelve months' training, then GP work for eleven months, then another sudden switch—back to a lowly resident in paediatrics.

Two years there—not so lowly second year—took her up to two weeks before he'd appeared on her veranda with his 'knight in shining armour' routine. And the new job was in a training post for paediatric oncology—he'd told her that—a follow-on from what he'd been doing.

She was puzzling over the shifts and possible reasons for them when she heard Grant's footsteps entering the kitchen. Not wanting to appear furtive, she remained where she was, the papers spread in front of her, and when he entered the room she gave him what she hoped wasn't a furtive smile.

'You did tell me to check your credentials. I just never got around to it.'

He remained where he was, just inside the door, looking at her in a way she couldn't read.

'You stopped and started at odd times, and the gap after you left A and E—did you go overseas?'

He didn't answer, though his eyes remained fixed on her—or were they on her? She couldn't be sure, but what she did know was that some new tension had entered the room—not with him, but emanating from him now.

'I'm sorry. I should have asked first—it was ages ago you said to look.' She gathered up the papers but in her haste knocked the briefcase to the floor so the folders she'd half pulled out spilled to the floor, opening enough for papers to flutter everywhere.

'Oh, I'm sorry. I'll pick them up.'

She reached out, lifted a bundle and was about to shove them back into the closest folder when she saw the photo that lay beneath them. Grant was by her side, so she didn't miss his reaction either, didn't miss the tremor in his hand as he reached out to lift it, moving it out of her grasp—out of her sight.

Instinct made her grasp his wrist and stop him hiding it. Instinct took her further so she knelt closer to him and reached out her free hand to turn his face towards her.

'I guessed a baby, but I don't know any more. You're far better at changing Cassie's nappies than I am—you had to have had experience. Let me see him, Grant. Tell me.'

He didn't answer, neither would he look at her or reveal the image on the photo he held protectively against his chest.

Kate traced the lines that had deepened on his face.

'They're lines of pain—I knew that when you first returned. But wouldn't sharing it help you take the next step to recovery? Isn't there enough of our old friendship left for me to be the one you talk to?'

He lifted his head and what she saw in his blue eyes terrified her. It wasn't grief, but a kind of blankness—like the bewildered terror of a child who'd lost his way.

Kate forgot the photo and wrapped her arms around him, drawing him close and rocking his body against hers.

'Let's forget it for a while. Leave the papers here. Come with me, we can lie on my bed. We don't have to talk but at least I can hold you—we can hold each other. Everyone needs someone to hold occasionally.'

He didn't argue, though he did help her to her feet and allow her arm to stay wrapped around his shoulders as they walked into the bedroom.

Stay asleep, Kate willed the baby as she pulled back the sheet and guided Grant's obviously numbed body down onto the bed. Then she lay beside him and, as promised, held him, resting his head on her shoulder, running her fingers through his hair, stroking his back and kneading at his shoulders.

The words, when they came, were muffled, but though Kate's heart hurt when she heard Debbie's name, when Grant spoke of the casual relationship that had resulted in a pregnancy, she said nothing.

'Debbie wanted to keep working for at least another year—it would have given her the seniority she'd need for future jobs. And though I knew I'd have to give up A and E—the hours were too erratic for a family man—I stayed on until Robbie was born, so I could get some paternity leave and do a lot of the caring for those first three months.'

He paused, and Kate could picture him, though little Robbie would have had more cuddles than the occasionally surreptitious ones she knew Grant gave to Cassie.

'Then I went into a GP practice for training, and Debbie worked part time. My mother minded Robbie in between, and things were fine.'

But not ecstatic from the sound of your voice, Kate thought, then regretted it, as she knew it came from a jealousy she had no right to feel.

'Until he was nine months old, when he became listless, failed to thrive. We took him to doctors and finally to specialists. It was diagnosed as a brain tumour, a glioma, in the brain stem, inoperable and, practically speaking, untreatable. Robbie died six months later. Debbie and I had stayed together until then, but with nothing left to bind us that ended as well.'

The words stopped, and Kate's grip tightened. With tears flowing unchecked from her eyes, she used her hands, and the warmth of her body, to try to offer comfort that could never be put into words. A heaviness in Grant's body told her the telling of Robbie's story had left him exhausted, and when his deep, steady breathing suggested he might sleep for a while, she slipped away, covered him with a light cotton blanket, then lifted Cassie, crib and all, and carried her out of the room.

No good taking her into the small bedroom—Grant would still hear her when he woke.

Kate's heart fluttered as she imagined the agony Cassie's cries must already have caused him—unknowing reminders of his tragedy.

'We'll sleep in the living room,' she told her still sleeping baby. 'You have your crib, I'll take the couch.'

But though Cassie slept, Kate couldn't emulate her, too distressed by Grant's story to turn her mind off the baby he'd called Robbie. And, in spite of the fears that beset her daily about her own small infant, it was for Grant she feared through the dark watches of the night. For the laughing carefree teenager who'd already suffered the loss of his beloved home, then had rebuilt his life, only to be hit by another tragedy.

So many things had fallen into place with the telling of the tale—why he was so determined to do further study, why he'd chosen paediatric oncology, why he was so adamant that he'd be gone in a couple of weeks...

Kate could understand it all, but it didn't make the loneliness it prompted any easier to bear. It was as if she'd secretly—subconsciously—been hoping he would stay— that the fairy story which had begun with her knight's arrival would have a 'happy ever after' ending.

'Which is nothing more than self-pity, so don't go there,' she warned her head. 'Think of Grant instead.'

Kate found herself hoping that Linda was good to him— that she understood his pain and could, in some small way, alleviate it.

Then wishing it was herself, not some unknown woman, who had the right to hold him when the memories crowded in on him and his eyes ached with unshed tears.

Cassie gave a quiet cry, prelude to the demand, and Kate leapt off the couch, then realised she'd forgotten to bring a dry nappy from the bedroom. Were there some still in the dryer? Or was that pack of disposables in the pantry?

She picked up the baby before her cries could bother Grant, dropped a kiss on her head and carried her through to the kitchen. Yes! Disposables. They'd do for one night. She changed Cassie on the kitchen table, marvelling at her growth and beauty, refusing to even contemplate the existence of baby-killing tumours.

'It's so rare, it certainly won't happen to you,' she assured her little one, then she lifted her into her arms and carried her back to the living room. 'Statistically as unlikely as a tourist flight to the moon tomorrow.'

Cassie dropped off to sleep as she finished her meal, and Kate returned her to the crib, then stood, looking down at her. Thinking of another baby, and the aching loss she'd heard in Grant's voice.

She tiptoed to the bedroom door and cracked it open. Grant lay in a tangle of sheets which were becoming even more tangled as he tossed restlessly. The breeze coming through the open door was cooler now, and she moved closer, thinking to straighten the top sheet and cover him as she'd covered her baby.

But he stirred as she tried to unwind the soft cotton material from around his legs and groaned, then shifted restlessly, his hand touching her arm. As if comforted by finding her, finding something to anchor him, he grabbed it and pulled her close, until she found herself nestled up against his body—again!

And thinking things she shouldn't—again!

But Grant needed comfort, someone to hold onto until his dreams and pain subsided. Someone to be there for him in the dark watches of the night, when the death of his baby boy returned to haunt him.

OK, so she wasn't the right someone but she was the only person available. And she loved him—there, she'd admitted it, so the least she could do was be there for him just this once.

She banished confused and confusing thoughts to concentrate on Grant—and his need—tonight. And moved closer so her body fitted itself to his, and she could hold him.

Grant knew it had to be a dream—it wasn't the first. He'd had one just like it since he arrived back in Testament. But this time Katie felt real, and her sweet, soft body was snuggled up against him, as if this was where she was meant to be.

And if she was meant to be here, he could kiss her neck like this, and nuzzle that place below her ear where he'd discovered sensitive skin so long ago. And the buttons on the shirt she wore to bed seemed to have come undone, so he could touch her breasts, hold the heaviness, tease the nipple so she'd make the funny little noise of wanting only Katie had ever made.

So he kissed her, and it certainly didn't feel like a dream. Surely in the dreams she hadn't kissed him back.

Fuzzily, he began to remember—Katie on his bed, the papers dropping, Robbie's photo.

More recollection—this was Katie's bed, and Katie's body stretched beside him.

No! She'd left earlier—it *had* to be a dream.

And if it wasn't a dream, it was a disaster, for if there was one thing he knew above all others, he was only seconds away from making love to Katie Fenton. And leaving Katie Fenton—hard though it was going to be anyway—after making love to her would be well nigh impossible.

She was touching him, unbuttoning his shirt, running her fingers through the fine swirl of hair on his chest, sliding her hands lower…

But Cassie came with Katie, and he was already halfway to loving the tiny baby.

He tried to analyse the situation more rationally but the

tight buds of her nipples brushing across his chest suggested she was as aroused as she must surely know he was.

Was she here because she felt sorry for him?

The thought was abhorrent, but he'd better mention it—just in case.

'I don't want pity, Katie.'

Damn! He hadn't meant to say it that way, but it came out harshly enough for her to recoil, but, like Katie of old, she didn't go far, standing up to his challenge with all her old defiance.

'I am not offering you pity, Grant Bell, I'm offering you comfort, and if comfort includes sex, well, that's on offer, too—just for tonight—because of Robbie.'

She'd sat up so he could see the upper half of her body silhouetted against the light from the veranda doors.

'And if you're worried about Linda, then so am I, but if she never knows than it can't hurt her...'

Already confused by emotion, arousal and the still clinging remnants of sleep, the mention of some unknown woman's name tipped Grant's mind into total bewilderment.

'Who the hell is Linda?' he demanded, and felt, rather than saw, Katie recoil. She was out of the bed in a flash, positively gasping with whatever emotion his seemingly innocent remark had generated.

'And to think I felt sorry for you!' she snapped, snatching the sheet off the bed so swiftly she almost tugged him out as well, then holding it to her scantily clad body as she stalked out of the room.

'Then it *was* pity,' Grant snapped right back, but she was already gone and if she heard, she didn't answer.

'Damn and blast all women to hell!' he muttered to himself as he sank back against the pillow. He'd remembered Linda now, but what he remembered far more clearly—far too clearly—was the feel of Katie's body snuggled up to his, the ripples of sensory excitement in his skin as her heavy breasts had brushed across his chest.

His head ached, probably from the telling of Robbie's story, which always brought with it such a burden of defeat. His desire refused to subside, so he was feeling pain down there as well, and his mind had ceased to function so he couldn't work out where to go from here—what to do or say to make things right again.

Eventually he slept, but not before he'd heard Cassie cry and felt the familiar spurt of tension and remembrance the sound always caused.

Kate was in the kitchen, precautionary tales about drinking coffee while breastfeeding set aside as she gulped down a strong black brew. After a totally sleepless night, she needed something before she faced Mr McConagle.

It wouldn't help with facing Grant, of course. Cyanide might, but she didn't have any on hand and, anyway, it wouldn't be right to leave Cassie an orphan.

The thought of her baby made her shiver. What had happened to all her good intentions—her determination to be the best possible mother for her daughter? Was nestling up to Grant in bed the way a responsible mother should behave?

Of course it wasn't.

And as for him—and his 'Who's Linda?'.

What kind of man forgot his own fiancée's name?

She was mulling over whether she was more angry with herself or Grant when the phone rang.

'School bus accident at Four Mile Creek and the ambulance has taken Mrs Stubbs to Craigtown. I'm on my way. Can you come?'

Kate recognised the voice of Dick Harris, the police sergeant, and wasted no time assuring him she'd be there. As she dialled Tara's number, Mr McConagle knocked and came through the back door.

'Could you wake Grant and tell him he's needed?' she said to the handyman, then explained to Tara's mother what was happening. 'So could you send Tara over?' she said into the phone. 'Cassie's not long been fed, and there's boiled water in the fridge if she's desperate before I get back.'

Grant appeared as she put down the receiver, Mr McConagle following.

Kate explained briefly, asked Mr McConagle to mind the baby until Tara arrived and to let Vi know what was happening, then she led Grant out to the car.

'Did Dick say how bad it was?' he asked, steering her towards the passenger seat as he added, 'I'll drive.'

'No, just that he needed us. It's at the Four Mile.'

They drove swiftly and in silence until they were several kilometres from town when Kate saw emus stalking long-leggedly towards the road.

'Emus,' she warned, though she knew Grant had probably seen them, the silly birds racing along the verge as if in competition with the car.

Grant slowed, but couldn't stop to see which way they might dodge as the thought of injured children was in the forefront of both their minds.

The birds, six in all, veered away, then suddenly one skittered back towards the car in a wild, suicidal dance.

'Damn!' Grant muttered, as the bird brushed into the side of the car. 'Silly bloody thing!'

'It's probably all right,' Kate told him, but her assurance didn't soften the grim set of his lips. Remembering the emotional toll his telling of Robbie's story must have had on him the previous evening, she understood an injury to the bird would take on extra significance. Hoping, needing to offer comfort, in spite of where that need had led last night, she rested her hand on his thigh and kneaded it gently.

The flashing lights on the top of the police car, and be-

yond that the red bulk of the fire engine, told them the crash
scene had come into view, and the bus, tipped sideways
into a ditch, told its own story. As Grant pulled up behind
the police car, Kate grabbed her bag and leapt out.

'We've got all but three of the kids out, and the driver's
also trapped,' Dick told her, motioning to where volunteers,
who'd apparently appeared from nowhere on the isolated
country road, were comforting a group of resting children.
'The firemen are using cutting tools.'

'I'd better go in and see if anyone needs stabilising before he or she is moved,' Kate said, putting down her bag
and moving towards the bus.

Grant grabbed her arm.

'Don't be stupid! You check the ones who are out—I'll
go in there.'

She twisted out of his grip, and kept going.

'Look at the bus—you'd never get in there. I'm smaller,
I'll go. You see to the others.'

For a moment she thought he'd argue, then he nodded
and turned away, picking up her bag as he strode towards
the huddle of children.

Kate squeezed through the emergency exit window at the
back of the bus and crawled along the passage between
twisted metal bars and vinyl seating. Ahead of her, a fire-
brigade volunteer was using heavy pincers to cut metal
away from a small boy, and farther towards the front another child whimpered.

'A couple of our chaps are cutting towards the driver
from the front, and once they get him out, we should be
able to get the two kids from the seat behind him. This
one's legs are caught beneath their seat. He's unconscious
but he's breathing and there's no obvious blood loss.'

Kate reached around the man, feeling for the child's
wrist, feeling the rapid flutter of his pulse. Something
grasped her arm and she saw blood on the small fingers.
From where she was she couldn't see the child but, know-

ing he or she was conscious, she knew she had to get closer, if only for reassurance.

She gave the fingers a reassuring squeeze, then said, 'I'm coming, darling. I'll stay with you.'

'Can you let me past?' she asked the man, whom she now recognised as Richie Webb's father.

He wriggled closer to the seat and she squirmed past him, managing to turn so she could face the seat where the other two children were trapped. Outside, the wail of approaching sirens announced that at least one ambulance was finally arriving. Grant would get some help.

From where she was it became obvious the bus had rolled before coming to rest on its side, and the roof had caved in more seriously here in the front section. The trapped driver was hidden from her view by the back of his high seat, and the two children were wedged between it and their own seat, which had been squashed almost flat by the roof.

She pushed her hand towards what she could see of school uniform, felt the rounded leg beneath material, felt warmth and no wetness, and prayed the little one still lived. Then she edged closer into the narrow space and pushed her hand farther, finally encountering the arm of the second child. Once again small fingers found her arm, and then her hand, and, knowing there was nothing she could do until the driver was released, she held the little hand and talked about the day outside, the blue sky they would soon see when the roof was lifted off the bus.

The raw screeching of the power tools cutting into metal set her teeth on edge, and tightened the child's grip on her hand.

'It's just a saw—probably your dad has one,' she said, while behind her she heard Mr Webb grunt in exultation as the metal he was cutting finally gave way.

'I can lift this one backwards now,' he said to Kate. 'Will you come out and check him?'

'Dr Bell's out there, but can you lift him, seat and all? Perhaps just drag the seat backwards and wait until the roof comes off so he can be checked before he's moved. If he has spinal injuries, the seat will protect him. Do you need a hand?'

'No, you stay there,' the man said. 'The roof's moving so they must be close to lifting it. I heard Bob Willis's crane arrive. It should be able to peel the top back as easy as opening a sardine cane.'

'There are some similarities,' Kate commented, then she felt the movement as well and a sudden rush of air as the roof was lifted and blue sky appeared above them.

Also Grant Bell. He glanced her way, nodded as if assuring himself she was OK, then turned his attention to the driver. An ambulance officer handed Grant a neck collar, then a short backboard, which Grant slid between the back of the seat and the driver's body. Straps fastened around his chest and legs fashioned the board into a sling, and men with gentle hands lifted the injured man from his seat.

Within minutes the seat was also removed, allowing Kate her first glimpse of the two children behind it. The owner of the hand, a girl of about seven, smiled at her, but the lad beside her— 'He's my brother, he's asleep' —didn't move.

Then Grant was there, helping Kate to her feet, then strapping a neck and back brace onto the girl before lifting her in his strong arms and stepping out of the bus to pass her to rescuers. Kate bent to examine the boy. His pulse was strong, and he was breathing, but a large bruise already darkening the skin behind his left ear suggested the cause of his concussion.

Kate felt his body, seeking blood, then ran her hands over his arms—the left one gashed but not deeply—and down his legs. His right ankle, which had taken the brunt of the driver's seat when it had collapsed backwards, was certainly broken, but there was no other obvious damage.

'You climb out, I'll get him ready to be lifted.'

Grant was back, his hands on Kate's waist, ready to lift her out as well.

'I can manage,' she told him, but he took no notice, and one look at the determination in his eyes warned her not to argue. Firm, warm, safe hands lifted her onto the outside of the bus where others helped her to the ground.

She crossed to the ambulance where the little girl was being treated, a catheter already inserted into her arm and a drip about to be attached.

'Where's Robbie?' she asked, and Kate, though momentarily taken aback, quickly realised she must be talking about her brother.

'The other doctor is bringing him out now,' Kate said, brushing chips of safety glass out of the child's tangled hair.

'Will he be all right?'

Kate crossed her fingers superstitiously behind her back, and said, in her most definite voice, 'Yes, he will.'

Then Grant was there, the child in his arms.

'This is Robbie,' he announced, smiling broadly at Kate. 'He actually told me his name.'

Kate sighed her relief. Robbie must have remembered his name as he'd regained consciousness, which was an excellent sign. She tried not to think of Gareth, now convalescing at his home, and crossed her fingers again.

'It doesn't work, crossing fingers,' Grant said, taking her hand and uncrossing them, then lifting the imprisoned hand to his lips and dropping a kiss on the palm. 'What does work is medical knowledge most times, and love and faith at others.'

He paused then added, 'And when those don't suffice, it isn't because we didn't know enough, or do enough, or care enough, but because there's some grand plan that we don't understand, which decrees a person's time has come.'

Kate was so startled by his words she gaped at him. This

hardly sounded like the man so shattered by the death of his baby son he was about to dedicate his life to knowing more about what had killed him.

'You don't mean that,' she said, bending to help the ambulance officer strap young Robbie gently onto the stretcher and roll it into position beside the one on which his sister lay. The children's mother climbed in beside them, and the ambulance officer shut the door.

'I didn't for a long time,' Grant said, his voice quietly convincing, 'but I do now. Lifting this Robbie out, seeing him open his eyes, I remembered the good things about my Robbie, and thought of him without the depth of pain I hadn't, until now, been able to avoid.'

Kate felt as if her heart might break—but whether with sorrow for the love she had for him but could never reveal to him or with happiness that he was started on a real path to recovery, she couldn't tell.

She looked around, seeking some distraction, then realised the other children had already been transported, either home or to the hospital, where they'd be kept until checked again by either her or Grant.

'We have to get back,' she said, pretending she'd been thinking about work all along. 'There'll be a queue at the hospital and a lot of edgy patients in the surgery.'

Grant glanced her way but said nothing, merely collecting her bag and following her towards the car.

But as they drove home, quietly discussing the various theories the rescuers had offered about the cause of the accident, they passed the place where the emu had run into them and saw the fallen body with its long frilled feathers lying beside the road. And beside it, another emu, peering down at the lifeless form, poking at it with its beak.

Once again, Kate felt her heart swell with sadness, and this time she didn't try to stem it, letting it wash over her as if empathy with the big bird might relieve some of her own pain.

'It must have been its mate,' she murmured, the words catching in her throat, coming out far too huskily. 'Emus mate for life. Did you know that?'

She glanced at Grant, but he was looking fixedly ahead, as if piloting her car back to town took all his concentration.

CHAPTER ELEVEN

GRANT went to the hospital while Kate, knowing the badly injured victims had been taken straight to Craigtown, checked with Tara that the baby was still sleeping, with Mr McConagle that he had everything he needed, then headed for the surgery to tackle the backlog of patients.

Having heard about the accident, those waiting were understanding but anxious to hear details and reports on young friends, so every consultation seemed to take for ever. Stopping to feed Cassie put her further behind. Eventually Grant arrived and, using the treatment room for consultations, helped her through the session.

Kate thanked Vi, but as she carried the baby back to the house she felt the emptiness of deep disappointment.

Was it simply that she'd wanted to talk over the accident with him—to talk it out of her system—or was she missing him already, knowing he'd soon be gone? She phoned the hospital and found all but one of the children seen there had been discharged and the one remaining was asleep, his mother by his side. Still edgy, she phoned Craigtown hospital, where medical staff assured her that the bus driver and three children were all resting comfortably.

'And you're not much company,' she told the sleeping Cassie. 'It's night-time feeds you're supposed to sleep through now you're getting older. Not the daytime ones.'

She slouched about the house, getting in Mr McConagle's way until he started to dismantle a wall and shooed her off, telling her to take the baby out for a walk until he was finished making a mess. Maybe a walk wasn't such a bad idea, she decided, lifting Cassie into her stroller and slapping a wide-brimmed hat on her own head. She'd

172

get paint for the walls of the small bedroom. After all, Grant had said he'd help her paint it, though she could hardly paint it while he was sleeping in it, paint fumes being what they were. She'd have to wait till he was gone.

The brightness of the day failed to lift the weight of depression that settled more firmly on her shoulders with this thought, but then her daughter, waking to smile at her as they walked towards the town, reminded her of why she'd shifted to Testament and of the commitment she'd made when Cassie had been little more than a fist-sized foetus.

'We *will* be happy here,' she promised the wide-eyed baby. 'And you and I will make a wonderful life together. For a start, we'll buy some Christmas decorations, things we can keep from year to year, making a tradition for our little family. We'll get a special tree that can be packed away and little ornaments to hang on it, and bright tinsel for the walls. Or is tinsel tacky?'

'I don't think so.'

Grant's voice startled her out of her determinedly cheerful conversation. He'd emerged, again, from Codger Williams's bakery.

Confused by the rush of physical sensation his appearance had caused, Kate took refuge in business, looking pointedly at her watch before saying in a remarkably controlled voice, considering how edgy she was feeling, 'I thought you'd be back at the surgery by now.'

Grant's smile, which had, understandably, been missing all day, twitched about his lips, but all he said was, 'I've five minutes before I'm due to start. I think I'll make it back by then.'

And with that he was gone, striding away, leaving Kate with the lost sensation she'd felt on returning home to find him gone.

'He'll be gone for good before long,' she reminded herself, 'so you'd better get used to it.'

She pushed on resolutely towards the shops, focussing her mind on Christmas decorations, wondering how one cooked a turkey—were they much more complicated than chickens?

Which reminded her of the emu and she sighed.

'You know, Cass,' she said softly to the baby, pausing in the shade of a peppercorn tree to adjust the stroller so the sun didn't strike the chubby limbs, 'I think I might be like the emu. I'm beginning to think things didn't work out with Mark because he wasn't my mate for life, and deep down I knew it. Though, if I'd never met Grant again…'

She couldn't go on, knowing with a deep conviction that infiltrated every cell in her body that *he* was her mate for life.

And he belonged to someone else.

'I guess that happens to hundreds of thousands of people,' she told Cassie, although the baby had drifted back to sleep and probably hadn't been following the conversation too well. 'They don't meet that one person or, if they do, it's the wrong time or place or circumstances.'

On that gloomy note, she pushed the stroller into the newsagent's and with a total lack of excitement or enthusiasm surveyed the array of Christmas decorations the shop had on display.

'I need a tree, and things to go on it, things that will last but nothing poisonous if the baby sucks it, and probably nothing too fragile that will break if she clutches at it, and some tinselly stuff—though she might eat that, mightn't she…?'

Young Jill Ellis, who'd come to serve her, frowned at these requests.

'Won't Grant Bell still be working for you over Christmas?'

'Yes, he's here till the New Year,' Kate replied, annoyed with the young woman for offering a reminder she didn't need. 'What's that got to do with anything?'

'Well, he's just bought a whole heap of Christmas decorations, including our top-of-the-range tree. He asked Dad to deliver them to your place and we guessed he was helping you set up.'

Jill hesitated, then lifted her fingers to her lips as if to take back the words, adding, 'Gosh, it was probably a surprise for you, and I've gone and put my foot in it. But it seemed silly, both of you buying trees.'

'Yes!' Kate said, then she wheeled the stroller around, ready to march out of the shop and back down the street to the surgery, where she'd demand to know what Grant Bell thought he was doing—buying *her* Christmas decorations. Unfortunately, the stroller wheel caught a turntable displaying Christmas cards and the flimsy structure toppled, spreading cards in all directions.

Cassie, jolted awake, began to cry, and by the time Kate had comforted her and helped Jill collect the cards, much of her anger had faded.

Though Grant still had a cheek!

The morning's accident meant some patients had switched from the morning to the afternoon surgery session, so it was late by the time Grant crossed the garden and pushed through the back door of the house.

The house was quiet and he found Katie sitting on the lounge, an assortment of boxes and plastic bags in front of her. As she heard him come in, she turned, then shook her head.

'I went up to buy them and Jill told me you'd already done it.'

Her words were so bleak he hurried over to her, squatting in front of her and taking her hands in his.

'I'm sorry if I spoiled your fun,' he said, massaging her cold fingers, 'but I was up there and I couldn't resist.'

She shrugged as if it didn't matter, confirming this when

she said, 'I don't think I'd have found it as much fun as confusing.'

'So what else is wrong?' he asked, resting his free hand against her cheek.

Another shrug.

'Nothing. Everything.'

She twisted her head away and removed her fingers from his other hand.

'I suppose you know about cooking turkeys as well.'

'Of course, *and* I've ordered one,' he said, standing up and dropping a kiss lightly on the top of her head. What he really wanted to do was take her in his arms and hold her close and promise her everything would be all right, but he wasn't certain that it would be. Not yet. 'So stop fretting about Christmas, and don't start on that perfect mother thing again because Cassie needs love, not perfection, and you've got love by the bucketload, Katie Fenton.'

She looked up at him as she spoke, and the confusion in her eyes proved too much for him. He took her hands in his, drew her to her feet and wrapped his arms around her body, drawing it in to feed warmth into it from his own.

'You're the most generous, sharing, caring person I know,' he said, murmuring the words into her ear. 'And Cassie is the luckiest girl in the world to have you for a mother.'

He tilted up her head and looked deep into her eyes.

'Believe me?'

She shook her head.

'No, but it made me feel better.'

Then she pushed away from him, but not before he saw the sadness still lingering in her lovely eyes.

Grant grabbed her hands and drew her close again.

'I love you, Katie Fenton,' he said quietly. 'Can you hold that thought until I come back?'

She spun away again, glaring now, obviously unaffected by his declaration.

'Come back from where?' she demanded.

'Sydney,' he said, grinning at her wrath. 'Well, Brisbane first and then Sydney. You did say I could have the weekend off, didn't you? And Dr Darling's visiting some old friends and has agreed to fill in for me for the morning sessions tomorrow and Friday. Codger's giving me a lift to Craigtown in the morning and I'll fly to Brisbane, then go on to Sydney Friday afternoon. I'll be back Monday afternoon so, if you could get Tara to mind Cassie and do that morning session, I'll do the evening.'

He paused, then couldn't resist adding, 'I do hope it doesn't interfere with your date with Brian.'

'It's not a date and don't tell me how to organise my practice,' Kate snapped at him, hurrying into the kitchen before his too-perceptive eyes saw her despair. 'How did you know about Dr Darling? And is he qualified to practise still? He's got to be about a hundred.'

Kate knew her anger was misdirected, but she had to release it or go mad, so she fumed on, blaming Vi, blaming anyone, when all along her heart was breaking because she knew exactly why Grant was going back to Sydney. He was going to see Linda.

He might love Katie Fenton—as a friend he'd known for a long time—but Linda was his lover, his fiancée...

His mate for life?

The thought hurt so much she had to close her eyes for a moment, willing tears she no longer shed so freely to remain at bay and the painful thudding in her chest to subside.

With hands that barely trembled, she peeled vegetables for their dinner, put lamb chops under the grill, even made a salad.

You knew all along he'd be going, she kept telling herself, but the desolation in her heart, over his departure for just a few days, suggested she'd been subconsciously harbouring the most ridiculous hopes and dreams.

Somehow they got through the meal, conversation about patients covering an underlying tension so brittle Kate wondered their words didn't crackle in the air. Grant excused himself to pack—she wanted to ask how long it took to pack four Hawaiian shirts and three pairs of board shorts— and she washed the dishes, then willed Cassie to wake up so she'd have an excuse to disappear into her bedroom.

He was gone by the time Kate got up in the morning, leaving a note with his mother's address and phone number in Sydney 'in case you need to contact me about a patient or if there's anything you'd like me to pick up in the city.'

Angry and frustrated because she knew she had no right to be, Kate tore the note up, then had to retrieve all the pieces with the number and sticky tape them together in case she *did* need to contact him about a patient.

Mr McConagle arrived and because it was going to be a sawdusty day, she packed up what Cassie would need and took her down the road to Tara's.

'I'll just see Dr Darling has all he needs, then be back to feed her,' she explained to Tara. 'Then I suppose I could take her for a walk uptown. Honestly! I'd have been better off doing all the surgery sessions myself. I don't know why Grant got Dr Darling to come in.'

'Because the old fellow loves to keep his hand in,' Tara's mother told her, 'and the folk in town who knew him love to see him again. He's always done a few sessions when he's been visiting.'

Kate left their house, grumpier than ever. Why hadn't she known that?

And if Dr Darling liked to do a bit of locum work, why hadn't Vi contacted him instead of Grant?

The puzzle prodded her into asking Vi, who merely smiled at her, shrugged her shoulders, then said, 'Grant was available and, though you mightn't realise it, he needed help as much as you did, Kate. Needed to get away from the city for a while as well.'

Kate was about to point out that he *had* been away from the city at the time, but Dr Darling arrived at that moment, greeting her with a warm hug and assurances that he could still remember most of the medicine he'd learnt.

'I've got old, Katie, not stupid,' he said, smiling delightedly at her. 'Now, where's this baby of yours? When am I going to meet her?'

He was so like the kind and loving man she remembered that her bad mood subsided and she found herself inviting him to come to lunch—to see the house and what she was doing to it and to meet Cassie.

Collecting Cassie from Tara, she returned home, tidied up and prepared salads for their lunch, trying desperately to keep her mind off planes winging towards the city and a certain passenger on a certain plane...

The day dragged slowly by. She phoned Brian. He'd been so hurt when she'd turned down his offer of a loan and had accepted the bank loan instead that she hadn't liked to cry off the dinner-dance. But now she did, using Grant's absence as an excuse to avoid the Christmas party, but in her heart knowing Grant had been right—it would have been a date, and to go on a date with Brian, now she realised how she felt about another man, would have been unfair.

The weekend brought its usual spate of minor accidents, and the casualties coming into the hospital kept her busier than usual. So much so that as she sank, exhausted, into bed on Sunday evening, she reminded herself to contact the Health Department. If they didn't have a doctor starting at the hospital in the New Year, she'd have to rev up the board and community and organise protests and petitions to the local members of parliament.

At least, she thought, smiling wryly into the darkness, it

would keep her mind off Grant's departure, and the heart-break and loneliness she knew would follow it.

On Monday morning, she left Cassie at Tara's place again so Mr McConagle could hammer and saw without thought for the baby, and as she walked back to start surgery she looked around her, recalling the joy she'd felt as she'd walked these streets when she'd first returned, re-membering the certainty that had told her she'd done the right thing.

Now Christmas decorations flapped on telegraph poles and Christmas lights were strung across the street, and though she knew that every day she spent with Grant would make his final departure that much harder, at least she'd have his company for Christmas and memories of that special day to hold in her heart for ever.

Morning surgery seemed to go on endlessly, and by the time it finished she was so anxious about Grant's return she collected Cassie from Tara and walked up to the bakery, casually asking Codger, as she bought a loaf of raisin bread, if he was picking up his friend from Craigtown.

Codger looked startled, then shook his head.

'Hell, I hope not! I'm sure he didn't mention it—and if he did, I've forgotten. The Monday flight comes in at about eleven.'

He frowned at Kate, then added, 'Actually, I was under the impression he was driving back.'

More confused than ever, she walked home, realised Mr McConagle was still hammering and, after a quick lunch, sought refuge in the surgery, Cassie sleeping in her basket there while Kate caught up on some paperwork.

So when the strange car pulled into her drive, she had a good view of it—and a vague impression of someone in the passenger seat. She moved to the window to get a better view. Grant was driving and there was definitely a woman sitting beside him.

He'd brought Linda back with him!

Kate's heart faltered so badly she had to put a hand against the wall to steady herself. Of course he'd want to spend Christmas with his fiancée, she told herself, but the aching emptiness of unacknowledged love drained all the energy from her body and left her so weak she wondered how she'd get through the rest of the day, let alone another fortnight of Grant's presence in the town.

Then she steadied herself and straightened up, stiffening her spine and tilting her chin. For a start, he could shift to Vi's. She'd tell him she needed to decorate the small bedroom for the baby.

Then she needn't see him at all. He'd do some sessions, she'd do others, and their paths needn't cross.

But he was going to cook the turkey, an inner voice wailed. And you were waiting until he returned to put up the decorations.

'He can damn well take them to Vi's as well,' Kate muttered to herself, then she leaned closer to the window, realising for the first time that he had a trailer hooked on behind the car. A loaded trailer covered by a grey tarpaulin.

Maybe it was another motorbike—maybe Linda rode one as well.

A light tap on the door, then Grant was there, opening his arms to her as he had on the day he'd first arrived.

'I'm back,' he said, smiling so broadly he seemed to shine with an inner radiance.

'So I can see,' Kate said crisply, determined not to let the radiance thing get to her—or to reveal her own devastation.

'Well, aren't you going to kiss me?' he asked, holding out his arms again.

'Why the hell should I kiss you?' Kate demanded. 'You're my locum, not my lover.'

And though he should have been put firmly in his place by that pronouncement, the wretch continued to smile, and the twinkle in his eyes positively gleamed with delight.

'Ah, but we were, and could have been again, remember.'

'That was different,' Kate muttered, aware the heat burning inside her must have washed colour into her cheeks.

'Was it, Katie?' he said softly, moving closer. 'Oh, I know you said it was just comfort you were offering, but it seemed very much like love to me. Isn't comfort an element of love?'

'I don't know what you're talking about, and even if I did I wouldn't listen,' Kate snapped, as angry with the foolish hope that had risen in her heart as she was with this two-timing male in front of her. 'I don't know how you can talk that way, with Linda outside in my garden.'

'Linda in your garden?' Grant looked genuinely confused, then his face cleared and he laughed with such delight Kate wanted to hit him. 'That's not Linda, that's Mum. Actually, Linda doesn't exist—never did—and I thought Cassie needed a grandmother so I brought Mum back to get started with that side of things. She'll stay with Vi, of course, but mind Cassie for you—for us—whenever we can't get Tara.'

Kate shook her head. This was a worse conversation than they'd had the day he'd ridden into Testament four weeks ago. But there was so much she didn't understand that she didn't know where to start. With 'Linda doesn't exist'? Heavens! Her heart was cavorting so madly she was afraid she might have misheard him, in which case she'd better not ask...

Then there was the 'us' thing he was going on about...

She was still hesitating when he took the last step needed to bring him into touching distance, so her physical reaction caused further chaos in her mind.

'Kiss me, Katie,' he murmured. 'Kiss me then tell me there's no us!'

The last working cell in her brain registered that he'd often seemed to know exactly what she'd been thinking, then she gave in to the hands drawing her closer and lifted her face towards his, accepting his kiss and kissing him back.

Then she remembered Linda, and pushed away.

'What did you mean—Linda doesn't exist?' she demanded, hope battling with apprehension—but she had to know.

'I made her up,' Grant told her, his smile so broad she knew he thought this had been sheer brilliance, though all it was to her was unbelievable.

'Made up a fiancée? Why on earth would you do that?'

'So you'd feel safe with me, not feel threatened having a man about the house—you know, after Mark…'

Kate didn't know, but her body, still close enough to Grant's to feel his warmth, seemed delighted to learn that Linda was pure fiction.

Though when she considered the anguish this fictional woman had caused her…

She was about to give voice to her disapproval of this tactic when Grant drew her close again, and this second kiss blanked out her mind completely, leaving room only for emotion and the physical responses as old as time itself.

Grant felt the passion in her response, and the final coil of terrible tension he seemed to have carried for so long unwound from his body.

'I love you, Katie,' he said, drawing her close against him and burying his head in her fragrant, tangled hair. 'I think I realised that soon after I came back, but I wasn't over Robbie's death—couldn't handle commitment that included another baby—so I tried to ignore it. I told myself specialty training was more important anyway—that what I'd learn or might discover could benefit so many babies in the future. But when I lifted the other Robbie out of that bus, I knew that you do what you can in this life, and contributing happiness, any time or any place, is just as important as contributing to great scientific discoveries.'

He felt the woman in his arms move and added, 'Well, maybe not quite as important, but I was an average student at best, and a man or woman twice as bright as me will now have the opportunity to do the work I thought I wanted to do.'

This time the movement was more definite—in fact, the woman to whom he was so ardently professing his love was actually pushing him away from her. He looked down and saw the fire flashing in her green eyes.

'Are you telling me you've given up the speciality training?'

Uncertain what was angering her, and knowing it was best to tread warily with his Katie in this mood, Grant nodded.

'To do what?' she demanded, her eyes narrowing dangerously.

He grinned, couldn't help it, and held out his arms again.

'To be the hospital doctor at Testament. Though, actually, when I talked to the Health Department people, I did mention they might be able to restructure the position so I've rights of private practice and we can sort of run the hospital and surgery jointly—the two of us, you know…'

His voice tailed off as he realised she looked, if anything, even fiercer.

'And you didn't think to mention any of this to me? You say you love me then rearrange both our futures without any consultation whatsoever? How do you think I feel, having you sacrifice your dream of paediatric oncology for me? What kind of burden is that for me to carry?'

'Ah!' Grant murmured, and drew her close again. 'So that's what's got you fired up!' He tilted up her chin so their eyes met. 'It was no dream, no sacrifice, Katie. When Robbie was born I set aside my first dream, to have a property again, replacing it with the wonderful vision of fatherhood. Then, when he died, that dream died with him. I went in the direction of paediatric oncology because I was so lost I didn't know what else to do, and I knew that drifting aimlessly would lead to disaster.'

He saw a softening in her eyes and knew she understood, and when she murmured 'And then?' he continued, confident now that he'd found his way again.

'I came back to Testament, and remembered all I'd loved about life in the country. I felt at home again, and more at peace than I'd been for a long time. You were part of that healing—seeing you again, being with you, feeling that intensity that had been missing from my life for so long.'

'But you still didn't share any of this with me,' she protested, but so weakly he knew it was a token argument.

'I wanted to make sure I *could* come back—that I could get out of my commitment in Sydney without leaving the department short-staffed. I also needed to know if I could get a job out here. I spoke to officials over the phone, but had to be interviewed in Brisbane. I didn't want to get your hopes up then let you down—but if it hadn't been now, it would have been soon that I'd have come back because, having found you again, my mate for life, I was darned if I was going to lose you.'

Kate was so overwhelmed by all this information she forgot the other questions and objections she might have made, and when he leaned forward to kiss her again, she gave herself up to the delight of being in his arms, and with all her heart and soul returned the kiss.

The sound of Cassie's waking cry broke them apart and, though Kate moved towards the door, it was Grant who got there first, picking up the baby girl and cradling her in his arms, his face glowing with the love he was now unafraid to show.

'I'd better introduce her to Mum, then get the trailer unpacked. We can leave the furniture in the garage until we get Cassie's room painted. I'll start on it this week.'

Kate, still bemused by the rapidity of the changes taking place in her life, followed him out of the surgery. She'd been about to ask, And where are you going to sleep? when a tide of heat rushed through her. She knew exactly where Grant was going to sleep. Not only tonight, but every night for a very long time.

By Christmas Eve the new bathroom was finished and the altered guest bedroom restored to its original purpose. Cassie's room was not only painted and decorated, but furnished with white baby furniture, brightened by small decals of ducks and ducklings—the precious furniture Grant had brought with him on the trailer.

Grant and Katie stood beside the crib, looking down at the sleeping infant.

'I want to adopt her, you know,' Grant said, 'so she's officially mine as well as just belonging to me.'

Katie felt her heart swell with so much love she wondered it could all be contained within the confines of so small a part of her—then she remembered how Grant's love seemed to permeate all of her, not just her heart.

Permeated the whole house, so it was in the air she breathed, the food she ate.

'Don't you want me to?' he asked, shocking her out of her fantasy.

'Of course,' she said, turning to look at him so he'd know she meant what she was saying. 'It's just that you continue to surprise me—to overwhelm me—with your love. You take my breath away.'

'I know other ways I can do that,' he suggested, and Kate knew, from his smile and the light in his brilliant blue eyes, that her love for him had also worked some magic. Grant had come as her knight in shining armour, charging to the rescue of the maiden in distress, but together they'd vanquished the dragons of the past, and she and Cassie had brought him safely home.

CHRISTMAS IN PARIS

by

Margaret Barker

Margaret Barker has enjoyed a variety of interesting careers. A State Registered Nurse and qualified teacher, she holds a degree in French and Linguistics and is a Licentiate of the Royal Academy of Music. As a full-time writer Margaret says, 'Writing is my most interesting career because it fits perfectly into my happy life as a wife, mother and grandmother. My husband and I live in an idyllic sixteenth century house near the East Anglian coast. Our grown up children have flown the nest but they often fly back again bringing their own young families with them for wonderful weekend and holiday reunions.'

CHAPTER ONE

ALYSSA paused at the foot of the wide, sweeping steps that led to the revolving glass door. *Une grande porte à tambour,* Pierre had called it. She was relieved to find that her French was coming back, although she'd found that her conversation with the taxi driver coming across Paris from the Gare du Nord station had been a bit of a strain. She could understand Parisians who spoke like her mother, but the taxi driver had had a strong accent from the south of France, and he'd chatted so quickly it had been difficult to follow him.

Alyssa hadn't spoken much French in the eight years since she'd worked in this very building with Pierre. The knot in her stomach tightened as she thought about him, his wonderful eyes when he'd turned to look down at her, the touch of his tantalising fingers on her skin...

She shivered, as if someone had walked over her grave. Maybe she shouldn't have come back here. Perhaps it was all going to be too poignant, walking along the white corridors of the Clinique Ste Catherine when Pierre was no longer there.

A young, tall, fair-haired man was hurrying along the road towards the *clinique*. He stopped and smiled at Alyssa, pointing to her suitcase, which she'd dumped on the pavement whilst she indulged herself in poignant memories of that other time, now so long ago.

'Puis-je vous aider, mademoiselle?'

Alyssa smiled at the helpful young man, replying in French that it was kind of him to offer to help her, but she

5

could manage to carry her suitcase up the steps to the *clinique*.

The young man smiled back, giving a Gallic shrug which seemed to imply that he wasn't going to allow a small, slightly built blonde to carry a heavy suitcase up the steps when he was going that way. Bending down, he heaved up the suitcase as if it were an empty plastic bag.

Frenchmen are so gallant! Alyssa thought as she walked beside him, relieved that she didn't have to carry that heavy suitcase any more. It had been bad enough getting it from the Eurostar into a taxi and from the taxi to the foot of the steps.

The young man introduced himself as Dr Jacques Suchet. *'Et vous êtes…?'*

'I'm Alyssa Ferguson.'

'Ah, our new English doctor. Welcome to the Clinique Ste Catherine. I thought maybe that was who you were, but your French is so good you could almost pass for a Parisian.'

Alyssa smiled. 'You're very kind. My mother was born in Paris and I used to speak fluently with her as a child, but I've spoken only English for the past eight years,' she said as she negotiated the revolving doors behind Dr Suchet.

He looked very young to be a doctor and couldn't have been qualified very long. He had that devil-may-care, zest-for-life attitude that had typified Pierre when she'd first met him. She'd followed Pierre in through these very doors so often. Sometimes he'd turned to give her a clandestine kiss, laughing at her prim concern when she'd glanced over to look at the staff on the reception desk.

She'd been so young then, only twenty-one, and Pierre had been twenty-nine. Her own age now, so Pierre must be thirty-seven. She reckoned he would still be handsome, and probably tanned from all that sun out there in the West Indies. He'd used to have a permanent suntan here in Paris from jogging every day in the Bois de Boulogne, she remembered fondly, and he'd looked so fantastic in that dark blue tracksuit she'd helped him choose in the sports shop on the Rue de Passy.

She swallowed hard. Yes, it had been a mistake to come back here, but she had to make the best of it now.

Whatever had possessed her to answer that advertisement in that medical magazine? Nostalgia was a terrible affliction! But she'd felt drawn to come back. It was as if a magnetic force was dragging her away from London to make this journey to Paris. Deep down she was hoping that she would be able to lay the ghost to rest. Get rid of her constant yearning for those idyllic days of her affair with Pierre.

'I expect you'll have to report to our medical director.'

Dr Suchet put her suitcase down on the tiled floor in the reception area, looking down at Alyssa enquiringly. 'What exactly are your instructions, Dr Ferguson?'

'Oh, please, call me Alyssa.'

'What a beautiful name! And you must call me Jacques.'

Alyssa hesitated. 'Jacques, I was told to come to the *clinique* and…'

Her voice trailed away and her legs seemed to turn to jelly. She put out her hand to place her fingers on Dr Suchet's arm, in case she fainted with the shock. The tall, dark man coming towards her looked unmistakably like Pierre. But he couldn't be Pierre! Pierre wasn't here. Pierre lived and worked in the West Indies. There wasn't the remotest chance that this was happening. It was a dream. She must have fainted and dreamed that…

'Hello, Alyssa.'

The dream was holding out his hand. And there was no

mistaking the voice. She would know that voice anywhere, and the handshake—firm, deeply disturbing. Frissons of excitement tinged with apprehension ran through her.

'Pierre, why are you here?' Her faint voice sounded strange even to her own ears.

His dark eyes held her gaze. 'I could ask you the same question, Alyssa. What made you come back?'

Dr Suchet gave a discreet cough. 'I believe that introductions do not seem to be necessary, so I will leave the two of you together. Obviously, Dr Alyssa Ferguson, you have previously met our *médecin-chef*—the medical director of the *clinique*—Dr Pierre Dupont.'

Alyssa stared at Pierre, her heart beating rapidly. Had she heard Jacques correctly? Was Pierre really the medical director of the *clinique* now?

'But I was interviewed by Dr Cheveny. He told me he would be here as director when...'

'Dr Cheveny had a heart attack last week. I happened to be in Paris on a three-month holiday. François Cheveny is an old friend of mine and he asked me to take over the *clinique* temporarily until he has recovered.'

Pierre glanced around the reception area, where work seemed to have stopped. All eyes of the clerical and nursing staff were on the couple in the centre of the tiled floor.

'Come into my consulting room,' Pierre said quietly. 'We can't talk here.'

He bent down and picked up her suitcase.

As she followed Pierre down the white corridor her head was spinning at the completely unexpected turn of events. Pierre looked exactly the same. Still handsome—slightly older, perhaps. In the brief moment when their eyes had met she'd noticed a tired expression which hadn't been there when she'd first known him. But his dark hair was still thick and luxuriantly shining, with a couple of strands falling over his face, though she'd detected the beginnings of lines on his forehead and at the sides of his eyes.

As she walked through the door of his consulting room she was still in a state of shock. But beyond the feeling of shock she was deeply aware of the turbulence of her emotions. When she'd written that letter to Pierre, eight years ago, she'd planned never to see him again. It was madness to meet up like this! And if Pierre was medical director here she would have to come into contact with him every day. And he would ask her why…

'Do sit down, Alyssa.'

Pierre was holding the back of a deep, buttoned leather armchair. She sat down, rigidly at first, and then more relaxed as Pierre released his grip on her chair and moved over to the other side of the large, beautifully polished mahogany desk. For a moment she allowed her eyes to roam around her surroundings, admiring the book-lined walls, the deep pile of the luxurious carpet. She'd forgotten just how luxurious the Clinique Ste Catherine was. A great deal different from the hospital where she'd been working in London.

'So, how are you, Alyssa?' Pierre's voice was cool and impersonal as he faced her across the desk.

'I'm fine. How are you, Pierre?'

This was ridiculous! Two ex-lovers conducting an excruciatingly embarrassing conversation. Alyssa longed to get up from her chair, kick off her shoes, run round the desk and put her arms around Pierre. He was looking as uncomfortable as she felt.

'I'm in good health,' Pierre replied. 'A little disconcerted by the fact that you're here. It was only this morning that I checked through the latest staffing arrangements and saw that you were coming to join us. I must admit it was the last thing I expected.'

'I didn't know you would be here, Pierre,' Alyssa said quietly.

'Well, obviously!' Pierre's brown eyes flashed.

He leaned back in his chair, placing the points of his long, slender, tapering fingers together in front of him. It was an endearing gesture that Alyssa remembered so well. It meant he was giving the problem his undivided attention. She leaned forward to explain, but Pierre continued after the pause.

'You made it quite clear in your last letter that you never wanted to see me again.'

'I'm sure I wasn't as brusque as that.'

Pierre waved a hand in the air, as if to dismiss her argument. 'You were utterly explicit that you wanted to end our affair. You said that you found it difficult to continue to commit to a serious relationship whilst you were studying to be a doctor. And you said that when you were qualified your career would come first.'

Alyssa winced inwardly. Had she really been so brutal to the man she still loved with all her heart? But, because she loved him, she hadn't been able to tell him the real reason. That really would have broken his heart. No, she'd had no choice. She'd had to call a halt, sooner rather than later, so the white lies had been inevitable.

'I was finding it hard to concentrate on my work when…'

'Are you sure that was the real reason?' he said, with steely calm. 'Obviously our relationship meant nothing to you. I found it hard to believe that you could cool down so quickly.'

If he'd only known the agony she'd been going through at the time! Yes, she would have loved to put her head on his shoulder, to sob her heart out and have him commis-

erate with her misfortune, but that would have only prolonged the time before their inevitable split.

She took a deep breath. 'Pierre, I don't think I'll be able
to work here at the *clinique* now that I know you're the
medical director. I realise that it would be difficult for you
to have me working on your staff, so...'

'Oh, please don't give up so easily! You're committed
to a contract, remember? Or is any kind of commitment
onerous for you?'

Looking across the desk at the hard expression on
Pierre's face, she felt as if a knife was being driven through
her heart. She leaned back in her chair and closed her eyes
for a moment, to blot out the sight of the man she still
loved. It was her love for him that prevented her from
explaining the truth to him.

A deep weariness was stealing over her. The train journey through the channel tunnel had been slow, due to a
temporary breakdown, and it was hours since she'd left
London this morning. She couldn't take much more of this
cross-questioning that would lead nowhere. Nor could she
bear to work with the man she loved under these hostile
conditions. Unbidden, a tear escaped from underneath her
tightly shut eyelids. Her head felt light—as if it was full
of cotton wool.

'Alyssa, are you all right?'

She felt Pierre's hand on her shoulder and opened her
eyes, aware that they were moist and displaying far too
much emotion. Looking up, she saw deep concern etched
on Pierre's strikingly handsome face. For a brief, mad moment she expected him to bend down and kiss the tears
away from her cheek. But that was yesterday—long, long
ago. This was today, when her life had changed so much.

'Yes, yes, I'm OK,' she said quickly.

Pierre reached for a tissue from the box on his desk and, leaning forward, dabbed her eyes with his gentle touch.

'I don't know why you're crying,' he said, his voice oh, so soft, just as she remembered it used to be. 'Do I have such a terrible effect on you that you can't bear to be near me?'

She raised her hand and caught hold of his wrist. His tender expression changed to one of surprise and he stood stock still, looking down at her.

She cleared her throat. If only she could tell him the truth! No, she mustn't! She let go of his wrist, clasping her hands in front of her so that she wouldn't be tempted to make physical contact again.

'I'm just tired, that's all,' she said quickly. 'Travelling always has this effect on me. I remember coming over on the boat train to France with my mother as a child. I was always exhausted when we arrived at the Gare du Nord, and my mother would put me straight to bed when we reached Grand-maman's apartment.'

Pierre leaned back against the desk, his expression more relaxed and open. 'How is your mother, Alyssa? I never met her, but you told me so much about her when you were here in Paris before that I feel I know her.'

'Maman…' Alyssa faltered, as she always did when she thought about her mother. 'Unfortunately, she developed an incurable cancer. She died some years ago.'

'I'm so sorry.'

Alyssa swallowed hard. 'I would have liked you to meet her.'

Now, that was the sort of remark she mustn't make if she was going to see this contract through! It must be strictly professional from now on.

'Yes, it was a pity I didn't meet her when we…when

you were in Paris before,' Pierre said quietly. 'Now, let's get down to business.'

He returned to the other side of the desk. 'I'd like to suggest that we don't refer to…to what happened between us again. You obviously had your reasons for terminating our affair and I will respect that. Simply do your job as efficiently as you can. Dr Cheveny hopes to be back here after Christmas. That's when I have to return to the West Indies. It's now November, so we only have to work together for a few weeks. Do you think you can manage that?'

Alyssa nodded. 'Of course. I'm looking forward to working here as a doctor. Eight years ago—as temporary medical assistant and general dogsbody, at the end of my third year of medical school—some of the work I had to do was pretty boring and repetitive, but now…!'

She smiled, feeling herself relax again. Yes, it would work. She would *make* it work.

Pierre smiled, and Alyssa could see some of his erstwhile boyish charm returning. 'You were a very pretty general dogsbody, if I may say so.'

Alyssa wanted to tell Pierre that he mustn't make remarks like that if their professional relationship was going to work. But, looking at the glorious smile on his beautifully shaped mouth as she watched him across the desk, she tried to tell herself she could handle the occasional compliment from him. She'd been starved of this sort of warm feeling for far too long.

'I understand I qualify for a room in the medics' quarters now,' Alyssa said quickly.

Pierre nodded. 'I'll ask the housekeeper to show you up there.' He picked up the phone and gave the necessary instructions. 'You don't start work until tomorrow, so you'll have time to settle in.'

Now he was standing up, very much the efficient medical director who wanted to terminate this interview and get on with his important job.

The housekeeper arrived to escort her to the medical staff quarters. Alyssa gave a backward glance as she left Pierre's room, but he was already immersed in his paperwork, giving the impression that she was just another employee who'd taken up his time.

As he listened to the sound of Alyssa's small feet retreating down the corridor Pierre closed his eyes and leaned heavily against the back of his chair. The shock of seeing Alyssa again had been emotionally shredding. Eight years ago, when he'd received that heartbreaking letter, he'd been unable to comprehend how Alyssa could do such a thing. He'd adored her, worshipped her, known without a shadow of a doubt that she was the only woman he could ever love.

And then, out of the blue, her letter had arrived, tearing his heart into pieces and turning him into a nervous wreck for weeks on end. He'd thought of phoning to see if Alyssa was ill, or had taken leave of her senses, but then he'd reprimanded himself severely. The plain fact of the matter was that he'd obviously misjudged Alyssa's character. They'd only known each other for three months, after all. She must have been putting on an act for him until it was time for her to return to England.

For eight years he'd tried to be sensible about the situation. He'd told himself to get on with his life and forget Alyssa. But he couldn't forget her. She'd been his whole world for three months and he'd planned to spend the rest of his life with her. Whenever he'd tried to enjoy a brief relationship with someone he'd found himself comparing them with Alyssa, the love of his life, and had given up on the idea of continuing.

So how was he going to handle this situation? He could simply have agreed with Alyssa when she'd said they couldn't work together and that she ought to leave. That would have been the sensible course of action. But, having met her again, he couldn't bear to have her disappear once more. That was why he'd reacted so sharply—worried that she might simply stand up and walk out through the door.

He would try not to become emotionally involved, because obviously Alyssa was the sort of girl who didn't want a serious relationship. Just having her near him until his temporary directorship of the *clinique* ended after Christmas would be enough...wouldn't it?

He would have to play it cool, as he hoped he'd done just now. Alyssa mustn't have any idea how he longed to reach out and take her in his arms, to feel that soft silky skin against his hardening body. Perhaps if Alyssa thought he'd got over their affair she might agree to come out with him one evening on a light-hearted date—something like a trip to the theatre with supper in a restaurant afterwards, perhaps a trip in a *bateau mouche* on the River Seine one evening, with dinner in the floating restaurant, looking out at the twinkling lights of Paris on either side of the river.

Nothing too romantic, of course! He would be happy just to be with Alyssa. But she mustn't know how deeply he felt about her or that would send her running away again.

Pierre's internal phone was ringing. He picked it up and listened to the voice of his secretary.

'Excuse me, sir, the doctors for the medical conference you asked for will be assembled in the lecture hall this evening. They would like to know how long you will require them to be in conference with you.'

Pierre glanced down at the notes he'd prepared for his inaugural talk with the senior medical staff of the clinic. 'About an hour, Sidonie.'

He put down the phone, rose from his desk and went over to the window. Henri, the middle-aged gardener, was getting ready to cut the tall hedge at the end of the garden. Pierre remembered him from the time he'd last worked here. Dr Cheveny had told him that Henri had lovingly taken care of the large *clinique* garden since he took over from his father when he'd retired twenty years ago. Earlier on Pierre had seen Henri carefully tending the rose beds which were always so impressive during the summer months. Even now, in November, there were still a few blossoms among the green leaves.

The sight of the roses in the beautiful garden always revived Pierre's spirits. They reminded him of the lovely garden that surrounded his home on the island of Ste Cécile in the West Indies. He closed his eyes so that he could visualise it again. He could almost hear the enchanting sounds of the tropical birds who came every morning to be fed outside the kitchen door. Oh, he had such a wonderful home on his beautiful island! The only thing it lacked was the woman he loved—the woman he'd asked to be his wife.

Soon after he'd met Alyssa for the first time he'd known. That feeling of completeness, of oneness with another soul, could only come once in a lifetime. He was sure of that. And, foolishly, he'd thought he knew that Alyssa felt the same way, so he'd gone ahead and made his dreams into concrete plans.

He'd planned to marry Alyssa here in Paris, then take her out to the West Indies and start the family he longed for. Eight years on, his garden would by now be resounding with the noise of their children playing under the tall palm trees. Alyssa herself would perhaps be sitting in the shade of the veranda, feeding the latest baby. Alyssa knew he loved babies.

They'd discussed it just before she'd gone back to England, he remembered, on the night he'd asked her to marry him. She'd said she loved babies too, but wanted to finish her medical training before she thought about marriage. She'd wanted them to keep in contact with each other, and she'd given him absolutely no inkling of the fact that she had decided to call a halt to their relationship. At that point in time he'd had no idea that she was determined to remain independent for the rest of her life.

He turned away from the window, pressing his hands against the sides of his head, knowing that he mustn't dwell on what might have been. He would never put himself through the misery of having his heart broken again, so his emotions must remain on ice for the whole time Alyssa was working here at the *clinique*. He would enjoy an evening out with her if she agreed, just for old times' sake, but that was as far as it must go.

Alyssa's room at the back of the *clinique* faced west, so that now, looking through the open casement window, she could see the sun slanting down over the Bois de Boulogne. She was lucky to have a view of the immaculately maintained garden. This must be one of the most expensive gardens in Paris, because land and property prices in the sixteenth arrondissement didn't come cheap. The *clinique* could sell this land to a property developer and get a huge sum. But it was a well-established garden, and the *clinique* considered it essential that their patients should enjoy beautiful surroundings. It was all part of the healing process.

Although it was already the middle of November, there

were still roses in the garden, and splendid, carefully tended perennial shrubs. Out there, at the end of the garden, the gardener was standing on a ladder cutting a high hedge. Screwing up her eyes, she could see that it was the same friendly man who'd looked after the garden when she was first here. What was his name? Henri? Yes, that was it. She'd chatted to him sometimes when she'd sat on that seat over there and luxuriated in the summer sunshine.

The rasping hum of Henri's electric saw was disturbing the peace of the late afternoon, but the garden was an idyllic sight and she didn't mind the noise. It blended in with the general hum of Paris which was always there in the background, just like she remembered it had been when, as a child, she'd used to visit her grandmother in the nearby Rue de la Pompe. She would lie in her little bed, with its curved mahogany ends which had reminded her of a boat, listening to the continual, fascinating sounds of this great city, longing to be grown up so that she could go out at night and become a part of the excitement that she knew was always out there.

Her mother had always looked so glamorous when she dressed up and went out to the theatre. There had never been any lack of men-friends from her mother's former time in Paris, more than willing to escort a beautiful young widow to the theatre or a concert. And when her mother had gone Alyssa would sneak out of her room and go into the salon, where her grandmother would be working on her needlework.

She would tell her grandmother she couldn't sleep and Grand-maman would put down the needlework and open her arms towards her. Alyssa would run over to the sofa and snuggle up, knowing that she wouldn't have to go back to bed until she'd had a hot chocolate drink and maybe another of those *petit beurre* biscuits…

She sighed and sank down on to the bed. It was no good indulging in nostalgia all the time. Just look where it had got her! She lay back against the pillows as she cast her eyes around the room that was to be her home whilst she worked here at the *clinique*.

It had its own little shower room, complete with bidet and loo. Very French! The white cotton bedroom curtains were lined with a heavier linen mix material and looped back against the walls with ties; the shelves on the walls looked sadly empty as they waited to be filled with the few books Alyssa had been able to carry with her. She would have the joy of buying some more French books now she was in Paris again. But the afternoon sun, streaming through the windows, made up for the stark uniformity of this anonymous, functional room.

The last time she'd worked here at the clinic she hadn't qualified for a residential room. She'd been obliged to find her own cheap room on the ground floor of a nearby prestigious apartment block in the Rue de l'Assomption. In reality, it had been a *chambre de bonne*, a maid's room, which the owner, who didn't have a live-in maid, had decided to rent out. There had been a shower and loo down the corridor, she remembered, but she'd hated having to leave the safety of her room to visit those shared conveniences after dark.

But the deprivations of her living accommodation hadn't dispelled the euphoric feeling of happiness that had constantly enveloped her during the wonderful three months of her affair with Pierre. She'd never taken Pierre back to her room. The concierge would have fixed her with his beady eye as she'd walked past his little office. Visitors to the maids' quarters were actively discouraged. But she'd spent many nights at Pierre's apartment further down the road.

Pierre's apartment was where their baby had been conceived. That poor little mite who'd never stood a chance because he'd never got further than her left Fallopian tube. If only he could have found his way down into her womb she would have been able to nourish and cosset him and bring him to full term, and then…

She swallowed hard. She didn't like to dwell on the memory of that ill-fated ectopic pregnancy: the pain, the horror of knowing that she'd lost Pierre's baby—the baby she hadn't known was developing in her Fallopian tube when she'd said goodbye to Pierre at the Gare du Nord on that sunny September afternoon, her heart so full of love and longing to return to him as soon as possible.

She was only glad that Pierre had never known she'd been pregnant when she'd left him here in Paris. Pierre, who couldn't wait to be a father, who'd told her that he longed for a large family. Pierre, who'd begged her to marry him, to leave medical school and go with him to the West Indies so that they could start their wonderful family and live happily ever after.

But the dream had been well and truly shattered when her left Fallopian tube had been excised, with the unviable embryo inside it, and she'd been left with only one Fallopian tube together with some abdominal scarring and internal adhesions. Her gynaecologist had told her that it was unlikely she would be able to conceive again. So, loving Pierre as she did, knowing how much he wanted children, she'd taken the decision to put an end to their relationship.

It had been necessary to be cruel to be kind. At least by giving him his freedom from a relationship with her she was making sure that he could find someone who could have the babies he wanted.

She gave herself an inward shake and made a determined effort to climb off the bed. It was no good lying here expecting her case to unpack itself!

She suddenly realised that it was all quiet in the garden. The gardener must have finished his hedge and packed up for the day. She looked out of the window and as her eyes focused on the hedge she gave an involuntary gasp of dismay.

Henri had indeed finished working, but he was lying at the bottom of the hedge beside his fallen ladder and from where she was standing it looked as if he'd sustained a seriously damaging fall. He was completely silent and motionless.

Alyssa picked up the phone. Pierre's internal number was the only one she'd written on her notepad since arriving here. She dialled. *Please be there, otherwise…*

'*Allo? Oui…*'

Pierre's comforting voice helped to calm her. Yes, he would go out into the garden at once… Yes, her help would be invaluable…

Seconds later she was bending over Henri's motionless form while Pierre, who had already alerted extra staff, was making a clinical assessment from the other side.

A porter with a trolley came hurrying up the path.

'We need to put Henri on an orthopaedic slab before we take him inside on the trolley,' Pierre said quickly. 'There could be some damage to his neck. He had the ladder fully extended and he's fallen in an awkward position.'

The porter hurried back inside to return with a rigid plastic slab, specifically designed for trauma patients who might have suffered neck injuries. Carefully, Pierre and Alyssa eased their patient on to the slab, strapping him down so that Henri would sustain no further damage to his spine or limbs. With the help of the porter, they lifted him on to the trolley. As they did so, Henri opened his eyes.

Trying to move his head, their patient was irritated to find he was restrained by the head brace.

'Lie still, Henri,' Pierre said gently.

'What's happened?' Henri asked in a croaky voice.

'You've fallen from your ladder,' Alyssa said, taking hold of the frightened man's hand. 'We're going to take you inside the *clinique*.'

'My leg hurts.'

Alyssa held her patient's hand as they moved off down the garden path towards the door that led into the *clinique*. 'We're going to take care of you, Henri.'

'Have we met before?' Henri said, screwing up his eyes as he looked at Alyssa. 'Aren't you that little English girl who used to bring me coffee in the garden?'

Alyssa smiled. 'That's me. I've come back to work here.'

Henri momentarily winced with pain, but tried to carry on with his conversation. 'You haven't grown much, have you? You're still *très petite*.'

'Alyssa's a doctor now,' Pierre said, glad that the conversation was helping to keep Henri's mind off his unpleasant situation.

'She doesn't look like a doctor,' Henri said, in his brusque yet jocular manner. 'Anyway, it's nice to see you again, Alyssa. *Mon dieu!* Don't they have any painkillers in this—?'

'Coming up,' Pierre said as he reached for the syringe he'd prepared.

Looking down at Henri, Alyssa could see that he was a tough man. But the pain he was feeling now in his right leg was reducing him to tears. It was obvious from the unnatural angle of the leg that there was a multiple fracture around the area of the ankle.

She'd already removed Henri's shoe because his foot

was rapidly swelling. As soon as they got him inside they could make a real assessment of the damage.

Pierre helped the porter to manoeuvre the trolley into one of the treatment rooms and Alyssa found a pair of scissors and cut up the sides of Henri's trousers to expose the damaged limb.

Pierre's face was grave as he looked down at the splintered tibia bone which had pierced through the skin.

'Fractured tibia made worse by the fact that the talus bone appears to have been pushed up into it,' he said quietly to Alyssa. 'We'll get an X-ray.'

'Is my leg broken?' Henri asked.

'I'm afraid so,' Pierre said. 'We're going to have you X-rayed so that we'll know exactly how to treat it. I'm just going to give you an injection that will help with the pain.'

'Thanks, Pierre—I mean Dr Dupont. I heard that you'd taken over since Dr Cheveny's heart attack, so you're very important now.'

Pierre smiled. 'I'm just Pierre to old friends.'

Henri groaned with pain again. 'More painkillers, *s'il vous plaît*. My leg feels awful.'

'It looks as if you took the full weight of your fall on that one leg, Henri.' Pierre said, as he and Alyssa accompanied Henri into the X-ray department. 'I can't find any other area that's affected.'

'In that case can I come out of this neck brace? *Mon dieu!* It hurts like hell!'

'Not until we've had your neck X-rayed and you've been seen by a neurologist,' Alyssa said. 'You were out cold for a few minutes, and after a fall like you've sustained we've got to be sure your spine is uninjured.'

The radiographer took over for a while, to get the relevant X-rays.

As they waited in the ante-room, Pierre looked across at Alyssa. 'I read in your CV that you've had extensive experience in orthopaedics.'

'Yes, I toyed with the idea of specialising,' Alyssa said evenly.

Alone with Pierre again, even with the busy hospital staff in the next room, she was beginning to feel the strain of pretending that they'd never meant anything to each other.

'So why didn't you?' Pierre asked quietly.

'I was also very interested in obstetrics and gynaecology, so I would have had to make a difficult choice. And at the same time…' She hesitated. 'I felt I needed a change from my life in London. I needed to get away,' she said slowly, careful not to blurt out too much.

'So you thought you'd give Paris one more try, did you?' Pierre said lightly. 'Do the lights of Paris shine brighter than London?'

'Sometimes,' Alyssa said, remembering that she was supposed to be an independent, fun-loving woman whose interests revolved around theatre, entertainment, restaurants and enjoying herself.

It would be difficult to keep up this charade, but Pierre must never know how she longed for a home and babies. On her next birthday she would be thirty, and she could almost feel her biological clock ticking away inside. Thirty wasn't old, but it was time to take stock of her life. The emptiness of her constant social round in London was beginning to get to her, and Paris still had a warmth about it—mainly because she'd once been happier here than she'd ever been in her whole life, either before her relationship with Pierre or afterwards.

The radiographer, a tall, slim woman of about forty, came into the room with Henri's X-rays and switched on the screen which displayed them. Pierre and Alyssa went carefully through each one.

'You can see here where the foot took the full impact, forcing the talus up into the tibia, causing it to shatter into all these pieces we see floating around,' Pierre said, pointing to the injured lower leg.

Alyssa nodded. 'So, we've got massive problems with the ankle.'

'Our orthopaedic consultant is on his way over from another hospital. As you know, we have a number of consultants who work both here and at other hospitals in Paris. Yves Grandet is one of our top specialists. I've alerted the theatre staff about the possibility of an orthopaedic operation this evening, but we'll wait to see what Yves thinks when he arrives. He should be here any—'

Pierre broke off and smiled as a small man of about fifty in a dark grey pinstripe suit came into the room.

'Yves!' Pierre shook the newcomer by the hand. 'Thank you for coming so promptly. This is Dr Alyssa Ferguson, who has joined the staff today. She comes from England.'

Yves Grandet smiled and held out his hand towards Alyssa. 'I am so glad to meet you, Alyssa...may I call you Alyssa? You look about the same age as my daughter.'

Alyssa smiled back, and as they shook hands she formed an instant rapport with this small, rotund, friendly man.

The orthopaedic consultant turned to look at the X-ray screen, his face taking on a serious expression as he pointed out the various sections of the injury.

'Some of these little fragments of bone aren't going to be viable,' he murmured thoughtfully. 'But until I've opened up the leg in Theatre I won't know exactly how I'm going to approach the problem. I may have to fuse the ankle here.'

'We have a theatre ready, if you're going to operate this

evening, Yves,' Pierre offered. 'Or Henri could have his leg fixed on a back slab for the night. We could keep him well sedated and you could operate in the morning. The neurologist has checked our patient and reported that there is no damage to the cervical spine.'

'I'd prefer to operate this evening,' Yves said quickly. 'I'll go up and start getting ready for Theatre. I need to see that everything is exactly how I want it. Nurse! Yes, you!'

A startled young nurse hurried over.

'Come with me. I have a long list of things for my creature comforts before I start operating: a bottle of pure mineral water, some biscuits, very plain...'

Pierre smiled at Alyssa. 'Yves is always like this before a lengthy operation. And I think we both appreciate that this operation will take a long time.'

Alyssa nodded. 'That's what I was thinking.'

Pierre stood looking down at her, his eyes far too tender for her to feel easy about the situation.

'I've got a meeting in a few minutes.'

'I'll stay with Henri until the orthopaedic staff take over,' she said quietly.

'Thanks.' He hesitated. 'Good to have you on board, Alyssa.'

'It's good to be here.'

She watched as he turned and walked away.

Yes, she could handle this unnatural situation. The old days were over. This was a completely new situation. It wasn't going to be easy, but she wouldn't give in so long as she kept her emotions under control.

Easier said than done!

CHAPTER TWO

WHEN she first opened her eyes, Alyssa couldn't remember where she was. This wasn't her bedroom in east London. There was the steady hum of a city in the background, but outside her window the immediate sounds were different. Light was filtering through the curtains of her little room, trying to make sense of ill-defined objects and furniture, but Alyssa still felt completely disorientated.

Then she remembered. She was here in Paris, back at the *clinique* where it had all started, where her life had taken on a new meaning one wonderful summertime until, so agonisingly, her dreams of a perfect future had shattered.

She propped herself up against the pillows as she looked out towards the garden. There was no sound of activity in the garden this morning. Poor Henri would be lying in bed after his operation. She hoped it had been successful. You could never tell at this early stage. Orthopaedics was a slow business, and a great deal of patience was necessary by both patient and medical staff alike.

Lowering her feet to the floor, Alyssa felt the first chill of the morning as she walked barefoot from the bedside rug over the woodblock floor to the tiny *cabinet de toilette*. The heating from the radiator was beginning to make its presence felt, but it was obvious that winter was just around the corner.

As the hot water from the shower cascaded over her she felt her tense, tired body relaxing. Yesterday had been a long day. Getting here from England and meeting up with

Pierre again had been emotionally exhausting. Was she glad she'd come back to the *clinique*? Had it been a wise move?

She stepped out of the shower and reached for the *clinique* issue towel. Soft, fluffy and luxurious. The *clinique* never stinted on expense. Yes, she was glad she'd come back here. But, no, it hadn't been a wise move!

Rubbing herself vigorously with the towel, she remembered the number of times in the night when she'd awakened and tried to put Pierre from her mind so that she could sleep. But the image of his handsome, expressive face was always there to haunt her.

Alyssa went back into the bedroom and reached down into the depths of her still unpacked suitcase. Her new black suit would make her feel professional again.

Looking at herself in the mirror, she was pleasantly surprised. Yes, with the addition of her white silk blouse she looked efficient, professional—as if she *wasn't* scared stiff of people wondering all the time whether she was a proper doctor. Being small had its disadvantages, but she should have got used to it by now. In her social life it didn't make a scrap of difference, but in professional situations where everybody—patients and medical colleagues alike—towered over her, she longed to have a few extra inches of leg.

She gave a vigorous brush to her still damp blonde hair, glad that she'd let the hairdresser cut it short enough to be easily manageable. It had just the faintest hint of a wave which made the style less severe as it framed her face.

She told herself that so long as she did her job to her own satisfaction that was all that mattered. Well, perhaps not all that mattered. She also had to keep her emotions under control. Maybe she wouldn't have to see too much of Pierre. She had mixed feelings about that. Half of her wanted to avoid him whilst the other half, the wayward, wanton, emotional half, yearned to be with him every minute of the day.

Picking up her stethoscope, she opened the door and went out into the corridor, hoping that she could still find her way to the medical staff room. They served an excellent cup of black coffee, as she recalled.

Down on the ground floor, she found that the location of the staff room hadn't changed. When she pushed open the door the aroma of coffee assailed her nostrils. Mmm! She headed over to the serving counter, which was always referred to as the bar. A pleasant, diminutive middle-aged waitress in black dress and small white apron asked Alyssa what she would like.

'Un petit café noir, s'il vous plaît,' Alyssa replied.

'Ah, *mademoiselle*! I remember you!' The waitress leaned forward across the bar to shake hands with Alyssa. 'The little English girl. You were here a long time ago. You haven't changed at all. *Toujours petite!'*

Alyssa smiled. 'No, I haven't grown, Christine.'

She picked up the small cup of coffee. Nothing had changed here either.

She turned around to look for a table. And that was when she saw Pierre, seated by the window, looking out over the garden. He hadn't seen her. She ought to sit down at this table by the bar, pretend she hadn't...

Too late. As if drawn by the same magnetism that propelled her, Pierre turned and automatically raised his hand when he saw her, indicating that she should join him. Her heart began beating rapidly, but she allowed the magnetic force to move her across the room.

'Bonjour, Alyssa. Tu as bien dormi?'

Pierre was standing up in his gallant way, waiting for her to be seated before he resumed his own seat. Asking

Alyssa if she'd slept well was merely a customary morning greeting between friends or acquaintances. If he only knew how he'd been responsible for her lack of sleep!

She wouldn't enlighten him. Alyssa merely said that yes, she had slept well, and she took her place at the other side of the small, round, wooden table.

'No one working in the garden today?' she remarked, looking out of the window. 'Have you heard how Henri is?'

'Yes, Yves phoned me just before midnight to say that he was pleased with the outcome of the operation but the next few days will be critical. It was a difficult operation. Due to the pressure from the talus bone, which had been pushed up into the tibia in the impact of the fall, the tibia had shattered into more than twenty pieces. Yves had difficulty fixing them into position. Some of the smaller pieces of bone were completely unviable—as he thought.'

Alyssa nodded. 'So, did Yves have to do a complete reconstruction of the ankle?'

'Yes, he had to put in a steel plate and nail the bones into a viable position; he's hoping that there will still be some mobility in the ankle. He's put a plaster on the leg from below the knee, but left a window in the plaster so that we can keep a constant check on the wound.'

Alyssa took a sip of her coffee. 'That's always a good idea. Where there's an extensive wound such as Henri has we need to know how the healing process is progressing. And there's always the problem of a secondary infection in the post-operative stage.'

Pierre was watching her with a questioning expression on his face. 'I know you're interested in this case, so I thought you'd like to start work on the orthopaedic floor. As you probably gathered when you were here last time, our doctors have to work in all areas of the hospital and we call in specialists from other hospitals to advise or perform surgical operations when required. Last night you expressed an interest in orthopaedics, and also in obstetrics and gynaecology, so—'

'I'm quite happy to work wherever you think I would be most—'

'I'd like you to have the opportunity to work in obstetrics and gynaecology after you've had a short spell in orthopaedics,' Pierre continued, as if Alyssa hadn't interrupted.

Alyssa took a deep breath. Somehow she didn't think working with babies was going to be such a good idea if Pierre was likely to be anywhere in the same building. But in her contract she had agreed to work wherever she was assigned.

'Well, you're the *médecin-chef*,' she said lightly.

A shadow passed over Pierre's face. 'Do I gather that you would prefer to stay in orthopaedics? I thought you liked working with babies.'

'As I said, both orthopaedics and obstetrics are extremely interesting,' Alyssa said evenly. 'That was one of the things that drew me to working here at the *clinique*. The opportunity to move around from one area to the other. I enjoy being versatile in my work. It's so different to London, where I had to commit to—'

She broke off as she saw the hardened expression on Pierre's face.

'You don't like to commit yourself, do you, Alyssa?' Pierre murmured. 'Keep moving. That seems to be your philosophy.'

She could feel a lump in her throat. She longed to be able to tell Pierre why she hadn't been able to commit to a lasting relationship with him, but she knew she had to keep up the charade.

'It works very well for me,' she said, in a false, facetious tone, hating the image she was portraying.

'I'm sure it does,' Pierre said evenly.

'And how about you, Pierre? Have you made any strong commitments since I last saw you?'

'If you mean the ultimate commitment of marriage, then the answer's no,' he replied smoothly. 'I've had a few affairs since we last met but…but no. *Je suis toujours célibataire.*'

Alyssa ran a hand through her short blonde hair. 'I'm not sure *célibataire* is the right word. I know it's the French word for bachelor, but I wouldn't imagine you've remained celibate.'

Pierre raised an eyebrow. 'Did you expect me to remain celibate after we parted?'

Alyssa pushed back her chair and stood up. Whatever kind of conversation she and Pierre enjoyed, it would always turn to their previous relationship. They'd shared so much together. It was hard trying to be just good friends.

'I'm going to the bar to get a croissant.'

Pierre was already on his feet. 'I'll get it.' He moved swiftly to take her by the arm. 'Sit down again, Alyssa. We haven't finished our discussion about your work role here.'

Reluctantly she sat down, telling herself she must remain unemotional until they'd finished their conversation. No more references to the past. No more questions about how they'd lived during the past eight years of separation. Like hers, Pierre's private life had to remain private if they were to survive until after Christmas.

The thought of Christmas in Paris would have excited her so much if she and Pierre had still been lovers. She remembered how they'd always walked hand in hand beside the Seine, looking into the swirling waters, discussing anything and everything…and how much they loved simply being together…

He was returning to the table. She put on a bright smile and assumed her role of platonic friend, chiding herself for her momentary lapse from her assumed character.

'Christine is bringing over our *petit déjeuner*,' Pierre said. 'She insisted.'

Alyssa smiled. 'One of the perks of being the *médecin-chef*.'

Pierre smiled back and Alyssa felt her heart lift as she saw the way his facial features lit up in that interesting and expressive way when he was happy. This was the Pierre she remembered. Carefree, looking forward to the future.

'Yes, there are advantages to being the boss,' Pierre said lightly.

Christine was now setting out croissants, bread, butter and apricot jam on the table.

'Christine remembers me when I was a young doctor here, one of many—don't you, Christine?' Pierre looked up at the waitress with a whimsical smile.

'You haven't changed, *monsieur*.' Christine patted Pierre's shoulder affectionately before returning to her work behind the bar.

Pierre looked across the table at Alyssa. 'Oh, but I have changed,' he said meaningfully. 'I'm not half as trusting as I used to be. I never take anything for granted.'

Alyssa broke off a piece of flaky croissant and spread it with apricot jam. When she raised her eyes she saw that Pierre was still looking at her.

'That's called experience,' she said quietly. 'Life is a learning curve. You learn from what happens to you, then leave all that baggage behind and move on.'

'Move on?' he repeated softly. 'Is that what you're doing, Alyssa? Then why have you come back here?'

'Good question,' she said slowly, playing for time until she could compose her thoughts into some kind of order. 'I suppose I felt there was some unfinished business here. I had to completely lay the ghost.'

Pierre leaned back against his chair, putting both hands behind his head as he eyed her with a puzzled frown. 'Is that what I was? A ghost?'

'Oh, you know what I mean. It's just an English expression. It means to get rid of the past...of the baggage from the past... Oh, I don't know—stop twisting my words.'

An amused smile was hovering on Pierre's lips. 'So I can choose whether I want to be called a ghost or a piece of baggage, can I?'

'Oh, Pierre!' Alyssa brought her hand down on the table in exasperation. 'You know what I mean...'

Pierre leaned across the table and took hold of her hand, bringing his face oh, so tantalisingly close to hers. The faint scent of his aftershave was causing havoc with her emotions. She remembered this cologne so well—it was the one he'd applied to his body after a particularly exciting shower they'd taken together. And then he'd applied it to both of them, and...

'Just teasing!' he whispered.

Alyssa realised that the room had gone quiet. The medical staff enjoying their *petit déjeuner* were all looking across at the newly appointed *médecin-chef* with his English friend, whose role at the *clinique* had yet to be defined.

Alyssa decided to ignore the curious looks as she wallowed in Pierre's attention. A girl could drown in those dark brown expressive eyes!

'You always did like to tease me,' she said softly. 'But in those days I knew how to handle it. Now…'

She took her hand from his grip and leaned back in her chair, putting a safe distance between them.

'Now the situation is different,' she said, half under her breath, as she tried to bring her emotions under control.

'Yes, the situation is different.' Pierre took a sip of his coffee. 'We are…how do you say it in English?…we are just good friends. And so, as just good friends, I wondered if you would like to come out to the theatre with me this evening. I bought a couple of theatre tickets last week, hoping I could persuade some beautiful unattached young lady to accompany me.'

Alyssa could feel her spirits lifting. Pierre was certainly playing along with her charade now, and the thought of an innocuous, no strings attached evening with him was exciting.

'I'd love to go to the theatre…that is unless the *médecin-chef* asks me to work this evening.'

Pierre smiled. 'Oh, I don't think he would be so hard-hearted as to prevent a young lady going out to see the bright lights of Paris after her first full day here. After all, the *médecin-chef* knows he must keep his staff happy. Some members of staff like to have a quiet night in, but others, like yourself, prefer to… How do you say it in English? Go out on the town? Yes, that's what you like to do, isn't it, Alyssa?'

He was standing up now, the smile still on his face as he looked down at her. 'I'd like to take you along to the orthopaedic unit now. Yves Grandet is calling in to see how Henri is after last night's operation. He's asked the orthopaedic team to meet him up there, so if you come along with me now I could introduce you to the staff and—'

'Pierre? Before we go up to the orthopaedic ward I...'

Alyssa stood up but still found herself craning her neck as she looked upwards towards the lofty Pierre. Yes, she was anxious to get started on her work here, but Pierre's quip about the bright lights was still stinging. How little he knew about her real self! About what she really wanted in life. But she couldn't enlighten him. She had to go on playing the role she'd set herself.

'Yes?' he asked, waiting to hear what she had to say.

'Oh...er...what time shall we meet tonight?'

'I'll meet you in the foyer of the *clinique* at seven. We can have a drink somewhere before the play starts.'

They walked in silence to the end of the corridor. Pierre pressed the button which would summon the lift. They waited a couple of minutes, still maintaining an awkward silence. Nothing happened.

Pierre tapped his fingers against the wall impatiently. 'I think there must be a problem with the lift. We'll have to use the stairs.'

As they mounted the stairs side by side Pierre found difficulty in maintaining a reasonable space between them. He was longing to reach out and take hold of her hand, as he would have done in the days long ago when they were lovers, but he knew if he reached out and showed his true feelings the possibility of friendship would be dashed.

With an effort he concentrated his thoughts on the work ahead of them. Alyssa's interest in orthopaedics had surprised him. He'd been sure she would have preferred obstetrics, from what they had discussed the last time she was here. Orthopaedics required physical strength—and, with the greatest will in the world, you only had to look at Alyssa to know that physical strength wouldn't be her strong point.

He glanced down at her now and caught her eye.

She looked up and gave him a nervous smile. 'Do the staff of the orthopaedic ward know I'm coming in today?'

'Don't worry, they won't bite you, Alyssa. The sister in charge of the ward, Sylvie, is a great friend of mine. If you'd been unable to go to the theatre this evening I would have asked her.'

Somehow that didn't make Alyssa feel any happier!

'It's a purely platonic friendship, of course,' Pierre said lightly.

'Of course.'

'Just like our friendship is now, Alyssa.'

Her pulse quickened. 'Don't tease me, Pierre. You know that friendship between a couple who've been lovers can never be truly platonic. There's always that underlying factor that has to be stamped out. Or perhaps...' She hesitated. 'Perhaps you and Sylvie have been lovers?'

She held her breath. It was much too bold a question, and quite out of character, but she knew she would find it difficult to work with someone who had experienced an affair with Pierre.

Pierre's eyes flashed dangerously. 'No, we haven't. Not that it's any business of yours.' He paused, running a hand through his dark hair with long, sensitive fingers. 'But if you're going to ask personal questions like that, then so am I. Is there any special person waiting for you back in England?'

Alyssa was relieved that her London life was now so uncomplicated that she could be utterly truthful with Pierre. She smiled across at him.

'Only my cat, who's being looked after by a neighbour.'

Pierre smiled back. 'Cats are incredibly independent creatures. Rather like you. I'm not surprised you have a cat as a companion.'

They had reached the top step and Pierre decided that he dared put a hand under Alyssa's arm to steady her.

As Alyssa paused to regain her breath, she looked up at Pierre, willing herself not to be too unnerved by the touch of his fingers under her elbow. His comment about her not needing anybody was still stinging. She couldn't let it pass. Pierre had to know that she was still human.

'I had a husband once,' she said quietly.

She realised almost at once that she was in danger of blowing her cover by mentioning Mike.

Pierre stared down into her eyes with that piercing appraisal she remembered so well, as if he was looking right inside her soul. Surely if she told him now that she couldn't have babies, and that was why she'd had to break off their— No! She mustn't! She'd got this far, and their new platonic relationship would work out if she kept her cool.

'You had a husband?' His voice was low. 'What happened? Was it one of those totally free marriages where each partner goes their own way and—?'

'Don't, Pierre!' She pulled free from the constriction of his hand. 'You wouldn't understand.'

'Oh, but I think I would!' He took a deep breath. 'I don't want to pry. Especially not here at the *clinique*. We owe it to the patients to remain calm, and if either of us becomes emotional…'

The sound of footsteps resounding on the corridor made Alyssa nervous of the situation. 'Let's leave it, Pierre. We can talk tonight.'

Pierre pulled himself to his full height and began to move away, indicating that Alyssa should follow him. He was once more the eminent *médecin-chef*, pausing briefly to reply *'Bonjour,'* to the white-uniformed nurse who greeted him in the corridor.

They reached the orthopaedic ward and Pierre pushed open the swing doors.

Alyssa took a deep breath as she followed him through. She wasn't normally nervous when coming on duty, but this morning was different. This morning she had to give a good impression to the nursing staff, who would want to feel they could trust her skills and knowledge.

Pierre headed for the room where their patient Henri was settled back against his pillows, with his injured right leg propped up high on a special orthopaedic cradle.

The small, plump figure of the orthopaedic consultant, wearing a dark suit this morning, was surrounded by what looked like a positive crowd of doctors, nurses and medical students. He was bending over the leg, adjusting the angle of a drainage tube.

One of the medical students was pointing out the size of the consultant's posterior as his back was turned towards them.

Medical students never change! Alyssa thought, hiding a smile. It was amazing how they turned into capable doctors.

She scanned the faces of Yves Grandet's entourage and was pleased to recognise someone she knew. Jacques Suchet, the friendly young fair-haired doctor who'd carried her suitcase up the steps yesterday, smiled across at her. She smiled back. It was good to know she already had a friend on the orthopaedic team.

'Bonjour, Yves,' Pierre said to the consultant.

Yves smiled as he straightened up and turned round. 'Bonjour, Pierre—et bonjour, Alyssa.'

Alyssa smiled as she returned the greeting. She liked this friendly consultant very much already. He exuded the confidence and capability of a highly successful surgeon whilst remaining very down to earth and approachable.

'It was important I call in on my way to another hospital, to check on my very special patient,' Yves said, addressing his medical colleagues in the tone of voice he adopted when giving lectures. 'I don't like to spend hours operating on a patient who doesn't behave himself, and I felt Henri might pose a problem.'

Their patient knew he was joking, and smiled around at the assembled medical staff. The consultant leaned across and patted Henri on the shoulder.

'But I'm glad to say that Henri is being a perfect patient so far. Apart from running too high a temperature, he's doing fine. I'm going to put all of you in the picture so that you can take good care of Henri when I'm not here.' He glanced at his watch. 'I'll be brief, because I have to be on the other side of Paris in an hour.'

Alyssa studied her patient's leg, taking in the full details of the case as Yves outlined the operation he'd performed. It was much as Pierre had already explained to her when they were having their *petit déjeuner*.

'So, I think intravenous antibiotics should be continued,' Yves was saying, in conclusion of his instructions. 'The high temperature is worrying at this stage. Because of the open wound there is a high risk of infection.'

'Has a swab been taken from the wound for histology?' Alyssa asked, examining the area where the surgical incision had been sutured through the window in the rigid plaster.

'That's all under control,' said a quiet composed voice as the sister in charge of the orthopaedic ward stepped forward. 'We are expecting results from the pathology laboratory this morning.'

'I'd like to know the results as soon as they come in, Sylvie,' Pierre said, giving her an approving smile.

Sylvie smiled back and the rapport between the two wasn't lost on Alyssa.

Alyssa looked across at the dark-haired, blue-uniformed sister, and her first impression was one of a young woman who was extremely competent, devoted to her job, highly efficient…and with long, slim legs that seemed to go up to her armpits!

Alyssa told herself to concentrate on the task in hand and not allow jealousy to get in the way of caring for the patient.

'We can close up the window in the plaster now,' Yves said. 'The wound should remain covered as much as possible, but nevertheless we need to keep an eye on it.'

After Yves had gone, Pierre introduced Alyssa to the rest of the orthopaedic team.

'Pierre, would you like me to show Dr Ferguson round the orthopaedic ward?' Sylvie asked. 'I know you must have a million other things to do.'

'Thank you, Sylvie, that would be very helpful.' Pierre turned to look down at Alyssa. 'I'll leave you in Sister's capable hands.'

He moved away quickly and left the unit.

Alyssa looked around her, feeling decidedly apprehensive about her new job.

'This way, Dr Ferguson, *s'il vous plaît*,' Sylvie was saying.

Alyssa felt completely dwarfed as she walked beside the tall sister, but as the ward round continued she found she was enjoying herself. It was good to be working again, and she enjoyed meeting the patients and checking up on their case notes, which were all attached in folders to the foot of the beds. It was a mixed ward to the extent that some bays were female, others male, and there was freedom to move around for the more ambulant patients, which, meant that they didn't get too bored with their incarceration.

Alyssa found Sylvie was extremely helpful and thorough in her explanation of the treatment the patients were undergoing. She told Alyssa that very few patients were confined to bed. The policy on the ward was to get the patients moving as soon as possible, even if it meant they had to walk around with heavy steel fixators in their limbs to keep the bones in place.

Patients who had extreme difficulty with walking were given wheelchairs, so that they could circulate amongst the other patients or even take the lift down to the ground floor and go out into the garden.

'Dr Ferguson, this is Jean-Claude,' Sylvie said, as the two of them were almost mown down by an enthusiastic young man speeding his wheelchair away from one of the bays. 'He thinks he's a racing driver so you'd better be careful when he's out of bed.'

'Sorry, Sylvie!' Jean Claude called out as he whizzed off in the opposite direction from them. 'Didn't see you!'

'He's a cheerful patient.' Alyssa smiled. 'What's his diagnosis, Sister?'

'He was climbing in the Pyrenees when he fell down a rockface and cut his leg. A local doctor put stitches in. The wound healed over but after a few months Jean-Claude's leg became very painful. Yves Grandet operated to open up the leg and discovered extensive gangrene in the lower part of the tibia. Years ago he would have had to have a below-knee amputation, but Yves was able to excise the affected part of the bone and replace it with a steel rod.'

'Has he had plastic surgery to cover the wound?' Alyssa asked.

Sylvie nodded. 'The front part of the steel rod has been covered with a flap of flesh and skin, but the posterior part will need further treatment to make the steel rod less visible. We're liaising with the plastic surgery team about a future date for further surgery—'

Sylvie broke off and smiled down at Alyssa. 'You've probably seen enough of the patients for the moment. Now that you know your way around you'll find all the information you need in the notes, and you can always ask the rest of the team. Would you like to come and have coffee with me in the office, Dr Ferguson?'

'I'd love to—and do call me Alyssa.'

Sylvie pushed open the door of her office. 'And you must call me Sylvie. Everybody does. We don't stand on ceremony at the Clinique Ste Catherine. Our *médecin chef* is calm and relaxed about protocol and I'm pleased that Pierre hasn't changed anything now he's taken over. How do you find Pierre?'

Momentarily, the question threw her. Alyssa had no idea how she was going to reply as she sat down near Sylvie's desk. Watching her new colleague as she poured strong coffee from a *cafetière* into two tiny cups, she thought how different this was from the mugs of instant coffee she was used to in her London hospital. But then, this was Paris.

As the ward sister handed her one of the cups Alyssa couldn't help wondering just how platonic *was* this friendship that Sylvie and Pierre were having? And how much did Sylvie know about her own previous relationship with Pierre?

'I only arrived yesterday,' Alyssa said, playing safe. 'So I haven't had much time to—'

'Yes, in spite of his friendliness, it takes time to get to know Pierre,' Sylvie said. 'I've been out with him a few times, but even though we are friends I still don't feel I know much about him.'

Alyssa stiffened.

'I mean, he's such a handsome, intriguing man!' Sylvie went on enthusiastically, her rapid French breaking into Alyssa's thoughts. *'Ça m'étonne qu'il est toujours célibataire!'*

'Yes, it is surprising that he's still a bachelor,' Alyssa said, echoing Sylvie's words. 'But—'

'It's just impossible to get close to him—and he doesn't talk about his past relationships. He's told me about his wonderful life in the West Indies, but there's something lacking in his emotions. It's as if— *Excusez-moi...*'

Sylvie broke off to answer her phone.

'Oui...j'arrive tout de suite.'

Sylvie put the phone down and stood up. 'I've got to go back on the ward, Alyssa. *A tout à l'heure.* I'll see you later. And don't forget—if I can be of any help while you're working here...'

Sylvie swept out of the door, leaving Alyssa feeling that she should have broken through the flow of Sylvie's enthusiastic description of Pierre to explain her own previous relationship with him.

She put down her coffee cup and stood up. She would go round the patients once more, to familiarise herself with all the current treatments, and she would go back to see the young woman who'd complained that the site around the intravenous canula in her hand was painful. The patient had been on intravenous antibiotics for over a week now, so it looked as if a change of canula into the other hand was indicated.

Work always took her mind away from her problems, she thought as she went back into the ward. Tonight, when she was once more with Pierre, would be time enough to consider whether she could handle this new platonic relationship.

CHAPTER THREE

ALYSSA paused at the end of the corridor as she looked across the foyer at the handsome stranger who was waiting to take her out that evening. In reality, Pierre wasn't a stranger, but the eight years they'd been apart had caused a rift wider than the widest canyon. A rift that neither of them must cross. Tonight they must be platonic friends having a date in the most wonderful city in the world.

Pierre hadn't seen her yet. He was standing with his back to the reception desk, looking out towards the large plate glass windows where the twinkling lights of Paris were illuminating the darkness of this chilly November evening. Soon the whole of Paris would be lit up with Christmas decorations. Frosted illuminations would span the wide boulevards like fairy bridges and excited shoppers would gather round the enticing displays of Christmas presents in the windows of the shops and little boutiques.

Alyssa felt a sense of apprehensive anticipation as she thought about the impending Christmas season and all it had meant to her in the past. What would this Christmas bring now that she had met up again with Pierre? She felt her heart beating rapidly as she watched him by the window. He was wearing a dark grey suit, impeccably tailored to fit his lean, athletic figure. She guessed that he hadn't put on even half a kilo in the eight years they'd been apart.

She was trying desperately to get a hold on her emotions, but all she could feel was an overwhelming desire to rush across and fling herself into Pierre's arms. And the way she was feeling at the moment made her want to suggest to him that they cancel the theatre date and stay in tonight, just the two of them, so that...

He turned and saw her. She felt the most annoyingly telling blush spreading across her cheeks. How long did she have to keep up this pretence? Pierre had said he was in charge here until just after Christmas. Could she hold out that long without giving in to her turbulent desires?

Pierre smiled and his face lit up with pleasure as he came towards her.

'Ah, there you are. How did you get on today? We haven't lost any patients, so I presume you've been making yourself useful.'

Alyssa stiffened as she felt his hand gliding under her elbow to guide her towards the revolving door. Outside on the steps he paused, standing back so that he could take a better look at her.

'You're looking lovely tonight, Alyssa. Am I allowed to say that, now that we're just good friends?'

She ran a hand through her short blonde hair, still damp from the shower, and wondered if Pierre realised how long she'd agonised over what to wear. Deciding on this cream woollen skirt and jacket had been a major decision, despite how many times she'd told herself she wasn't supposed to be trying to impress Pierre.

'Oh, I'm happy to receive compliments,' Alyssa said, smiling up at Pierre, his face so familiar but so untouchable now.

She swung into step beside him as they walked along the road.

'We'll get a taxi at the corner here,' Pierre said. 'The traffic is pretty dense, but eventually we'll get there.'

'Why don't we take the Métro, like we always used...?' Alyssa's voice trailed away as nostalgic emotions threatened to get the better of her. She mustn't keep referring to their previous life together.

Pierre looked surprised. 'I thought now that you were more sophisticated you would prefer to take a taxi.'

'I'm eight years older but I'm no more "sophisticated" than I was when we last met,' Alyssa said quietly. 'I like taking the Métro. It's always nice and warm down there, and it's usually quicker when the traffic's bad.'

As they walked along the Avenue Mozart Alyssa paused briefly to admire the Christmas-themed window of one of the shops where her grandmother had often taken her as a child. A small tinsel-draped Father Christmas was standing with his elves and reindeer amid the cheeses and hams.

Pierre raised one eyebrow. 'A bit premature to start the Christmas decorations in November, don't you think, Alyssa?'

She smiled. 'Not at all. Christmas will soon be here, and it catches everyone by surprise if we're not reminded to start getting ready. It's pure nostalgia for me, and it makes me feel I'm very young again.'

Pierre laughed. 'You *are* young, Alyssa.'

They made for the Ranelagh Métro station, which was the nearest, and ran down the steps. Pierre produced a couple of tickets from his *carnet*, the book of tickets in his pocket, and they went through the *guichet* to the platform.

'It's a long time since we were on this station together,' Pierre said, in a voice smoothly devoid of emotion.

'I was thinking that,' Alyssa said, deliberately focusing her eyes on the advertisement posters plastered over the walls.

'I remember exactly when it was,' Pierre said, his voice husky with emotion. 'Don't you?'

Alyssa steeled herself for the nostalgic experience he would inevitably conjure up.

'I think so,' she said carefully, knowing full well the wonderful evening Pierre was referring to.

Pierre smiled. 'We took the Métro over to the Rive Gauche, as I recall, and had supper in that little café overlooking the river. The one where the waiter always used to try and listen in to our conversation. And afterwards we came back here and—'

'It's all so long ago,' Alyssa cut in quickly, before Pierre had time to refer to that night of pure magic, her last night in Paris, the night before she'd gone back to London to continue her studies at medical school and then discovered that she was pregnant—only to lose the most precious baby in the world.

'Yes,' Pierre said softly. 'Difficult to believe it all happened. I've often wondered if…'

The roar of the Métro train approaching drowned his words. Alyssa climbed aboard, trying to remain calm when her shoulder was pressed against Pierre's side as they sat together. Physical contact with someone you loved desperately was an unnerving experience which threatened to blow away all her resolutions not to revive their previous relationship.

'I've often wondered if things would have been different between us if you'd stayed on in Paris.'

Pierre was looking sideways at her as he resumed what he'd been going to say before.

'You mean, if I'd given up my medical studies?'

'No, if you'd perhaps taken a year out to think about the situation. Maybe I pressurised you too much into the idea of marriage. You were very young, after all, and you—'

'Pierre, it wouldn't have made any difference to the situation,' Alyssa said, hating herself for not being able to explain the real reason. 'I was… Circumstances change, and I felt that marriage to you wasn't the right thing.'

'So you married someone else.'

Alyssa could hear the deep emotion in Pierre's voice and it tore at her heartstrings. No wonder Sylvie had said she couldn't get close to him. Pierre was a man whose heart had been broken by her own refusal to marry him. And he was still carrying the scars.

'Yes, I did marry someone else, but—'

'We get out here,' Pierre said, putting out a hand to help her rise from her seat.

Amid the noise and the crowds as they emerged into the busy street it was impossible to continue. Pierre's arm was comfortingly on the small of her back as they negotiated a path through a group of lively young students to secure a table outside a small café. An overhead heater was dispelling the November chill in the air and the bright lights from the theatre opposite were creating a carnival atmosphere, reminiscent of the balmy summer evening when they'd last been here. That had been another momentous occasion, almost as poignant in retrospect as her last evening in Paris.

Alyssa looked at Pierre across the small wrought-iron table, with its red and white checked tablecloth, and her heart felt as if it would burst if she had to keep a hold on her emotions much longer.

'You shouldn't have brought me here…to this café…to this table,' she said, her voice quivering with feeling as she remembered how they'd come here so often—holding hands across the table, feeling the electric current passing from fingertip to fingertip, until it had consumed their entire bodies and they'd had to hurry back to Pierre's apartment so that they could consummate their love once more.

He feigned surprise. 'Why not? I thought you liked it here.'

'I do, but...'

'You were telling me about your husband, remember?' he said evenly. 'What I can't understand is how you could tell me that you were dead against marriage and then off you go—'

'Like I said, situations change,' she interrupted quickly. 'I'd finished my final exams; I'd qualified as a doctor. Mike was a fellow medical student, a good friend who qualified at the same time, and we started going out together. We got on well...and it seemed like a good idea to get married.'

It sounded lame even to her own ears. She would have to come up with something better. But, whatever she told Pierre, she wasn't going to say that she'd found she couldn't bear a lifetime of loneliness and that one of the other reasons she'd felt she could marry Mike was because he'd said he didn't want a family.

He had, in fact, been completely against the idea of having babies when they'd first married. He had said he didn't even like children and felt that family would just get in the way of his career. So when Alyssa had told Mike, before she'd agreed to marry him, that she probably couldn't have a baby, it hadn't affected him in the slightest. He'd seemed relieved.

That had been at the beginning of their marriage. But two years later, Mike had changed his mind completely out of the blue and had announced that he'd like a family after all.

For two years they'd tried for a baby, but Alyssa hadn't got pregnant. And it had been at that point that Mike told her he was having an affair, his girlfriend was pregnant and he was going to go and live with her.

Pierre leaned across the table. 'You're looking very solemn all of a sudden. From the way you're reacting there doesn't seem to have been much romance in this marriage.'

'Oh, it had its moments.'

She swallowed hard as she tried to remember if she'd ever really fallen in love with Mike and came to the conclusion that she hadn't realised that it would be impossible to get over Pierre. No wonder Mike had left her! She'd only had half a heart to give him, and after the heartbreaking two years of trying to get pregnant, she had accepted that she was childless. As friends they'd got on well; as married partners it had been a disaster.

She raised her eyes to Pierre's and saw her own deep sadness reflected there. Why did they have to torture each other like this? Why couldn't it be like it was before she lost their baby?

Because that's life, said the still, small voice of reason. You have to take the good times with the bad and make the best of it. You can't change the fact that you can't give Pierre a baby, so it wouldn't be fair to marry him.

The waiter was placing their drinks on the table. A pastis for Pierre and a kir made from crème de cassis and white wine for Alyssa. Nothing has changed as far as our drinks are concerned, she thought, as she watched Pierre pouring water from the little jug into his glass, making it cloudy.

'Who broke up the marriage?' Pierre asked quietly.

'Mike left me…for my best friend, Rachel. She was one of our theatre sisters.'

'That must have been awful for you.'

'I'd realised that something was going on between them. I wasn't surprised.'

'But weren't you devastated?'

She weighed her words carefully. 'To be honest, I think

it was a relief. You see, we hadn't been getting on very well for some time so…'

She paused, unable to continue because of the way Pierre was looking at her.

'As far as I can see, first of all you drifted into a boring marriage with an unsuitable partner when you really didn't want to get married anyway. And then, having found out the situation was awful, you weren't sad when it all ended and you could go back to your exciting life as an independent bachelor girl.'

She took a larger sip of her drink and forced herself to smile. 'You sound like a psychiatrist who specialises in analysing marriage break-ups.'

'Do I? OK, if that's how it looks to you,' he said, placing his elbow on the table and one hand at the side of his face as he leaned over. 'But tell me, Alyssa, do you think you will you ever try marriage again?'

She took a deep breath. 'What do you think?'

'I thought not. But all men aren't like your unfortunate Mike, you know.'

She wanted to tell Pierre that most men wanted to have a family, and that was something she couldn't give to anyone. But she simply remained silent.

Instead she leaned forward. 'Now it's your turn to tell me what *you've* been doing for the past eight years.'

Pierre remained silent for a few seconds as he contemplated just how much he should tell Alyssa. The main problem since they'd split up had been his efforts to forget her. Just when he thought he'd got Alyssa out of his system, something would happen to remind him of her and he would be back to square one again. But he wasn't going to mention any of this.

'I've got this fabulous house on the island of Ste Cécile in the West Indies. Fully staffed, of course. All the domestic side of work is taken care of, so I spend my off-duty time on the sea. I love taking friends out on my boat, exploring the coastline, picnicking under the palm trees on the beach—'

He broke off and smiled across the table at Alyssa. Was he painting too alluring a picture for her? Was he trying too hard to convince her that he enjoyed life without her?

Alyssa smiled back. 'It sounds idyllic. No special girlfriend, then? I thought you would have married by now, knowing how you long to have a family.'

Pierre drew in his breath. 'A family is still my dearest wish,' he said, his voice husky. 'I was an only child, an adopted child...but I believe I told you this when you were here in Paris last time, didn't I?'

'Yes, you did,' Alyssa said quietly. 'I remember you said that you wanted to have your own flesh and blood around you, to create a Dupont dynasty. Being adopted yourself, you were determined to have a real family of your own.'

'Did I say that? What a brilliant memory you have, Alyssa.'

'Yes, it made a big impression on me. That's why I thought you would have made a start on your family by now.'

'Haven't met the right mother for my children yet—that is apart from...apart from one or two girls I thought I'd fallen for. But I was quickly disillusioned.'

'You're probably being too choosy,' Alyssa said lightly, assuming her role of platonic, carefree friend. 'Someone will come along and you'll immediately know she's right for you.'

Pierre swallowed hard and leaned across the table to take hold of Alyssa's hand. 'I hope so.'

Alyssa stared down at her hand, imprisoned in Pierre's.

Oh, the feel of his fingers was far too pleasurable! Carefully, she withdrew her hand and leaned back in her chair.

'Give it time, Pierre,' she said quietly.

They finished their drinks and crossed the road to the theatre. The noise of Paris night-life had always excited Alyssa, and tonight was no exception. Amid the busy traffic Pierre took hold of her hand, to lead her to the safety of the pavement, and she didn't try to pull away. This could only be construed as a friendly gesture, so she tried to ignore the frisson of desire that flickered through her at the touch of his fingers.

Alyssa enjoyed every moment of the play. She also enjoyed being escorted to the bar in the interval by the most handsome man in the theatre audience. They kept their conversation deliberately light, discussing the play, the plot, the actors and actresses.

'It's good for me to see a contemporary play in France,' Alyssa said, as she sipped her drink. 'My French needs updating. Back in London I rarely use it. Since my mother died I've spoken only English.'

'How long is it since your mother died?'

'It was my last year at medical school. I was living with her so that I could take care of her, and our house wasn't too far from the hospital or the medical school. About half an hour on the Underground. I continued to live at home after she died and took over the mortgage. Mike moved in with me when we married.'

'And your father? I remember you said he lived in Australia. Do you have any contact with him?'

Alyssa shook her head. 'Not since he left my mother when I was very small. Maman came over from Paris to be an au pair in her summer vacation from university. She met my father and he persuaded her to stay on in London.

She got pregnant with me and so they married. My father left home when I was about six months old.'

'You didn't tell me that before,' Pierre said softly.

'There's lots I haven't told you,' she said quietly, putting down her drink.

'The second half of the play is about to begin,' Pierre said, standing up and holding out his hand towards her.

Automatically, before she could think, she took hold of his hand, revelling in the feel of his fingers wrapping around her own. Walking hand in hand together into the auditorium couldn't do any harm...

The rapport between them was now palpable. However hard she tried, Alyssa was never going to be able to shake off her love for Pierre. She realised, not for the first time, that they were made for each other. They could try, but nothing was ever going to change that.

Pierre guided her through the crowded foyer at the end of the play and they walked down towards the Seine. The restaurant where Pierre had made a reservation was equally crowded, but the waiter showed them to a secluded corner table. Alyssa was relieved that this was a restaurant where they hadn't been before. Too much heart-rending nostalgia was wearing down her resolve.

'I don't remember ever having been here,' Alyssa said, settling herself on the banquette and looking up at the ornate alabaster ceiling which was punctuated with a myriad of tiny halogen lights. 'Very smart.'

Pierre smiled. 'I couldn't afford to bring you here in the old days. Way beyond my wallet then. I knew you'd be impressed with the place.'

Alyssa laughed. 'Is that why you brought me here? To impress me?'

'I bring all my girlfriends here,' he said, in a bantering tone.

'Well, they'd expect only the best restaurants from the *médecin-chef* of the prestigious Clinique Ste Catherine,' Alyssa said, in the same half-joking manner, although the thought of Pierre taking girlfriends anywhere was agonising in the extreme.

'You must try the *escargots*,' Pierre told her. 'They serve small portions as a starter and they are exquisitely cooked in garlic and butter.'

'Mmm…sounds great. Just like my grandmother used to cook them.'

'And their fish is magnificent. So fresh it—'

Pierre broke off to speak to the waiter who was going to take their order.

Alyssa sat back in her chair and watched him giving precise instructions. This had always happened when they'd had a meal together. They both got an idea of what they wanted to eat and rarely consulted the menu. Pierre was looking enquiringly across the table at her and she nodded, yes, to his question about whether she would like the sole *meunière*.

Of course she would like it, if that was what Pierre was recommending. Oh, dear, she was falling so easily back into the easy relationship they'd had. There was nothing platonic about the electric vibes that were crossing the table at the moment.

She sipped a glass of chilled white wine as she tried to still her turbulent emotions. Even in a completely new restaurant the nostalgic feelings followed them. They had too much history behind them to make a transition into the present and the unknown future.

As the meal progressed their conversation flowed easily—both of them now seeming to make an effort to avoid referring to the past. When they'd discussed this evening's play Pierre asked Alyssa about what was on in London at the moment. She was able to describe the theatres she'd been to most recently, and that was a completely safe subject.

Alyssa put down her coffee cup at the end of the meal and smiled across the table. 'That was superb.'

'Glad you enjoyed it. How about a liqueur?'

Now he really was being nostalgic! How many times had she sipped her favourite liqueur, with its piquant flavour of oranges, at the end of an evening with Pierre? But not tonight! That would be the ultimate undoing of all her resolutions. The white wine she'd drunk had already made her feel far too mellow towards Pierre, and too much off her guard.

'No, thanks,' she said quickly.

Pierre arched an eyebrow. 'That's unusual for you. I'm not trying to seduce you—I've got the message, you know. We're just good friends on a platonic night out. So you're quite safe if—' His mobile phone was shrilling. '*Allo? Oui, c'est Pierre Dupont içi…*'

Pierre was looking serious now. Alyssa drained her coffee cup. He seemed to be dealing with some kind of medical emergency. They were both off duty but Pierre, as director of the *clinique*, would often be consulted during his own time.

'*Oui, j'arrive tout de suite,*' he said tersely, before cutting the connection.

'What's the problem, Pierre?'

He was standing up, signalling to the waiter to bring the bill.

'A multiple pile-up on the Périphérique. All hospitals in Paris are on alert and we've been asked to take some casualties at the *clinique*.'

Outside on the pavement, Pierre was able to flag down a cab. The traffic had eased since the early pre-theatre rush.

She sat bolt upright next to him, aware of the tense atmosphere. The romantic ambience that had surrounded them all evening had dissipated at the realisation that they would have to become professionals again.

'I'll come into the *clinique* and work with you, if you need me,' Alyssa said, thinking that a multiple pile-up on the Périphérique, the fast-flowing ring-road that surrounded Paris, would be an extremely serious situation.

'Thanks, that would be a great help, Alyssa. Your experience and knowledge of orthopaedics will be useful. I'll phone Sylvie and see if she's available to come back and take charge of her ward. The night staff are very efficient, but Sylvie always likes to be on her ward if there's an emergency.'

Alyssa could hear Pierre speaking to Sylvie now. Yes, it sounded as if she was going to come in. And it also reaffirmed the fact that she and Pierre had a good relationship between them.

Alyssa tried to convince herself that she was glad about that, but failed miserably. She wanted Pierre to find someone he could be happy with. Someone who could give him the family he so desperately craved. But standing on the sidelines and watching it happen wasn't going to be easy.

An ambulance was parked outside the *clinique* and an inert figure was being stretchered inside, using the entrance at the side of the *porte à tambour* which didn't have any steps. This entrance led straight into the area which served as their emergency department, although in the normal course of events the *clinique* didn't cater for emergency patients.

Alyssa and Pierre followed the stretcher inside, where they found another patient already being treated by Yves Grandet.

The consultant turned to acknowledge Pierre and Alyssa. 'I was at a dinner party with friends in this arrondissement when the call came,' he explained. 'I was able to get here very quickly. Can you get the X-ray department up and running, Pierre?'

'I've just phoned a radiographer. She'll be here in a few minutes, I hope. I'll deal with this man here—Alyssa, could you take that patient into a cubicle and…? Ah, there you are, Sylvie…'

Pierre looked relieved to see his orthopaedic sister arriving.

Alyssa bent over her unconscious patient. He was breathing normally but there was no other sign of life. She placed her stethoscope and listened to his heartbeat. Too slow. She checked out his head. Amid the stubbly dark hair of his crew cut she could discern the development of an ominous bruise. Checking out his limbs and torso, she couldn't find any further signs of injury.

Everything pointed to concussion. She noted the time so that she would know how long he'd been unconscious.

'*Il est là!*' A petite, smartly dressed Parisian lady came rushing into the department and burst into Alyssa's cubicle. '*Oui, c'est mon mari, Hubert!* But he's so still and quiet. Has he been awake since you brought him in?'

'I believe Hubert has been knocked unconscious during the crash,' Alyssa said. 'We're going to admit him to the *clinique* for tests so that we can ascertain—'

Alyssa broke off as her patient opened his eyes. He stared around him. 'Where am I?'

'You're in the Clinique Ste Catherine,' Alyssa said gently. 'You were involved in a road accident on the Périphérique. The car you were driving was—'

'I wasn't driving a car. My mother says I can learn to

drive as soon as... Is my mother here? Does she know I came home early from school and...?'

'Hubert, what on earth are you talking about?' said his distraught wife. 'I'm here, darling...'

The patient frowned up at the excitable woman. 'Who are you? Don't you dare call me darling! I want to see my parents, not you—whoever you are.'

'I'm your wife!'

Hubert began to laugh in a giggling, childish manner. 'Don't be so stupid. You're much too old to be my wife. I'm only fourteen, so how can I possibly be married?' He looked up at Alyssa with pleading eyes. 'Get this woman away from me. I've never seen her before in my life.'

'I'm Giselle,' the woman cried. 'Look at me, Hubert!'

Hubert turned his head away from his wife as Alyssa put restraining hands on her narrow shoulders.

'I'm afraid this is all part of the concussion, Giselle,' Alyssa explained gently. 'It sometimes happens that concussed patients regress into childhood. Usually not for long. I would hope that we might see some improvement soon, but it's difficult to say how long it will take. If you'd like to give me some details about your husband, I'll admit him to a ward and you can come back in the morning. It's too stressful for him if you remain here while he's feeling unsure of what's happening.'

Giselle became calmer as she listened to Alyssa's words. After a few seconds' hesitation she was able to give Alyssa the details she required about Hubert, both personal and medical. Hubert, it seemed, was a successful lawyer who had been returning home this evening. He'd telephoned his wife to say he would be about an hour late because he was with an important client. Giselle had been entertaining their dinner guests as she'd waited for his delayed arrival.

When the phone call had come from the police, who'd

checked Hubert's wallet and diary, Giselle had left her guests and driven straight to the *clinique*.

'So, shall I go home and come back in the morning, Doctor?' Giselle asked in a tearful voice.

'That would definitely be the best course of action,' Alyssa said soothingly. 'Meanwhile I'll have Hubert checked out by a neurologist and I'll be able to give you a much better prognosis tomorrow.'

Giselle leaned across the stretcher and attempted to kiss her husband, only to be roughly rebuffed by him.

'Get off me, you dreadful woman. Doctor! Take this woman away...'

'Yes, yes, Hubert. Giselle is just going.' Alyssa took hold of Hubert's hand, feeling terribly sorry for the other woman as she left with tears in her eyes.

The patient clung to her hand as if it was a lifeline. 'Can I see my parents now?' he asked in a small voice. 'They'll need to write a note to my teacher if I'm going to stay in hospital. And I want to ask them if I can go on the skiing trip with the school party in February. Will I be better by then?'

'We'll have to see,' Pierre said, coming up behind Alyssa. He lowered his voice. 'I saw you were having problems, Alyssa. I've contacted our consultant neurologist and he'll be in later tonight. We could well find that his memory has returned by the morning, in which case we shall only have to keep him in for observation for a few days.'

'And if his memory doesn't return?' Alyssa asked Pierre.

Pierre frowned. 'Then we've got problems. But we've got a good neurology team who'll do all they can.' He turned to their patient and held a mirror in front of him. 'Would you like someone to comb your hair, Hubert?'

The patient stared into the mirror. 'That's not me; that's my dad!' He stared more closely. 'No, it's not Dad. But it's not me, either. You're trying to play a joke on me. Give me a proper mirror.'

'Hubert, you've lost part of your memory,' Pierre said patiently. 'But hopefully it will return when you get stronger.'

'You took a nasty knock on the head when all the cars smashed into each other,' Alyssa said gently. 'We're going to take you up to the ward now and make you comfortable.'

A nurse took over from Alyssa and walked beside the trolley as a porter pushed it away along the corridor.

'Hubert is actually forty-four years old,' Alyssa told Pierre.

'I know. He's a very distinguished lawyer. His wife must be distraught with worry about him.'

'She is. Let's hope the neurologist can do something to help him...'

'Ah, here comes our consultant. Perhaps you could fill him in on the details of the case, Alyssa, while I deal with another patient?'

In the early hours of the morning the emergency area resembled the aftermath of a battle. Doctors and nurses had tried to cope with the chaotic situation, but it wasn't until the last patient had been discharged or admitted to one of the wards that they were able to restore some kind of order to the department. One by one, the staff left. An exhausted Sylvie said goodnight to Alyssa and Pierre before going away to her room in the medical staff quarters.

Alyssa began to clear the trolley she had used, throwing everything disposable into the nearby bin. She realised that she was working like an automaton, her mind having ceased to function. She and Pierre were the only staff.

'I think you ought to go and get some sleep, Alyssa,' Pierre said, coming up behind her and putting his hands on her shoulders. 'You feel very tense. What you need is a long hot soak in the bath first.'

For a few seconds, under the guise of being a doctor, Pierre was able to massage the tense knots of muscle around Alyssa's shoulderblades.

'Mmm, that feels wonderful,' Alyssa said, instinctively closing her eyes as she leaned back against Pierre's chest.

Whatever am I doing? she thought, without opening her eyes. If she stopped all rational thought just now, she could put the clock back eight years and give herself up to the erotic sensations that were claiming her senses. She could collapse into Pierre's arms and...

'No!'

She was so dead on her feet that she hadn't realised she'd actually spoken out loud. She swung round to look at Pierre and saw the tender expression in his eyes.

'I think you're right about the bath,' she said quickly, in as normal a voice as she could possibly muster under the circumstances. 'Trouble is I've only got a shower, and that's not half as soothing.'

'I've got a wonderful bath—big enough for two.'

Pierre's answer was predictable. Alyssa realised she was boldly holding his gaze but she couldn't help flirting. She was so tired that her brain had simply stopped functioning. How could she be so brazen when she was trying so hard to remain platonic? She felt as if she herself had been in the car crash on the Périphérique and had come out of it with no memory of the last eight years. She and Pierre were still lovers. Any moment now he would carry her off to his apartment, run a hot, scented bath, lift her in, run his tantalising fingers over her skin and…

'It really is time you went off duty.'

Pierre's seductive voice brought her back to the present.

'You'd better forget my offer of a bath for two,' he said gently, reaching out to touch the side of her cheek. 'That really doesn't fit into our lives any more, does it?'

She put up her hand to touch his fingers as they rested on her cheek.

'No, it doesn't,' she said, trying hard to convince herself.

It would be so easy to give in to her natural inclinations. They were the last of the medical staff left. Nobody would see them slipping away down the road if… But they mustn't.

Pierre bent his head and touched her cheek with his lips. *'Bonne nuit, ma petite princesse, dors bien.'*

She hadn't thought Pierre would call her his little princess ever again. It was the name he'd given her when they were lovers. The name he'd always said in their most tender moments. But maybe it had been a slip of the tongue, because he'd already turned from her and was striding purposefully away.

She put her hand to her cheek, on the place where he'd kissed her. It was too poignant a moment to be alone. She wanted to erase the last eight years, to run after Pierre and tell him none of it had happened. They were still young and carefree and…

With a sigh, she forced herself back to reality.

Outside, on the steps of the *clinique*, Pierre paused to take deep breaths of the cold night air. He needed something to calm his emotions. He'd almost given in and confessed that he'd been living only half a life since Alyssa had broken up their relationship.

How long would it take to get her out of his system? At times Alyssa seemed exactly like the young girl he'd known. But then something would happen to change their new rapport and she would be at pains to make it obvious that now, eight years on, she was a totally different woman. An independent woman who didn't want him to interfere in her new life.

He ran down the remaining steps, moving quickly along the deserted street to the door of his prestigious apartment block. An apartment block 'of great standing' was how it had been described in *Le Figaro* when he'd first bought it, ten years ago. He'd rented it out when he went to the West Indies and it had provided a sizeable income for him over the years. It was fortunate that his tenants had been moving out just at the time he'd come back for his three-month holiday.

Some holiday this had turned out to be! He punched in the numbers of the code necessary to open the large front door, crossed the woodblock floor of the foyer and took the thickly carpeted stairs to the second floor two at a time. The lights of the corridor were dimly lit as he made for his oak front door, with its discreet spyhole that helped him to sort out the desired from the undesired visitors when he was on the other side.

Turning the key in the lock, he reminded himself that he would have to be firm with his emotions if he was to survive until Christmas in this strange, unreal relationship with Alyssa. As soon as Dr Cheveny returned from sick leave he could relinquish his post and go back to the West Indies. Once more in the sun, with the surroundings of his established life, it would be easier to forget Alyssa.

But meeting her each day like this, it was far too tempting to believe that she hadn't really changed, that she would open up to his advances and decide that she could compromise on her idea of total independence. Why on earth had she come back? If all she wanted was to be independent, it didn't make sense for her to stir up the past.

He bent down and picked up the letters from the mat, carrying them through into his sitting room. He sank down on to the sofa where he'd so often made love with Alyssa, and suddenly gave a deep sigh. One of the things about coming back here was the wonderful memories of Alyssa that it evoked. Burying his head in the sofa cushions, he tried to conjure up the scent of her body, the feel of her skin against his.

No! He must pull himself together. Quickly he leapt off the sofa and headed for the bathroom. This wouldn't do! Anyway, the apartment needed complete refurbishment. Nearly everything in it was ten years old. Time for a total change. He would just have to accept that Alyssa was a different woman, and that trying to resurrect the past was futile.

As the water from her shower cascaded over Alyssa she closed her eyes and turned her head upwards, feeling the soothing spray on her eyelids. This way she hoped she could blot out all thoughts of Pierre. Because if she didn't, even though she was dead tired, she would find it impossible to sleep.

Just one evening spent with Pierre and her feelings for him had become stronger than they'd ever been. She was eight years more mature now, with a woman's needs and feelings, and at this moment she wanted Pierre so badly she was physically hurting inside.

CHAPTER FOUR

ALYSSA accepted the cup of coffee which Sylvie was holding out towards her. The two of them were taking a midmorning break whilst reviewing the treatment of their patients.

'Not much we can do about Hubert Legrange,' Sylvie said. 'He's simply refusing to let us move him to the neurology unit.'

Alyssa took a sip of her coffee. 'He told me he likes being in this ward. This was where he was first admitted and I think he feels safe with the people he's got used to.'

Sylvie frowned. 'His wife wanted to have him moved to a private room but he refuses to be parted from Alain, our motorbike crash victim.'

Alyssa smiled. 'Well, Alain is only eighteen, and Hubert, who's still convinced he's fourteen, finds him a good friend.'

Sylvie nodded. 'I'd hoped we would make some progress in three weeks, but Hubert is still in the same state as when he came in.'

Alyssa leaned back against her chair. 'Three weeks! I can't believe I've been working here so long! In one way it feels like only yesterday since I first arrived, and in another it feels like years. We've admitted so many different patients, and I feel I've learned so much since I came here.'

'You've settled in as if you'd been here for years,' Sylvie said, putting the last set of case notes on the pile

67

that had to be returned to the ward. 'The orthopaedic team will be sorry to see you go next week.'

'Next week? I'm not going anywhere, as far as I'm concerned…'

The door of the office opened and Pierre stood in the doorway, as if waiting to be invited into Sylvie's inner sanctum, as everyone called it. Coffee in here was strictly by invitation only. Pierre might be the director of the establishment but he knew his place.

Sylvie's face brightened. 'Do come in, Pierre. Coffee? I was just saying to Alyssa—'

'I didn't know I was moving,' Alyssa said, looking enquiringly at Pierre.

He lowered himself into an armchair next to Sylvie, stretching out his long legs in front of him.

'I was going to discuss it with you, Alyssa, but I've been so busy it simply slipped my mind. I remember when you first came you said you'd be happy to move on to obstetrics when you'd had a spell in orthopaedics. You thrive on versatility, you told me.'

'Yes, but now that I'm settled here I…'

Pierre raised an eyebrow as he looked across at her. 'Settled? I didn't think you were the settling kind.'

Alyssa drew in her breath. Really, Pierre could be so infuriating! During the last three weeks she'd had to cope with her feelings of longing to be alone with him whilst knowing that she mustn't give in. And, not content with simply being around far too much for her emotional stability, Pierre was constantly referring to her desire for independence, her need to move on.

They hadn't repeated the experience of going out together again. The whole of that evening had been far too poignant. On the one hand Alyssa was relieved that Pierre hadn't asked her for another date, but on the other, her perverse side, she longed for another attempt at achieving a platonic friendship. Anything was better than the situation now, of working with Pierre in the *clinique* and wondering how he was spending his off-duty time.

She swallowed hard. 'I'm equally interested in obstetrics and gynaecology,' she said evenly. 'So if that's where I'm required I'll be happy to move on.'

'Splendid!' Pierre said in a relieved tone. 'We'd like you to move to obstetrics in a couple of days.'

'Fine!'

Alyssa deliberately averted her eyes from Pierre. It was the best way of keeping up a professional relationship with him.

'We'll be sorry to see you go, but you'll love it down there,' Sylvie said. 'They have a great time at Christmas on the obstetrics ward. There's such a happy feeling when a new baby is born around Christmas. The patients and staff make a point of having a special celebration.'

'Sounds great!' Alyssa managed to smile, hoping that she would be able to cope with the emotional aspect.

She would have to be totally professional and not allow herself to become sentimental over the new Christmas babies. Her eyes moistened as she thought about the tiny little baby that she and Pierre should have had. Looking across the room, she saw that Pierre was watching her with an anxious expression in his eyes.

'Are you feeling OK, Alyssa?' he asked, gently.

'I'm fine—absolutely fine.'

'You don't look—'

There was a light tapping on the door before a young nurse burst in. 'Sister, Hubert Legrange is creating a terrible fuss. He's dangerously excited and nobody on the ward can calm him down. I'm afraid that he might harm himself.'

The junior nurse hovered uncertainly in the doorway.

'I'm coming!' Sylvie was on her feet, racing out through the door, followed quickly by Pierre and Alyssa.

They found Hubert standing by his bed, shouting down the ward, 'I want my wife! Where's Giselle? Get me out of this place. What am I doing here?'

Pierre took hold of Hubert's arm and began to speak to him in calming tones.

'Please, Hubert, don't make any more fuss. We're all here to help you.'

Hubert looked around him, his expression one of bewilderment, but he took hold of Alyssa's outstretched hand.

'You've been looking after me, Doctor, haven't you?' Hubert said in a quiet voice. 'There's nothing wrong with me, is there? I remember I was driving home on the Périphérique, and…and then it's all blank. I just woke up now, in this bed, and nobody will tell me…'

'Hubert,' Pierre said in a firm but gentle voice, 'you've been here three weeks—since you were involved in a car crash. You were suffering from memory loss and thought you were only fourteen, so—'

'But that's ridiculous! I'm forty-four. How could I…?'

'It sometimes happens,' Pierre said.

'But what about my wife? Has she been in to see me?'

'You didn't know who she was,' Alyssa said carefully. 'So the neurologist who was treating you thought it best she didn't visit you any more. If you'd like to see her now…'

'Well, of course I'd like to see her now!'

'I'll get a message to Madame Legrange immediately,' Sylvie said soothingly.

Hubert leaned forward, towards Sylvie. 'And if you could find me a private room, Sister, I would prefer to be on my own. I need to get back to work as soon as possible. Ask my wife to bring in my laptop, and any paperwork that's accumulated since my accident.'

Pierre assigned a specialist neurology nurse to remain with Hubert until the neurological consultant arrived. As they moved away from Hubert's bed Pierre asked Alyssa if she would come down to his office for a few minutes.

'Of course. What did you want to see me about?'

Pierre smiled. 'Don't look so worried! I simply wanted to explain the new work roster.'

'You mean you thought you should explain why Sylvie knew about my move to obstetrics and gynaecology before I did,' Alyssa said quietly.

Pierre hesitated. 'That does come into it, yes. If you've time to come down now...?'

Alyssa nodded. 'You're the boss.'

Neither of them spoke as they went down in the lift together. The professionalism that was needed cloaked any feelings they might have for each other. Alyssa was utterly scrupulous in observing protocol whenever she found herself working with Pierre. It was the only way she could survive the maelstrom of her emotions.

Once in Pierre's office she sat down at the other side of the desk from him, looking across as she waited for him to elaborate.

Pierre cleared his throat. 'I made the work roster when you first arrived, Alyssa. I assure you that you really did give me the impression that you enjoyed a certain versatility in your work. So I'm sorry if you would have preferred to stay in orthopaedics. Sylvie tells me that she's spoken to the sister in obstetrics and the entire team is looking forward to having you work there.'

'It seems everybody knows about this move except me.'

Pierre ran a hand through his hair. 'Alyssa, there just hasn't been an opportunity to talk to you in the last few days.'

'Yet you found time to talk to Sylvie.'

'We happened to be having dinner together and Sylvie asked me how long you would be working in her department.'

Alyssa could feel a cold hand clutching at her heart.

'And where were you and Sylvie having dinner together?' she asked quietly, hating herself for being so petty but unable to stop the jealous query from escaping her lips.

After a long pause, Pierre finally spoke. 'Well, well. I won't flatter myself by presuming to think you're jealous. But if you'd really like to know we were at the restaurant where I took you before the theatre, three weeks ago. And, yes, before you ask, the fish was superb—as always. But Sylvie doesn't like *escargots* so she had the *pâté maison* instead, which she said was delicious. Anything else you'd like to know about our evening?'

Pierre was trying to glare across the desk at Alyssa, but glaring wasn't something he was any good at. He tried to look fierce and knew he'd failed miserably. How could Alyssa expect him not to hope that she might have feelings of jealousy where other women were concerned?

He sighed. 'Alyssa, Sylvie and I are just good friends, nothing more. I want to make that clear, even if it makes no difference to you.'

Alyssa put a hand to her forehead, resting her elbow on the arm of her chair. She couldn't bear being at loggerheads with Pierre. This situation was all her own fault. She shouldn't have come back here, searching for something that would lay the ghost of her affair with Pierre. When she'd found that the ghost was well and truly alive she should have gone straight back to London. She mustn't meddle in Pierre's life any more. She must allow him to get on with it and not interfere. But still, she couldn't suppress the feeling of relief that he and Sylvie were only friends.

For an instant she closed her eyes, to crystallise what she was going to say. The next thing she knew, Pierre's arm was around her shoulder and he was leaning over her. 'What's the matter?'

'I'm feeling tired, that's all,' she improvised, opening her eyes to look up at Pierre.

Just making eye contact threw her completely. This was the first time she'd looked into his eyes in three weeks, and at such close quarters the experience was turning her legs to jelly. It was a good thing she was sitting down otherwise she might have fallen into his arms.

'It's all such a strain,' she admitted weakly. 'Being here with you, in this same building where…where it all started. Sometimes I think…'

He knelt down beside her, putting comforting arms around her, holding her head against his chest. His jacket had fallen open and she could feel the smooth texture of his silk shirt against her cheek, whilst the distinct scent of his cologne aroused those sensual memories.

'Sometimes you think what, *ma princesse*?' he whispered huskily in her ear.

'Don't, Pierre! Don't call me by that name. You know how—' She broke off as she felt her treacherous body reacting to his closeness.

Gently, he took hold of her hands and pulled her to her feet, so that he could mould his body against hers. She sighed as she felt the beloved contours of his body fitting against hers, as they had done so often before in that fantastic other world of years gone by. This was where she belonged, and she knew nothing could ever change that.

His lips claimed hers and she gave in, lovingly, to his gentle kiss. But a gentle kiss was not enough. She couldn't hold back her longing to be taken completely. This small token of love would always have been the precursor to something more satisfying. Her body needed consummation.

As his kiss deepened she revelled in the frisson of excitement, the liquid desires stirring deep down inside her, the feeling that this was so right for both of them, that they simply had to come together and make love until all their passions were spent…

'No!' She moved suddenly as the feeling of wild abandon threatened to engulf her senses. Looking up into his eyes, she smothered a groan. She wanted Pierre so much, but she mustn't allow herself to be carried away.

'Oh, Pierre,' she said softly, 'what are we going to do?'

He gazed down at her, his eyes, so full of love and longing, mirroring her own.

'You're the one who changed the rules, Alyssa. Are you telling me that you still have feelings for me in spite of…?'

'If you only knew!' she said, her body aching with the frustration and futility of the situation. 'If only—'

She broke off. She'd said too much already.

Pierre dropped his hands to his sides and took a step backwards, leaving a fair distance between them.

'Look, we can't go on like this.' He shook his head in despair.

Alyssa gazed at him, the object of all her affections, and longed to be taken in his arms again. But he was making an effort and so must she.

'Would you like me to leave the *clinique*?' she asked quietly.

He hesitated, before taking a deep breath. 'No, I think we can work this out together. It won't be long before I leave the *clinique* myself, and the problem will be solved anyway.'

He turned away and walked over to the window, staring out over the garden. 'Christmas is on its way, and then…' He turned, forcing himself to smile. 'What we need is some time together that isn't fraught with emotion. Let's go for a walk in the Bois de Boulogne, like we used to do when we had a problem to think through.'

She smiled back, her spirits lifting. 'When did we ever have a problem in those days?'

He took a step towards her, seemed to think better of it and began organising the top of his desk, his eyes intent on the task in hand.

'Oh, we had a few minor hitches, as I recall… Look, go and get out of that ridiculously severe suit and into something that won't spoil if you find yourself rolling amongst the leaves.'

Warning bells began ringing in the sensible part of her mind. 'I hadn't intended to roll in the leaves, Pierre.'

'Joke, Alyssa!' he said in an exasperated tone. 'It was supposed to be a joke. I know your days of rolling around on the ground having fun are well and truly over. You're much too sophisticated for anything so ridiculous.'

She bridled. Was that how he saw her now? A serious, sophisticated career woman? Well, that was the image she'd tried to portray, so she mustn't complain if she'd well and truly succeeded.

'I thought I was supposed to be on duty,' she muttered.

'There's nothing the orthopaedic team can't handle without you,' Pierre said firmly. 'And you need a couple of days off before you start on your new ward. Take the rest of the day off, and that's an order.'

As she turned to move towards the door he looked up from his desk. 'I'll come up and collect you from your room in about an hour. I've got to clear my desk and explain what's happening to my secretary.'

She turned at the door. 'And what *is* happening?' she asked softly, her heart beating so loudly she was sure he would hear it from the other side of the room.

He raised his eyes to hers. 'It's called getting to know you second time around—in a platonic way. We can't go on as we have been during the past three weeks, so it's off with the old and on with the new. And out there in the fresh air, with all those joggers flying past us, we can't get up to any mischief, can we?'

He was grinning at her, that wicked boyish grin that always made her body melt with longing. She yearned to go back into his arms, tell him that she didn't want to form a new relationship. The old one was all she needed.

In her room, Alyssa pulled off the detested suit. She'd thought she looked so smart in it, that it was perfect for her role of doctor in a prestigious *clinique*, but obviously Pierre didn't like the new image she portrayed.

She sat down on the bed for a moment, looking at the crumpled heap of clothes on the floor. Pierre had always preferred her in casual clothes, which were the only kind of clothes she'd possessed when she was last here. So he would approve of the old jeans she was going to put on for their walk in the Bois de Boulogne.

But should she really be seeking Pierre's approval? Did she want him to look at her and admire the way she looked? Wasn't she supposed to be keeping this relationship cool so that neither of them would hurt too much when it finished around Christmas?

She put the probing thoughts to the back of her mind, knowing full well that she wanted Pierre to look at her and admire her in the way he always had during their affair.

She'd always delighted in finding something that made his eyes sparkle with admiration, made his fingers reach for the fabric to check what it was made of. And then, at the end of the day, he would slowly remove the new garment, toss it on the floor and...

This kind of reminiscence would get her nowhere! If Pierre could make the effort to form a new workable relationship, then so could she. After all, it was harder for him. He was the one who thought she'd chosen to break up their affair. She was the only one who knew the truth.

Reaching into the bottom of the wardrobe, she pulled out the old jeans she'd stashed away in a pile of garments that she'd thought she probably wouldn't wear. At the time, when she'd unpacked her suitcase, she'd wondered why on earth she'd brought such a tatty pair of jeans from England. Likewise the white polo neck sweater that she'd mended where it had snagged when she and Pierre were in the woods one time.

But now she remembered quite clearly how she hadn't had the courage to throw out these two items from her wardrobe at home. She'd kept them because they reminded her of her wonderful walks in the Bois de Boulogne with Pierre. And, yes, once they had rolled in the leaves. It had been September, and some of the leaves had started to fall early. They'd been red and gold; she remembered the vivid colours as if it were only yesterday. Pierre had picked up a handful and tried to push them down the neck of her sweater, and they had finished up rolling on the ground, laughing as she made valiant but useless attempts to stop him from behaving like a demented teenager.

So that was why she'd brought these clothes to Paris in her suitcase! Simply to have them here as a dangerously nostalgic reminder of what had happened long, long ago in another life...

Someone was knocking on her door. Please don't let it be Pierre! I'm not ready…

She pulled up the zip on her jeans and struggled into the white sweater, smoothing it down over her tummy.

Running to the spyhole in her door, she looked through. Pierre's brown eyes stared back at her. She unlocked the door, running a hand through her very ruffled hair as she stood back to allow him to enter.

'I hadn't expected you so soon,' she said breathlessly, wishing she hadn't wasted so much time. 'I haven't finished my make-up, and…'

He stood near the door, looking down at her, his eyes full of undisguised admiration. 'I prefer you without make-up. I meant to tell you that before, but I didn't think it fell within my job specification as *médecin-chef* of the *clinique*.'

He looked around him. 'So this is where you live.'

'Small, but cosy, and I'm getting used to living in one room again. Although I have to say I hadn't intended to entertain the boss here.'

Pierre smiled. 'I thought it would be better if we didn't meet in the foyer, where everyone would see us going off for a walk in the middle of the day.'

'A perfectly innocuous walk.'

'Absolutely!'

She drew in her breath. 'Don't look at me like that, Pierre!'

He put his hands on her shoulders, his fingers smoothing over the rough texture of her sweater.

'Like what?' he said with mock innocence. 'I was simply trying to think where I've seen this sweater before, and now I remember.'

She held her breath. 'And where was that?'

'On the floor of my sitting room—and I do believe those are the jeans that went with it.'

'Pierre, don't remind me of—'

She broke off as she looked up into his eyes. It was no good. She couldn't hold out against this powerful feeling of love.

'Don't remind you of what?' he asked huskily.

'Pierre, I'm trying hard to control my feelings, but it's almost impossible. So...' Hesitantly she began to outline the plan that had sprung into her mind. 'I've been wondering if...if this new platonic relationship we're supposed to be having could include some innocuous lovemaking. Do you think we could have a light-hearted affair that will end at Christmas?'

He stared down at her with mock solemnity. 'You mean a sort of hello, goodbye, been nice knowing you sort of affair?'

His fingers tightened on her shoulders. She groaned with the agony of her frustration.

'Yes, yes—but don't make it sound so cold-blooded. I still feel... I'm still very fond of you, and being with you would...'

He lowered his head and covered her quivering lips. She sighed. Another second and she would have wept if Pierre hadn't kissed her. She knew she was being weak by giving in like this, but a light-hearted affair was the only solution that would save her sanity until she and Pierre had to split up again.

As she felt the excitement coursing through her she knew her body was out of control. With a sigh of delicious anticipation she gave herself up to the out-of-this-world experience that she knew would follow.

Pierre's hands were caressing her, gently fingering the restrictive garments. She tugged at her sweater, helping him to remove it. Slowly he unbuttoned the shirt underneath before reaching for the clasps at the back of her bra. She leaned forward to help him and put her hands on his chest to unbutton his shirt. She could feel the sensual pace quickening. They were both impatient to feel their skin touching, to feel the electric current of passion that had always shot through them at this point.

Gently he carried her over to the bed, shedding garments on the floor as they moved. She moaned with anticipation as he laid her down. As his body covered hers she gave herself up to the thrill of his caresses. His tantalising fingers were moving, exploring, turning her body into a fiery furnace of passion where the flames were growing hotter and hotter.

She strove to melt herself into his adored body, to make herself one with him, and when he entered her she gave a gasp of sheer ecstasy at the wonder of their renewed bonding. Her passions rose higher and higher as the rhythm of their coupling increased. Feeling him moving inside her, she wanted to weep with joy at this unbelievable union of souls who should never have been parted. And as the ultimate climax drove her to the heights of sensual delirium she cried out at the wonder of an experience made in heaven…

It was the shrilling of a mobile phone that wakened her. The distinctive sound wasn't her mobile, so whose was it? Then she remembered. Turning her head, she saw that the head on the pillow next to hers was Pierre's. The phone was still ringing, but he ignored it as he brought his lips down on hers.

'Let them leave a message,' he whispered huskily. 'I'm in no state to put on my *médecin-chef* voice and make decisions.'

She revelled in the touch of his lips, the saltiness of his damp skin. She couldn't recall how many times they'd made love. It had been the most momentous reunion of all time!

The phone stopped ringing. Pierre, taking his time, rolled out of the small bed and searched in his trouser pockets for his mobile. He climbed back into bed after checking the message. 'It's only my secretary. She says it's not urgent but she'd like me to call within the next hour. I'll get it over with so that we can go out for that walk we promised ourselves.'

He lay back against the pillow as he phoned his secretary. Alyssa smiled as she heard him saying how delightful it was to be out in the Bois de Boulogne. The trees were a bit bare but...

Alyssa smothered a giggle as Pierre's hand strayed across her breasts whilst he was speaking. He was talking in an efficient, no-nonsense voice that would convince his secretary that everything was under control. He might be taking a few hours off, but he still had his finger on the pulse.

He put the phone down and rolled over to look at her. 'Sidonie wanted to know which surgical consultant she should call in for an operation scheduled for two days' time. The surgical firm can't come to an agreement and I have the casting vote on these occasions. I've given her the names of two suitable consultants that she can contact. Now, where were we...?'

'Don't you think we should go for that walk now?'

Pierre grinned. 'I think you're right. Otherwise we could be here a long time.'

He reached forward and kissed her gently on the lips. 'It's so wonderful to be with you again, Alyssa. I wish we'd thought of this sooner. A light-hearted affair that will finish at Christmas. What a brainwave!'

She swallowed hard as she felt the tears pricking at the back of her eyes. The thought of splitting up from Pierre again was impossibly cruel. She wouldn't think about it while they were together again. She would live for the moment, as she was doing now.

Quickly she pulled herself away and got out of bed. 'Race you to the shower!'

Pierre's long legs overtook her, and he was able to pull her—all the while making mock protestations—into the tiny shower with him. He turned on the wrong tap and cold water cascaded over them, causing her to scream. Laughing, he found the other tap, holding her against his comfortingly warm body, caressing her gently. And then he was rubbing scented foam over her as the water soothed her.

Her nerve-endings were still highly charged, sensitively alive with the excitement of their lovemaking. She was still on cloud nine. Even the cold water that had initially startled her couldn't dampen her high spirits. But at some point she knew she would have to return to earth.

Somehow Alyssa managed to convince herself that a walk in the Bois de Boulogne was a better idea than returning to bed with Pierre. From the vibes she was getting she knew that Pierre thought otherwise, but she wanted to see how their new relationship would hold up when they got outside into the cold afternoon.

It was an unreal situation that they were in. They'd both gone back to the easygoing rapport that had existed between them before. It had been so easy to make love together, so natural, and yet so out of this world. It was as if they'd never been apart, and yet, at the back of her mind, Alyssa had to accept that it was only a temporary situation.

She had to enjoy every stolen moment and then steel herself to say goodbye.

Christmas would be a time of parting.

Pulling on her sweater, she turned to look at Pierre, who was fully clothed and waiting for her already.

'When exactly is Dr Cheveny coming back?' she asked, trying to sound light-hearted and failing miserably.

'He's making good progress and should be back around Christmas. Just before or just after. His cardiac specialist isn't sure when it will be, but apparently François is keen to take up the reins again. At the moment he's convalescing at his house in Provence, but he's due back in Paris next week.'

She swallowed hard. 'It will be good to see him again. I always found him to be very sympathetic—especially so when I had my interview.'

She turned away so that Pierre couldn't see the moistness in her eyes. 'Come on, let's go for that walk.'

As they crossed the little bridge over the old railway line at the top of the street they looked down into the small park beyond. The red and golden leaves had fallen from the trees and, interlaced in the stark brown winter branches, chains of pre-Christmas lights twinkled, giving the impression of glow worms at the height of summer. The façades of the grand houses around the park, where preparations for Christmas were well under way, had shining lights beamed upon them from their well-tended gardens.

A couple of joggers passed them on their way to the paths that criss-crossed the Bois, and it seemed only natural that Pierre should hold her hand. She wondered how the other medical staff would view them if they were to meet anyone they knew. But she found she didn't care what anyone thought, so long as Pierre didn't. He was the one with something to lose. He was the one who had to find himself a suitable wife at some point. Whereas she only had to content herself with a light-hearted affair.

They walked along the path they'd usually taken before, which led to the Lac Supérieur, the larger of the two lakes in the Bois. The afternoon sunshine was quite warm and they sat down on a seat, watching the sparkling of the sun on the water.

Pierre's fingers firmly enclosing hers gave her a false sense of security. If she closed her eyes now she could return to those heady days when their future together had seemed secure. But she knew she must keep reminding herself that this was only temporary. They had three weeks to enjoy their affair, and then...

'When are you planning to go back to the West Indies, Pierre?'

She was trying so hard to sound as if it didn't affect her, but even to her own ears it didn't sound like that.

'I have to be back there at the beginning of the New Year. My post has been covered by a locum for three months. Every couple of years the medical service out there gives me a three-month holiday. I usually spend part of the time in Paris and then travel somewhere.'

'It sounds an idyllic life.'

'It is.' He hesitated, knowing he was pushing his luck. 'You're not tempted to join me?'

She drew in her breath. 'That's your life, Pierre, not mine. I...I must make my own life.'

'I can see you're still hell-bent on being independent,' he said quietly. 'And I can't help admiring you for sticking to your principles. But I wonder how you'll feel as you grow older and—'

'Don't, Pierre! Please leave me to make my own decisions,' she said quickly. 'Tell me, what exactly do you do when you're working in the West Indies?'

'I'm in charge of the medical care of the inhabitants of a group of islands. Ste Cécile is a beautiful French-speaking island, where I run the medical centre. It's the island where I was born. My father was the doctor there before me. When he retired eight years ago I applied for the post and was accepted.'

'Eight years ago,' Alyssa repeated softly. 'So that was when you left the *clinique*.'

Pierre nodded. 'That was after I asked you to marry me, so that you could come with me and share my life. When you went back to England you gave me the impression that as soon as you'd finished your medical training—'

'Pierre, it wasn't as simple as that. Please don't—'

'OK, OK, I'm sorry. I get the message. I don't understand what you're trying to do, but I'm sure you've got it all worked out in that complicated head of yours. You seem to be a bit mixed up, and you're sending out some weird signals, but I'll leave you to work out your own future. Even though I can't help worrying about your happiness.'

He put an arm round her shoulders in a comforting gesture. 'I'd forgotten that we were supposed to be having a light-hearted affair. It's so easy to slip into our old relationship when we're sitting together here on our favourite seat.'

He jumped up decisively, taking hold of her hands and drawing her to her feet. 'Let's walk again. Talking about the past only makes it worse. We've got to live in the present and enjoy it while we can.'

They took a narrow path through the woods, Pierre hurrying ahead as the remains of the autumn leaves rustled beneath their feet. Alyssa longed for him to turn round and take her in his arms. That was how he would have behaved in yesterday's romance. But she knew that in this new, artificially constructed temporary relationship they mustn't be too demonstrative in public. Besides, they were eight years older and possibly eight years wiser.

When he finally turned to look at her, as they reached the main road that encircled the Bois, he was smiling his assured, confident smile. Alyssa could see that he'd obviously come to terms with their new situation.

'Would you like to come back to the apartment for supper? Something simple, like one of my omelettes?'

Alyssa smiled. 'You must have read my thoughts. I'm absolutely starving.'

He touched the side of her cheek as he looked down at her with a fond expression. 'So am I. It's been an energetic day and we missed lunch, as I recall.'

'I'd forgotten all about lunch,' she said, looking up into Pierre's eyes as she felt the inevitable stirring of excitement at the prospect of a whole evening with him.

'We had better things to think about,' he murmured huskily. 'Come on, it's getting dark.'

'And cold,' Alyssa said, shivering.

Pierre put his arm round her, as she'd hoped he would. Maybe he wasn't too worried about them being seen in a compromising situation after all. Her heart lifted in spite of the fact that she reminded herself once more she was in a temporary situation. There was no harm in enjoying every moment of her time with Pierre.

CHAPTER FIVE

PIERRE'S apartment was just as Alyssa remembered it. Nothing had changed. The sofa and chairs were still comfortably squashy. Slightly shabbier now, but as infinitely inviting as they always had been. She sank down on to the sofa and put her head back on one of the cushions.

'I was afraid you might have changed everything, Pierre.'

He laughed wryly. 'No chance. I hate change. That's why I'm still living on the island where I was born. But I know I'll have to have this place refurbished soon, or I won't be able to get any tenants to rent it when I go back home to Ste Cécile.'

'I don't think you should change anything,' she said quickly. 'Have you got tenants lined up for next year?'

'Not yet. That's when I was planning to have the refurbishment done.'

An embryonic idea was stirring in her mind. 'If the rent isn't too exorbitant I'd love to take it on.'

'You?' Pierre was staring at her with a puzzled expression on his face. 'Why on earth would you want to live here? I thought you were going to move on again when your contract expired with the *clinique* next May.'

'Well, for a start it's more spacious than my room at the *clinique*,' she improvised. 'And I may want to stay on in Paris—extend my contract, if that's possible, or find another position if it's not.'

She knew she mustn't explain that it would mean she could always be in touch with Pierre. Once she'd con-

quered her jealousy at the thought of him having a relationship that would lead to marriage and a family she could
see him from time to time. That way her heart wouldn't
break whenever she had to say goodbye. Having renewed
their love again, she knew goodbyes would be agony.

'Well, if you're sure you'd like to rent it we'll come to
some amicable arrangement,' he said slowly.

'Why don't I take it on for six months from January?'
she suggested. 'That will see me through to the end of my
contract with a little time at the end to sort out what I'm
going to do next. I can let you know in the spring what
my plans are.'

By the spring she hoped she would have made up her
mind what she was going to do with the rest of her life.
Starting an affair with Pierre again was going to be a life-
shattering experience. She no longer knew what she
wanted from life, nor where she wanted to go. For the
moment she would simply coast, get through one day at a
time until it was time to say goodbye. Maybe then her
rational thoughts would crystallise, but for the moment all
she wanted was to be with Pierre, to love him and be loved
by him until the time came for him to go back to the West
Indies.

'OK, that's a deal,' he said, his expression still curious.
'But if you change your mind…'

'I won't.'

'It has been known,' he said evenly.

She swallowed hard. 'Yes, but in matters of…er…business
I'm always scrupulously correct.'

'Glad to hear it. So, do you think you could whisk up
some scrupulously correct eggs while I nip out for some
salad and fresh bread? It's after five o'clock so the *bou-
langerie* will have freshly baked baguettes.'

'Mmm, yummy! Hurry back! I'm starving.'

*   *   *

Alone in Pierre's kitchen, Alyssa found herself singing quietly to herself as she whisked up the eggs.

'*'Il y avait les gros crocodiles et les orangoutans…*''

She smiled to herself as she realised it was years since she'd sung the little song she'd learned at the kids' club on a beach in Normandy where her grandmother had rented a holiday house one summer. She must be feeling happy and carefree again.

Looking around her, she felt a warm glow deep down inside at the realisation that this was going to be *her* kitchen soon. She would be able to close the doors on her own little kingdom, curl up on the sofa with a good book and feel that in some indefinable way Pierre was still part of her life.

'I'm back!'

Her heart lifted at the sound of Pierre's voice from the tiny hallway. She could hear him kicking off his shoes, putting his jacket in the hall wardrobe, padding over the soft carpet and then into the kitchen. He tossed a fresh baguette along with packets of lettuce, tomatoes, garlic and fresh herbs on to the wooden table.

'You look as if you've moved in already,' he said, coming up behind her and placing his arms around her waist.

She turned in his arms and standing on tiptoe lifted her face to his. Slowly he brought his lips down on hers. She savoured the kiss before gently pulling herself away.

'Your eggs are ready for the difficult omelette operation, sir. I've separated the yolks from the whites so you can do your fantastic soufflé omelette—which I remember used to be the *specialité de la maison* here in this kitchen. Is there anything else you would like me to do? Do you require a scalpel, scissors, local anaesthetic…?'

'You could wash the salad and then sit beside me on this stool and look beautiful.'

She laughed as she picked up the lettuce and walked over to the sink. 'I don't feel very beautiful in this old sweater.'

'You look radiant to me,' he said gently.

She knew that her radiance was something coming from within. She hadn't felt like this when she'd wakened this morning. But after spending most of the day with Pierre there had been a definite transformation.

They sat down at the wooden table when their meal was ready. Pierre sat at the head of the little table, Alyssa on his right side—just as they always had done.

The omelettes were delicious. Putting down her fork at the end of the meal, Alyssa reached across and took hold of Pierre's hand.

'The best omelette I've had in years.'

Pierre looked down at Alyssa's small fingers encircling his own. 'Haven't cooked an omelette like that for years.' He raised his eyes to hers. 'I've always stuck to the plain variety.'

The electric current throbbing between them as their eyes met was too poignant to bear. Looking at Pierre now, Alyssa could see he had that little boy lost look that always melted her heart. What was she doing, denying them both a future together? Why did their situation have to be so complicated?

She stood up and cupped his chin in her hands as she leaned forward to kiss him gently on the lips. 'I'm unsure about everything,' she said sadly. 'But I'm glad we're to-gether again for this brief time.'

He stood up and took her in his arms. 'It doesn't have to be brief. We could—'

Gently she put her finger against his lips. 'Trust me. It's for the best,' she whispered.

'Then let's make the most of every minute,' he said, his voice husky with passion.

She sighed with joyous anticipation as Pierre scooped her up into his arms and carried her through to his bedroom. Gently he laid her on his bed. This time their lovemaking was slow and unhurried—the lovemaking of a couple who'd satisfied every fibre of their physical being earlier in the day but still wanted to reaffirm their love for each other.

She leaned back against the pillows, running her hands over his strong, muscular, athletic body as his caresses started to drive her wild. This night would be their eternity. She would pretend there was no ending to this blissful encounter…

Alyssa awoke with a start and reached out to silence the phone before realising that she wasn't in her own bed. Her body tingled with the aftermath of their lovemaking. She had never experienced such magical passion with Pierre before.

Still remaining in her relaxed euphoric state, she felt a pang of dismay when she heard Pierre telling whoever it was on the phone that he would be at the *clinique* as quickly as possible. Yes, he would meet them there.

She rolled on her side. 'Who was that?'

'Henri Fontaine's wife. You remember Henri? The *clinique* gardener with the shattered leg?'

'Of course. He went home about two weeks ago. What's the problem?'

Pierre was already out of bed, pulling on his trousers, buttoning up his shirt and reaching for his jacket.

'Henri's wife says he's running a high temperature. She

didn't know who to call at the *clinique* so she rang me here. I've told her to bring him back to the *clinique* immediately.'

Alyssa leapt out of bed and reached for her clothes. 'I'll come with you. Sounds as if there could be some infection—either in the bone or the surrounding tissues.'

'Let's hope not. But whatever it is, we must deal with it quickly.'

The lights of the *clinique* were dimmed as Alyssa and Pierre made their way in through the side entrance that led to their small emergency area. Alyssa prepared a patient trolley as they waited for Henri and his wife to arrive. As their car pulled up in front of the *clinique*, they hurried outside.

Madame Fontaine was distraught with worry.

'When I realised how high Henri's temperature was tonight, I knew I couldn't ignore his fever any longer.'

'How long has Henri had a high temperature?' Alyssa asked, as she helped Pierre to manoeuvre the trolley into the treatment area.

'About five days. I thought it was a cold coming on, or a touch of *la grippe*.'

Alyssa nodded. *La grippe*—or flu, as it was called in England—was common in Paris during the winter, and did cause a high temperature, so she could understand Madame Fontaine coming to that conclusion. But with Henri's history of a recent orthopaedic operation it might not be the correct diagnosis.

She looked down at Henri, lying so uncharacteristically still with a worried expression on his face. 'Don't worry, Henri. We'll soon find out what's the matter with you and—'

'It's my leg, isn't it?' Henri said plaintively. 'It's got

nothing to do with *la grippe*. I told Marcelle to bring me back to the *clinique* two days ago, but...'

'Well, you're here now, Henri,' Pierre said quickly. 'Now, I'm just going to open up the window in your plaster to take a look at what's happening.'

Alyssa leaned across their patient as Pierre removed the section of plaster which had been left as an observation window. She could immediately see that there was inflammation and redness around the post-operative wound, which was a clear indication that there was internal infection.

She looked across at Pierre, waiting for him to explain the situation to Henri.

'I'm going to remove your plaster entirely, Henri,' he said carefully. 'We need to see exactly what's going on, but it looks as if there is some infection in your leg. I'm going to put you on intravenous antibiotics and call in Monsieur Grandet—the surgeon who performed your operation.'

'Whatever you say, Doctor,' Henri said in a resigned tone.

'I'll fix a canula in Henri's arm for the antibiotics,' Alyssa said. She turned to look at Henri's wife, who was once more voicing her worried concern about her husband. 'Would you like to take a rest in the little sitting room at the top of the steps, *madame*?'

Madame Fontaine agreed that she would, seemingly relieved to let Alyssa and Pierre take over from her. She'd obviously had a worrying time since Henri fell from his ladder. Pierre had told Alyssa that the *clinique* was continuing to pay Henri's wages, but with the serious state of his leg his wife must have been wondering if her husband would ever be able to continue in his physically demanding job. Coupled with her concern for Henri's health, she had a heavy load on her shoulders.

After Pierre had removed the plaster Alyssa examined the site of the wound. It was badly infected. Pierre drew her to one side to discuss the situation.

'When Yves arrives I think he'll want to take Henri to Theatre,' Pierre said. 'The night staff will provide me with a couple of theatre nurses. I'll arrange for an anaesthetist to come in. In view of your past experience of orthopaedic surgery, would you be willing to assist Yves?'

Alyssa nodded. 'Of course. I'm thinking it could be the steel plates holding the bones in place that are the source of infection. It sometimes happens in patients who've had a complicated fracture—especially if the fractured bones were exposed through the skin at the time of the accident. If there is some infection, it will gravitate and stay around the steel plates. Some patients tolerate internal plating better than others. My guess is that Monsieur Grandet will take out the plates and put external steel rods through the bones to hold them in position.'

'That seems a very good solution to me,' Yves Grandet said, coming in through the door and overhearing what Alyssa was saying.

'*Bonsoir*, Yves,' Pierre said. 'Yes, I think Alyssa will prove to be a good orthopaedic assistant for you.'

'I'm sure she will.'

'I'll be on hand to help if there are problems with closing up the skin,' Pierre told Yves. 'The infection has eroded the area around the initial wound, and some skin grafting may be necessary to help the healing process.'

Yves nodded. 'I remember you specialised in plastic surgery at one point in your career, didn't you? That could be useful to me.'

Alyssa looked up at Pierre questioningly. 'I didn't know you'd worked in plastic surgery.'

'There are a lot of things you don't know about me,' Pierre said quietly. 'I worked in a specialist burns hospital just outside Paris soon after I qualified.'

'You would have made a very fine plastic surgeon,' Yves said, as he leaned over their patient to take a better look at the injured leg. 'But I remember talking to Claude, your father, when he came back to Paris one time. He told me you had this dream of living in the sun on the island where you were born, surrounded by your own large family. He was looking forward to all those grandchildren. Can't think why you're still a bachelor, my boy.'

Alyssa glanced at Pierre and was relieved that he remained silent, his expression giving nothing away.

As the genial orthopaedic consultant examined Henri's leg his expression swiftly changed to concern. Quickly he outlined what he was going to do in Theatre, giving his patient as much information as he thought he would understand.

'So I'm going to Theatre now, am I?' Henri asked in surprise.

Yves nodded. 'The sooner I take a look and find out why your leg is infected the better.' He turned to Pierre. 'How long before the theatre will be ready?'

'It's ready now. And I've almost completed organising the theatre team. As I said, Alyssa will assist you. She's had wide experience of orthopaedic surgery and—'

'Oh, I know all about Alyssa's credentials,' Yves interrupted. 'I checked her out when she first arrived here and went to work with the orthopaedic team. I have to say I've been impressed with her work. She's a very good doctor. Now she'll have to prove to me she's a good orthopaedic surgeon.'

'But you'll be doing the operation, *m'sieur*, won't you?' Alyssa said quickly.

Yves Grandet smiled benignly. 'Of course. But I'll need your expert help.'

With the rest of the theatre team gathered around the operating table, fully gowned and masked, Alyssa waited for Yves to begin the operation. She watched as he carefully opened up the wound from the previous operation. Inside the tissues were inflamed, but the bones appeared to be healthy.

Alyssa leaned forward and took a swab from the infected tissue before placing it in a sterile test tube. Handing it to a nurse, she instructed her on how to label it so that it could be taken to the path lab for histology. Once they had discovered which specific organism was causing the infection they could deal more easily with an antibiotic cure.

Holding back the surrounding tissues with sterile retractors, Alyssa ensured that the orthopaedic consultant had a clear view of the infected area.

'You were quite right, Alyssa,' Yves muttered. 'The infection is all centred around the plates. I'm going to take them out and—'

He broke off, glancing towards Pierre who, also fully gowned and masked, was awaiting further instructions. 'Have you got the steel fixators I asked for, Pierre?'

'They've just arrived,' he said, handing the sterile steel rods to Alyssa.

Yves proceeded to discard the infected plates, before taking the rods from Alyssa and screwing them through the bones to hold them in place. When four fixators had been screwed through the tibia—the main bone running down the front of the leg—and the calcaneum—the heel bone—Yves stood back for a moment to review the situation.

'What do you think, Alyssa?' he said, peering at her over the top of his mask. 'Will that hold the bones in place, do you think?'

He was one of the few men who were barely any taller than she was, and Alyssa felt very comfortable looking eye to eye with this eminent surgeon and giving him her opinion.

'I think the fixators will hold the bones. But there isn't a very good blood supply in that area. Henri's legs are particularly thin around the ankle, so I was wondering if we should do a flap.'

Yves nodded approvingly. 'That's what I was thinking, Alyssa. You've obviously worked on this problem before. Yes, if I turn back a flap of flesh to cover the affected area we'll get a better blood supply to aid the healing process.'

'But turning back a flap will mean that a sizeable area of the leg is exposed without skin, so...' Alyssa looked across at Pierre. 'That's where we'll need your help, Pierre. Can you find a suitable donor site from which to transpose the necessary skin?'

Pierre nodded. 'Yes, I know exactly what I'll do.'

'Don't know why I bothered to come in,' Yves said, with the hint of a chuckle in his voice. 'The two of you could have managed very well without me.'

Yves turned to look at Pierre and Alyssa could see that the eyes above the surgeon's mask were smiling. 'So, where do you propose to transpose this skin from, Pierre?'

'Top of Henri's left thigh...just here,' Pierre said, leaning forward to prepare the donor site. 'Good healthy skin like this is going to serve the purpose.'

Pierre scraped small slivers of skin from the surface epithelium of Henri's thigh, leaving the lower layers of the skin intact, before transferring the tiny slivers to the exposed skinless area of the lower leg. Then he fixed a string of special gentamycin beads near the surface of this area of tissue.

The junior theatre nurse, who hadn't seen gentamycin beads used before, asked Alyssa to explain their purpose.

'Gentamycin beads give antibiotic cover inside the leg for three to four weeks,' Alyssa told the nurse. 'So in about a month, when they've served their purpose, we'll remove them.'

'Does that mean Henri will have to have another operation?' the nurse asked.

'Just a minor operation under local anaesthetic,' Alyssa explained.

As Alyssa finished sewing up the wound at the end of the operation she was careful to leave one of the gentamycin beads outside the wound, to indicate where they were. After this, she stood back to take a critical look at Henri's leg. Pierre moved forward to inspect the finished results more closely.

'Well done, Yves!' Pierre said, before looking down at Alyssa. 'And well done to your surgical assistant.'

Watching Pierre now, Alyssa could see that his eyes were full of admiration.

'Thank you, *m'sieur*,' she said demurely.

'Henri can go to the orthopaedic ward as soon as he comes round,' Yves said, pulling off his gloves and throwing them in the general direction of one of the bins. 'Will you be able to stay on, Alyssa? The first few hours will be critical, and I need a good orthopaedic doctor to be on hand.'

'Of course,' she said. 'I'd like to make sure that nothing goes wrong.'

Yves nodded approvingly. *'Bon!'* He glanced at Pierre.

'Not only beautiful, but talented as well. What a find! I hope you're going to extend Alyssa's contract at the *clinique* for a long time, Pierre.'

'Actually, Yves, it won't be up to me,' Pierre said quietly. 'François Cheveny will be returning around Christmas to take over again.'

'Ah! Well, you must give Alyssa a good report when you speak to François. How is he, by the way? I heard...'

The two men were deep in conversation as they left the theatre, and Alyssa was glad that neither of them had asked her whether she *wanted* to extend her contract. For the moment she wasn't going to think any further than next June. She was going to make the most of her few weeks with Pierre, then she would work through the New Year and the spring, enjoying the fact that she was living in Pierre's apartment.

Earlier in the evening, the idea of staying on as long as she could at the *clinique* and in Pierre's apartment had seemed appealing. But now she wasn't so sure she could handle the emotional turbulence she would experience when Pierre finally found himself a wife. Remaining emotionally detached from a situation like that would be well-nigh impossible.

Better to finish her contract at the end of May, stay on for a couple of weeks to get the apartment ready for the next tenant and then move on. But where she would move to was utterly uncertain. Being with Pierre was proving to be an earth-shattering experience that was causing emotional and mental turbulence. Her future plans were becoming more and more complicated and uncertain...

Someone had put a hand on her shoulder. Alyssa opened her eyes and found a junior nurse smiling down at her.

'You fell asleep, Doctor. Would you like *un petit café noir*?'

Alyssa smiled back, accepting the tiny coffee cup that the nurse was holding out to her. The lights in the orthopaedic ward were being switched on as the nurses began their morning routine. She took a sip of the coffee before placing the cup on her patient's bedside locker. Standing up, she began to readjust the flow of Henri's intravenous drip.

Her patient opened his eyes. 'You still here, Dr Alyssa? I thought you'd have gone to your bed by now. Have you been here all night?'

'Yes, I have, Henri.' She leaned over to examine Henri's leg. Carefully, she adjusted the tube which was draining the infected area. She'd fixed the leg on a rigid plaster back slab to keep it immobile after the operation.

'What are those spikes sticking out of my leg?'

'Those are holding the bones in position, Henri. We had to take out the steel plates because they were acting as a source of infection. That was why you were getting such a high temperature. Your temperature is almost normal again this morning, thanks to the antibiotics.'

'Thanks for all you're doing for me, Doctor.' Henri looked up as Pierre arrived at the bedside. 'I was just saying to Dr Alyssa, it's time she went to bed.'

'That's precisely what I was going to tell her, Henri,' Pierre said.

Alyssa turned and smiled at Pierre. 'I'm OK. Once I've handed over to the orthopaedic team I'll get some sleep. I actually fell asleep in the chair for a little while.'

'I'm not surprised. I'll stay with Henri until Sylvie comes on duty,' Pierre said firmly. 'Take the rest of the day off, and tomorrow as well. Like I said, you need a break before you start work in obstetrics.'

'Alyssa isn't leaving us, is she?' Henri asked anxiously.

Alyssa smiled down at her patient. 'I'm afraid so. But I'll keep popping in to see how you're getting on, Henri.'

'I hope you will,' Henri told her.

Pierre waited until Alyssa had said her goodbyes to the patients she'd worked with most recently. She had to promise all of them that she would return to visit them from time to time. As she made for the swing doors that led away from the main ward, Pierre caught up with her.

'May I see you this evening?' he murmured.

She smiled. 'What did you have in mind?'

'I'll try to get tickets for one of the pre-Christmas concerts at the Ste Chappelle. A small choir and orchestra are doing a series of concerts performing baroque music with a Christmas theme.'

'Sounds interesting.'

'And afterwards I thought we could walk along the Seine, find a little restaurant somewhere and...'

'You just talked me into it,' she said, hoping that she would be able to sleep for a few hours now that she was livening up again. She didn't want to be tired this evening. There weren't many more evenings with Pierre left.

As Alyssa walked into the obstetrics and gynaecology unit she was greeted by the sister in charge. Jacqueline Montigny, a tall, imposing woman in her early fifties, hurried down the ward towards her.

'Ah, Alyssa. How nice to see you again,' the sister said.

Alyssa smiled as she shook the outstretched hand. She'd been introduced to Jacqueline soon after she'd arrived at the *clinique* and found the sister to be friendly and helpful.

'Welcome to obstetrics. According to Pierre, you've had a lot of experience in obstetrics and gynaecology, so I'm sure you're going to be a valuable member of our team.

A new patient has just arrived and I'd be grateful if you could give me some help. Her name is Marie Lefevre.'

Alyssa walked back down the ward with Jacqueline, who paused in front of the bed of a young woman who was sobbing quietly, her hands clutching the sheet that covered her.

'The doctor is here to see you now, Marie,' Jacqueline said, handing a case history file to Alyssa. 'There's very little information in here yet, Doctor, so I'll leave you to it…'

Alyssa bent over her patient and took hold of her hand. 'Now, tell me all about yourself, Marie.'

Marie stifled her sobs. 'I've got this awful pain, Doctor—down here.'

Alyssa pulled the curtains round her patient and turned back the covers on the bed. Marie was indicating the lower right side of her body. Alyssa placed her fingers gently on the affected area and her patient winced.

'I haven't had a period for three months, Doctor, and I know I'm pregnant, although I haven't checked with my doctor. I haven't even told my husband yet, because I've already had two miscarriages and I was waiting until this pregnancy was more established before I told him. Charles is just longing for me to have a baby and I don't want to disappoint him again.'

Alyssa, palpating the abdomen, could feel the tense muscles guarding the tender area. Her awful suspicions were being confirmed and it was all too close to home for her. She was trying to be professional, but flashes of memory kept on reminding her of the devastating time when she herself had been rushed into hospital suffering from an ectopic pregnancy.

'I'm going to examine you, Marie,' Alyssa said in a calm, professional tone.

As she turned to take a pair of sterile gloves from the trolley which a staff nurse had wheeled in, she steeled herself against any emotional involvement. She owed it to this poor, suffering patient to give her all the help and expert care that she needed.

Gently she examined inside the patient's vagina. It wasn't necessary to examine too far because the tell tale signs were there. A brownish discharge—usually referred to as the prune juice discharge—pointed to the obvious diagnosis. Further examination revealed extreme tenderness over the affected Fallopian tube, where Alyssa suspected a tiny embryo had implanted itself instead of into the wall of the womb.

Alyssa peeled off the sterile gloves and glanced at the temperature reading which the staff nurse had produced. She swallowed hard. All the cardinal signs of an ectopic pregnancy were there in front of her. A much-wanted baby was about to terminate its struggle for survival. It held no chance as it grew in the Fallopian tube, and if they didn't get this patient into Theatre and remove the affected tube as soon as possible the tube would rupture with dangerous consequences. The mother's life was at stake as well.

'We're going to take you to the operating theatre, Marie,' Alyssa said gently.

'There's nothing wrong with the baby, is there? I only went to the doctor this morning because I had a pain down here. As I said, I hadn't even told the doctor I thought I was pregnant and... Oh, say I'm not going to lose this one, Doctor. Go on—say it...'

Jacqueline came hurrying through the curtains. 'There, there, Marie. What on earth is the matter?'

The sister glanced at Alyssa's ashen face. 'Are you all right, Doctor?'

'Yes, I'm fine, Sister,' Alyssa said briskly. She lowered

her voice. 'I've examined Marie and I think we should take her to Theatre for an immediate laparoscopy. If, as I suspect, this reveals a tubal pregnancy we'll need a laparotomy to ligate bleeding points and remove the tube.'

'I'll phone Theatre now,' Jacqueline said quickly. 'Staff Nurse will prepare the patient and—'

'Minimum preparation,' Alyssa instructed. 'The main thing is for Marie to be operated on as quickly as possible. She may need a blood transfusion, so I'm going to take a blood sample for grouping and cross-matching, and then I'll set up an intravenous saline drip.'

Jacqueline nodded in agreement before hurrying away.

'I'm going to lose the baby, aren't I, Doctor?' Marie said, her voice shaky but quiet and resigned now.

Alyssa straightened up from taking the blood sample, her heart full of compassion for the ordeal her patient was going through. And she knew, from her own traumatic experience, that the agony had barely started. When the full realisation that this much-wanted baby wasn't going to make it set in...

Alyssa cleared her throat. 'We're doing all we can, Marie. I can't predict how things will go in Theatre, but you're in good hands. I'll make a point of being here when you get back.'

Marie reached out and took hold of Alyssa's hand, squeezing it tightly as the tears ran down her cheeks.

'Make sure you're here, Doctor. You seem to know what I'm going through.'

Alyssa reached for a tissue, dabbing at the moist patches beneath her patient's eyes. She was being most unprofessional, she knew, but even though she was a doctor she was only human. She was beginning to find it impossibly difficult to cope with a situation that provoked so many unhappy memories.

'I'll be here, Marie,' she told her patient, in a calm voice which belied the traumatic turmoil of her emotions.

'So, how did your first day in obstetrics go?' Pierre asked as they sat in a little bar overlooking the Seine. 'You've been unusually quiet all evening. I'm beginning to get the impression you're not happy about something.'

Alyssa took a sip of her wine. The concert they'd attended should have been an uplifting occasion, but she'd found it difficult to concentrate on the music.

There had been no tickets available for the concert in the Ste Chappelle two days ago, so Pierre had bought tickets for this evening, and Alyssa had been looking forward to hearing the prestigious choir and orchestra performing Christmas music. But caring for her ectopic patient, seeing her go through the agonies that she herself had gone through, had been so traumatic that she felt unable to switch off and relax.

Explaining to Marie the implications of the surgical removal of her Fallopian tube when she'd come back to the ward after the operation had left Alyssa feeling drained and emotionally exhausted.

'I'm perfectly happy with the obstetrics unit,' Alyssa said with false brightness. 'I'm a bit tired, that's all. But the concert was so wonderful tonight—it helped to raise my spirits again. I thought the Bach was superb, and listening to it in such a beautiful setting made the music seem to soar up to the high ceiling and pour out through those exquisite stained glass windows…'

'Alyssa, you're not a music critic, preparing your piece for the culture page in *Le Figaro*,' Pierre said gently.

He reached across the table and covered her hand with his own as he interrupted her eulogy. 'You don't fool me one bit. Tell me why you don't like working in obstetrics and then we'll go on to discuss the concert. Until I know what's troubling you I—'

'There's nothing wrong. I do like working in obstetrics. I really do.' Alyssa swallowed hard, hesitating before she continued, 'I got a bit upset about one of the patients who was having a hard time, that's all.'

'You mustn't let yourself become too involved,' he said gently. 'Who was this patient?'

'Oh…a patient called Marie Lefevre. She…she was suffering from an ectopic pregnancy. The foetus was growing in her Fallopian tube, so I arranged for her to be taken down to Theatre and—'

Alyssa could hear her own voice breaking up. She couldn't go on in front of Pierre. It was all too reminiscent of her own traumatic experience eight years ago.

'Go on, take your time, Alyssa.' Pierre's eyes were both sympathetic and questioning. 'I've read the report on Marie, but I can't see why it should affect you like this. Yes, ectopic pregnancies are always traumatic. But you must have experienced numerous ectopic pregnancies during your career. I would have thought—'

'I need some fresh air.' Alyssa stood up. 'It's too stuffy in here. Let's go outside.'

She hurried outside, walking across the cobbled road to lean against the wall that flanked the footpath at the side of the river. Staring out across the deep swirling waters of the Seine, she tried to dispel the images of her own trauma when she'd come round from the anaesthetic to be told she'd lost the baby, had the affected tube removed and, because of complications, would be unlikely ever to conceive again.

She didn't turn as she heard Pierre's footsteps behind her. His arm encircling her shoulders gave her comfort, but she still felt terribly alone in an impossible situation.

'Let's walk along the river path, Pierre.' She moved away from the warmth of his arm.

He took her hand in his, holding it firmly as they walked side by side. She glanced up at the pale December moon. There had been a moon like this peeping through the hospital window on that fateful night when she'd lost their baby.

Suddenly Alyssa knew she couldn't go on alone. This was a problem she had to share with Pierre. Whatever the outcome, she couldn't continue to shoulder this awful burden.

She stopped walking and turned to look up at Pierre. 'You said you thought I must have experienced ectopic pregnancies before and coped with them... Well, yes, I have. Quite a few, in fact. One in particular was...'

'Go on, Alyssa,' he said gently, putting his hands on either side of her shoulders and drawing her towards him.

'I experienced...I went through an ectopic pregnancy myself,' she said, trying to put herself on automatic pilot so that she could continue without breaking down. She didn't know why she was telling Pierre now. It would only make matters worse. But she needed to confide in him, to unburden herself of the secret she'd kept from him so long.

She looked up at the moon again, seeking some kind of inspiration as to how she could best get all this off her chest without hurting Pierre too much.

'There was a December moon just like this on the night I lost my baby,' she said, her voice quivering with emotion.

Pierre's expression was agonisingly tender as he looked down at her, his hands tightening on her shoulders before he moved round to encircle her in his arms.

'A December moon? How long ago was this, Alyssa?' For a few seconds she remained silent. But she knew she must go on and tell Pierre everything. She'd got this far. She had to finish what she was going to say to him.

One of the long Parisian *bateaux mouche* was slowly gliding past them. Alyssa looked at the bright lights fixed to the sides of the boat, twinkling out across the water, and realised that this was the moment when everything would change between her and Pierre. But she couldn't find the right words. She remained rooted to the spot, staring at the illuminated interior of the boat which was decorated in a Christmassy fashion for the happy diners who were sampling a Christmas menu.

'The ward was decorated ready for Christmas when I came back from Theatre, Pierre,' she said quietly. 'I remember looking up at a paper streamer above my head. One of the nurses had fixed it there, specially for me. I think it was meant to cheer me up, but…'

She couldn't go on.

Pierre held her so close now that she could feel the pounding of his heart.

'When was this, Alyssa?' he said softly.

'It was…it was eight years ago.'

Pierre released his grip and took a step backwards, staring down at her, his eyes registering bewilderment and disbelief.

'You were pregnant with our child and you didn't tell me?'

'I'd only just found out. I hadn't missed a period,' she said quickly, her thoughts gathering momentum now that she'd made the initial revelation. 'As we both know, that sometimes happens when the pregnancy occurs outside the uterus.'

She mustn't stop now. She could see the sadness in Pierre's expression, but she had to continue.

'I'd done a pregnancy test only the day before, because

I'd been experiencing nausea for a few weeks and my abdomen was beginning to feel tight and swollen. When the test turned out to be positive I phoned you, but all I got was your answering service. I didn't want to leave a message for you to call back because I was on duty for the rest of the day, and I didn't want to have to tell you in front of... Anyway, there was an emergency just as I was going off duty, and by the time I was free it was the middle of the night.'

'You could have wakened me,' Pierre said plaintively. 'With wonderful news like that I—'

'Don't, Pierre! Yes, it was wonderful news. And I thought I had plenty of time to tell you. But in the early hours of the next morning a searing pain in the area of my left Fallopian tube woke me up. I could feel the tense muscles over my abdomen and I knew...I just knew that I was going to lose our baby...'

'*Oh, ma petite princesse,*' Pierre whispered, gathering her back in his arms again. 'Why didn't you call me? I would have come straight over to be with you in hospital. You shouldn't have been alone. It was my baby as well as yours...'

'I knew how sad you would be if I did lose it, and I was hoping that the doctors would say there hadn't been too much damage. If they'd given me a healthy prognosis I would have called you after they removed the affected Fallopian tube and...and the tiny embryo inside. But...but the obstetrics consultant came to see me soon after I came round from the anaesthetic. He told me it had been a difficult operation which had left me with scar tissue and adhesions. He said it was unlikely that I would ever get pregnant again.'

'But that was straight after the operation, Alyssa!' Pierre

cupped her face in his hands, gazing down at her with an anguished expression. 'You would have healed and—'

'No, no.' Alyssa shook her head.

'I was married for four years. Mike had said he didn't want children when I told him I was unlikely to conceive, and at the beginning of our marriage he was relieved about that. After two years Mike changed his mind. Until that time I'd been taking the Pill, because Mike was so dead against starting a family and insisted I take it just in case. When he had this change of heart I stopped taking it. After two years I still wasn't pregnant. That was when Mike told me he was having an affair with Rachel, one of our friends. She was pregnant, so he decided to leave me and move in with her.'

'Sounds like you were well rid of him. But I can't understand why you haven't told me all this before.'

She looked up into his eyes and couldn't bear to see the anxious, hurt expression.

'It's because I love you, Pierre,' she said brokenly. 'I want you to move on and be happy with someone who can give you the family you want. Someone who—'

'But I don't want anyone else. I want you!'

CHAPTER SIX

ALYSSA stared at Pierre, deeply moved by his passionate outburst. She hadn't expected him to believe so positively that a childless relationship between them would be enough for him.

'Yes, I can believe, at this moment, that you think our relationship is worth more to you than having a family,' she said slowly.

'But it is! It's all that matters to me.' Pierre drew her closer in his arms, bending down so that his face was nestling against her hair.

By the pale light of the moon and the overhead lights from the riverside road, Alyssa could see a young couple walking hand in hand towards them. She could feel the trembling of Pierre's body against her own. This wasn't the place to discuss life-shattering problems.

Gently she released herself from Pierre's arms. 'Take me home, Pierre.'

He held her at arm's length, looking down at her with a wistful expression. 'Home? Where's home?'

She gave him a sad smile. 'That was a slip of the tongue. I think I meant your apartment…soon to be my apartment…for a little while. That's where I feel most at home.'

Pierre drew her to him. 'We'll go up to the embankment and get a taxi.'

Alyssa curled her bare feet underneath her on the sofa, reaching up to take the glass of cognac that Pierre was holding out towards her.

'Sip that slowly, until you feel warmer and stronger,' Pierre said. 'It's purely medicinal—I usually find it works on patients who're suffering from shock.'

Alyssa studied Pierre's solemn expression. 'Yes, Doctor. But I thought you were the one who'd had the shock.'

He sat down beside her, cradling his own brandy glass with both hands. 'I've had a tremendous shock. But the full effect of *your* suffering has been delayed for eight years. I could tell you were reliving your traumatic experience down there on the footpath beside the river.'

Alyssa took a sip of her cognac, feeling strength flowing through her again as the fiery liquid revived her body.

'I've relived the experience every day of my life since I lost the baby,' she said slowly.

'But it would have been so much easier for you if you'd shared it with me, Alyssa.'

She turned towards him. 'I couldn't do that, Pierre. You would have tried to persuade me that the fact I can't have children doesn't matter to you…just like you're doing now. But I know that sooner or later you would have regretted being married to me. You want a family so much.'

'We could have adopted a baby.'

Alyssa leaned back against the cushions and closed her eyes. 'Do you remember that conversation we had eight years ago, when you said you wanted your own flesh and blood as family?'

Pierre was silent for a few moments. 'Yes, I remember saying that.'

'You were speaking from your own experience, weren't you? Because you yourself were adopted?'

He nodded slowly. 'Yes, that's why I feel like I do. Because I was an adopted child myself.'

'But you were born on the island of Ste Cécile, where your father was the doctor, weren't you?'

'I was,' Pierre said quietly.

He looked down into the golden liquid he was swirling around in his glass. Alyssa could hear the rasping sound of his laboured breath. She should tell him she didn't want to hear the details and spare him what seemed to be an ordeal.

'Pierre, if you don't want to tell me any more, I—'

'I want you to know everything about me,' he said quickly, turning his face towards hers. 'It's important you know exactly why I've always had this longing for my very own family.'

She remained silent as she looked up into his eyes, feeling deep compassion for the emotions he was experiencing.

'My birth mother was a young girl who ran away from home with her boyfriend. I was told that they camped out on the beach until my adoptive father noticing that my birth mother was pregnant, suggested they move into our house where he and Sabine, my adoptive mother, could take care of them. Sabine couldn't have children, and she was over the moon when a baby was born in our house.'

Alyssa reached across and took hold of Pierre's hand. Her heart ached for him as she felt the tremors of emotion that were running through him.

'My birth parents readily agreed to the idea that I should be adopted by Claude and Sabine. So as soon as Claude's lawyer had dealt with the legal side of the adoption the young couple—who were only seventeen—left the island. Claude told me my real father was an impoverished student and my mother came from a prominent family who didn't want the news about their scandalous daughter to reach the press. That's all I was told.'

'But didn't you want to know more?'

'I was told that the young couple...my real parents…just wanted to get on with their lives and didn't want anything more to do with the baby…with me.'

'That must have been hard for you to accept,' Alyssa said softly.

Pierre's eyes flickered. 'I was twelve when my father…when Claude told me I was adopted. I prided myself on being a tough guy so I didn't let it upset me. And as for finding out that my real parents didn't want me…' Pierre shrugged. 'I can understand what they did. They were only seventeen, with all their lives in front of them. And it was the answer to a prayer for Sabine. She was the one who begged to be allowed to adopt me. Sabine had miscarried several times and she was desperate to have a child. Claude told me they regarded me as a gift from heaven.'

'At least you must have always felt wanted.'

'Oh, yes, I couldn't have wished for more attentive parents. But after I knew that Claude and Sabine weren't my real parents I felt different, somehow. And so I've never wanted to put another human being through what I went through after I discovered the truth. That's why I never even contemplated adopting a child when we talked about having a family.'

'I can understand why you feel like that,' Alyssa breathed, moving closer to Pierre.

'But that was then, Alyssa. Being with you again has proved to me that none of this matters any more. The only thing that matters is that we should be together…for the rest of our lives.'

He looked deep into her eyes. 'Alyssa, will you marry me?'

'Pierre, I can't! Sooner or later you would resent the fact that I can't give you the family you want.'

'No, I wouldn't. You're the most important part of my

life. For the joy of having you as my wife I would happily give up everything else. Now that you've told me why you broke off our relationship before, now that I know you're still the same Alyssa I knew, not some carefree, fun-seeking, shallow and unrecognisable woman, I'm not going to see you go away again. Please, Alyssa, say you'll marry me and—'

'Pierre, I want to marry you. But I know it wouldn't be fair. However you protest to the contrary, I know how passionately you feel about a family of your own, and I can't destroy your dream.'

Pierre leapt to his feet and began pacing the room. 'Alyssa, if you won't commit yourself now, would you consider seeing a gynaecologist and having an examination? If, as could happen, something can be done about your conception problem, would you then be willing to marry me?'

She stared across the room at him. He was standing by the window. They hadn't drawn the curtains and his tall, athletic body was framed by a background of stars and the glow of Parisian lights illuminating the night sky. At this moment she loved him more than she'd ever done. She wanted so much to believe that her childlessness wouldn't affect him, but she was convinced that it would eventually kill his love for her.

'I don't want to sound pessimistic, but if I couldn't conceive in two years...'

'Think positive, Alyssa. At least give it a try.' He crossed the room with easy strides, his eyes pleading as he bent over her. 'It doesn't matter to me whether you can give me a family or not. How can I convince you that you're all I want in life? If I can't convince you, then promise me you'll go and see a gynaecologist.'

'I'll think about it,' she whispered, almost to herself. 'Yes, yes—I'll get myself checked out.'

She heard Pierre's sigh of relief. His lips were hovering close to hers. She leaned forward and sought comfort in the balm of his kiss. Here—here was where she belonged. If only she could blot out all other considerations she would stay with Pierre for ever. As his kiss deepened she tried to immerse herself in the feeling of belonging, pushing away all the sensible considerations about how long Pierre would want her if she couldn't give him his much-wanted family.

Once bitten, twice shy, was the phrase that sprang into her mind. She closed her eyes as she remembered the distress she'd felt when Mike had rejected her because she couldn't give him a child, in favour of his pregnant girlfriend. She'd never loved Mike as she loved Pierre, but still, it had been hard to take. Rejection from Pierre would be impossible to bear.

He was holding her oh, so close now, his caresses soothing away her distressing thoughts. She moulded herself against his body, trying to fit herself into every muscular contour so that she would become one with the only man she'd ever really loved.

She sighed as he lifted her in his arms and carried her through to the bedroom. As he laid her down on the bed she allowed herself to drift off into a blissful state of mind where only the present had any meaning. The past was over, the future none of her concern. Only tonight mattered. They would live in their perfect world for a few hours…

Pierre's hand was on her shoulder, gently shaking her back to reality. She looked up and smiled the dreamy smile of someone whose body was utterly slaked with the passionate consummation of a night of lovemaking.

'I've brought you coffee,' Pierre said, sitting down on the edge of the bed.

He was wearing a black towelling robe and she could smell the aroma of his soap and aftershave. She must have slept on while he was splashing around in the adjoining bathroom.

'You haven't changed your mind, have you, Alyssa?'

She leaned back against the pillows as she reached for the coffee cup.

'About what?' she asked, playing for time as she tried to get her brain back from the realms of deep, love-saturated sleep.

'Will you definitely go to see a gynaecologist?'

She took a sip of her coffee. 'Yes, I'll go, but—'

'No buts!' Pierre said firmly, reaching forward to kiss the tip of her nose. 'And then, when you've seen the gynaecologist, will you reconsider my proposal of marriage?'

'I've already thought that one through. Pierre, let me see the gynaecologist and then…yes, I'll reconsider.'

'If you found yourself pregnant, would you marry me?'

'Of course I would! Finding myself pregnant would be a dream come true. But…' She stared at Pierre. 'Just because I've agreed to see a gynaecologist doesn't mean that a miracle will happen. I've still got the same scarred body, the same lack of function in…'

'Shh, you'll only upset yourself. Last night was the first time I didn't use a condom. Now that I know the problem, now that I believe there's a chance your surgical scars might have healed, I'm going to do my best to make you pregnant,' Pierre said, reaching across to remove the coffee cup from her hands. 'And there's no time like the present…'

Alyssa gave him a languid smile. Her body was still tingling from the aftereffects of their lovemaking. As she'd wakened this morning she'd thought she was totally satiated, but now, as Pierre's warm breath fanned her face, she felt the excited stirrings of liquid desire deep in the depths of her body…

Later that morning, Pierre and Alyssa hurried into the foyer of the *clinique*. It seemed natural to her that Pierre should still be holding her hand, but she couldn't help noticing the surprised but discreet glances from the medical staff.

They agreed to meet back at the apartment when they came off duty that evening. Pierre had insisted he would make the necessary arrangements for Alyssa's gynaecological examination. He was going to contact an eminent consultant in another hospital to make an appointment, and he was also determined to come with her.

'Gynaecologists usually prefer to meet the patient's partner, don't they?' he'd argued earlier this morning as she'd emerged from the shower to step into the large fluffy towel he was holding out for her. 'It makes sense to get the full picture. After all, it takes two to make a baby,' he'd added gently.

His caressing arms, encircling the towel with her inside it, had completely thrown her ability to think logically.

'Yes, they do,' she'd admitted. 'But announcing that we're a couple is a big step. It's tantamount to saying that…'

'It's saying that we're committed to each other,' he'd told her quietly.

Now, as she looked around the crowded foyer, she felt that everything was happening too fast. She was being manipulated. Strings were being pulled. She didn't feel in command of her future any more. After eight years of coming to terms with the fact that a family was a futile dream for herself, she now found she had to accept a whole new set of rules.

She'd steeled herself to accept what her gynaecologist had told her after he'd removed her Fallopian tube, along with the precious non-viable embryo, and after Mike's rejection she'd painfully accepted that she couldn't have a baby. But now...

She looked up at Pierre as he released her hand. For an instant she felt a sense of panic. What was she letting herself in for? Why had she come back and stirred up this hornets' nest which could only bring her more pain and suffering?

But as she saw the tenderness in his eyes she knew that her love for Pierre was the driving force that had brought her back to this situation. She had to go forward, for Pierre's sake. She couldn't disappoint him by refusing to be examined when he had such high hopes. Whatever the outcome, she owed him this.

'*A bientôt*, see you soon, *ma princesse*,' he whispered.

For a moment Alyssa thought Pierre was going to kiss her, but he merely turned and walked purposefully in the direction of his office.

She hurried away down the corridor, anxious to escape the questioning eyes. Standing in the lift, she pressed the button for the orthopaedics floor. She would go in and see her old patients and colleagues before she went back to obstetrics. At a time when you were feeling like a little-girl lost, you needed to see a few familiar friendly faces.

Alighting from the lift on the top floor, she reached for the nearest internal phone, calling obstetrics to let them know where she was. Jacqueline assured her that she wasn't required for another half-hour, when the consultant would do his round of the patients.

'Marie Lefevre has been asking for you, but I've told her that you'll be in later,' Jacqueline added.

'How is she?' Alyssa said, anxious to hear whether her ectopic patient was more settled than when she'd left her yesterday after her operation.

'She's much better physically. Emotionally she's still a bit down, but that's only to be expected,' Jacqueline said briskly.

As she put down the phone Alyssa reflected that Jacqueline was a no-nonsense professional. She cared for her patients with an expertise acquired over many years of hard work. It was unlikely she ever allowed her patients' problems to affect her own life when she went off duty. Not like she herself had done yesterday evening.

And look what that had got her! A proposal of marriage that she couldn't possibly accept under the circumstances. Nothing had changed in her body. Nothing had changed in her resolve not to tie Pierre to a childless marriage.

She put on a professional, confident smile as she walked in through the swing doors of orthopaedics. Whatever happened today she was going to give the patients her full, undivided attention, and leave her problems until this evening.

Making her way towards Henri Fontaine's bed, she found herself rewarded by the look of happy surprise on his face.

'You've come back, Dr Alyssa! What's the matter? Don't you like all those screaming babies?'

'Just called in for a few minutes to see how everybody is getting along. Can't keep away from you, Henri,' Alyssa quipped.

'We all miss you, Alyssa,' Henri said. 'I was asking Dr

Pierre yesterday how you were getting on delivering babies, and he told me it was your first day of actually working in obstetrics so he didn't know. He was planning to take you out last night to find out.'

Henri gave Alyssa a suggestive wink and lowered his voice. 'How did it go? The evening, I mean. I always thought you two should have got it together by now. I remember thinking to myself the last time you were working here at the *clinique* that you two were made for each other. What happened? Why didn't you meet up again sooner?'

Alyssa glanced round the ward. Nobody was remotely interested in their conversation, and with the clattering of the trolleys and trays nobody could hear what they were saying.

'Life happened, that's all,' she said quietly, and sat down on the chair at the side of Henri's bed. 'Don't you sometimes find, Henri, that circumstances beyond your control make it impossible for you to have everything you thought you might have?'

Henri pulled a wry face. 'Well, of course I do. But you're going to make it happen this time, aren't you, I mean you and Pierre...?'

Henri's big, kind eyes staring at her were almost pleading.

'I don't know. It's very complicated, Henri. Look, we shouldn't be discussing me. I've come to find out how you're getting on. How's the leg?'

She stood up and moved round to examine the badly injured leg, with its one gentamycin bead peeping out of the extensive wound.

'The wound looks much healthier to me,' Henri said. 'Those gentamycin beads that Pierre put in are a good idea.

He told me that they give off antibiotics for about three or four weeks which helps to get rid of any lurking infection.'

Alyssa nodded. 'That's right. When they've done their job, we'll remove them.'

'Does that mean another operation?'

'It's a fairly simple process. We'll just give you a local anaesthetic around the wound before we take them out.'

'Will Pierre do it?'

Alyssa smiled. 'I think he might, if you ask him nicely. It will depend on his schedule, of course, but why don't you check with him?'

'I'll do that,' Henri said. 'Trouble is, now that he's so important I don't like to keep on asking him favours.'

'Ask away, Henri,' Alyssa said, as she bent over the leg to examine the drainage tube. There was still quite a lot of fluid draining from the internal tissue of the leg.

'How long will it be before I'm up and about, Alyssa?'

She hesitated. She wasn't on the orthopaedic team any more, so it wasn't up to her to make a prognosis.

'You'd better ask your consultant, Henri,' she said carefully. 'It's going to take quite a while before everything is healed enough for you to start bearing weight on that leg.'

Henri nodded. 'That's what I thought. I'm resigned to it now. Can't hurry things. At the end of the day, for all the high tech equipment and knowledge you medics have, it's Mother Nature who's in charge, isn't it?'

'Very true, Henri,' Alyssa said, thinking how much this applied to her own precarious situation.

Sylvie was hurrying down the ward towards Henri's bed. 'Good to see you again, Alyssa. Would you like a coffee?'

Alyssa glanced at her watch. 'Just a quick one. Got to get back to obstetrics.'

'How are you getting on down there?' Sylvie asked, pushing open the door of her office.

Alyssa sank into one of the shabby but comfy armchairs. 'It's early days for me. I've only worked one day. I love delivering babies, but hate the trauma when things go wrong.'

'I thought you were looking a bit peaky when you walked out of the *clinique* last night. I was standing in the foyer and you looked straight through me as you went outside.'

Alyssa took a sip of her coffee. 'Did I? I'm sorry. I didn't see you, Sylvie.'

'I expect you were also in a hurry to go out on your date with Pierre,' Sylvie added with a huge smile.

Alyssa gave a start. 'How did you know about that?'

'It's the talk of the *clinique*! One of my nurses saw the pair of you walking along the path by the Seine last night, so deep in conversation that you nearly pushed her and her boyfriend into the river. And then our orthopaedic registrar just told me that he saw you both at a concert in the Ste Chappelle.'

Alyssa put down her cup. 'We both enjoy Bach's music. It was a very good concert.'

'And you were holding hands,' Sylvie finished, as if she hadn't been interrupted. Suddenly she laughed and clapped her hands together in delight. 'I am so pleased for you both! Pierre is a wonderful man and a great friend. I do hope—'

Sylvie broke off as someone tapped on the door. Alyssa stared up at Pierre as he stood in the doorway.

'Didn't expect to find you here, Alyssa,' he said in a bland, professional tone.

'Can't keep away,' Sylvie said, smiling at Pierre. 'If you ask me, I think she prefers orthopaedics to obstetrics.'

Alyssa stood up. 'I'm just on my way there. There's a ward round in five minutes. Thanks for the coffee, Sylvie.'

The sleeve of her jacket touched Pierre as she brushed past him. He looked down and smiled. 'I'm coming along to obstetrics later this morning. I have to write up a report on Marie Lefevre, our ectopic pregnancy patient, and I haven't got enough information in the notes I've been given.'

Alyssa nodded. 'I'll be there.'

She moved away quickly, desperately aware that Sylvie was scrutinising her as she stood so close to Pierre. Soon the whole of the *clinique* would be speculating on their relationship. They would be in the spotlight, and Alyssa wasn't looking forward to fielding questions about what was happening between Pierre and herself when the situation was still so unsure.

The ward round had been a useful way for Alyssa to get to know the patients. Frederic Massenet, the obstetrics and gynaecology consultant, was a patient, experienced, mature man who explained the patients' symptoms, diagnosis and treatment as his medical team followed him around the ward. Alyssa found that she was gaining a lot of knowledge about each patient, but one of the difficult aspects of obstetrics and gynaecology was that the turnover of patients was rapid. It was rare for patients to be in the ward for more than a few days, so she didn't get to know them as well as she would have liked.

But with Marie Lefevre it was different. She felt she had known this patient for a long time already. So many aspects of her situation were similar to her own, and she felt a deep empathy running between them. As soon as the ward round was finished she made a beeline for Marie's bed.

'How are you really feeling, today, Marie?' she asked gently. 'You seemed to be putting on a brave face during the ward round.'

Marie wearily raised her dark sad eyes.

'Well, you were there, Doctor. You heard the consultant telling me that the remaining Fallopian tube is scarred and may not be of any use when I try to get pregnant again. In effect he was saying he thinks it's useless, even though he used a lot of high-falutin medical jargon and tried to wrap it all up a bit. So how do you think I feel? Charles and I had set our heart on a big family. It just isn't fair.'

Alyssa was aware that someone was pushing through the curtains that she'd pulled as the tears started falling down Marie's cheeks.

'No, it isn't fair, Marie,' Pierre said sympathetically as he moved forward to sit on the bed so that he could take hold of the patient's hand. 'But it's happened before, to other patients, and eventually they've come to accept it.'

Standing there, looking at the tender scene which was too close to home, Alyssa could feel a lump in her throat that wouldn't move. Pierre was such a caring doctor. He would make a very caring father... She wished she could look into the future and see how this was all going to turn out.

'I don't think we will ever accept that we can't have children,' Marie said in a barely audible voice. 'We talked about having a family even before we got married, and—'

She broke off, unable to continue.

'I've come to help you, Marie,' Pierre said gently.

Alyssa sat down on the other side of the bed and wiped Marie's wet cheeks with a tissue as she listened to what Pierre was saying.

'We're in touch with a counselling service. I'm going to explain your situation to an experienced counsellor, who will then visit you here in hospital and help you to cope with the immediate future. Later on, when you feel stronger, you'll be able to see her again, and she'll explain the various options that are open to you when you decide to try and start a family again.'

'You mean fertility treatment, adoption and all that, Doctor?'

Pierre nodded. 'But those options will be a last resort. The body has a remarkable way of healing itself, given time. If you're patient, you may find that you can conceive naturally. Dr Massenet hasn't ruled that out entirely.'

Marie looked up, her face brightening. 'That would be wonderful. But I don't think it's going to happen somehow.'

'Yes, it's best not to be too optimistic at this stage,' Alyssa said quietly. 'You'll have to be very patient.'

Pierre looked across the bed at Alyssa, the expression in his eyes tender and sympathetic. 'I know we shouldn't raise our hopes too high, but there's no harm in being optimistic, is there? If there is a chance of natural pregnancy then it's more likely to happen to a happy patient than someone who's given up on the idea.'

Alyssa swallowed hard, knowing that he was referring to their own situation as well as their patient's. She turned away to reach for another tissue, this time for herself.

Pierre was writing something in the case file on his lap. 'Now, if you'd like to tell me about yourself, I'll take a few details and get in touch with our counselling service. That's if you'd like me to do that, Marie. It's up to you.'

Their patient hesitated before turning towards Alyssa. 'I'd prefer to give *you* my details, Doctor.' She turned back to look at Pierre with an apologetic expression on her face. 'Nothing personal, but I'd find it easier to talk to a woman doctor than a man.'

Pierre smiled and patted his patient's hand. 'Of course you would.' He looked enquiringly at Alyssa. 'Have you got time?'

Alyssa smiled. 'I'll make time for a patient as important as Marie.'

'Could you have your report on my desk by lunchtime?'

'I'm sure I could.'

Alyssa let Marie ramble on in an unstructured way, occasionally prompting her patient to get her back on course, and wrote down the details relevant to her case. Marie's overwhelming desire for a family was the most obvious factor in the case. Alyssa hoped that the counsellor would be able to give Marie some positive help in coming to terms with the uncertain situation.

As she closed the file and stood up Alyssa couldn't help wondering how she would have felt if she'd been offered counselling. She would have clutched at any straws back in those dark and desperate days, but would it have given her the courage to contact Pierre and enlighten him about her situation? It was purely academic now, so there was no point in speculating.

Drawing back the curtains from around Marie's bed, Alyssa smiled down at her patient. 'I'll come back later to see you, Marie.'

Marie's eyes pleaded with her. 'Thank you so much, Doctor. I feel you understand. It's almost as if you've been through this yourself.'

Alyssa remained silent, forcing herself to continue smiling. It wouldn't help the patient if she broke down and sobbed in sympathy. She had to remain professional if she was going to be a good doctor and help her patient get through the dark days ahead.

CHAPTER SEVEN

ALYSSA tapped lightly on the door of Pierre's office.

He stood up, going round the desk and coming towards her as she went in.

'I've brought the report on Marie you asked for,' she said, taking care to maintain her professional mode because she was unsure whether Pierre's secretary was still in her small room adjoining his office.

'Thanks, Alyssa.' Pierre said, taking the file from her.

He closed the door and, turning towards her, took her in his arms.

Feeling distinctly ill at ease beside Pierre's office door, knowing that at any moment they could be disturbed, she tried to release herself from his arms. But he was holding her too closely.

'Pierre! Don't you think someone might just walk in here?'

'Does it matter?'

She looked up at him. 'I don't know. I'm not the one in charge of the *clinique*.'

Pierre gazed down at her with a confident smile. 'Well, if that's your only concern, then…'

He bent his head and kissed her gently on the lips. Releasing Alyssa, he held both her hands in his while he stepped back to take a more careful look at her.

'I especially asked you to call in at lunchtime. As you know, everything stops for lunch in France, so I hope you'll have lunch with me.'

'I'd love to, but I haven't got much time. Spending half the morning with Marie has put my working schedule out.'

Pierre smiled. 'That's the English side of you talking! The English don't know the importance of relaxing in the middle of the day and having a good lunch. Lunch is essential to life in France, and especially in Paris. With the exception of medical emergencies, work can wait. As director of this *clinique*, I'm committed to looking after the health and welfare of my medical staff.'

She smiled up at Pierre. His boyish enthusiasm was infectious. 'Well, I could spare half an hour, perhaps, but...'

'Half an hour isn't long enough for a proper lunch!' Pierre said in a scandalised voice as he raised his hands in disapproval. '*Mon dieu!* We would barely have time to reach that small café in the Avenue Mozart, and I'm planning to take you along to a little restaurant near the Champs-Elysées where...'

'Pierre, perhaps we could go there this evening. I really do have to...'

'OK,' Pierre said grudgingly. 'We'll go along to the dining room. That won't take too long.'

'The dining room?'

Alyssa took a step backwards as she thought of the implications of being seen lunching with the *médecin-chef*. After her first day, when she'd had breakfast in the medical staff room, she'd been scrupulously careful not to be seen in any social situation with Pierre at the *clinique*.

'Yes, the dining room,' Pierre said, his eyes twinkling with amusement. 'Amazingly, that's where they serve lunch in this establishment. If we were in England we would have to go out and find a crowded pub, balance ourselves on a precarious bar stool and gulp down a curled-up cheese sandwich so that we didn't waste any time over our so-called lunch. Then we would spend all afternoon suffering from indigestion and working in a highly inefficient way.'

Alyssa gave a mock groan. 'You're incorrigible when you go all French with me. Don't forget I'm half-French, you know.'

He took hold of her arm and led her towards the door. 'Well, come and have a French lunch, then.'

The *clinique* dining room was crowded. All eyes seemed to be on her as Alyssa followed Pierre to a corner table that was still empty. It was at the far end of the room and she was aware that the noise of conversation had dropped dramatically.

She slid into one of the padded seats that flanked the walls.

'*Soupe, madame le docteur?*'

Alyssa, recognising the voice, smiled as she looked up at the black-and-white-uniformed waitress. Christine, who'd been here for years, not only served coffee and croissants in the medical staff room each morning, but also helped with lunch in the dining room.

'*Oui, s'il vous plait, Christine.*'

'*Et monsieur le médecin-chef?*'

Pierre smiled up the waitress. 'Do we have to be so formal, Christine? Couldn't you call me Pierre, like you used to before I was promoted to these great heights?'

Christine giggled. 'Not if I want to keep my job, *monsieur*.' She twinkled as she placed a bowl of spinach soup in front of Pierre. 'It's good to see the two of you together again. I was beginning to think you'd fallen out with each other since the last time you were both here.'

Alyssa looked across the table at Pierre as soon as Christine had left them alone again. 'Everybody in the *clinique* seems to be speculating about our relationship.'

Pierre gave her a grin. '*Eh bien*, what's wrong with that?'

Alyssa picked up her soup spoon, keeping her eyes deliberately on her plate. 'Well, I thought we should be a bit cautious while the situation is so delicate.'

'That's why I wanted to see you this lunchtime,' Pierre said softly. 'I've been in touch with Pascal Coumau, the gynaecologist I'd like you to see. He really is one of the top gynaecologists in Paris and he's agreed to see you next week. I'll make sure your work is covered by the obstetrics team for the entire day so that you can relax and take it easy afterwards.'

'Thanks, Pierre.' Alyssa put down her soup spoon. She'd eaten half the soup, but suddenly she didn't seem to have any more appetite.

'You're worried, aren't you?'

'Well, of course I'm worried… Sorry—I didn't mean to sound so fierce but it's bringing it all back to me and…'

Pierre reached across the table and took her hand in his. 'That's why we've got to get this problem solved once and for all. The uncertainty of not knowing can wear you down.'

Alyssa stared across the table at Pierre, grateful for his concern but sensing in her heart of hearts that it was most unlikely that her scarred body would have repaired itself so miraculously. She'd lived with the idea of sterility for eight years, and suddenly to have her hopes raised and probably dashed again fairly quickly would be heartrending. She couldn't help remembering how careful her gynaecologist had been to suggest that she should resign herself to most probably being childless.

As a doctor she knew that the body could sometimes heal itself, against all the odds, but she'd long since stopped believing in miracles.

Alyssa managed to swallow some of her main course. The *pommes frites* were delicious and the *pintade*—roast guinea fowl—was done to perfection. But she couldn't banish the worries at the back of her mind. Now that Pierre was involved it was ten times harder for her. If the examination proved her to be permanently sterile there would be two people plunged into despair.

Her mobile phone was ringing. She reached into her bag. It was Sister Jacqueline on the obstetrics ward. Across the table, Pierre was watching her enquiringly.

'No problem,' she told Jacqueline in answer to her short message. 'I'll come now.'

Switching off the phone, she stood up. 'Sorry, Pierre. An emergency situation on the obstetrics ward. Two patients in the final stages of labour and not enough staff on the ward.'

He stood up. 'I'll come with you. I should have been told there was a staffing problem.'

'Jacqueline says it's only just arisen,' Alyssa told him as they hurried out of the dining room. 'Two of the obstetrics medical team became ill and went home during the morning suffering from *la grippe*. Jacqueline thought the midwives could handle the workload, but now admits they need help.'

'I'll work with you, Alyssa,' Pierre said, as he pushed open the swing door that led into obstetrics.

'Delivery suite—*vite, vite!*' Jacqueline called as soon as they stepped inside the ward. 'Pierre, I was going to contact you to report that—'

'That's OK, Jacqueline. I understand the situation and I'm here to help. Don't worry,' he added as he saw the surprised look on the sister's face. 'I've had obstetrics training and a great deal of experience during my career. I've lost count of how many babies I've delivered—and not always in super-technical surroundings like we have here at the *clinique*.'

Alyssa and Pierre hurried down the ward, followed swiftly by a junior nurse carrying sterile gowns and masks for them to put on as soon as possible. After scrubbing up at the sink in the ante-room adjoining the delivery room, they hurried to take their places at either side of the delivery table in the first room.

Neither of them spoke as they prepared themselves. They were simply professional colleagues, all other personal considerations didn't exist for the moment.

'There's a problem here,' Catherine, the midwife, told them quietly. 'Labour has been prolonged—much longer than we expected.'

'Is the baby showing signs of distress?' Alyssa asked quickly.

The midwife nodded. 'Within the last few minutes there were signs that the baby is suffering, so—'

'Pierre!' Jacqueline appeared in the doorway of the delivery room. 'I need help in the next room. My patient is haemorrhaging.'

'I'll come now,' Pierre said, glancing across the table at Alyssa. 'You can handle this patient, can't you?'

'Of course,' Alyssa said, although she felt a moment of panic as Pierre disappeared into the next room. She'd delivered many babies herself, with varying complications, but Pierre's presence in the room had been very comforting.

Alyssa leaned over her patient, checking the monitor to find out for herself just how distressed the baby was. She glanced at Gabrielle, the young mother-to-be, and noted the signs of exhaustion showing.

'I can't hold out much longer, Doctor,' Gabrielle said.

'I can feel the baby pressing down on me and… Ooh, can I push now…?'

'Breathe into the Entonox mask,' Alyssa said, placing it over her patient's face. 'Hold off pushing, please, till I've checked that your baby is in the right position for delivery. Sister, take over from me here, please.'

As the midwife took over at the Entonox machine Alyssa quickly bent down to examine the birth canal. At the top of the canal the neck of the womb was fully dilated, but instead of the head presenting itself Alyssa could see part of a small buttock.

'It's a malpresentation,' Alyssa said. 'We've got to get this baby out now, Sister.'

Alyssa's mind was racing ahead as she thought of the options open to her. She could opt for a Caesarean section under general anaesthetic, or she could attempt to deliver the baby in breech position. Neither option was going to be easy at this late stage in the labour.

She decided to make one last attempt to deliver the baby down the birth canal before she had to resort to Caesarean section. She'd delivered several babies in breech position during her medical career. It was never easy, because each case was different, but she'd never lost a baby yet. And setting up a Caesarean section would involve calling in the anaesthetist, which would waste valuable time and cause more distress to the unborn baby and its mother.

Reaching her gloved hand up inside the birth canal, Alyssa felt her fingers make contact with the tiny buttock. She could tell that the baby was lying on its side; one tiny foot was already partially protruding through the neck of the womb. Grasping the foot gently but firmly, she eased most of the leg through the neck of the womb. The attached body was sliding with it; she could feel the buttocks coming along behind the leg and now the other leg, curled up against the small body, was being released.

Alyssa glanced up at her patient. The midwife was leaning over her, still holding the Entonox mask over Gabrielle's face.

'Gabrielle, can you give me one last push when you feel a contraction coming on?' she asked her patient gently. 'Your baby's nearly here; just one last effort from you and then…yes—yes…he's here. He's here…I've got him…'

Blood and mucus flowed out of the birth canal, but Alyssa was holding the slippery baby safely in her hands.

'*C'est un garçon*—it's a boy,' she told the young mother happily.

Carefully cutting the cord, she gave the tiny infant to its mother.

'He's wonderful!' the exhausted mother said, her buoyant spirits returning as she cradled her baby against her breast. 'I'm going to call him Thibault, after my father, who died earlier this year. He would have loved to see him but it wasn't to be.'

There was a movement at the door and the new father appeared. 'Sorry I had to go out, Gabrielle,' he said sheepishly. 'I would have fainted if I'd had to stay any longer.'

Gabrielle was smiling happily as she held her precious son.

'Fat lot of use you were, Gaston! You were supposed to give me moral support. But I'll forgive you if you promise to have the next one yourself.'

'Thank God that's not possible!' Gaston said, attempting to take hold of his newborn child and having great difficulty in holding the head in the right position. 'I think you're much better at this sort of thing than I am, Gabrielle.'

Alyssa was talking to the midwife about the postnatal

checks they were going to carry out on the baby and the mother when she heard the swing doors opening once more. Pierre walked into the delivery room.

'Everything OK here?'

'Mission accomplished,' Alyssa said, in a satisfied voice. 'A slight problem with a breech delivery, but the midwife and I coped.'

'Dr Alyssa was brilliant, sir,' the midwife said. 'I have to admit I was a bit worried. There was no time to lose if we were to save this baby.'

'And a lovely baby he is too,' Pierre said. 'May I hold him?' he asked the young father.

Gaston gave a beaming smile as he handed over the baby. 'What do you think of my son, Doctor?'

'I think he looks very healthy—and sounds it too!' Pierre was smiling as he handed over the lustily crying baby to the midwife so that she could start the postnatal checks. 'Doesn't sound to be anything wrong with this baby's lungs!'

'Thanks, all of you!' Gaston said, looking round the room at all the medical staff. 'I've brought a bottle of champagne so we can celebrate our baby's safe arrival. Have we got some glasses?'

Alyssa smiled as she watched the new father produce a bottle which had been smuggled in under cover of the voluminous green theatre gown he'd been made to wear. She'd never known this happen before in the hospitals she'd worked in—but then this was Paris, where life was always exciting.

The midwife produced some disposable paper cups from the ante-theatre, and Gaston did the honours.

'Well done, all of you!' Pierre said, raising his glass towards Alyssa. 'Here's to the doctor who brought little Thibault into the world. *Santé*, Alyssa!'

'*Santé*, Alyssa!'

Alyssa found herself blushing with embarrassment as the toast reverberated around the delivery room.

'I was only doing my job,' she murmured.

Jacqueline poked her head round the door. 'When you've finished in here, Dr Dupont, our patient would like to see you again. No hurry, of course. She's out of danger…'

'I'll be with you in a moment,' Pierre said, putting his plastic cup in the wastebin by the door.

Alyssa moved away from the table so that she could speak privately to Pierre. 'What was the problem with your patient?'

'Part of the placenta had been retained in the uterus after birth, so my patient had started to haemorrhage. Fortunately she'd been given an epidural anaesthetic so I was able to put my hand into her uterus and separate the placenta from the uterine wall. The bleeding is under control now and she's receiving blood intravenously.'

He lowered his voice. 'Don't forget to come to the apartment this evening, will you? We still haven't visited that restaurant on the Champs-Elysées I was telling you about.'

She smiled as she heard the shift in tone from professional to personal. Nobody in the room seemed remotely interested in their conversation.

'I'll certainly come to the apartment,' Alyssa murmured. 'But can we make a decision on the restaurant when—?'

'Dr Alyssa, would you come and look at baby Thibault?' Catherine called. 'Do you think he's showing signs of neonatal jaundice?'

'*A bientôt*—see you later,' Pierre said, disappearing into the next room.

Alyssa went over to look at the new baby. 'I noticed a slight tinge of yellow to the skin when the baby arrived,' she told the midwife. 'But it's not pronounced enough to need any treatment at this stage. I'd planned to take some blood so that we can ascertain the serum bilirubin level.'

'Is something wrong with my baby?' Gabrielle asked anxiously, raising herself from the pillows that had been placed behind her head and leaning over on her elbow to get a better look.

'It's just a slight discolouration of the skin, which is perfectly normal in some newborn babies, Gabrielle,' Alyssa told her patient quickly. 'We call it physiological jaundice and it's due to the normal breakdown of red cells. This occurs in all babies after birth, but in some of them the rate of breakdown is greater than the rate of elimination of bile pigments from the bloodstream. This accounts for the jaundice—the yellowing of the skin.'

Alyssa smiled sympathetically. 'There's absolutely nothing to worry about. It's only a tinge in the skin at the moment. If it becomes more pronounced later on we'll give baby Thibault some phototherapy.'

'What's that?' Gabrielle asked.

'We'll put him in a little cot with a blue spectrum of light above it. This will convert the fat-soluble bilirubin into water-soluble bilirubin, which can be excreted into his nappy. Meanwhile, I'd like you to drink plenty of water. You're planning to breastfeed, aren't you?'

Gabrielle nodded. 'Of course.'

'Well, we may step up the feeds if baby's jaundice becomes more pronounced, so you'll need plenty of milk.'

'What will happen if I haven't enough milk, Doctor?'

'We would give supplementary feeds with a bottle. But don't worry about that now, Gabrielle.'

'Thanks, Doctor. And thanks for explaining everything to me. It's good to know what's happening.'

Alyssa smiled and patted her patient's hand. 'You're both doing fine, Gabrielle.'

By the end of the afternoon the workload on the ward had eased considerably, and Alyssa found herself able to catch up on the routine work she'd intended to do that morning. The patients, who'd been waiting all day to see her, were very understanding when she explained the reasons for her delay in arriving at their bedsides.

It was dark outside when Alyssa hurried down the Rue de l'Assomption to Pierre's apartment.

Pierre thrust a glass of champagne into her hand as soon as she arrived.

Alyssa smiled up at him, clinking her glass against his. 'What's the celebration?'

'A continuation of the celebration we started in the delivery room. Only this time we don't have to drink from plastic cups...and this time,' he added carefully, 'it's looking ahead to a hopeful future for the two of us.'

Alyssa sipped the delicious champagne as she reflected that Pierre was taking their future together very much for granted. She was glad he hadn't said anything about babies, but she knew that was what was uppermost in his mind. She was certain that in his own mind Pierre was toasting the baby he hoped she would be able to have. It made her more and more nervous of the situation she'd found herself in.

'I haven't yet booked a table at the restaurant because I wasn't sure how soon you could get away,' Pierre said, placing both glasses on the coffee table in front of them as he drew Alyssa against him on the sofa.

'Would you mind if we stayed in tonight?' Alyssa kicked off her shoes as she leaned against Pierre. 'I'm feeling tired and it might be easier to talk here rather than in a crowded restaurant.'

'Of course I don't mind.' Pierre dropped a kiss on her head. 'What did you want to talk about?'

'Can't you guess?'

'Your gynae consultation?'

'Of course! What's he like, this consultant?'

'Pascal Coumau is kind, gentle and very thorough. We'll be in good hands.'

'We? I thought I was the one who was going to have the examination.'

'I'm in this with you all the way, Alyssa. If Pascal finds that there's no hope of a natural pregnancy then we'll go for fertility treatment.'

Alyssa stared at him. 'But I remember you saying that you wouldn't want to have to go through fertility treatment. I remember quite clearly. It was when we were sitting on that bench—our favourite bench—at the side of the Lac Supérieur in the Bois de Boulogne. We'd been discussing some new advances in fertility treatment that had appeared in a French medical magazine I'd borrowed from you. I'd only known you a couple of weeks, but you started to tell me about your dream of a big family and you said…'

Pierre's expression was troubled as he turned sad eyes towards her. 'Alyssa, that was eight years ago. That was what I believed in those far-off, carefree, idealistic days. But life changes and we change along with it.'

Alyssa reached out and took hold of Pierre's hand. 'I wouldn't want you to be tied to me if there was no possibility of a baby,' she said quietly. 'Pierre, you must see that if everything fails and—'

'Shh! Let's wait and see what happens, Alyssa.'

Pierre held her close to him, his lips seeking hers, and

as their bodies came together Alyssa felt the tug of desire rising again inside her. The physical act of making love with Pierre would soothe away her anxiety...

The sky was dark, with no sign of the moon this evening as Alyssa pushed back the curtains to look out over the rooftops of Paris. Through a gap in the tall buildings she could make out lights at the far side of the Seine. She turned her head to look at Pierre, still sleeping.

She reflected that there had been a certain poignancy about their lovemaking this evening. It was as if both of them had known that they were starting out on a great adventure. Alyssa would soon find out whether she could conceive naturally or whether she would have to embark on fertility treatment.

But what happened if everything failed? She stood up and crossed the room, easing herself back into the snug, warm bed, curling herself up against Pierre.

He stirred in his sleep and then opened his eyes. 'I dreamed you left me,' he said, still half asleep. 'But you've come back.' He pulled her closer against him. 'Alyssa, why don't you move into the apartment with me? After all, you did say you felt more at home here than anywhere else.'

Alyssa hesitated. 'That's true,' she said quietly.

Once again she felt that life was moving ahead too quickly for her. But she couldn't back out now she'd embarked on this adventure with Pierre. Still tingling from their ecstatic lovemaking, it was hard for her to make a decision. She had to put herself in Pierre's hands now and believe him when he said that she was more important to him than having a family.

He raised himself on one elbow, looking down at her with tender, expressive eyes. 'Was that a yes?'

'I think it was.'

'In that case you won't need to get up again tonight,' Pierre said sleepily as he drew her even closer into the circle of his strong, muscular arms.

'Or any other night,' Alyssa whispered, almost to herself.

But even as she snuggled against Pierre, feeling her strong desires blending with his, the doubts were still there. Her ultimate fear was rejection by Pierre when he regretted he was trapped in a childless relationship. She would never be able to forgive herself for changing her initial resolution—nor would she be able to bear the agony of rejection by him.

But—as she had to keep reminding herself—she couldn't back down now. And as Pierre's caressing hands coaxed her tingling body into a new sensual delirium she closed her eyes and gave herself up to the wonderful moment when their bodies would unite once more in ecstatic fulfilment…

CHAPTER EIGHT

ALYSSA looked along the street to the tall impressive building of the prestigious *clinique* that Pierre was pointing out to her and felt a moment of panic.

She'd insisted they take the Métro to the foot of the hill that led to the heart of Montmartre. Sitting in her seat close to Pierre as the carriage had rattled through the long, dark tunnels she'd felt as if time didn't exist any more. As long as she didn't reach journey's end she could still imagine that nothing was about to change between Pierre and herself.

But as they'd walked up the steep, cobblestoned road, with the impressive cathedral of the Sacré Coeur looking down on them, and as the minute hand on her watch had moved relentlessly nearer the time of her appointment, she'd been riddled with doubts.

Her eyes had been drawn to the shimmering silvery decorations festooned across the street for the festive season. Coloured lightbulbs adorned the façades of every building, and she'd tried desperately to forget her worries and absorb the spirit of Christmas. In spite of the cold, the doors of the little shops were open and blasts of enticingly welcome hot air had fanned her face as she'd walked past. She'd caught a glimpse of brightly coloured Christmas wrapping paper, cards, books and party clothes in the dazzlingly sparkling shop windows, but, however hard she'd tried, she hadn't been able to get rid of her apprehension.

Pierre, as if sensing her mood, had put his arm around her waist and drawn her towards a seat at the foot of the steps leading up to the Sacré Coeur. An artist who'd set up his easel close by, intent on capturing the beauty of the cathedral set in its well-tended gardens, had smiled at them as he paused between brushstrokes.

To Alyssa, he'd looked young, happy, and as carefree as she and Pierre had been in those far-off days when their love affair had been new and untried. She'd looked up at the clear blue sky, knowing that it was impossible to put the clock back. She had to go forward.

A wispy cloud crossed the sun, blotting out the feeble warmth. She shivered. Even though the sun was shining this morning, it had very little effect on the cold December day. A couple of days ago she'd had to buy herself a warm winter coat, and Pierre had pulled out a tailored black overcoat from the back of his wardrobe that morning. He'd asked her if she thought he would need it today and she'd advised him to wear it.

To all intents and purposes they were a real couple now. Living in the same apartment, eating together, sleeping together, making love together. In the week since they'd had lunch in the *clinique* dining room they seemed to have become accepted by the majority of the staff.

Alyssa hugged her own doubts about the situation to herself. She couldn't help realising that these doubts threatened the whole of her future with Pierre. But for the moment…

'You don't have to go through with this if you really don't want to,' Pierre said gently, drawing her hand into his, removing her new leather glove so that he could press her cold fingers to his lips. 'It's not too late for me to cancel the appointment.'

She turned to look at him, her heart so full of love for this wonderful man that she knew she would go through fire for him. But could she allow him to pledge his whole future to someone who might shatter his dreams?

She hesitated before her thoughts crystallised. 'I want to find out the truth.'

'So do I.'

Carefully he replaced her glove, raising his eyes to hers.

For a moment they remained close together, their eyes locked in a tender mutual understanding, before Pierre drew Alyssa along the ancient cobbled street towards the *clinique*.

'I'm relieved that we've come here,' Alyssa said as Pierre pressed the bell on the brass nameplate. 'Think of the rumours that would have flown around if I'd been examined at our own *clinique*.'

'That was one reason why I chose this place,' Pierre said. 'That and the fact that Pascal, besides being one of the best gynaecologists in Paris, is a friend of my father's.'

A look of concern crossed Alyssa's face. 'Your father?'

'My adoptive father—Claude.'

As the door was opened by a white-coated young man Alyssa felt uneasy about the fact that the eminent Pascal Coumau should be a family friend. She would have preferred to remain in a more detached, professional situation, where personal considerations didn't come into the equation, but it was too late now.

Once inside the *clinique*, Alyssa's first impression was one of quiet, calm, opulent surroundings, and subdued lights emphasising the sheen that appeared on the polished oak of the doors and wood panelling. Barely had they been asked to sit outside the great man's room before they were whisked inside by a dark-haired nursing sister in starched navy blue, with a shining silver buckle at her trim waistline.

'Pierre—good to see you again.'

Alyssa watched as Pascal Coumau, a tall, steely-grey haired man, probably in his mid-fifties but looking much younger, came forward from behind a huge mahogany desk, his hand outstretched towards Pierre. Briefly the men shook hands before the gynaecologist turned to look at Alyssa.

He gave her a genial smile which helped to put her at her ease. 'Welcome, Alyssa—may I call you Alyssa? Pierre has told me so much about you that I feel I know you already. Do sit down.'

Pascal returned to the other side of his impressive desk and wrote something on the case file in front of him. Alyssa had barely time to wonder what the consultant could possibly have deduced from their brief introduction before he began asking her questions.

An hour later Pascal was still questioning her. She looked sideways at Pierre, who was looking solemn. Her attention was beginning to flag, and she began to wonder whether all these questions about her previous medical history and her present general health were really necessary. Surely a physical examination would reveal more than she could possibly tell the gynaecologist.

As if reading Alyssa's thoughts, Pascal put down his pen and leaned back in his large leather chair. 'I think we all need a break. Would you like coffee?'

Pascal spoke into his intercom, instructing someone in the adjoining room to bring in a tray. 'Or tea, perhaps, Alyssa? Being half-English you might prefer...'

Alyssa smiled. '*Un café noir, s'il vous plaît, monsieur.*'

Now that the pressure was off her for the moment, Alyssa found she could relax. Sipping her coffee, leaning back against the plush, leather-buttoned armchair, she was able to look around at the tasteful surroundings. The book-lined walls, the antique pictures of old Paris all helped to take her mind off what might lie ahead of her.

'You're probably thinking I'm taking an extraordinary amount of details from you, Alyssa,' Pascal said at last, putting down his coffee cup on a small silver tablemat in the centre of his desk. 'But if you're to be my patient then I need all the background information I can get.'

'As a doctor, I can appreciate that,' Alyssa said, carefully placing her own cup on the silver tray at the front of the desk. 'But obviously I'm anxious to know what kind of physical examination or perhaps surgical operation you propose to perform on me.'

The gynaecologist placed both elbows on his desk and pressed the tips of his fingers together in a pyramid. He seemed to be considering Alyssa's question.

'Now that I've got the full picture of your background, Alyssa, we can proceed with the diagnostic and prognostic considerations. I'm relieved that both you and Pierre have been so frank with me.'

Pascal stood up and came round the desk. 'Firstly,' he said in a brisk tone, 'I'm going to perform an ultrasound scan on you to determine the extent of the injuries the ectopic pregnancy inflicted on your reproductive organs. Then I'll give you my findings and we'll take it from there.'

Pascal pressed a button at the side of his desk and the navy blue-uniformed sister came through from the adjoining room.

'If you'd like to follow Sister, Alyssa, I'll be with you in a few minutes.'

He turned back to look at Pierre. 'I think it would be a good idea if, initially, you stayed here, Pierre. I'll give you a thorough report at the end of the ultrasound scan. So if you'd like to make yourself comfortable...'

* * *

Lying on the ultrasound scanning table, looking up at the bright lights, Alyssa waited for Pascal to begin his examination.

'Was the coffee part of the pre-ultrasound treatment?' she asked the gynaecologist, nervously feeling a need to chat to him before the examination got under way. 'I've often had to remind patients not to empty their bladders before their ultrasound scan. Then I have to explain that ultrasound works best that way, and we get a better picture.'

The nursing sister, who was smearing ultrasound cream over Alyssa's abdomen, gave Alyssa a conspiratorial smile.

'As soon as Monsieur Coumau orders coffee for a patient I know I must get everything ready for an ultrasound scan,' she said.

Pascal smiled. 'Now, just relax, Alyssa. Have you got a good view of the screen?'

Alyssa assured the gynaecologist that she had an excellent view of the screen, which had been switched on above the end of the table.

'I'm just trying to orientate myself,' she said quietly, feeling her heart beating more rapidly as the picture of the various internal organs of her abdomen became clearer.

Pascal Coumau was moving the ultrasound scanner over her abdomen whilst keeping his eyes firmly on the screen. 'Here we've got the area where the left Fallopian tube was excised…looks like the ovary is missing as well… Yes— no ovary on the left side.'

'That's what I thought,' Alyssa said resignedly, closing her eyes for a moment as she remembered the first and last time she'd had an ultrasound scan. It had been six weeks after she'd lost the baby and the Fallopian tube in which it had tried to grow. The tissues around the affected area had been so badly scarred and damaged that it had been difficult to determine whether the ovary on that side had survived or not.

Apparently not. She opened her eyes and looked up at the screen again. 'What about the other side?' she asked. 'Can you move the…? Yes, leave it right there, please.'

She felt a pang of excitement as she saw her remaining Fallopian tube. From where she was lying she couldn't detect any abnormalities, but closer observation might reveal some flaws.

'The last time I saw this remaining Fallopian tube, soon after my operation, it looked completely unviable. The sides seemed to be attached to each other by adhesions. There was absolutely no way that an egg could travel down from the ovary. From the number of adhesions I saw eight years ago I couldn't understand why the surgeon hadn't excised this Fallopian tube as well as the one from where they took…they took the embryo.'

She drew in her breath to steady her nerves. She'd never dared to hope for a miracle, but this seemed the nearest thing. She looked up at Pascal.

'Would you like Pierre to come in and see this?' he asked gently. 'I didn't want him to be here if the injuries to your reproductive system were as bad as I first suspected. But I think you'll agree with me that—'

'You think there's a hope that I might conceive?'

Alyssa found she was holding her breath as she waited for the gynaecologist's answer.

'Let's get Pierre in first.'

It was mere seconds before Pierre arrived and took his place beside Alyssa. Taking her small hand in his, he looked up at the screen, narrowing his eyes as he focused on the picture.

'I'm no gynaecological expert, Pascal, but I would say—' Pierre broke off, his voice elated. 'That looks like a healthy Fallopian tube to me—and the ovary looks…' He glanced up at Pascal. 'Come on, you're the expert. What's your pronouncement on Alyssa's chances of conceiving?'

'Well, she's only firing on one ovary, and the egg has got to travel down this previously scarred Fallopian tube. But if all other conditions are right I think we might…'

'What other conditions are you talking about?' Alyssa asked quickly.

'Well, if I didn't already know, this is the point at which I would check on your social conditions,' Pascal told her. 'With patients whose background I'm not familiar with I would enquire if they were in a stable, settled relationship with a loving partner. That is one of the most important considerations. There must be no tension in the relationship.'

Pascal broke off and glanced at Pierre. 'Forgive me for mentioning this, but I gained the impression, from what Alyssa told me, that there was a great deal of tension in her previous marriage. This might have been an important factor in the reason why she couldn't conceive. The more settled and relaxed the situation between the prospective parents, the more chance we have of producing a baby.'

The gynaecologist gave them both a beaming smile. 'From the impression you've both been giving me, I presume you're planning a settled, permanent relationship?'

'Of course,' Pierre said quickly. 'I've asked Alyssa to marry me and…' He turned to look enquiringly at Alyssa, his tender eyes pleading for an answer. 'I know this is a strange place to ask you for the third time…'

'The third time?' Pascal's voice conveyed his amazement.

'Yes, the third time,' Pierre said. 'Eight years ago Alyssa asked me to wait until she'd finished her medical training. Then, only last week...'

'Excuse me while I leave you two lovebirds alone for a little while,' Pascal said, hurrying towards the door. 'I'll be back in a few minutes.'

Pierre leaned forward to kiss Alyssa's cheek with such tenderness that it brought tears to her eyes.

'I'm hoping I'm going to be third time lucky,' he told her huskily. 'Alyssa, will you marry me?'

'I will,' she said, softly.

Pierre drew her towards him, his kiss deepening as his lips claimed hers.

'I think you've just ruined your suit,' she said, as finally he pulled away. 'You've got ultrasound cream all over it.'

Pierre grinned. 'It doesn't matter. Nothing matters except that we're going to be together for ever.'

Pierre began planning their wedding as soon as they were in a taxi, heading down through the busy streets of Paris. The sky was darkening and the chill in the air had increased as they left the *clinique*.

'It looks as if it could snow,' Alyssa said, glancing out of the taxi window for a moment as she tried to rearrange her thoughts about the impending wedding.

When she'd awakened this morning, full of apprehension about her appointment with Pascal Coumau, she hadn't imagined that everything would happen quite so quickly.

'You're not taking this wedding seriously, Alyssa,' Pierre said, taking hold of her hand.

She turned back to look at him. 'Oh, but I am, believe me, Pierre. I'm just overwhelmed by the enormity of our new situation. I can't believe that I might be able to—'

She broke off, her eyes moist with tears. She didn't want to cry, here in the taxi, not when everything seemed to be working out for them.

Pierre drew her close and kissed her damp cheeks. 'Shall we leave the details of the wedding until later? You're understandably tired and—'

'No, let's talk about the wedding now—let's talk about it all the time,' she said, suddenly feeling happiness surge through her as she realised she could look into the future with hope again.

She and Pierre would be together for the rest of this year, for the whole of next year and for years, and years to come...

She put her hands on the sides of Pierre's face and drew his lips towards hers. 'I'm so happy,' she whispered, ignoring the fact that the taxi driver was watching them in his rearview mirror. 'Just now, when you suggested we get married before Christmas, I thought you were mad. I couldn't see how everything could be arranged in time. But now I can see that we don't need to worry about minor details.'

'Exactly! Leave the licence and all the paperwork to me, Alyssa. Just find yourself a beautiful wedding gown.'

'Couldn't we have a simple civil ceremony? Perhaps with a blessing in a church after Christmas, when we've got more time?'

Pierre hesitated. 'We've got to tell my parents yet. And when we do I have a feeling Sabine will want to be involved in the planning. She once told me she wanted me to be married in the church where she and Claude were married.'

'Where is this church?' Alyssa asked, a feeling of unreality sweeping over her.

'It's down in the south-west of France, on a craggy

promontory that overlooks the sea. My parents have retired to live in their holiday house down there. It's very beautiful—with a wonderful, rugged coastline—rather like our family home in the West Indies.'

'But would Sabine be able to organise a church wedding so quickly? It's less than two weeks to Christmas now.'

'Sabine is a very determined character. She will be able to get her own way with the clergy involved. She was born very near to the house she and my father now live in and knows lots of influential people in the area.'

Alyssa remained silent as a feeling of unreality swept over her once more.

'So, are you happy for me to give my parents the good news?' Pierre asked.

The taxi driver had pulled up in front of the apartment. Alyssa smiled up at Pierre.

'Of course. I look forward to meeting them. They must be quite a tough pair to have taken on someone like you from birth.'

'My father once said he hadn't much choice in the matter. Sabine gave him an ultimatum. Either he adopted me or she was leaving the island to go back to France.'

Pierre broke off to pay the driver, before putting his arm around Alyssa's waist and leading her up the stairs.

'Sabine sounds like my kind of woman,' Alyssa said with a wry smile as she waited for Pierre to unlock the door.

'You mean bossy?'

'Not at all! Strong, confident...'

'Same thing,' Pierre said as he swept her up into his arms and carried her over the threshold.

Alyssa laughed. 'What was that for? We're not married yet.'

Pierre pushed the door closed with his foot. 'No, but we soon will be.'

Carrying her through to the bedroom, he laid her down on the bed. 'I know you said you were tired earlier on, but...'

'I'm never too tired to make love with you, Pierre,' Alyssa whispered.

CHAPTER NINE

ARRIVING at the *clinique* next morning, Alyssa felt the world around her was totally unreal. It was less than two weeks to Christmas and it was an even shorter time to her wedding!

Pierre had gone in early because of a surgical emergency, so she'd had time to herself to think about everything she had to do. One of her first priorities must be to choose a dress. Perhaps she could fit that in this afternoon, if she could finish her scheduled work in time.

Stepping through the *porte à tambour*, she almost collided with one of the porters who was unloading a huge Christmas tree in the foyer.

The young man grinned. 'Sorry, Doctor! I've got to get this tree erected so you doctors and nurses can trim it this morning.'

'Come on, Alyssa,' Jacqueline said, as she hurried down the corridor into the foyer, followed by a couple of nurses from obstetrics. 'It's traditional that we all trim the Christmas tree, so I've left a skeleton staff on the ward while we work here for a few minutes. After that we'll trim our own tree up on the ward. The porters are bringing the boxes of decorations... Here they are... We always put the fairy on the top of the tree. That's when we need a tall man... Pierre!'

Pierre, arriving at the foyer desk, smiled as Jacqueline beckoned him over.

'I wondered how long it would be before I was needed,' he said, unwrapping the carefully cherished fairy. He

155

looked down at Alyssa as he held the fairy in his hands. 'It's going to be a wonderful Christmas,' he whispered. 'Are you all right, Alyssa?'

She smiled. 'I'm fine.' She hesitated. 'A bit over-whelmed, but...'

'I'll help you all I can.'

'You can't help me choose a wedding dress,' Alyssa said firmly. 'I thought I could go round the shops this afternoon—unless I'm needed here.'

'I'll make sure you're not.'

Alyssa bent down to decorate one of the lower branches of the tree with silver stars. Pierre stooped so that he could whisper in her ear.

'I thought we ought to make an announcement about our wedding. How do you feel about that?'

Alyssa turned her face to look up at him and felt over-whelming love surging through her.

'Everyone will have to know soon, but will you make the announcement...perhaps when I'm out at the shops this afternoon...?'

Pierre leaned forward and squeezed her hand. 'Don't worry. They'll all be delighted with the news.'

More doctors and nurses were arriving in the foyer, un-packing the boxes of coloured glass balls, silver stars and tinsel. A porter hurried in with a trolley on which there were huge sacks of presents. These were to be stacked under the tree ready for Christmas Day, when they would be given to the children of a nearby residential home.

Jacqueline came round the tree to speak to Alyssa.

'I think we can be spared to go back to obstetrics now that half the staff seem to have arrived. We've still got our own tree to do. I've left a couple of nurses putting up coloured lampshades in the shape of stars. Come and see what you think, Alyssa.'

Alyssa looked at Pierre. 'I must go.'

Pierre looked down at her. 'Hope you find a beautiful dress this afternoon.'

Alyssa smiled up into his eyes. 'I feel as if I'm in a dream.'

Pierre bent down and whispered, 'So do I. A wonderful dream!'

As Alyssa started to walk away she noticed that Jacqueline was waiting for her at the end of the corridor. The knowing look on her face said it all. Nobody was going to be the least bit surprised when Pierre made his announcement this afternoon! But, unless there was an emergency, she would be shopping for her wedding dress when the grapevine began to buzz...

Alyssa's heart pounded with excitement as she went into the little boutique on the Rue de Passy. She'd often wandered past it on her way to the fruit market and she'd admired the elegant white dresses in the window. Now she was the one who had to choose.

A chic, immaculately coiffured elegant lady of a certain age came towards her.

'Mademoiselle désire...?' she enquired.

Alyssa swallowed hard. 'I'd like to look at wedding dresses.'

The lady smiled. *'Pour mademoiselle?'*

'Yes—yes, it's for me.'

'Félicitations—congratulations, *mademoiselle*! Come this way, *s'il vous plaît.'*

Alyssa was led into a large room at the back of the boutique, where several dresses were displayed on dummy models and many more were hanging on racks at the side of the room. Almost immediately her eyes fell on a chic white silk and lace creation which hung on one of the models. The tight bodice had puff sleeves and then fell in folds from the waist, fairly straight at the front but more generous at the back, so that it formed a small trailing train. The veil which crowned the outfit was of fine lace with a richly embroidered edge, not so opaque as to hide her face, but dense enough to create a little mystery, so that her face would only be revealed after she and Pierre were pronounced man and wife.

Her heart seemed to turn over at the thought, and she found herself shivering with excitement at what lay ahead of her.

'I'd like to try that one,' she said quickly.

A discussion on sizing followed, before the owner of the boutique helped Alyssa into the beautiful dress. It was—of course—too long for her, but she was assured that a seamstress would have no problem in making the creation fit her perfectly.

Alyssa stared at the stranger in the mirror. Was that really her? Was she really going to walk down the aisle of a church to where Pierre was waiting for her and…?

'I'll take it!'

'An excellent choice. *Mademoiselle* will make a perfect bride! One moment while I call my seamstress to check on the alterations, and then if you would care to return in three days' time the dress will be ready for you.'

Outside in the icy street, Alyssa felt as warm as toast. She positively glowed with happiness. The dress was the most expensive garment she'd ever bought, but she didn't mind dipping into the money her grandmother had left her. She felt sure she would have approved.

Her feet barely touched the ground as she hurried through the crowds of Christmas shoppers, glancing occasionally at the charmingly decorated shop windows. Her mind buzzed with the arrangements that she would have to make before she could be married.

Who could she possibly find to give her away in the church? It would have to be an old family friend. One of her mother's admirers who still lived here in Paris, perhaps? Yes, she knew the very one—and his phone number was in her address book.

The wedding was finally arranged for two days before Christmas. There had been a great deal of discussion between Alyssa, Pierre and his parents about whether it would be possible to have the wedding on Christmas Day, but in the midst of it all Pierre had stated quite clearly to his parents that he and Alyssa wanted to return to Paris on Christmas Eve.

They were both agreed that they wanted a quiet Christmas, on their own, in their own apartment, after all the excitement of the wedding and the organisation and plans leading up to it.

As Alyssa looked out of the window of Pierre's parents' house she reflected that she had been right in her assumption that his mother was a strong, confident character. As soon as Pierre had phoned to say that he and Alyssa were going to be married Sabine had wanted to take over all the organisation, right to the very last detail.

Initially Alyssa had been happy to go along with this. She had still been heavily involved with her work at the *clinique* and had had little time to spare. But on the question of which day they would marry neither she nor Pierre had given in to the parental idea that they should remain in the south-west until after Christmas.

Pierre had pointed out that he had to be back on the island of Ste Cécile early in the New Year, so would need time in Paris to organise his apartment and hand over his work at the *clinique* to Dr Cheveny.

Alyssa and Pierre had discussed the idea of spending Christmas in Paris with each other and decided that it *wasn't* selfish of them to want to be alone together, living in their apartment. After all, it would be their honeymoon.

From the moment Pierre had announced they were going to be married their time hadn't been their own. They'd both continued to work each day at the *clinique*, but had been overwhelmed by social invitations from the rest of the medical staff who all wanted to be a part of the happy couple's life.

They'd been invited to so many pre-Christmas parties that Alyssa had felt exhausted. They'd even hosted their own pre-wedding party in the Christmassy *clinique* dining room, which had been combined with a leaving party for Pierre now that Dr Cheveny was soon to return as *méde-cin-chef*.

They'd driven down from Paris the day before, and now they had a whole day in which to make final preparations. She wouldn't disturb Pierre, who was sleeping in a bedroom further down the landing. His final work schedule at the *clinique* had been excessive, and during their drive from Paris yesterday he had seemed very tired. As they'd driven off the ring road that skirted Bordeaux and headed out towards the coast Alyssa had insisted she take over the driving for the last few kilometres.

On arriving at the house Pierre had made an effort to be sociable with his parents, who had greeted both of them very warmly, but after a light supper they'd retired to their rooms. It seemed strange to be apart from Pierre in the night, but Alyssa had adhered to the sleeping arrangements which her hostess and soon to be mother-in-law had made for them. Sabine came from an older generation where the bride didn't sleep with the bridegroom until after they were married.

This evening they would go through a civil wedding ceremony in the nearby town of Arcachon, after which Pierre's parents were hosting a family dinner, but until then their time was their own.

Alyssa continued to gaze out at the beautiful view, wondering if she dared to slip out of the house and run down to the sea without waking anybody. The sea was angrily pounding on the shore at the end of the garden, the white-capped waves spreading their foam over the rocky beach. She turned to reach for the warm sweater she'd tossed on to a chair the night before.

The door was opening.

Pierre, wearing an old, unfamiliar brown robe, obviously borrowed from his father, came into her room, crossing the thick-carpeted floor in bare feet.

'I've missed you,' he whispered, taking her in his arms.

Alyssa sighed as she snuggled against the all familiar body of the man she loved so much. 'I've missed you too.'

Pierre looked longingly towards Alyssa's bed. 'Why don't we…?'

Alyssa adopted a mock scandalised expression. 'I'm saving myself for tomorrow night—my honeymoon night.'

Pierre groaned. 'In that case, let's go for a walk to burn off my frustration. I'll go and get dressed.'

Pierre unlatched the little garden gate that led immediately on to the shore and they ran hand in hand towards the pounding waves. Alyssa screamed with excitement as a huge wave bore down on them and they had to retreat to the safety of the upper tide mark, with its piles of seaweed and driftwood.

'The tide's going out,' Pierre said, drawing Alyssa close

against his side. 'I remember being brought here as a child for a brief holiday sometimes. It's been my parents' holiday home since they were married. Before that it belonged to Sabine's uncle, who left it to them in his will. They always made a point of coming back to France once a year, if my father could get away from his work in the West Indies.'

'Sounds idyllic!' Alyssa said. 'Living most of the year in the sun and then coming over to France for a holiday.'

'That's what I'm intending *we'll* do, Alyssa,' Pierre told her, as he kissed the tip of her nose in a playful gesture. 'You're cold. Let's go back into the warm house.'

'Not yet. I don't mind the cold. And I want you all to myself for a while. Let's walk; that will keep us warm.'

They walked briskly along the shoreline, talking excitedly like children making plans for a great adventure— except the adventure was their future together. As they ran a mock race back to the house Alyssa felt an overwhelming sense of belonging, of being exactly where she wanted to be, with the man who was exactly right for her.

The town hall was lit up brightly, as if to proclaim its importance at this festive season, declaring the pride that the citizens should feel for their town council. The imposing façade was festooned with chains of lights leading up to a huge star of Bethlehem at the apex of the collonaded front. Alyssa, following Pierre in through the covered portico, noticed a rough wooden shade which housed a nativity scene with the three kings bearing gifts for the infant in the cradle.

Reaching the main hall where the civil ceremony was to take place, she felt her heart lifting at the sight of the Christmas stars adorning the walls. Yes, Christmas was almost upon them, and here she was, at last going through the first part of her wedding ceremony. Tomorrow in the church would be even more daunting.

The room was crowded with people. Nervously smoothing down the skirt of her newly purchased, expensive Parisian suit, Alyssa looked around her. She hadn't a clue who most of these people were. She was grateful when Sabine, resplendent in a heavy silk dress with matching coat and a tiny hat perched on the top of her highlighted grey hair, introduced some of them to her, but the names didn't stick in Alyssa's mind. Seemingly most of the people were relatives or distant cousins of Claude and Sabine, who lived in the area or had travelled down from Paris.

A large, important, official-looking man called for silence and the conversation died down. Alyssa felt she was in a dream as she made the required responses in French. She glanced sideways at Pierre, who looked so handsome in a new grey suit. His responses were loud and clear. Alyssa had no idea what hers sounded like. The only important thing was that she made those vows...and meant to keep them. She prayed with her whole heart that Pierre felt the same way.

As they were pronounced man and wife Pierre turned to her. His kiss was brief, but oh, so sensual, giving a hint, a promise, of what was to come when all the ceremony had been dispensed with.

The waiting for the civil ceremony to begin had seemed endless, but now it was all over and Alyssa was caught up in a crowd of friendly, excited people, all wanting to kiss the bride, shake hands with the groom and congratulate them both.

Pierre succeeded at last in helping Alyssa into the beribboned car that was waiting outside for them. The driver began to sound his horn as soon as they drove away from the kerb.

'French tradition after a wedding,' Pierre said, in explanation of the honking of the horn which continued as they drove down the road that skirted the Bay of Arcachon.

Alyssa smiled. 'I know. I used to hear the sound of wedding cars when I was trying to sleep at my grandmother's as a child.'

'And to think we've got to do it all again tomorrow,' Pierre said, as Alyssa snuggled against him now that they had left the town behind them and were climbing the steep coastal path.

'I'm looking forward to our wedding in church,' Alyssa said quietly. 'The civil ceremony was only a formality, but tomorrow…'

'Formality or not, we're married, Madame Dupont,' Pierre said huskily, kissing her with a tenderness that took her breath away.

'I'm half-French you know,' Alyssa said, eventually forcing herself to move out of the circle of his arms. 'So I do know that tradition dictates we don't sleep together until after the church ceremony.'

Pierre groaned again. 'That's the second time today you've put me in my place. But I'm warning you, the honeymoon will be something out of this world.'

Alyssa leaned up to kiss his cheek. 'I certainly hope so.'

The car was coming to a halt outside Pierre's parents' house. Alyssa ran a hand through her hair, trying to restore it to the style which the visiting hairdresser had imposed upon it that afternoon.

'Leave your hair as it is,' Pierre said, ruffling her short blonde strands even more. 'I prefer you with the casual look. This is how I always used to remember you during the eight years we were apart.'

For an instant Alyssa could feel tears pricking behind her eyes. All those years she'd wasted without being close to Pierre. But now she could make up for it. Now she could begin to be a wife to him…and maybe…just maybe…the mother to his children.

The house seemed strangely quiet as they walked into the entrance hall, but then Pierre's mother came hurrying out of the salon to greet them. She had taken off her silk coat but remained in the tailored dress, which showed off her slim figure to perfection. Sabine was a handsome, well-preserved woman, and Alyssa could only guess at her age…late sixties, perhaps? Pierre's white-haired father was well into his seventies, and suffered with arthritis that forced him to walk painfully with a stick. But Sabine was still sprightly and full of boundless energy.

'We're in the salon, having an aperitif. Our dinner to-night is for close family only, so there will be just five of us.'

Alyssa looked at Pierre, who appeared as puzzled as she did. Five? Who was the other person who qualified as close family?

As Alyssa went into the sitting room she looked around at the Christmas decorations. Strands of silver paper were looped across the room and the Christmas tree, taking pride of place in the large window area looking out over the sea, was heavy with presents and coloured decorations of every shape and size.

A log fire blazed in the hearth. It was like any family gathering at Christmas…except who was the unknown man standing beside the Christmas tree? Alyssa remembered seeing him at the back of the crowded room in the town hall. No one had introduced her then, so she'd assumed he was one of the distant, obscure cousins.

He was a tall, distinguished-looking man, probably in his early fifties, his dark hair flecked with grey. He stepped forward now and came towards them, holding out his hand towards Pierre.

Pierre automatically put out his hand to the stranger.

'I'm very nervous about meeting you,' the man said quietly, still holding on to Pierre's hand. 'I'm André Filou…your father.'

Alyssa, watching Pierre's reaction, saw the blood drain from his face.

'You're…you're my father?' Pierre said, in a hoarse voice that was barely audible.

Alyssa swallowed hard. The moment was too poignant to bear. She held her breath as she waited for Pierre's reaction. He had every right to be upset with the father who'd abandoned him when he was a baby, but she knew that bitterness wasn't a part of Pierre's character.

Pierre reached towards his father. With a sigh of relief, André Filou put his arms around his son and held him in a firm bear hug for several moments.

The sound of a champagne cork popping brought Alyssa back to earth. The whole scenario had seemed unreal, but now Claude was holding out the bottle he'd just uncorked and the foaming champagne was spilling on to the carpet.

'One of you youngsters come and do the honours,' he called out from his chair. 'We've all got a lot to celebrate tonight.'

Pierre poured champagne for everyone and then, holding up his glass, he gave the first toast. 'To my beautiful bride.'

Alyssa smiled round and, raising her own glass, proposed a toast to her wonderful bridegroom.

'And I'd like to propose a toast to André,' Claude said, sitting bolt upright in his chair and holding his glass high in the air. 'It took some courage for him to come here and meet his son. To André!'

Curiosity was eating away at Alyssa. She longed to know all the answers. Why had it taken André so long to make contact? And why had he finally made the effort?

It transpired that André was a consultant surgeon at a hospital in Poitiers. He was married to a gynaecologist and they had two children, a boy and a girl, both studying medicine in Paris. The similarities in their lifestyles seemed endless, but Alyssa was still avid to know more about these newly acquired relatives.

During the course of the evening, whilst they were drinking their aperitifs and during the prolonged family supper, the story of what had really happened emerged.

André and Dianne had met when they were sixteen, on a skiing holiday in the Alps where different schools were amalgamated in one skiing course. This was how André, from a relatively poor family, had met up with the well-heeled Dianne. According to André, it had been love at first sight for both of them, and they'd taken every opportunity to be together.

A couple of months after returning home to Poitier André had got a phone call from Dianne. She was pregnant and desperate to know what to do. Her father was a prominent politician and Dianne hadn't dared tell her parents. André, being young and idealistic, had felt it his duty to protect Dianne. He'd drawn out savings from his bank, sent a cheque to Dianne and then the pair of them had flown, independently, to meet up on the island of Ste Cécile, with very little idea of what they were going to do when they got there.

Pierre reached across the table and topped up his father's glass with red wine.

'Thanks, Pierre,' André said, raising the glass to his lips. 'You've all made me so welcome since I arrived here today. And you especially, Pierre. I'm glad you're not angry with me.'

'Why should I be angry?' Pierre said. 'I have wonderful parents who have looked after me all my life. Claude explained to me when I was old enough to be told I was adopted that my mother had been very young and unable to keep me. Later he told me that she belonged to a prominent English family who would have disapproved of her having a baby when she was unmarried.'

'An English family?' Alyssa queried.

André smiled across the table at her. 'Yes, Dianne's mother was English. That was part of the charm for me—her beautifully accented French. When she was angry with me she would shout in a mixture of French and English which I found fascinating, and then...' André gave a sigh. 'But you don't want to hear about our stormy romance.'

'I gather you were very much in love with Dianne?' Alyssa said quietly.

André nodded. 'Yes, I was. But it didn't last. It was a young and immature love that didn't survive. My money didn't last very long out there on Ste Cécile. I bought a small tent, which I pitched under the palm trees near the beach.'

'And that was the first time I saw you, André,' Claude said. 'You were sitting on the beach with your heavily pregnant girlfriend and I started to worry about the pair of you.'

'I remember you persuaded us to move into your house so that you could look after us. Dianne was nearing her time and she'd had no medical examinations. I was so glad when you took over her antenatal care.'

'As I recall,' put in Sabine, 'Dianne needed very little persuasion to move out of that tent into a comfortable bedroom in our house. She was in a huge panic and didn't know what to do.'

Pierre nodded slowly. 'I understand what the poor girl must have been going through. Was that when the idea of adoption arose?'

Sabine nodded. 'Dianne begged me to adopt you. She said then she'd know her baby would have a good home. I was desperate to have a child myself, but my gynaecologist had told me I couldn't have children and…'

'That was when I phoned my lawyer in Paris,' Claude said, taking over the story from Sabine, who was overcome with emotion at the poignant memories. 'He drew up the necessary papers, and after baby Pierre was born in our house the lawyer flew over to finalise the details.'

'But why have you made contact now, André?' Alyssa asked quietly.

André's face clouded. 'Dianne was killed in a riding accident a couple of months ago. I'd had no contact with her since…since we left Ste Cécile, but I read it in the papers.'

'So did I,' Claude said. 'I knew that it was Dianne who hadn't ever wanted to make contact, so when I knew Pierre and Alyssa were going to be married I thought it was a good time for a family reunion. I know how Pierre has always longed to have his own flesh and blood around him.'

'You've been the best father I could ever have wished for, Claude,' Pierre said, his voice husky with emotion. 'But now that I've met my real father I feel totally complete. Alyssa and I will look forward to having you and your family joining up with my own family.'

André smiled across the table. 'I look forward to that. Are you planning a big family?'

'We're hoping so,' Pierre said in a confident tone. 'But if it's not to be we shall be happy in other ways.'

Alyssa held her breath as yet another toast was proposed, this time to their unborn children.

She couldn't bear to disappoint Pierre now.

CHAPTER TEN

THE ancient church stood on the walls of a small medieval town which was set on a rocky promontory on the shores of the Gironde. Usually cars were not allowed inside the walls of the town, but today the stately wedding car drove through the ancient stone gateway and drew up in front of the church already decorated by the congregation in preparation for Christmas.

Silvery lights shone around the porch and up the aisle. Roses, carnations and ferns had been arranged around the old stone windows through which shone the last rays of the late-afternoon sun.

The church seemed to be packed with everybody who'd attended yesterday's civil ceremony alongside other guests and well-wishers. Alyssa was poignantly aware of the beautiful, haunting music as she walked down the aisle, but the people, craning their necks to get a better view of the bride in her fabulous white gown, were a blur through her heavy white lace veil.

As she peered through it Alyssa knew that if she kept her eyes on that tall, dark-suited man waiting for her at the altar, she would survive the seemingly interminable walk.

She was holding on to the arm of an old friend of her mother's, who'd driven down from Paris for the occasion.

When Alyssa had phoned Jean Beauvois in Paris he'd said he would be honoured to give Alyssa away on her wedding day, and had admitted to a secret unrequited love for her mother many years ago.

171

Alyssa had been deeply relieved that Jean had agreed as she hadn't seen him since she was a child. Most of her grandmother's friends and relatives had moved away from Paris or had died, and her mother had been an only child. There had been no contact with her father since he'd walked out on them and Alyssa had long since accepted that he didn't want to acknowledge his first marriage.

The music stopped and she stood beside Pierre, making her responses, listening to his. The church was hushed and silent apart from the occasional cries of a small child who was rapidly taken outside by his mother so that the service wouldn't be disrupted.

And then Pierre was lifting her veil, kissing her gently, leaving a promise of their wedding night hanging in the air as he took hold of her hand and led her through the crowded church out into the cold December sunlight.

The church bells were ringing out into the air, the sea-gulls gave their distinctive cries as they swooped down, and the swishing of the waves on the shore formed a continual background of natural sound. Pierre was squeezing her hand and she felt her heart would burst with happiness.

'We're married,' he whispered as they stood in front of the flashing lights of the photographers.

'Can't believe it,' Alyssa whispered back.

The guests were beginning to move away down the hill to the hotel where the reception was to be held. Not long before they could be alone now...

It was only later that night, when all the guests had departed from the hotel, that Pierre and Alyssa were finally able to be alone. Alyssa looked around the bridal suite and drew in her breath.

Gently Pierre stooped down and began to undo the tiny silk-covered buttons at the back of her silk gown.

She looked down at the marks along the hem of her gown and smiled up at him. 'Most of the men I danced with have managed to leave their footprints on my dress.'

Pierre laughed. 'Every man in the room wanted to dance with you. You must be exhausted, but may I have the last dance with my beautiful bride?'

Pierre pressed a switch beside the bed and the quiet strains of a slow waltz filled the bedroom. Alyssa stepped out of her dress, allowing it to fall to the ground like a silken waterfall as Pierre drew her into his arms for their final dance.

As the music stopped he carried her gently over to their honeymoon bed.

'Happy?' he whispered, as she snuggled against him.

'Mmm…what do you think…?'

The lights of Paris seemed even brighter than usual this evening. In addition to the normal street lights, chains of coloured bulbs ran along each side, while shops, hotels bars and cinemas, decorated with every conceivable kind of festoon and trimming, blazed with the spirit of Christmas.

'Well, it is Christmas Eve,' Alyssa said, as she looked out over the Seine.

They were sitting in a small café on the Left Bank. It was one of the restaurants they'd frequented during their first wild fling together, but this was their first time there during this second time around romance.

'I didn't want to bring you here before I knew you were really going to marry me,' Pierre said, putting his hand over hers.

They were sitting in their favourite corner table. Looking around the crowded room, Alyssa could see other romantic couples holding hands. The candles on the table and on the Christmas tree in the corner of the room flickered. The room was strung with Christmas lanterns and the windows adorned with sparkling decorations created to look like snow.

'We mustn't forget we've got to do the rounds at the *clinique* tomorrow,' Alyssa said.

Pierre smiled. 'I won't forget. Even though I might become a bit distracted by our own Christmas celebrations.'

They finished their meal and walked out to hear the sound of Christmas carols echoing down the narrow cobbled side street. Students from the nearby university were making the clear Christmas Eve air resound with their harmonies.

Pierre hailed a taxi, which swept them off to the foot of the Eiffel Tower.

'You've got to see Paris in all its glory on Christmas Eve,' Pierre told Alyssa as he led her up the narrow iron staircase, gripping her hand as they made it to the *deuxième étage*—the second floor.

Laughing at Pierre's enthusiasm and energy, Alyssa agreed that in spite of being breathless it had been worth the effort. The whole of Paris was laid out in front of them, the magnificent city sprawling out on either side of the stately Seine. And, yes, she had to agree that the lights of Paris were even more spectacular because it was Christmas Eve.

They were moving off again.

Alyssa put her hands on Pierre's shoulders as they descended the stairs to saunter across the bridge that took them back to the Right Bank.

'Not too tired?'

'No, I love being out in Paris on a night like this. Pierre, let's just walk—let's lose ourselves in the streets and soak up the atmosphere of Christmas Eve in Paris.'

How long they walked, hand in hand, Alyssa had no idea, but the atmosphere was so electric she didn't want to stop—the happy crowds of revellers, the music as the doors of bars and restaurants opened, the pavement cafés where people laughed and joked as they stamped their feet to keep warm...

And then they found themselves climbing upwards, taking the cobbled street that led past the *clinique* where Pascal Coumau had given Alyssa such hope for the future.

Neither of them spoke about the problem that was uppermost in their minds.

Alyssa's period had arrived that morning. When she'd told Pierre he'd said it didn't matter that she wasn't pregnant. They were together, that was all that mattered to him, and besides, he'd found his father—his own flesh and blood.

But she'd seen the wistful disappointment in his eyes before he'd put up his façade of indifference. Life was a compromise, she told herself now as they mounted the steps to the Sacré Coeur cathedral. She had everything she could possibly wish for now. Everything except...

She deliberately blotted out her disappointment as, hand in hand, they went into the great cathedral. At the far end the choir were singing a haunting Christmas anthem. Alyssa bought a candle and lit it. As the small light flickered she found herself making a plea to her favourite saint that her final wish might come true.

But if it didn't...

She glanced up at Pierre, who had been watching her.

He knew what she was wishing, but he didn't speak about it. They had each other and that was enough.

He led her through the maze of streets surrounding the cathedral, past the artists in the Place du Tertre, who were still painting portraits by the light of the overhead lamps, and took her into a small café-bar called the Butte des Vignes. A young man was playing an accordion—all the favourite tunes she remembered from her Parisian holidays staying with Grand-maman. She leaned back against the chair and sipped at the cognac which Pierre had prescribed to keep out the cold.

'Happy Christmas, Alyssa,' he said, his voice husky. 'Next Christmas we'll be in the sun. I hope you won't miss the cold?'

Alyssa shook her head. Wherever Pierre was she would be happy.

Christmas Day at the *clinique* was a festive occasion. In the beautifully decorated wards Père Noel, in the shape of the small, rotund Yves Grandet, was doing his rounds whilst uttering lots of 'ho, ho, hos' amid hilarious laughter from the patients.

Pierre and Alyssa stopped off in the orthopaedic ward to wish Henri a Happy Christmas. Sylvie told them that the infection in Henri's leg was finally under control and they were hoping to send him home for New Year.

'Congratulations on your wedding!' Sylvie said, as they all stood around Henri's bed.

'Thank you,' Alyssa said. 'And thank you for looking after me when I first arrived.'

'I recognised at once that you were the one for Pierre.' Sylvie nodded with a smile. 'You pretended you couldn't care less, but I sensed what was happening.'

'So did I,' Henri said. 'You didn't fool me. And I'll expect a slice of the christening cake!'

'Me too!' Sylvie said.

Pierre put his arm around Alyssa in a comforting gesture as he sensed her unease.

'We're in no hurry,' he said evenly.

Taking their leave, they went on to the obstetrics ward. Marie Lefevre had remained in the *clinique* for extensive tests and counselling following her ectopic pregnancy. She had seemed much brighter when Alyssa had spoken to her a few days before.

'Happy Christmas, Marie,' Alyssa said, smiling down at her patient.

'How was the wedding, Dr Alyssa?' she asked, sitting forward in the chair beside her bed to grasp Alyssa's hand.

'Out of this world,' Alyssa said. 'But we're both looking forward to having some time to ourselves.'

'You're going out to live and work in the West Indies soon, aren't you?' Jacqueline said, coming across the ward to see them.

She was holding the latest arrival on the obstetrics ward. 'Thought you might like to see our Christmas baby. Baby Beatrice was born at two minutes past midnight this morning.'

'She's beautiful,' Alyssa said, taking the tiny little blonde-haired infant in her arms. The dear little rosebud mouth puckered into the makings of a smile.

'I know that's supposed to be wind,' Pierre said gently, as he touched the little mouth with his finger. 'But I like to think that Beatrice is smiling at us.'

'It's obvious the pair of you love babies,' Jacqueline said. 'I expect you'll have a big family out there in the West Indies.'

'Could be,' Pierre said lightly. 'We're leaving Paris in ten days' time.'

'We're going to miss you both,' Jacqueline told them, stretching out her hands to take baby Beatrice from Alyssa.

'And we'll miss all our friends here, Jacqueline.'

Alyssa looked enquiringly at Pierre. The seemingly endless rounds of patients and staff were taking their toll on her strength. She longed for the peace and quiet of their apartment…

The small tree in the corner of their sitting room seemed very tiny compared with the huge trees which had adorned each ward at the *clinique*.

'It's big enough for the two of us,' Pierre said. 'And next year…well, maybe next year we'll get a huge one.'

'Yes, maybe next year,' Alyssa said, thankful that Pierre hadn't voiced his obvious thoughts.

Alyssa picked up their plates from the kitchen table and took them over to the sink. Having had endless wedding feasts and a huge Christmas lunch, they had made their supper a simple affair. Alyssa had requested her favourite light meal, so Pierre had cooked a soufflé omelette.

He came up behind her now, putting his arms around her waist and holding her against him. 'Shall we have an early night? Catch up on our sleep?'

Alyssa turned and looked up into his eyes, revelling in the tender expression that mirrored her own.

'Can't think of anything I'd like better.'

She knew the time for feasting and celebration was over. Their real life together was now beginning. She had no idea what the future had in store for her, but whatever it was she was sure that Pierre would always be at her side.

The last few days had cemented their love. Not only was Pierre her lover, her husband, but he was her best and most trusted friend. She couldn't ask for more than that.

Or could she…?

EPILOGUE

ALYSSA ran down the beach into the blue sparkling sea. It was a perfect morning. The sort of morning when she was used to settling herself amongst the rocks for an hour or so, before it was time to help Pierre with his morning clinic.

Out here on Ste Cécile she had more time for relaxing than she'd ever had in her life. For a couple of hours each morning she helped Pierre in the clinic adjoining their beautiful spacious house. After that, if there were patients to be seen on the surrounding islands, she would sometimes go in the boat with Pierre to lend a hand, or simply chat with her new-found friends.

She and Pierre made a point of having lunch together, either at the house or in one of the tiny restaurants here on Ste Cécile or on the surrounding islands. But usually by the middle of the afternoon they were free to spend time on the beach—swimming together, exploring the rocky creeks in their boat or simply lying under the palm trees, their fingers interlaced, as they talked endlessly about every subject under the sun.

Every subject except the one which was usually uppermost in their minds.

Pascal Coumau had told them to wait a year before they gave up the idea of having a baby naturally. He'd given Alyssa his personal phone number, telling her to call him any time she was worried. Only three weeks ago she'd been on the point of picking up the phone. One year on,

179

with Christmas almost upon them, there was no sign of their much-wanted baby.

But two weeks ago her period hadn't arrived. And she was always on time.

Slipping off her sandals, she remembered how she'd tried to contain her excitement. She hadn't dared to raise Pierre's hopes. For the first few months of their marriage she'd reported every little detail of her menstrual cycle to him, but lately she'd been more guarded.

There was no point in both of them breaking their hearts. They had a wonderful life here on the island—she couldn't wish for a more fantastic husband, their love grew stronger every day, and yet when a much-wanted child hadn't materialised...

'Hey, wait for me!'

She turned at the sound of Pierre's voice. He was running down the beach towards her, clad only in black swimming trunks. She held her breath at the sight of his firm muscular body. It was only a couple of hours since he'd held her in his arms and her body was still tingling from their lovemaking.

He flung wet salty arms around her. 'You do realise you've still got your dress on, don't you?' he said, laughing as the spray from the waves made them both even wetter.

'I didn't intend to swim,' she said, turning over on to her back, her cotton dress floating around her like petals on a large flower. 'I just got excited about something, and you were down in the clinic treating that patient who'd called in early, so...'

'Hey, steady on. What was so exciting that you forgot to take your dress off?'

His face in the water was oh, so close to hers as she continued to look up at the heavenly blue sky. A sky that would never look the same again now that the miracle had happened.

'I...I did a test...just now...and...'

'Tell me—tell me, Alyssa!' Pierre was holding her in his arms now.

She trod water. 'We ought to swim back to the shore. It would be such a pity if we both drowned now...now that...now that we're going to be parents...'

Pierre drew Alyssa on to her back as if he were lifesaving. 'Don't move another muscle, Alyssa. I'm holding you. Now, just relax and—'

'Pierre, I'm not ill. I'm going to have a baby.'

'I know, and it's the most wonderful day of my life. I love you so much Alyssa. I always did, but now...'

Calm and relaxed, now in dry clothes, Alyssa sat on the terrace holding a glass of freshly squeezed orange juice in her hand. Pierre had insisted she do nothing for the rest of the day, having decided that her early-morning dip had been too strenuous in light of her condition.

'You're not going to cosset me all through the nine months, are you, Pierre?'

He smiled. 'Of course I am. We're not going to take any chances with this one. I'll cosset you through your first pregnancy, but after that, when you're an experienced mum, we'll take it in our stride.'

'Don't you think we ought to start phoning people?' Alyssa said. 'All those pointed remarks that Sabine has been making to us. And what about André and his wife? They're becoming as bad as Sabine whenever they phone.'

'We'll tell them all together when they come out here for Christmas—our first real family Christmas together.'

'I'm so looking forward to Christmas this year.'

Pierre smiled lovingly. 'Make the most of it. It will

never be just the two of us again. Baby will make three. We'll be up to our eyes in nappies.'

'I don't mind if you don't,' Alyssa said softly, as she realised that, against all the odds, all her dreams had now—unbelievably—come true.

Pierre folded her in his arms. *'Ma petite princesse,'* he whispered. 'I love you so much. I've always loved you, since the first moment I saw you…but now…even more than I ever thought possible…'

Alyssa closed her eyes as she revelled in being oh, so close to Pierre. She would take such care of this precious baby inside her. She was strong and healthy now, but her experience of obstetrics had taught her never to take anything for granted in a pregnancy.

She gave a little shiver as a trace of doubt ran through her. Pierre held her away from him and his eyes searched hers.

'You're going to be fine! I just know that this time next year—'

Alyssa put her finger against his lips. 'Don't say it, Pierre,' she whispered, and she realised that he too, after all his medical experience had taught him, was having doubts.

EPILOGUE TWO

ALYSSA waved her hand as the hire car taking the last of the Christmas guests away disappeared down the drive. It had been a hectic Christmas and she was looking forward to having some time alone with Pierre and baby André. Looking at her son now, sleeping peacefully in Pierre's arms, she felt a surge of love for both of them.

'Let's have a drink on the terrace, Pierre, now it's just the three of us.'

Pierre smiled. 'I must admit I'm looking forward to having the pair of you to myself. Sabine can be so bossy where babies are concerned!'

Alyssa laughed. 'Sabine is an expert on everything! But she really enjoys herself spoiling André, doesn't she? And all those presents they brought!'

'And André is over the moon that his grandson is his namesake.'

Alyssa sighed contentedly as she gently took André from Pierre and sank down into one of the cane chairs on the veranda.

Pierre handed her a glass of champagne. 'It doesn't seem like three years since we married.'

Alyssa eased herself back against the cushions. 'In some ways it's flown past, but in others…'

She swallowed hard as she looked at Pierre.

He put out his hand and tilted her chin so that she was looking up at him. 'You were marvellous all the way through your pregnancy. You needn't have worried.'

'But I couldn't help worrying,' Alyssa said quietly.

Pierre nodded understandingly. 'Neither could I. But we needn't have worried, need we? And next time…'

'Next time?'

'I would say you're a natural at having babies, Madame Dupont.'

'Is that your considered opinion, Doctor?'

'Absolutely!'

'I'm glad about that, because it just so happens that I did a test this morning, and…'

'You're not going to tell me that—?'

Alyssa nodded and smiled.

'Alyssa—I think you're wonderful!'

'Well, you did give me some help. And I won't be scared of going through this pregnancy now that I know everything is OK. What shall we call this one? If it's a girl we could call her Sabine, and if…'

'Alyssa, let's leave all that for the moment and just think about ourselves,' Pierre said gently, taking their baby from Alyssa's arms. 'Come upstairs and we'll put André in his cot. We need some time alone together.'

'Don't worry. We'll always make time for each other,' Alyssa said softly as she walked up the stairs beside her husband and son.

And later, as she lay in Pierre's arms, listening to the sound of the waves on the shore, she knew that her dream, her wonderful dream, was going to get better as each year passed.

HOME BY CHRISTMAS

by

Jennifer Taylor

Jennifer Taylor lives in the north-west of England with her husband Bill. She had been writing Mills & Boon® romances for some years, but when she discovered Medical Romance™, she was so captivated by these heart-warming stories that she set out to write them herself! When not writing or doing research for her latest book, Jennifer's hobbies include reading, travel, walking her dog and retail therapy (shopping!). Jennifer claims all that bending and stretching to reach the shelves is the best exercise possible. She's always delighted to hear from readers, so do visit her at www.jennifer-taylor.com

CHAPTER ONE

'THERE'S something I want to ask you, Lisa. Will you marry me?'

'M-marry you?'

Lisa Bennett's hazel eyes widened as she stared at the man seated across the table from her. They were in the middle of having dinner at Dalverston's newest and most up-market restaurant, The Blossoms, when James had dropped his bombshell. It was two weeks before Christmas and the restaurant was filled to capacity that night. The steady hum of a dozen different conversations filled the elegantly appointed dining room so it was little wonder she was afraid that she might have misheard him.

'Don't look so surprised, darling. Surely you must have realised how I feel about you?' James Cameron reached across the table and took hold of her hand. 'I'm crazy about you, Lisa. Isn't it obvious?'

'I...well...um...' Lisa tried to marshal her thoughts but the announcement had come like a bolt from the blue. *Had* she had an inkling that James felt this way about her?

She searched her heart and sighed as she was forced to admit that there had been a number of signs in recent weeks that his feelings towards her had been deepening. They had met at a mutual friend's birthday party in the summer and had started going out together a short time later. Lisa had deliberately kept their relationship low-key in the beginning, but, if she was honest, she had sensed that James had been starting to want rather more than that. She had simply tried

5

not to think about it because it still made her feel a little guilty to imagine falling in love with another man.

She hurriedly pushed that thought to the back of her mind because there was no point thinking about the past when she had this present situation to deal with. 'I knew that you liked me,' she began hesitantly, then stopped when James laughed.

'It's a bit more than that, my love.' He gave her a rueful smile. 'I like an awful lot of people, but I don't go around asking them to marry me, I assure you!'

'Of course not,' she said hurriedly, wishing that she knew what to say to him.

If only Will was here then she could have asked his advice, she thought wistfully, then sighed again because at some point she would have to stop relying on Will to sort out her problems. She was a grown woman of thirty-three and held down a responsible job as a junior registrar on the children's intensive care unit at Dalverston General Hospital. Surely it shouldn't be beyond her to cope with a proposal of marriage without needing her best friend's advice?

The thought of not being able to turn to Will for help made her feel rather odd for some reason. Fortunately the waiter arrived at that point with the dessert trolley so she took her time choosing what she wanted to give herself a breathing space. By the time a crystal glass filled with white and dark chocolate mousse was placed in front of her, Lisa was feeling a little steadier even though she had no idea what she was going to tell James in answer to his proposal. Did she like him enough to want to spend the rest of her life with him?

'Look, sweetheart, I can tell this has come as a shock to you.' James picked up her hand and kissed her fingertips.

Lisa shivered as a frisson ran through her. She had noticed with increasing frequency how she responded to James's gentle kisses, his tender caresses. It had been reassuring to know that she could still respond to a man because for so long it had felt as though that part of her had died. Maybe her feelings for him were deeper than she had realised?

'It was a surprise,' she admitted, feeling her heart race at the thought. She summoned a smile, deeming it wiser to keep the mood light because she still wasn't sure what her answer was going to be. 'It's not every day that a woman receives a proposal of marriage.'

'I sincerely hope not!' James kissed her fingertips again, grinning when he felt her shiver once more. His expression was far more assured when he continued. 'I would be really worried if you confessed that this was your fourth proposal in as many days.'

'Fat chance of that. I spend my days surrounded by sick children and anxious parents. The only other man I see on a regular basis is Will, and I really and truly can't see Will asking me to marry him!'

James laughed and she followed suit, but there seemed to be a sting in the tail of that statement. Will certainly wouldn't ask her to marry him and she wouldn't expect him to, so what was wrong?

Will was her best friend, the one person in the whole world to whom she could always turn in a crisis. The boundaries of their relationship had been drawn up years ago and romance had never featured in it. Yet for some reason she found herself conjuring up a picture of how Will would look if he'd been sitting across the table from her at that moment.

His dark brown hair would be flopping over his forehead and there would be a smile on his mouth because Will was always smiling. It was one of the reasons why he was the most popular member of Dalverston General's paediatric surgery team. Everyone loved Will—staff, parents and especially the children.

He would be recounting some tale about what one of the children had done and his deep blue eyes would be sparkling with laughter. Naturally, he would have dressed for the occasion because dining out at The Blossoms was an event and ranked high on the 'must go there when I win the lottery' list that was pinned to the staffroom noticeboard. However, Will's ideas on what the well-dressed diner sported wouldn't be *quite* the same as everyone else's.

Lisa swallowed a chuckle as she imagined the mismatched shirt and tie Will would have chosen for the occasion. She'd never been able to decide if he was colour-blind or just plain crazy! She certainly couldn't imagine James wearing the kind of clothes that Will normally wore…

Lisa blinked and once again she was back in the present. She realised immediately that she had missed what James had said while she'd been daydreaming. She struggled to catch up, hoping that he hadn't noticed how abstracted she had been.

'And that's why I don't want you to give me your answer tonight, darling.'

'You don't?' she repeated, mentally filling in what had gone before. He must mean her answer to his proposal, she realised, and breathed a sigh of relief at being let off the hook for the moment.

'No.' He shrugged, his shoulders rising and falling beneath his suit jacket. James was a barrister and favoured the same kind of impeccable clothing out of work as he wore in court.

Lisa found herself thinking that Will didn't even own a suit—he wore sports jackets and trousers to work, and jeans and sweatshirts in his free time—before she forced herself to concentrate on the conversation. However, it was faintly alarming to realise how easily her thoughts kept wandering.

'You need time to think about this, Lisa, and I don't intend to put any pressure on you. I want you to be sure that you feel the same about me as I do about you. That's why I'm hoping that you will agree to spend Christmas with me at the cottage.' He squeezed her hand. 'I think it would help if we spent some time together, don't you?'

Lisa flushed because she understood what he was really saying. James had been very patient and hadn't tried to persuade her to go to bed with him even though she knew that he wanted to sleep with her. However, if she agreed to go to his cottage for Christmas then she would be agreeing to take their relationship a stage further, and maybe it *was* time that she did so, especially now that he had asked her to marry him. Surely, they both needed to be sure that the physical side of their relationship would be as pleasant as the rest?

'I...I think that would be a good idea,' she said huskily, then cleared her throat. It wasn't fair to James to make it appear as though she was agreeing to some sort of dreadful ordeal.

'I'd really love to spend Christmas with you,' she said more firmly, and saw his smile widen with delight.

'I'm so pleased, darling.' He leant across the table to kiss her then suddenly stopped and looked round. 'Hmm, probably not the best place to show you just how thrilled I am!'

Lisa laughed, although she couldn't help feeling a little disappointed by his lack of spontaneity. She dipped her spoon into the delicious chocolate confection in front of her and told herself sternly to stop acting like a child. A lot of James's important clients dined at The Blossoms so who could blame him for not wanting to make a spectacle of himself?

Still, Will wouldn't have done that. He wouldn't have given a damn who had been watching. He would have kissed the woman he loved right there in the middle of the busy restaurant and to hell with what anyone thought.

She frowned. How odd that she kept thinking about Will all the time.

'How's he doing?'

Will Saunders glanced at his colleague, Dave Carson, who was his anaesthetist that night. They were nearing the end of a gruelling five-hour-long operation to remove a metal stake from the abdomen of an eight-year-old boy called Daniel Kennedy.

Daniel had been climbing onto a garage roof to retrieve his football when he had slipped and fallen onto some iron railings. It had taken the emergency services almost two hours to cut him free. Will had gone to the scene of the accident, knowing that it was vital to have some idea what he would be dealing with when he got Daniel back to Theatre.

The metal stake had passed straight through Daniel's abdomen, missing his spinal column by mere fractions of an inch as it had exited through his back. It had caused extensive tissue and nerve damage, and severely damaged his large intestine, too. Just dealing with the massive amount of blood which the child had lost had been a major headache, and then there had been all the problems of realigning the torn muscles and blood vessels to stitch them back into place.

Infection would be their next, biggest obstacle to overcome, but Will knew that he mustn't look too far ahead. He had to focus on doing his job to the very best of his ability and leave the rest to his colleagues. It would take a team effort to pull the child through this ordeal.

'He's holding his own, but I'd be happier if you speeded things up,' Dave replied laconically from the head of the operating table. 'You'd think you would be a lot quicker at sewing up after all the practice you've had, Will.'

'Oh, he's not as slow as some I could mention.' Madge Riley, the Theatre sister, cut into the conversation. 'You should try working with Dr Maxwell and then you'd know what slow really means. It took him almost an hour to sew up after that emergency appendicectomy this morning. His hands were shaking so hard that he dropped the needle twice!'

'Give the poor guy a break, Madge,' Will exhorted. He waggled his eyebrows at her over the top of his mask. 'You know he's all fingers and thumbs because he's got a bit of a *thing* about you.'

'Can I help it if I have this effect on the younger men in the department?' Madge retorted, batting her eyelashes at him. Plump, grey-haired and on the wrong side of fifty, she kept threatening to retire, only she never quite got round to writing her letter of resignation. She was a superb nurse, though, and Will knew they were fortunate to have her working with them.

'Who said it was only the younger men who appreciated your charms?' he replied, his blue eyes glinting with laughter when she pulled a face at him.

He put a final stitch into the section of tissue he had been working on and nodded. 'Right, that should do it. We'll leave the wound open and pack it with gauze until we're sure there's no sign of infection setting in, although I doubt we'll be that lucky. Lord only knows what might have been on that lump of metalwork.'

He glanced at the chunk of iron railing which he had extracted from Daniel's body, thinking how amazing it was that the boy had survived this far. Now they would have to wait and see if he would pull through but, what with the blood loss and shock, the tissue damage and high risk of infection, the odds certainly seemed to be stacked against him.

Will tried to shrug off a momentary feeling of inadequacy as he left Theatre. It stemmed mainly from tiredness because an operation as complex as this one, coming on top of a full day's work, was bound to have been draining. However, he knew that it wasn't the only reason why he felt so flat. Lisa had been going out with James Cameron tonight and, try as he may, he couldn't shake off the feeling that there had been a reason why Cameron had taken her to The Blossoms for dinner. Was Cameron hoping that an expensive meal might persuade her into his bed, perhaps?

Will swore softly as he kicked open the door to the changing room. What business was it of his, anyway? Lisa was free to do whatever she chose, and if he was a true friend then he should be pleased that she had reached a point whereby she would consider having a relationship with another man.

She had been devastated when Gareth had been killed in that tragic skiing accident during their last year at med school together. Gareth had been an accomplished skiier but even he had been unable to do anything when a novice— who shouldn't have been on the advanced piste—had careered into him and knocked him off course. The Swiss police had explained that Gareth would have died instantly when he had hit the tree.

It had been Will who had flown out to Switzerland to identify his friend and bring him home, and Will who had made all the arrangements for Gareth's funeral. Gareth's elderly parents lived in Australia and had been too frail to make the journey to England, and Lisa had been far too upset to deal with it.

Her grief had known no bounds and Will had felt completely helpless as he had tried to comfort her. At one point he had feared that she would never get over Gareth's death, in fact. She had dropped out of college without sitting her final exams and he had honestly believed that she would give up medicine altogether. It had been almost two years before she had gone back to complete her studies, and in all that time Will had done his best to help and support her, spending long hours listening as she had talked about the plans she and Gareth had made for the future.

Gareth had been his best friend as well as Lisa's fiancé and Will had wanted to help in any way that he could. He had promised himself after the funeral that he would do everything in his power to make sure Lisa was happy for Gareth's sake. That was why he had invited her to share his flat when she had taken the job at Dalverston General, because it had meant that he would be around if she needed help.

Now it looked as though she was finally getting her life together and he should be glad about it, not feeling as though he were about to lose something more precious than life itself. Lisa had never been his in the first place so he couldn't lose her.

That thought just depressed him all the more so Will decided not to think about it as he shed his scrub suit and headed for the showers. The water was hot and he turned on the jets to full power, groaning half in pleasure but mostly in pain as the water pounded the aching muscles in his neck and shoulders. He'd spent most of the day in Theatre, plus a large chunk of the night, and his body was paying for the long hours spent bending over the operating table.

He turned off the water at last and briskly towelled himself dry then went back to the changing room to get dressed.

He was just taking his shirt off a hanger when there was a tap on the door and he looked round to find Lisa peering in at him.

'Can I come in?' she asked, hovering uncertainly in the doorway.

'Of course. I'm more or less decent.' He grabbed the shirt, feeling oddly uncomfortable about her seeing him half-dressed. Bearing in mind that they often bumped into one another coming out of the bathroom in the flat it seemed very strange, but he couldn't help it.

He quickly buttoned the shirt then pulled a tie from the rail. He glanced round when Lisa gave a choked little laugh. 'What?'

'Do you really think that tie goes with the shirt, Will?' she asked, a smile curving her mouth. She lifted warm hazel eyes to his and Will felt something inside him clench like a tightly bunched fist so that he had to force himself to breathe in then out before he could speak.

'I don't know,' he said, staring helplessly at the tie while he tried to work out what was wrong with him. Was having some sort of asthma attack, perhaps? Or had he developed a touch of angina? There was a definite pain in his chest and there was no doubt that breathing seemed to be a lot more difficult than it normally was. It was an effort to focus on the question Lisa had asked him when he felt so confused.

'What's wrong with it exactly?'

'It's green—*bright* green—and your shirt is blue.' She shrugged and once again he felt that iron fist grip his vital organs as he saw her small breasts rise and fall beneath her blue silk blouse. 'They…well…sort of clash.'

'Do they?' he muttered, dragging his eyes away and sucking in another desperate lungful of air which felt as turgid as steam. What on earth was going on? Why was he suddenly noticing things like *that*? He was Lisa's friend and a friend certainly shouldn't be having lustful thoughts about her body!

He cleared his throat, overwhelmed by a feeling of self-loathing. 'I hadn't realised they didn't go together. They look OK to me.'

'Obviously.' She gave him a quick grin them reached into the locker and took out a dark blue tie with a discreet cream leaf pattern sprinkled all over it. 'Try this and see what you think.'

Will took it simply because he didn't care one way or the other. What difference did it make what colour tie he wore when his whole world seemed to be hurtling out of control? He knotted the tie and turned down the shirt-collar but his hands were trembling and the tiny buttons that held it in place defeated his attempts to fasten them.

Lisa is my friend, he repeated desperately, but for some reason the words didn't sound the same as they had done in the past.

'Here, let me do that, butterfingers.'

Before he could summon up an aye, a yes or a no, she had stepped in front of him and briskly begun to fasten the buttons for him. Will held himself rigid, terrified that he would do something crazy like put his arms around her.

That was what he wanted to do—put his arms around her and hold her close—and although he'd done it a thousand times in the past when he had been trying to comfort her, he knew it wouldn't be the same if he did it now. He wanted to hold her now because all of a sudden his arms felt empty without her in them. He wanted to fill them with her and know that she needed him as much as he needed her...

'There! What do you think? Isn't that better?'

Will blinked and the delightful little scenario that had been unwinding inside his head switched itself off. All of a sudden he was back to reality and the reality was that he was Lisa's friend and if he hoped to remain so he could never, *ever* take her in his arms the way he had been longing to do.

'Um, yep, that's much better, isn't it?' He summoned a smile as he turned to peer into the tiny mirror set into the door of the locker, but he couldn't deny how shaken he felt by what had happened.

'Liar! Admit it, Will, you can't see any difference whatsoever, can you?' she demanded, glaring at him in a way that made him wonder what was wrong with her. Why on earth should it matter so much if he preferred her choice of necktie to his?

'Not really,' he confessed, his deep blue eyes searching her face for a clue to what was really going on. Something had obviously upset her and he had no idea what it could be until a thought suddenly occurred to him. A rush of anger hit him and he straightened abruptly, so abruptly, in fact, that he saw her take a step back.

'I was only joking, Will…' she began, but he shook his head.

'Forget the tie. It doesn't matter. What's happened, Lisa? I can tell something is wrong.'

He reached for her hands, although he had to make a conscious effort not to grip them too hard as the anger inside him grew to gigantic proportions. If Cameron had tried to *force* her to go to bed with him…!

'Not wrong exactly.' She gave a wistful sigh and his heart spasmed with pain because he couldn't bear to hear her sounding so troubled.

'Why don't you tell me what's wrong and then we can see if we can sort it all out,' he said more gently this time.

He let his hands slide to her wrists, feeling the steady beat of her pulse beneath his fingers. Its rhythm was a little faster than normal but not so fast that it alarmed him unduly, and he realised that he might have jumped to conclusions. Maybe Cameron had been the perfect gentleman and there was something else worrying her? He was just about to urge her to tell him when she spoke.

'James asked me to marry him tonight and I'm not sure what to do.'

She looked up and Will felt something inside him shrivel up in terror when he saw the plea in her eyes. 'I need you to help me make up my mind, Will. Do you think I should marry him?'

Lisa held her breath. Deep down she knew it was wrong to ask Will to help her make a decision like this, but she needed his advice more than ever. Will was always so clear in his views and she knew she could trust him to tell her the truth. If he didn't believe that James was the right man for her, he would say so.

A frown pleated her brow. Surely she shouldn't need anyone to tell her that? She should know in her heart whether or not James was the man she wanted to marry. But she had fallen into the habit of relying on Will to help her make any important decisions about her personal life. When it came to work then she had no such problems; she was always decisive in that area of her life. It bothered her to realise how dependent she was on him outside work, but it was too late to have second thoughts.

'I really don't think that's a question I can answer, Lisa.'

She jumped when he spoke, wondering why his voice sounded so harsh all of a sudden. There was none of the usual warmth and friendly concern in it that she had come to expect.

She shot him an uncertain look but Will was taking his jacket out of his locker and she couldn't see his expression.

It left her feeling rather as though she were floundering in the middle of the ocean without a lifeline to cling to, and it was a feeling she hated. Ever since Gareth had died Will had been there for her, her rock, her lifeline.

'I just wanted your advice, that's all,' she said quickly. 'I know you can't make up my mind for me.'

She gave a tinkly little laugh then grimaced when she realised how false it had sounded. 'Sorry. It came as a bolt from the blue, to be honest. I never expected James to ask me to marry him so I'm not sure whether I'm coming or going at the moment.'

'Which is why you decided I might be able to help?'

His tone was so flat that Lisa knew at once that he had deliberately removed any trace of emotion from it. The idea shocked her so much that she stared at him in amazement.

Will *never* tried to hide his feelings, mainly because he was so good-tempered there was no need for him to do so. His calm and equanimity were legendary amongst the staff at Dalverston General. He was always helpful, always caring, always…always just Will! The nicest, kindest, most compassionate man she had ever met. So what was wrong with him now? Was he upset at the thought of her marrying James?

The thought made her pulse race so that it was an effort to act as though everything was fine. 'Yes. Who better to turn to for advice than my dearest friend?'

'Thank you. At least you didn't say your *oldest* friend.'

He treated her to one of his wonderfully warm smiles and Lisa gave herself a brisk mental shake. Of course Will wasn't upset by the idea of her getting married! She was letting her imagination run away with her because it had been a stressful evening. And yet the nagging feeling that something had changed in their relationship wouldn't be dis-

missed. It was a relief when he looped a friendly arm around
her shoulders and steered her towards the door.

'How about we go to the café while we talk this through?
I'm suffering from a serious drop in my blood-sugar levels
and need a booster before I can think clearly.'

'Sounds good to me,' she said, eagerly grasping at the
return to normality.

She smiled up at him and suddenly realised how tired he
looked, although it was hardly surprising after the day he'd
had. She had bumped into Madge in the corridor and heard
all about the operation Will had carried out on the boy. That
kind of complex surgery was both physically and mentally
draining and it made Lisa feel guilty all of a sudden about
having dumped her problems on him.

She turned to him and her hazel eyes were full of concern.
'I really appreciate the offer, Will, but if you're too tired to
deal with this tonight, then say so. It will keep until another
time.'

'I'm sure it will, but we may as well try to sort things
out while we have the chance.' He shrugged, although she
couldn't help noticing how he avoided looking at her as he
opened the door. 'I doubt if you'll get much sleep if you're
churning everything round in your head all night, will you,
Lisa?'

'No-o...'

'That's what I thought.' He stepped aside and bowed and
once again the old Will was back, ready and willing to take
charge. 'After you, *madame*. Bacon and eggs coming right
up, with a side order of good advice to go with them!'

Lisa chuckled as she led the way from the room. It was
good to know that Will was there when she needed him.
She made her way to the lift and pressed the button then
felt her heart lurch as a thought suddenly occurred to her.

If she married James then she couldn't keep turning to

Will for advice. It wouldn't be right. And yet the thought of him no longer playing a major role in her life felt wrong somehow, strange.

She summoned a smile as Will came to join her because she didn't want him to guess there was anything wrong. But the nagging little thought wouldn't go away.

She simply couldn't imagine not having Will around.

CHAPTER TWO

THEY went to their usual haunt, a transport café on the bypass. A lot of the staff from the hospital went there after
they finished work at night and didn't have the energy to
make themselves a meal. Will parked his car in a gap between a couple of lorries and switched off the engine.

'Bacon and eggs for two, is it? Or are you still full from
your expensive dinner?'

'The food was delicious, but the portions they serve there
are *tiny*.' Lisa grimaced. 'I didn't like to ask the waiter if I
could have a bread roll in case James thought I was being
greedy!'

'Still at the stage of wanting to make a good impression,
are you?' Will said lightly, getting out of the car. He made
his way round to join her, praying that he wouldn't make a
complete hash of things. Lisa was depending on him to give
her some calm and rational advice yet he had never felt less
calm or less rational in his entire life.

What the hell was he going to do if she married Cameron?
How was he going to fill the void in his life? All of a sudden
the future spread out before him and all he could see in it
was loneliness. Without Lisa to think about, to worry about
and care for, then he had no reason to get up of a morning.

He sighed when it struck him how melodramatic that was.
Didn't he have a job he loved, dozens of friends *and* his
family? He had everything a man could wish for with one
notable exception, i.e. a wife, but now that it looked as
though his obligation to Gareth was coming to an end then
he could focus on his future. He'd always planned to have

children at some point and once Lisa was settled then he could set about finding the right woman to have them with.

The thought should have cheered him up but it didn't. He couldn't seem to see past the bad bits—the fact that Lisa might soon be leaving him—let alone focus on the good. It worried him that he seemed so ambivalent about the idea of her finding happiness when his main aim and objective for the past five years had been to bring that about.

A muggy wall of heat hit them as they entered the café. Will waved as Al, the owner, shouted a greeting. The place was packed but they managed to find a table in the corner and sat down. Al came over to take their order, bringing with him two huge mugs of wickedly strong tea.

Will grinned as he picked up the glass canister of sugar and poured a small mountain of grains into his mug. 'I wonder how long this has been stewing for?'

Lisa took a sip and shuddered. 'At least a week from the taste of it. It's pure tannin.'

'Just what I need to give me a lift.' He took a long swallow of the tea then put his mug down on the Formica-topped table. 'So, tell me all about your evening. What was the restaurant like?'

'Classy. All crisp white tablecloths and starched napkins, discreetly attentive waiters—you know the sort of thing.'

She gave a small shrug as she slipped off her jacket and draped it over the back of her chair. Once again Will felt that funny sensation grip his vitals as he watched her smoothing the lapels of her blouse and unwittingly drawing his gaze to the shadowy V of her cleavage.

He dropped his eyes to the table, praying that she hadn't noticed him staring. He had no idea why he was acting like this, but it couldn't have happened at a worse time. Lisa wanted to tell him about Cameron's proposal. She needed his advice about whether or not she should accept it and he couldn't afford to have his mind cluttered up by extraneous thoughts. And yet it was proving incredibly difficult to rid himself of them when he seemed to be aware of her in a way he had never been before.

'Will? Are you all right?'

He jumped when she leant across the table and tapped him on the arm. It was an effort to fix a carefree smile to his face when it felt as though all the worries of the world had suddenly descended on him.

'Fine. I'm probably a bit spaced out after the operation tonight. It was a bit of a stinker, to be honest.'

'I ran into Madge and she told me about it.' She grimaced as she stirred her tea. 'It sounded horrendous. Madge said that the boy was lucky to have survived long enough for you to get him back to hospital.'

'It was pretty nasty,' he agreed. 'I've rarely seen so much soft-tissue damage. Our biggest headache now is going to be dealing with any infection.'

'That's where we come in.' She smiled at him and her hazel eyes were warm with understanding. 'You can't do everything, Will. You've done the really difficult bit and now you have to leave it up to us to sort out the rest. We'll take good care of him, I promise you.'

'I know you will. Daniel couldn't be in better hands,' he replied sincerely.

Lisa's job in the paediatric intensive care unit meant that a lot of the children he dealt with came under her care. He knew how dedicated she was to her work, and that it wasn't just a job to her. She lavished an awful lot of love on the children she treated, gave each and every one that extra bit of support.

She would make the most wonderful mother, he found himself thinking, then quickly clamped down on that thought because it was of very little relevance. If and when Lisa ever had a family then he would be well off the scene.

The thought was so mind-numbingly painful that he found he could no longer speak and a small silence developed. Fortunately, Al arrived with their order and Will was grateful for the interruption. He had never felt in the least ill at ease around Lisa before but he felt so that night and it worried him. What on earth was going on? Surely he should be pleased for her, instead of feeling as though the bottom had dropped out of his world?

It was too unsettling to try and work out any answers so he applied himself to his meal, hoping it would help if he got some food inside him. It had been hours since he'd last eaten so maybe he hadn't been so far off track when he'd claimed to be suffering from low blood sugar.

They ate in silence until every last scrap had gone. Will heaved a sigh of contentment as he plucked a paper napkin from the dispenser and wiped his mouth. 'I might just live, although it was touch and go at one point, I can tell you.'

'I know what you mean,' she assured him, then grinned when he raised his eyes. 'OK, I know I've just dined at Dalverston's finest restaurant, but it always makes me feel hungry whenever I'm stressed.'

'And you're feeling stressed tonight because Cameron asked you to marry him?' he said quietly, knowing that he couldn't put off the moment any longer.

He settled back in his chair, praying that she couldn't tell how mixed up he was feeling. Of course he wanted to help her reach the right decision, but he wasn't convinced that any advice he offered would be totally unbiased. And yet what did he have against Cameron?

The man was an upstanding pillar of the community. He was rich, successful and unmarried—a real catch, as Will's own mother would have put it. If he'd been asked to compile a list of eligible suitors for Lisa then Cameron would have featured on it, and yet—and *yet*—the thought of her marrying the man stuck in his throat like a nasty dose of indigestion.

'Yes. It was such a surprise. I had no idea...' She broke off and sighed. 'That's not quite true, actually. I did realise that James was...well, attracted to me, but I tried not to think about it. It made me feel a bit guilty, you see.'

A wash of soft colour ran up her face and under cover of the table Will's hands clenched. It was an effort to force out a single word let alone a whole sentence as his mind played tag with the way in which Cameron was *attracted* to her.

'You mean it made you feel guilty because of Gareth?' His voice sounded somewhat strangled when it emerged, and he saw Lisa shoot him an unhappy look.

'You think it's wrong to encourage him, don't you? I can tell. You think I should remain faithful to Gareth's memory?'

'No, I don't think any such thing!' he exploded, realising that he was in danger of undoing years of hard work by acting like an idiot.

Making Lisa understand that she couldn't live solely on her memories had been his main objective since Gareth had died. He knew it was what Gareth would have wanted so week after week, month after month, he'd tried to convince her that she had to think about the future instead of the past. Lisa deserved to find love and happiness again with a man, even if that man wasn't him.

The thought almost blew him away because he had never for a second entertained the idea before. His feelings for Lisa were based on friendship, not...not *sexual* attraction! And yet when he looked at her sitting there across the table from him it wasn't only friendship he felt but a whole lot of other things as well.

It was as though the blinkers had been removed from his eyes and all of a sudden he was seeing her not as Gareth's fiancée but the most beautiful and desirable woman he had ever known.

Hell and damnation! What a time for something like *this* to happen.

'So you don't think it's wrong?' Lisa said uncertainly when she saw the grim expression on Will's face. She wasn't sure what the matter was with him that night but he seemed to be acting very strangely, snapping at her that way. She couldn't recall Will ever speaking to her so sharply before.

Just for a second she found herself wishing that she hadn't gone to find him after James had dropped her off at home. She'd felt so keyed-up by what had happened that she'd needed to talk everything through with him, but maybe it had been a mistake, after all. Maybe Will was growing tired of sorting out her problems, becoming resentful of her constant demands on his time?

A feeling of dread knotted her throat and she swallowed. She couldn't bear to think that she had become a nuisance to him but the facts had to be faced. Will had his own life to lead so why should he want to devote so much time to her all the time? It was hard to hide how upsetting she found that idea when he suddenly spoke.

'I don't think you should feel guilty about what's happened, Lisa. That's just plain silly and you know it is.'

The gentle understanding in his voice made her eyes prickle with tears and she stared at her cup. 'Do I?' she murmured, then looked up when he laughed, that wonderful, warm, *Will* laugh.

'Uh-huh! You're being a complete and utter idiot,' he assured her, tilting back his chair and grinning at her.

Lisa summoned a smile. 'Not that you are trying to insult me, of course.'

'Would I ever?'

His tone was teasing but beneath the laughter she could hear the concern. Will had sensed she was upset and he was trying to make her feel better. It made her see just how very special their friendship was.

'Look, Lisa, you have to take this a step at a time and think it all through.' He let his chair snap back onto all four legs and leant across the table towards her.

Lisa felt the strangest sensation flow through her as she caught the full force of his brilliant blue stare. She could feel heat flowing through her veins, making her heart race and her breathing quicken. Will must have looked at her a million times before but she couldn't remember it having this kind of an effect on her...

'Lisa? Are you listening to me?'

She jumped when he touched her hand and the warm feeling promptly evaporated, much to her relief. Her feelings for Will had always been clearly defined and she didn't want anything to change. Will was her best friend, the person she trusted most in the whole world. She needed that one constant to cling to when everything else was altering with such speed.

'Sorry. As I said, this came as rather a shock even though I knew that James was rather keen on me.'

'And how do you feel, Lisa? Are you *keen* on him, too?'

She pulled a face when she heard the teasing note in his voice. 'All right, I know that sounded a bit wet and like something out of a nineteen-twenties film, but you know what I mean.'

'Oh, I do, old girl!' This time he was openly laughing at her and Lisa sighed.

'You are an absolute pain, Will Saunders! Here am I trying to discuss the most important decision of my entire life and you're making fun of me.'

'Sorry, old bean,' he retorted, before he suddenly sobered. 'But you're right, of course. This really isn't a joking matter. So, seriously, how do you feel about Cameron? Do you think you're in love with him or what?'

'I don't know. That's the honest answer.'

She picked up a spoon and stirred her tea again, wondering why she felt so uncomfortable all of a sudden. She'd never had any difficulty discussing her feelings with Will in the past but she felt awkward about doing so now. 'I like James a lot. He's charming, attentive, kind and good-looking. He's also been very patient about...'

She broke off, wishing with all her heart that she hadn't said that last little bit. Did she really want to discuss the fact that James hadn't tried to persuade her to go to bed with him?

'About you not sleeping with him?' Will touched her hand, just lightly with the tip of his index finger, and smiled at her. 'Hey, this is me you're talking to, Lisa. You don't need to be embarrassed.'

'I'm not,' she said quickly, although it wasn't true. She *was* embarrassed about it, as much embarrassed by the idea of Will knowing that she hadn't slept with James as she would have been if she had done so, and she couldn't understand why she should feel that way. Why should it matter if Will knew about her sex life or, rather, the lack of one?

She hurried on, not wanting to delve too deeply into that question for some reason. 'James has been wonderful about it. Not many men would have been so considerate, in fact,' she said, wanting Will to know how much she appreciated James's forbearance.

'That's good to hear,' he said evenly. He picked up his mug and drank some of his tea then put the cup back on the table. And there was something almost too studied about the way he set it down exactly in the middle of the damp ring it had left on the Formica surface.

Lisa frowned as she saw what he had done. She had the funniest feeling that Will was deliberately keeping a check on himself, watching everything he said and did. It was so out of character for him to behave that way that she couldn't work out what was the matter with him. Unless Will had serious misgivings about her marrying James and was afraid to say so?

'Yes, it is,' she replied, trying not to let him see how unsettled she felt by the idea. Maybe it was silly to set too much store by Will's opinion but she couldn't help it. 'However, I can't expect James to wait for ever. Especially not after he has asked me to marry him.'

'So what's the plan, then?' Will said a shade gruffly.

Lisa shot him an uncertain look but he was stirring his tea. It should have made it easier to tell him what she was planning on doing, but all of a sudden she discovered that her heart was racing. How would Will feel about James's invitation?

'James has asked me to spend Christmas with him at his cottage. I...I think it would be a good idea, don't you?'

Will could hear a buzzing in his ears. It seemed to be getting louder so that he couldn't hear what else Lisa said, although it wouldn't have mattered if he had. His mind seemed to have stalled on that last question and he had to fight back a slightly hysterical laugh.

Lisa wanted him to give her a nice, tidy, *logical* answer when logic didn't enter into this. What this all boiled down to was feelings—how *he* felt about the idea of her spending Christmas with Cameron at his cottage and sleeping with him in his bed. Words couldn't begin to describe how gut-wrenchingly painful he found the idea!

'Will, your beeper!'

He nearly shot out of his chair when she shook his arm. He'd been so immersed in his own agony that he hadn't had a clue that the buzzing sound had been coming from his pocket. He dug out his beeper and checked the display, grimacing when he saw from the code that it was Theatre trying to get in contact with him.

'Looks like I'm needed,' he explained, hunting in the other pocket for his cellphone.

He quickly put through a call, feeling like the lowest form of pond-life as he eagerly agreed when a junior registrar from the general surgical team asked if he would mind returning to the hospital to deal with an emergency admission. The fact that he could feel relieved because there was a child in urgent need of his help filled him with disgust, but he couldn't help it. He desperately didn't want to have to discuss Lisa's dilemma any more that night, let alone come up with an answer for her.

'I'll have to go,' he explained, briskly standing and taking his coat off the back of the chair.

'Emergency?' she asked, quickly following suit. She slid her arms into her jacket, murmuring her thanks when Will picked up her bag and handed it to her.

'A four-year-old girl who's fallen out of an upstairs window. Multiple fractures,' he told her, swiftly heading for the door. They had almost reached it when he realised that he hadn't paid their bill.

He stopped and hunted through his pockets again, groaning when all he came up with was a handful of loose change and a button that had come off his jacket weeks ago. He'd intended to go to the cash machine on his way home, but he'd not had a chance once he'd received the call about Daniel Kennedy.

'I've no cash on me,' he explained. 'I meant to get some on the way home. Maybe Al will put it on the slate and I can pay him the next time I'm in?'

'Don't worry. I'll get it,' Lisa said, quickly taking her wallet from her bag. She went to the counter and Will heard her laugh at some comment Al passed.

He waited by the door while she made her way back across the room. It was warm in the café that night and the heat had added a touch of colour to her face and there seemed to be a definite sparkle in her eyes as well. It was a long time since he had seen her looking so animated, in fact, although her vivacity had been one of the first things he had noticed when Gareth had introduced them.

Lisa had been full of fun back then. It had only been after Gareth's death that she had grown sombre and quiet, sad. Now it was both a pleasure and a pain to see her looking more like she used to do because he understood the reason for it.

She looked different tonight because she was looking towards the future at last. It was painful to know that he hadn't been able to give her back her sparkle and that another man had.

'Al said to tell you that he likes your style. He's all in favour of women footing the bill in these days of equality.'

Will managed a sickly smile but the thought that he could be guilty of such a dog-in-the-manger attitude didn't sit easily with him. 'I hope you told him that I'm noted for my views on the equality of the sexes?'

'Oh, sure! So that's why you wouldn't let me paint the living-room ceiling the other week and insisted that you should do it instead? Come on, Will, you know very well that you could no more treat a woman as your equal when it comes to doing something dangerous than you could fly to the moon!'

'If you'd really wanted to paint the ceiling yourself then you should have said so,' he said stiffly. He opened the door and pulled up the collar of his jacket as a blast of icy December air hit them.

Lisa grinned as she huddled into her jacket. 'I didn't— not really. And don't go all prickly on me, because I wasn't getting at you. You have this overwhelming need to protect everyone, Will, and I for one wouldn't want you to change.'

'Sure?' he asked, wondering why it seemed so important to know that she was telling him the truth.

'One hundred per cent certain. I like you just the way you are, Will Saunders. Warts and all!'

She slid her hand through his arm and reached up on tiptoe to kiss his cheek. It was the sort of kiss they had exchanged countless times in the past and yet it had the most galvanising effect on him that night.

Will didn't have a clue that he was going to turn until he suddenly found they were facing each other. Lisa was still standing on tiptoe, her hand still resting on his arm, but her lips had skidded from his cheek when he'd turned and somehow ended up at the corner of his mouth. It was the easiest thing in the world to turn his head another fraction of an inch...

Will stifled a groan when he felt the softness of her lips make contact with his. His head spun as he became aware of a dozen different things all at once, like how sweet her hair smelled, how quickly she was breathing, how huge and bright her eyes looked as she stared up at him.

Her lids suddenly lowered and he felt a surge of something hot and wild race through him when she moved just a little so that their mouths settled more firmly together.

Maybe the kiss had started out as an accident but it had gone beyond that stage now.

He kissed her gently and with great tenderness then drew back and looked at her, knowing that he would remember this moment all his life. She looked so beautiful as she stood there with her eyes closed and her lips parted, her delicate oval face upturned to his. Her soft brown hair had started to come free from its elegant chignon and his stomach muscles bunched when he saw how the silky wisps had curled themselves around her small ears.

He lifted a hand, touched one gossamer-fine strand then breathed in and out just to be certain that he could still do something as mundane as breathe. It felt as though he were having an out-of-body experience, that he was looking down on himself and watching what was happening.

Was it real? Had it happened? Had he just kissed Lisa not as a friend but as a lover?

Her eyes suddenly opened and Will felt a wave of panic wash over him when he saw the confusion they held.

What in the name of heaven had he done?

CHAPTER THREE

'WILL, I...'

'Sorry! I didn't realise the ground was so slippery. Mind you, it's cold enough tonight to freeze, isn't it?'

Lisa blinked then looked uncertainly at the ground. There was indeed a shimmer of frost on the tarmac so was Will saying that he had *slipped* and that was how they had ended up kissing one another?

She tested out the theory, trying to spot the flaws in it, but deep down she wanted to believe him. She wanted to believe that the kiss had been pure accident and not design because it was less scary to do so. If it *had* been an accident then they could carry on as normal. But if it hadn't then she would have to decide what to do about it. How did she really feel about the idea of Will kissing her as a lover rather than as a friend?

The question brought a rush of heat to her face and she turned away before he could notice. 'Apology accepted,' she said huskily, starting off across the car park as though she were being hotly pursued by demons.

Will kept pace with her, whistling under his breath in a way that should have been soothing yet which made her nerves jangle all the more. Was he behaving just a bit *too* casually perhaps, trying too hard to act as though nothing had happened?

Lisa shot him a wary look as he unlocked the car but he didn't look as though he was trying to hide anything. She slid into the passenger seat, feeling almost weak with relief.

The kiss had been an accident. Will must have slipped and somehow their mouths had met and…

And did that also explain why it had been so wonderful that her knees had started knocking again just because she'd been thinking about it?

Lisa bit her lip, terrified that she might blurt out something unforgivable. Maybe the kiss had been wonderful but there was no way that she wanted her relationship with Will to change. She had enough to contend with at the moment, what with James's proposal and his suggestion that she should spend Christmas with him. Will was Will and her feelings for him were ones of friendship. End of story. He felt exactly the same about her.

Didn't he?

'I'll drop you off at the flat then go straight back to work. Heaven knows what time I'll get in so don't bolt the door on me.'

'What? Oh, no, of course not.' She hurriedly summoned a smile when he glanced at her, but that last question was giving her hot and cold chills. Will felt nothing but friendship for her. He certainly didn't fancy her. And yet the thought stubbornly refused to die.

'Typical that this should happen tonight,' she said quickly, in the hope that it might help to think about something else. 'You've had one difficult case and now it looks as though you've got another right on top of it.'

'A bit like buses—they tend to come in twos,' he replied, turning into the forecourt of the block of flats where they lived. He drew up outside the front door while she hunted for her keys. 'What time are you on duty tomorrow?'

'Six.' She grimaced as she jangled the key fob in her palm. 'I hate earlies, especially when I've been out the night before.'

'Well, I'll try not to disturb you when I come in.' He

checked his watch and groaned. 'Is that the time already? I
had no idea it had gone midnight. You'd better get to bed.'

'Shame you can't come, too,' she said without thinking,
then felt herself cringe when she realised how suggestive
that must have sounded.

She hastily got out of the car and waved as Will drove
away, but the fact that she had even paused to consider what
she'd said to him made her feel even more mixed up. Since
when had she needed to be aware of any sexual innuendo
creeping into their conversation? But that had been before
Will had kissed her. Had it really been an accident, as he
had claimed?

Lisa sighed as she let herself into the building. She was
in serious danger of building a mountain out of the proverbial molehill if she didn't stop this right away. Will had
explained what had happened and when had he ever lied to
her?

Of all the half-baked excuses to come up with, that one
should win an award!

Will scooped a handful of Hibiscrub from the dispenser
and lathered his forearms. He was in the process of scrubbing up before the operation, a task that left his mind free
to wander where it chose. The fact that it kept coming back
to that moment in the car park when he had claimed it had
been the icy conditions underfoot that had caused him to
kiss Lisa made him grind his teeth with shame.

What sane person came up with a story like that? She
was bound to see through it, guaranteed to spot it as the
snivelling lie it was, and then what would he do? How could
he hope to explain why he had kissed her like that when he
had no idea himself?

'There is being thorough and being masochistic. Give

yourself a break, Will. Whatever sin you've committed, it can't be that bad.'

Will looked round when Dave nudged him sharply in the ribs. He grimaced when he saw the anaesthetist shoot a meaningful look at his reddened forearms. 'Oh, I've got a lot on my mind at the moment. Take no notice.'

'Really? Well, there's only one reason I know of that reduces a healthy male mind to pure mush: a woman. Am I right or am I right?'

Dave turned to Madge before Will could say anything. 'Did you know that our Will has some woman on the go? It looks as though she's leading him a bit of a dance, too, from the pitiful state he's in.'

'And here was I thinking that you were faithful only to me,' Madge declared sadly, shaking out a sterile towel and handing it to Will. 'So who is she, then? She must be a looker if she's replaced me in your affections.'

'She's no one,' he said quickly, then realised his mistake when Dave smirked. 'What I meant is that there is no woman,' he said curtly. 'It's all down to Dave's overly fertile imagination.'

'If you say so,' Madge replied, winking at Dave as she handed him a towel as well. 'We'll believe you, won't we, Dr Carson?'

'Of course we will,' Dave agreed, completely deadpan. 'Did you happen to see those fairies in the corridor on your way in, Madge? There were at least a dozen of them from what I could count.'

'And there were half a dozen elves as well...'

'Oh, ha-ha, very funny!' Will glowered as the pair dissolved into fits of laughter. 'You two have missed your vocation. You would have made a superb music-hall act. Now, if we have finished with the jokes, boys and girls, maybe we can get started?'

'Aye, aye, sir.' Dave snapped to attention and saluted. He headed towards the anteroom where their patient was waiting, whispering to Madge in a loud aside that was meant to be heard, 'I'll find out who she is, Madge. Trust me.'

Will chose to ignore them as he went into Theatre to get ready, but he couldn't deny that Dave's parting comment had worried him. The thought that people might make the connection and realise that it was Lisa who was causing him so much soul-searching gave him hot and cold chills. It made him see that he had to nip this in the bud. Lisa was his friend and once he got that fact firmly re-established in his mind, there wouldn't be a problem.

It all sounded so easy in theory, but as Dave wheeled in their patient Will knew in his heart it could never be that simple. How could he go back to thinking of Lisa purely as a friend after what had happened that night?

The little girl's injuries were so severe that Will knew from the outset there was little chance of saving her. She had fallen thirty feet onto concrete flags and there wasn't a bone in her small body that hadn't been smashed. He did everything he could, working on long after he knew it was hopeless, but she was just too badly injured to be saved.

The silence in the operating theatre was testimony to the toll it took on the staff when they lost a child. Will glanced round at all the dejected faces and shook his head.

'I'm sorry. We did our best but sometimes it isn't enough.'

Nobody said anything as they got the child ready to be taken to the chapel so that her parents could see her. Will left Theatre and tossed his soiled gown into the basket then went through to the changing-room to shower. It was his responsibility to tell the parents the sad news and it was a job he always hated and would never get used to.

Little Tara's parents were in the waiting-room and the minute he went in he saw the fear in their eyes. He sat them down and gently explained that Tara's injuries had been too severe to save her. They both cried and he sat with them for a long time, reassuring them that she wouldn't have suffered even though he had no idea whether it was true. But people could only take so much and he wouldn't add to their pain when it wouldn't alter the outcome.

It was almost four by the time he left the hospital and the roads were empty, a thin layer of frost making the asphalt sparkle in his headlights as he drove home. He drew up outside the flat and let his head drop wearily onto the steering-wheel while he tried to summon enough energy to get out of the car. He felt a hundred years old, so tired that his bone-marrow ached, but in the end he managed to open the car door and stumble up the steps to let himself in.

He crept into the flat, cursing softly when he banged his shin on the table by the door. The whole place was in darkness and the air felt wonderfully warm and welcoming after the cold, lonely drive home.

He made his way along the hall, pausing when he came level with Lisa's bedroom. The door was closed and he couldn't hear any sound coming from inside the room yet he knew she was in there, sleeping. He could sense her presence and a pain so sweet and sharp hit him that he had to swallow a groan. He didn't need to see her to know she was there. He didn't need to touch her or speak to her, he just knew. Whenever she was about he sensed it.

Funny how he had never given any thought to it before tonight, but before tonight he hadn't had to think about what he would soon be losing. If Lisa married Cameron then she would no longer be in the flat when he came home. He wouldn't be able to stand in the doorway and simply feel her presence.

A wave of panic suddenly hit him. He didn't know how he was going to carry on living without her, yet at the same time he didn't know how he could stop her leaving. Whichever way he turned, someone would get hurt, and if it came to a choice then it had to be him.

So long as Lisa was happy, nothing else mattered.

Lisa had to drag herself out of bed when the alarm went off shortly before five the following morning. The late night combined with everything else that had happened had left her feeling drained. She stumbled into the bathroom, hoping that a shower would wash away some of her lethargy.

She towelled herself dry then put on Will's old robe because it just happened to be hanging behind the bathroom door. It was miles too big for her but she'd worn it so many times in the past that she barely registered the fact. Rolling up the sleeves the necessary dozen or so turns, she headed for the kitchen in the hope that a mug of coffee would wake up the bits the shower had missed.

Five minutes later, a mug of coffee clutched in her hand, she went into the sitting room and stopped dead at the sight that met her. Will was sprawled out on the sofa, fast asleep. He had taken off his shoes and tie but that was all. He was snoring gently and Lisa felt the oddest sensation start to bubble in the pit of her stomach as she watched his lips rhythmically pucker and relax. It looked for all the world as though he was inviting her to kiss him, and the thought sent her mind into a spin. All of a sudden she found herself transported back to those moments in the car park the night before…

'Humph…what time is it?'

She started so violently when he spoke that a wave of coffee slopped over the side of the mug. She let out a gasp of pain when the scalding droplets spattered her bare feet.

Will immediately swung his legs off the couch. 'Stay there while I get some cold water…'

'Don't fuss! It was only a few drops of coffee. I'll live.'

Lisa wasn't sure why she felt so annoyed all of a sudden. Will was only doing what he always did, trying to take care of her. But for some reason it irritated her that he apparently viewed her as some sort of pathetic creature who couldn't look after herself.

'Whatever you say,' he muttered, sinking back onto the couch and closing his eyes again.

Lisa chewed her lip, wondering why she felt equally annoyed because he had taken her at her word. She couldn't have it both ways. She either wanted him to look after her or she didn't. And yet the choice no longer seemed quite so clear-cut. Why did she suddenly find herself wishing that Will would see her not only as someone whom he wanted to take care of, but as a woman who had a lot to offer him as well?

'Any chance I could have some of that coffee?' he murmured, his eyes opening the barest slit.

'Of course.' She quickly passed him the mug, watching while he took a couple of needy glugs.

'That's better.' He opened his eyes fully this time and grinned as he handed back the mug. All of a sudden everything was back to normal again.

Lisa heaved a heartfelt sigh of relief. Of course she didn't want things to change! She wanted Will to carry on treating her the way he had always done. Why wish to change things when everything was fine the way it was?

'My brain has just about caught up with the rest of me now,' he declared.

'You and your morning coffee,' she teased, squeezing onto the couch beside him. He was still sprawled across the cushions and there wasn't much room. She felt a little spasm shoot through her when her hip rubbed against his, but steadfastly ignored it. She didn't intend to let anything rock the status quo again.

'I don't know why you can't arrange to have it served to you intravenously. That way you could get your morning fix of caffeine before you wake up.'

'Can I help it if I need a little help to get me going of a morning?' he protested mournfully. 'Anyhow, you don't look all that bright-eyed and bushy-tailed this morning, if you don't mind my saying so.'

'I don't feel it, but that's another story and I really don't have the time to bore you with it right now.'

She took a quick swallow of coffee, not wanting to go into the ins and outs of why she looked so tired. Maybe it was silly, but she couldn't face the thought of discussing James and his proposal at that moment. She needed to put a little more distance between herself and what had happened in the car park first. Once she'd got that safely sorted out in her head then she could deal with the rest.

'Anyway, I'd better get a move on or I'll be late for work. Do you want the rest of this?' She handed him the mug then got up and hurried to the door, pausing briefly to glance back. 'What time did you get in, by the way?'

'Just after four.'

Will took another gulp of coffee and Lisa felt that funny bubbling sensation start up once more as she watched him tip back his head and swallow the drink. He had unbuttoned the neck of his shirt and she had a perfect view of his strong, tanned throat. For some reason she found herself unable to look away as her eyes soaked up every familiar detail, only they no longer seemed quite so familiar all of a sudden.

Why had she never noticed just how firm his jaw was or how sensual his lips were? she wondered incredulously. And how had she ignored the fact that his eyes were the most beautiful shade of blue?

Her stunned gaze raced on, taking stock of thick black lashes, strongly marked brows, a nose with just the hint of a crook in it, mahogany-brown hair. It startled her to realise that Will was a very attractive man because she hadn't been aware of that fact before. Will was Will and whether or not he was good-looking hadn't mattered a jot.

Now Lisa felt her heart miss several beats as she found herself wondering if the discovery would affect the way she thought about him in the future. She sincerely hoped not, but deep down she sensed that already something had changed. Realising that Will wasn't just her best friend but an extremely attractive and personable man as well had altered the equation. It was no longer her plus Will equalled friendship. Adding his appeal had added a whole new dimension.

Quite frankly, the idea terrified her but the last thing she wanted was for Will to guess anything was wrong. 'I didn't think you'd be that late getting back,' she said quickly, hoping that he wouldn't notice the quaver in her voice. 'What happened about the little girl you operated on?'

'She died.' He shrugged but she could tell that he was upset. 'I knew there wasn't much chance of saving her from the outset. We did what we could, but it just wasn't enough in the end.'

'It wasn't your fault, Will,' she protested.

She came back and sat on the arm of the sofa, putting aside her own problems because she couldn't bear to see him looking so dejected. 'You mustn't blame yourself when you did everything possible.'

'It's hard not to. You should have seen how upset the parents were.' He sighed. 'It must be a nightmare when something like that happens, Lisa. I don't know how people cope. I'm not sure I could if it was my child.'

Lisa felt her heart lurch because the thought of Will's child had instantly conjured up an image of a small boy with tousled brown hair and a huge grin.

'You'd manage, Will,' she said softly, wondering what had come over her. She loved children and hoped to have some of her own one day, but she couldn't understand why the thought of Will's child should have awoken all her maternal instincts. It was an effort to dismiss the thought but Will needed her support.

'I know how upset the parents must have been, but most people come to terms with their loss eventually. You know that as well as I do,' she said gently.

'S'pose so.' He summoned a sad little smile. 'I know I shouldn't let it get to me like this, but it's hard not to. There can't be anything worse than losing a child. It doesn't bear thinking about.'

'It doesn't,' she agreed, her heart filling with tenderness because it was so typical of Will to feel this way. It was one of the reasons why he was such a wonderful doctor— he cared so deeply about the children he treated and their families. All of a sudden it struck her how much she admired him and it was yet another revelation coming on top of all the others she'd had that morning.

'It must help to get you through a situation like that if you have someone to turn to, like I had you when Gareth died.' She summoned a smile but it was unsettling to have to keep readjusting her view of him. 'I would never have coped half as well if you hadn't been here for me, Will.'

'And very soon you'll have Cameron to turn to, won't you?' He lifted the mug to his lips and drank some more coffee then shrugged. 'You won't need me then, Lisa.'

Of course I will! she wanted to shout, only she couldn't

do that. How could she lay any more of a burden on him than she had put on him already? Wasn't it time that she thought about his needs? Will had spoken about having children so he must have been thinking about it. Maybe he had met someone and that was what had triggered such thoughts?

The idea took her breath away. She had been so wrapped up in her own affairs since James had arrived on the scene that she had no idea if Will was seeing someone. Was he? Did that help to explain that comment about her no longer needing him if she married James? Had it been wishful thinking on his behalf because it would leave him free to concentrate on his own relationship?

It all seemed to fit and yet she couldn't describe how it made her feel to think about him and this unknown woman, didn't really want to have to think about it at all. It made her feel all churned up to imagine him falling in love with a woman.

Lisa rose swiftly to her feet, terrified that he would guess she was upset. Not that she had any right to be because Will was entitled to a private life. She should be glad if he had found someone to share his life, but she couldn't deny that the thought of him and another woman made her heart ache in the strangest way.

'I'd better run. I take it that you won't be coming into work this morning after your late night?' she said, hurrying to the door before she gave herself away. How would Will feel if he knew how selfish she was being when he had given up so much to take care of her.

'I wish!' He grimaced. 'I've a list as long as my arm and there is no way I can cancel any of the ops. Most of the kids have been waiting months to have surgery as it is.'

'Can't Ray Maxwell take over for you?' she suggested, thinking how unfair it was that he should have to put in a full day's work on top of the late night. 'I thought the whole reason for taking him on was to lighten your workload.'

'It will probably pan out like that in the end, but he's still finding his feet. It wouldn't be fair to drop him in at the deep end.'

He stood up and groaned. 'Remind me never to doze off on the sofa again, will you? I feel as though a herd of elephants has trampled all over me.'

'Go and have a shower then you'll feel better,' she advised as he staggered across the room. 'Better still, why don't you try and snatch another couple of hours' sleep? You don't need to be in work till nine, do you?'

'No, I don't. Good idea. That's what I'll do. I'll go and have a power nap, as all the top executives call it.' He grinned when she rolled her eyes. 'You can mock all you like, but I'll be the one tucked up all snug and warm in my bed while you're waiting in the cold to catch your bus.'

'Sadist!' she accused, but he only laughed.

Lisa went to get ready as he disappeared into his room. She slid into fresh underwear then chose a white blouse and tailored grey skirt to wear with it. She pinned her hair into its customary chignon and applied a little make-up and that was it. It had taken her a bare ten minutes to get ready but as she passed Will's room she could hear definite sounds of snoring coming from inside.

Lisa smiled as she left the flat and walked towards the bus stop. Knowing Will, he would be back to his normal self when she next saw him, ready to face whatever problems the day threw at him. It made her see just how strong he was because coping with the kind of workload he undertook on a daily basis would have been far too much for most people.

That was why they'd had such difficulty finding another paediatric surgeon to fill the new post at Dalverston General.

Budget cuts meant that staffing levels had been drastically reduced, which in turn put extra pressure on the people who worked there. In fact, several applicants had turned down the job once they had discovered what it entailed.

Will worked cripplingly long hours and thought nothing of doing a full day's work and then being on call at night as well. He was too dedicated to refuse to attend when there was an emergency involving a child, even though the general surgical staff were supposed to cover for him.

He gave one hundred per cent commitment to his work, just as he had given one hundred per cent effort to getting Lisa back on her feet after Gareth had died. Maybe it would be a relief for him to be able to shed part of his burden at last?

Lisa sighed as she put out her hand and signalled for the bus to stop. She hated to think that Will would be better off without her, but the truth had to be faced. She needed to set Will free from his obligation because it wasn't fair to carry on taking up so much of his time.

Marrying James would be the perfect solution and she would think seriously about the idea. Maybe she wasn't head over heels in love with him but she liked him and they got on well together so surely that was enough?

But no matter what happened she would have to make some changes because it was time that she struck out on her own and let Will live his own life. Knowing that he was happy would be some compensation for the fact that she was going to miss him dreadfully.

'We'll increase the antibiotics. We'll also need another set of cultures done so that we can pinpoint exactly which bacteria are causing the trouble.'

Will waited patiently while Lisa finished examining Daniel Kennedy, the eight-year-old who had fallen onto the iron railings. He had phoned the intensive care unit during his break and asked for an update on the child's status. Sister Matthews had informed him that there were definite signs of infection setting in, which was why Will had decided to pop down to see him.

It was what he had feared would happen because a wound like that left the body open to many different kinds of infection. Then there was the problem of the child's large intestine having been damaged, allowing its contents to spill into the boy's abdominal cavity. He knew that it would need a careful balance of antibiotic treatment to pull the boy through, but also knew that if anyone could achieve it, Lisa would. She never gave up if there was a chance she could help a child to get better.

A feeling of warmth ran through his veins so that it was an effort to act casually when she turned. Will saw a wash of colour run up her face when she saw him and the heat in his veins seemed to double in intensity even though he did his best to cool it down.

Lisa is just surprised to see me, he told himself sternly. But he couldn't shake off the feeling that she seemed to be aware of him in a way that she had never been before.

'I thought I'd call in to see how young Daniel is doing,' he explained, not wanting to go any further down that route. Letting himself get hung up on thoughts like that wouldn't help a jot. Lisa was only interested in James. She viewed *him* strictly as a friend. Nevertheless, it was harder than it should have been to dismiss the idea.

'Unfortunately, there seems to be a rapid spread of infection.'

She sighed as she glanced at the clipboard she was holding. Will could see that it held the observations that had been taken since the time Daniel had been admitted to the unit. The careful recording of vital signs—temperature, blood pressure, heart and respiratory rates—was essential in a case like this.

'I was hoping that we might be able to contain it, but it's no longer localised.'

'Not surprising when you consider the type of injury he sustained,' Will said, following her down the ward. 'Infection was almost bound to set in because of the damage to the large intestine. The fact that it took so long to get Daniel into Theatre meant that the bacteria and digestive juices that had escaped into his abdominal cavity had plenty of time to cause havoc.'

'Exactly. And then there's all the other micro-organisms that were introduced via the metal spike. Heaven knows what kind of a cocktail of nasties there is bubbling away inside him.'

She shook her head as she studied the child's notes. 'General antibiotic treatment is hopeless in a case like this. We need to know what we're dealing with. I've asked for another set of cultures so, hopefully, we'll have a better idea once we get the lab results back.'

'When is Leo due back?' he asked, following her into the ward kitchen. 'I've lost track of how long he's been away this time.'

Leo Harrison was the consultant in charge of the paediatric intensive care unit and Lisa's boss. Although Will accepted that Leo was excellent at his job, he disagreed with the fact that the man took so much time off. Leo was much in demand on the lecture circuit and had spent several months that year lecturing on paediatric intensive care regimes.

'After Christmas now, apparently.'

Lisa shrugged as she dropped the clipboard onto the table and went to pour them both a cup of coffee from the pot bubbling away on the hot plate. 'He was supposed to be back next week, but there was a note in my pigeonhole this morning to say that he has decided to take a week's holiday tagged onto the end of his current tour. Evidently, he's spending Christmas in Boston with friends.'

'Nice for some, but it does rather leave you in the lurch.' Will frowned as he accepted the cup of coffee. 'It means there's just you and Sanjay to keep everything ticking over here, plus the new houseman.'

'We'll manage,' she assured him. 'We'll have to.'

'But it still isn't right that you should have all that extra work put on you,' he protested, then looked up when she laughed. 'What's so funny?'

'What about you, Will? When you accepted the consultancy you were told that you would have a team of three paediatric registrars working with you, and so far you've got one. Your workload is far bigger than mine.'

'Maybe, but that doesn't mean it's fair for Leo to go swanning off all the time. I've a good mind to have a word with Roger Hopkins about it. After all, I have a vested interest in this department, bearing in mind so many of my patients end up here.'

'Roger must have given permission for Leo to take the time off,' she pointed out. 'He is the hospital's manager, after all.'

'Then maybe Roger should think about hiring a locum to tide you over. It might be an idea if I suggested it to him.'

'Will, this isn't your problem! I know how you love to play Mr Fix-It, but you can't solve all the problems in the world.'

'I wasn't trying to,' he said shortly, unaccountably hurt by the accusation. Didn't Lisa understand that he was worried about her?

'No, I know. And it was unfair of me to say that.' She took a deep breath and he wondered why he had a horrible feeling that she was about to tell him something he wasn't going to like.

'You were trying to help me and I appreciate it, Will, really I do.'

'But?'

He summoned a smile but his heart was pounding so hard that he felt physically sick. 'There was a definite *but* tagged on there, Lisa, so out with it.'

'*But* you can't spend all your time worrying about me. You have your own life to think about and it's about time I let you get on with it. That's why I've decided it would be better if I moved out of the flat.'

CHAPTER FOUR

LISA bit her lip when she saw the shock on Will's face. It made her feel dreadful to know that he hadn't been expecting her to make that announcement.

Just for a moment she found herself wondering if she should tell him that she hadn't meant it, but what would be the point? She had decided that morning it was time she took charge of her own life and left him free to get on with his. Maybe this was the perfect way to set things in motion.

'So when were you planning on moving?'

She shot him a careful look when she heard how strained he sounded. Was Will annoyed because she had dropped this on him without any warning? She hurried to explain, not wanting him to think that she had been making plans behind his back.

'I've no idea yet. I only decided this morning that it was time I made the effort to find a place of my own.'

'Is there any particular reason for it?' He shrugged when she looked blankly at him. 'I'm not trying to pry, Lisa, but if I've done something to upset you then I would far rather you told me.'

'You haven't done anything, Will! You've been kindness itself and I couldn't be more grateful. I just feel that it's time we each had a bit more space to get on with our lives.'

'Oh, I see.' He gave her a thin smile. 'It can't be easy, having me around all the time when you have James to consider. Sorry for being so dim, Lisa. I should have realised that you needed your privacy.'

'Privacy,' she repeated, then blushed when it hit her what

he meant. Will thought that she wanted to find a place of her own so that she could invite James to stay overnight with her, but that couldn't have been further from the truth.

'No, you've got it all wrong…' she began, then broke off when Angela Matthews stuck her head round the door.

'Sorry to interrupt but there's a call for Will in the office. A and E want you to have a look at a three-year-old who's been involved in an RTA, Will.'

'Thanks, Angela. Tell them I'll be right there, will you?'

Will put down his mug as Angela left and smiled at Lisa. 'Looks like I'll have to cut and run. But if you need any help flat-hunting, promise you'll tell me, although I expect Cameron will be keen to give you a hand.'

'I expect so,' she said quietly, her head whirling from the speed by which everything seemed to be happening.

Will hurried away and Lisa sat down at the table to drink her coffee but after a few sips she pushed the cup away. She couldn't help feeling a little hurt by the fact that he hadn't tried to persuade her to stay on at the flat. It made her wonder if he had been simply waiting for her to make the move and that thought was even more upsetting. It was one thing to wonder if she had become a burden to him and another to have proof that it was true.

She had grown used to relying on him but from this point on she had to stand on her own two feet. She was perfectly capable of doing so, of course, but she couldn't deny that not having Will to turn to was going to leave a big gap in her life. The scariest thing of all was wondering if anyone else would ever be able to fill it.

The morning flew past with all the usual traumas and triumphs that dealing with seriously ill children always entailed. Will's RTA case was sent up just before lunch, so Lisa left Angela to get the little girl settled and took the parents into the relatives' room. The young couple were obviously in a state of shock because of what had happened, not helped by the fact that they had both been injured in the accident as well.

'I'm Lisa Bennett, the junior registrar on the IC unit,' she explained as they all sat down. 'I'll be in charge of Chloë's care while she is with us.'

'What about that doctor we saw before—Mr Saunders, I think he said his name was? Won't he be looking after her?'

'Mr Saunders is the surgeon who operated on your daughter. Now that he has finished his part in the proceedings, Chloë will be cared for by staff from this unit.'

Lisa smiled reassuringly at Mandy Trent, the child's mother. 'Mr Saunders will still be involved, of course. In fact, he will be up later to see how Chloë is getting on so if you have any questions about her surgery then he will be happy to explain everything to you.'

'I see. I've no idea how everything works, you understand.' Mandy gave her a wobbly smile. She had a huge bruise on the left side of her face and her left arm was in plaster.

'I've never been in a hospital before and neither has Alan,' she added, referring to the young man sitting beside her. His right arm was in a sling and Lisa could see that his forehead had been stitched as well. It was obvious that the accident had taken its toll on the whole family.

'I'm sure it all seems very confusing at the moment, but you mustn't worry,' Lisa said gently. 'We all want to help Chloë and that's the main thing.'

'How soon will we know if she's going to get better?' Alan put in. 'Mr Saunders told us that he'd had to operate to ease the pressure on her brain and that's serious, isn't it?'

'It is. Chloë sustained a very bad head injury in the crash,' she explained gently. 'Her skull was fractured and Mr

Saunders had to remove the pieces of bone then drain away a rather large blood clot that had formed.'

'Does it mean that she'll be...*disabled*?' Mandy pressed a tissue to her mouth to stifle a sob. 'I've read about things like that in magazines, about how kiddies have been left like vegetables after they've hurt their heads.'

'It's impossible to say at this stage if the injury will have caused any lasting damage,' Lisa explained, knowing that it would be wrong to lie to them. 'However, the fact that Chloë received treatment so quickly will have gone in her favour, and Mr Saunders is a highly skilled paediatric surgeon who has performed this type of operation very successfully many times before.'

'But there's no guarantee that she'll not have brain damage,' Alan said bluntly. 'That's what you're really saying, isn't it, Dr Bennett?'

'I think it's best not to look too far ahead at this stage,' she said firmly. 'At the moment our main concern is stabilising Chloë and making sure that her condition doesn't deteriorate. The fact that she has come through the operation is a very positive sign so let's hold onto that.'

She stood up, knowing that no amount of reassurances would lessen the parents' fears for their daughter. 'Why don't you sit with Chloë for a little while? Don't worry about all the tubes and equipment she's attached to. It's there simply to tell us what is going on.'

She escorted the parents back into the IC unit and handed them over to Angela. It was lunchtime by then so she had a word with one of the nurses and told her to page her if she was needed.

The shortage of staff meant that she and Sanjay Kapur, the senior registrar, were having to work twelve-hour shifts at the moment. She would work until six that evening when Sanjay would come on duty and he would work through until six the following morning. Their young houseman, Ben Carlisle, was working from eleven in the morning to eleven at night so his hours overlapped with theirs.

There was no doubt that they were in desperate need of more staff because the workload was taxing. There were never enough free beds on any paediatric IC unit and Dalverston General's unit was no exception. As soon as one child was well enough to be transferred to a ward, another would arrive so there was never any let-up from the pressure.

However, Lisa loved her job and knew that she wouldn't wish to change it. Knowing how vital her role was made up for the long hours she worked, although if she did marry James she might have to think again about her choice of career. Would James be happy with a wife who spent so much of her time away from home?

It was a worrying thought but she decided not to think about it until she had made her decision about James's proposal. She took the lift to the sixth floor where the newly refurbished staff canteen was now sited. The day's menu was chalked up on a board by the door so she paused to study it. The canteen food had improved tremendously since the refurbishment had been carried out, thanks mainly to a local chef who had devised some new menus for them. It was hard to decide what she would have that day.

'I'd try the pork casserole if I was you.'

Lisa looked up when she recognised Dave Carson's voice. 'Good, was it?'

'Superb.' He smacked his lips. 'I'm thinking of bringing Jilly here for our wedding anniversary. Why pay top prices at some snooty restaurant when you can dine here for a fraction of the price?'

'Cheapskate!' she accused him.

'*Moi?*' He tried to look hurt. 'Just because I'm careful

with my hard-earned cash doesn't mean I'm being mean. We don't all earn the sort of money that allows us to wine and dine our loved ones at The Blossoms.'

Lisa rolled her eyes. 'I see the grapevine is working well as usual. Who told you I'd been to The Blossoms? Was it Will?'

'No. Mark Dawson popped in to book a table for him and Laura, and happened to see you there last night. Will never mentioned it, but I suppose he's got more important things on his mind at the moment.'

'He has?' Lisa's brows rose questioningly.

'Uh-huh.' Dave moved out of the way as several more members of staff arrived for lunch. He waited until they had gone inside the canteen before continuing. 'So who is she, then, Lisa? You must have an idea.'

'I don't know what you're talking about.'

'This woman Will's seeing, of course. He's obviously got it bad, because he was in a right state last night. Madge and I were tickled pink, to be honest. I don't think either of us thought we'd see the day when a woman got to poor old Will like this one has. So, come on, out with it, then—tell me who she is so I can tell Madge.'

'I've no idea.' It was hard to speak when her heart felt as though it had leapt right into her throat. She shook her head when Dave laughed. 'No, honestly. If Will is seeing someone, he hasn't told me about her, I swear.'

'Really? That does surprise me. I'd have thought you would be the first person he told, knowing how close you two are.' Dave shrugged. 'Still, I suppose there are *some* things you don't share even with your best friends.'

He winked at her then headed towards the lift. Lisa took a deep breath but her appetite seemed to have disappeared all of a sudden. She made her way along the corridor and opened the door to the rooftop terrace. It was bitterly cold out there that day, so cold that it took her breath away, but she stood there for some time, thinking about what she had learned.

It seemed that her suspicions about Will having met someone had been correct. It hurt to know that he had chosen not to tell her what had been going on, yet why should he have done? Will was a free agent and he certainly didn't need *her* permission to fall in love.

A mist of tears filmed her eyes but Lisa blinked them away. Will deserved some happiness after everything he had done for her in the past few years and she had no right to feel upset. They could still be friends, of course, although she was realistic enough to know that their relationship was bound to change. Now that Will had this other woman in his life, he would no longer have the time to worry about her.

She went back inside and it felt as though her heart had never felt so heavy as it did at that moment. Knowing that Will would shower the other woman with all the kindness and concern that he had shown to her left Lisa feeling bereft. The truth was that she was going to miss him such a lot.

It was a long day. As well as the list of children who needed elective surgery, there were two further emergency admissions. Will worked away with his usual dedication but he did so with a heavy heart.

Knowing that Lisa would be leaving sooner than he had anticipated had hit him hard, even though he knew how stupid it was to let it upset him. She would have left when she married Cameron so what difference did a few months make? he tried to reason, but it didn't work. He would give anything for a few days of her company, let alone several months.

It was almost seven before he put the final staple into the

last small patient and sent the child off to the recovery bay. Ray Maxwell had been assisting him for the past hour and Will grimaced as they left Theatre together. 'Been quite a day, hasn't it?'

'It has. I didn't realise just how heavy the workload here was going to be.'

Ray sighed as he flexed his shoulders. He was a good-looking man in his early thirties, a couple of years younger than Will was, in fact. His references had been excellent, which was why he had been hired for the job. However, Will had never been able to rid himself of a faint concern about Ray's commitment.

Ray had changed jobs at least a dozen times since qualifying. Although he had explained at his interview that it had taken him some time to find a post where he felt truly happy, Will suspected that he'd had another reason for moving around so much. Ray wouldn't be the first surgeon who had changed jobs because the pressure had become too much for him to cope with.

'Not having second thoughts, I hope?' he said lightly, opening his locker door. He bit back a sigh when he saw how uncomfortable the younger man looked. It was obvious that Ray had been wondering if he'd made the right decision by accepting the post at Dalverston General.

'I have to admit that I'm not a hundred per cent certain that I've chosen the right job,' Ray said. He shrugged when Will looked at him questioningly. 'Maybe you're happy not to have any social life, Will, but I'm not. I'm not one of those people who want to eat, sleep and dream about their work twenty-four hours a day.'

'Sounds as though you might have chosen the wrong profession, not just the wrong post,' he said dryly, trying to hide his dismay. It had taken them months to find anyone suitable to fill the vacancy and, from the sound of it, they might need to start advertising again shortly.

'Surgery is one of the most demanding areas of medicine that you can choose. It's both physically and mentally draining, no matter where you end up working.'

'Tell me about it!' Ray sighed as he took a towel from his locker and draped it around his neck. 'I was saying much the same to a friend of mine only last week. He made no bones about the fact that he thought I was mad to have gone in for surgery.

'He decided to opt out after he'd done a year as a houseman—he couldn't take the long hours and the poor pay. He's working for one of the big pharmaceutical companies now and you wouldn't believe the perks he gets with his job—company car, free medical insurance, five-star accommodation when he travels abroad. It makes me wonder why I'm doing this job, quite honestly.'

'Because you can make a difference to so many people's lives,' Will said flatly. 'That has to count for an awful lot in my view.'

'Even when it comes at the expense of having any sort of personal life?' Ray shook his head. 'Sorry, Will, but I'm just not as dedicated as you. I want to have some fun while I'm still young enough to enjoy myself. I'll be content to sit by the fire with my pipe and slippers quite soon enough!'

Ray laughed as he headed for the shower. Will slowly undressed but he had to admit that Ray's comments had touched a nerve. Was he in danger of becoming set in his ways, perhaps? He rarely went out of a night mainly because he had so little time to do so. And as for going out on a date... Well!

He wrapped a towel around his waist and padded, barefoot, into the shower room. Turning on the jets, he let the hot water drum down on his head and shoulders while he thought about how dull his life had become in the past few years. It consisted of work and evenings spent in the flat and, although he had been quite content up to now, maybe it was time that he made some changes, especially now that Lisa would be leaving.

He sighed. Everything seemed to hinge on that, didn't it? He had been content because what little free time he'd had in the past few years he had spent with Lisa. That was why he hadn't felt the need to go out and socialise.

They would open a bottle of wine and watch a movie together, maybe go for a pizza, although they hadn't done that for a while now, not since Cameron had become a permanent fixture in her life. But now all that was going to change because Lisa was moving on and moving out and *he* had to start getting his life back together, although he wasn't sure exactly where to start.

He frowned as he turned off the water and towelled himself dry. He could invite someone out, maybe one of the nurses from the children's ward. There were a number of unmarried women working there and he was friends with most of them.

Where to take her was a problem. It was so long since he had asked anyone out on a date that he wasn't sure what the form was nowadays. The cinema was always a reliable standby or maybe dinner. There were a number of new restaurants in Dalverston so he could make some enquiries and find out which ones were the best. At least it would be a start.

Only he didn't want to invite anyone to go out with him, did he? He didn't want to start a relationship, knowing that it could never really mean anything to him. It wouldn't be right and it certainly wouldn't be fair.

Will took a deep breath but the ache in his heart wouldn't

budge. The plain truth was that if he couldn't have Lisa then he didn't want anyone at all.

Lisa had been delayed because Daniel Kennedy had taken a sudden turn for the worse shortly before she'd been due to go off duty. It was obvious that the infection was spreading and that the increased dosage of antibiotics wasn't working.

Daniel's medical notes, which his GP had forwarded to them, showed that the boy had received several prescriptions for different antibiotic drugs in the past year. Unfortunately, that had increased the possibility that the child had built up a resistance to some of the more commonly prescribed antibiotics, making them ineffective in this instance.

Lisa phoned the lab but, as she had feared, the cultures wouldn't be ready for another twenty-four hours. It left her with no option but to try another broad-spectrum antibiotic even though she hated the feeling that she was batting in the dark. Until the lab identified which type of bacteria they were dealing with, she wouldn't be able to tailor the treatment to combat it.

She wrote Daniel up for the new drugs then explained to his parents what she was doing and why it was necessary. Like so many people, Mr and Mrs Kennedy had had no idea that different bacteria required different antibiotic treatment so it all took some time. However, Lisa didn't resent spending the time explaining it to the couple. It would help if they understood why Daniel hadn't been responding as they had hoped. Once he was started on the right treatment then she was hopeful that his condition would rapidly improve.

She left the IC unit at last and went to the staffroom to collect her coat. Angela Matthews was going off duty as well so they rode down in the lift together. They were jus crossing the foyer when Lisa spotted Will hurrying back into the building.

'Don't tell me you're still here,' she said, frowning. 'I thought you would have left ages ago.'

'I wish!' he declared.

'No rest for the wicked, eh?' Angela teased.

'Well, I must have been *really* bad somewhere along the line,' he retorted, grinning at her.

Lisa felt a little flash of awareness light up inside her when he included her in the smile. Once again she was struck by how very attractive he was, especially when he smiled like that. She couldn't believe that she had never noticed it before that morning.

Why had she been so completely unaware of his charms before? she found herself wondering, but there was no easy way to explain it. However, it was worrying to realise how much the situation had changed in a few short hours so that it was an effort to compose her features into a suitable expression when Will turned to her after Angela had hurried away.

'I was driving out of the gates when I had a call to say that one of the kids I operated on the other day had fallen over on his way to the bathroom and done himself some damage. Good job I hadn't made it all the way home, wasn't it?'

'I suppose so, but you really can't keep on this way, Will,' she said worriedly. 'You need to take some time off or you'll run yourself into the ground.'

'I'm off over Christmas so I'll get a break then. I'll probably sleep for the whole holiday!'

'Aren't you going to your parents' for Christmas?' she asked in surprise because she had assumed that was what he would do. She'd been invited to go with him several times since she had been living at the flat and had always enjoyed herself. Will's family were as easygoing as he was and always made her feel very welcome.

Her own parents had divorced when she was a small child so Christmases had been very quiet affairs while she'd been growing up. There had been just her and her mother to celebrate the day but they had always tried to make it special, even though there had only been the two of them.

She had missed her mother dreadfully after Helen Bennett had died so tragically of a heart attack while Lisa had been in her third year at med school. Fortunately she had been seeing Gareth at the time and he had helped her through that very difficult period. Will had also been wonderfully supportive, lending her a shoulder to cry on whenever Gareth hadn't been around. She didn't know how she would have coped without them both.

'Not this year, I'm afraid. Mum and Dad have decided to go away for Christmas for a change. Simon and Diane asked me if I'd like to go to them, but it's a bit of a drag, driving all the way to Devon for a couple of days, so I decided not to bother.'

'I see.' Lisa sighed because the thought of him spending Christmas on his own made her feel awful. Even when they had both been working, they had at least managed to have lunch together in the canteen. It would be odd not to spend any time with Will that Christmas.

'I could ask James if he would mind if you came to the cottage,' she suggested, thinking fast.

'It's kind of you, Lisa, but I really don't think it would be a good idea.'

'I'm sure he wouldn't mind, Will,' she insisted, wondering what had put that edge in his voice.

'Lisa, the last thing that Cameron wants is me hanging around.' He gave her a crooked smile. 'I'd feel exactly the same in his shoes, too. Remember that old saying about two's company and three is a crowd? Anyway, I've already made plans so you don't need to worry about me.'

'You have?' she said uncertainly, wondering if he was telling her the truth.

'Uh-huh.' He tapped the side of his nose and winked at her. 'I have something lined up, shall we say?'

'Oh, I see.' All of a sudden Lisa realised how foolish she was. Of course Will wasn't going to be on his own this Christmas! He was probably looking forward to having the flat all to himself so that he could invite his girlfriend round for the day.

Or the night, a small voice whispered.

The thought of him spending the night with some woman made her feel so sick all of a sudden that it was an effort to pretend everything was fine. 'Well, that's OK, then. As long as I know that you won't be on your own, I can go off and enjoy myself with a clear conscience.'

'I shall be fine,' he said firmly. 'And now I'd better get upstairs and see what's happened. Fingers crossed that it doesn't take too long to sort it all out.'

Lisa watched him hurrying towards the lifts then quickly left the building. It had started to rain but she barely noticed it as she made her way to the bus stop. She couldn't seem to rid herself of the pictures that were filling her head, pictures of Will making love to some faceless woman.

It shocked her that she should be having thoughts like that because it had never happened before. She had never *once* thought about Will in that context. It made her wonder what was wrong with her now and why she found the idea of him and this woman so difficult to deal with. Surely she couldn't be jealous?

Her breath caught because she didn't want to believe it was true, but how else could she explain the way she was feeling? Thinking about Will making love to another woman made her feel as though the bottom had dropped out of her world. It also made her see how impossible it would be to carry on living at the flat. It was bad enough imagining them together but how would she feel if Will invited his girlfriend to stay one night while she was there?

She would have to make a concerted effort to find somewhere else to live as soon as she could, although it was doubtful whether she could find anywhere before Christmas. But once Christmas was over, she would definitely move out of the flat.

Lisa sighed. She would have to move if she accepted James's proposal, but that didn't make her feel any better about the idea. Leaving Will was going to be very hard and it didn't make a scrap of difference what her reasons were for doing so.

CHAPTER FIVE

IT DIDN'T take Will long to work out what was the problem with his patient. Twelve-year-old Andrew Brown had been suffering from displacement of the upper epiphysis—the growing end of the femur. Because the bone was still growing, the epiphysis was separated from the shaft of the femur by a plate of cartilage, leaving an area of weakness that was susceptible to injury. When Andrew had fallen off a climbing frame during a school PE lesson a few weeks earlier, the epiphysis had slipped out of position.

Will had manipulated the displaced parts of the bone back into position and fixed them with metal pins. Unfortunately, Andrew had slipped in the bathroom that evening and wrenched the pins free. Will would now have to redo the operation, much to the boy's dismay.

'I'm sorry, son, but there really is no choice. If I don't realign the sections of your femur again, you'll carry on limping.'

'But that means I'll have to stay in hospital.' Andrew was doing his best not to cry. 'It's Christmas soon, Mr Saunders!'

'I know and it's really tough luck, but there really isn't any alternative.' Will patted the boy's shoulder, thinking how much he would have hated the thought of being stuck in hospital at Christmas when he'd been a child.

'It won't be that bad, Andrew. Honestly. The staff organise all sorts of things at Christmas—games and a party, even a visit from Santa Claus.'

'I'm too old to believe in Father Christmas,' Andrew muttered.

'Really?' Will shrugged. 'Then you won't be wanting the presents he brings for all the children in the ward, will you?'

'Well…' Andrew wavered, obviously not wanting to miss out on any treats.

Will laughed. 'Don't worry. You'll get a present even if you don't believe in Santa any more.' He lowered his voice confidingly. 'Just don't say anything to the little ones, will you? It would be a shame to spoil the fun for them.'

'I won't,' Andrew promised, looking a little happier at being entrusted to keep the secret.

Mr and Mrs Brown arrived just then, looking anxious as they hurried to their son's bed. Rachel Hart, the ward sister, had phoned to tell them about Andrew's accident and they wanted to know how much damage he had done to himself.

Will explained that he would have to redo the operation and that it would entail Andrew being kept in hospital a while longer. They were obviously upset to learn that their son wouldn't be home for Christmas, but they tried not to show it as they cheered him up by telling him what a good time he would have in the hospital.

They were the sort of parents whom Will enjoyed dealing with, full of common sense and wanting only what was best for their child. He left them talking to the boy and made his way from the ward, stopping off on the way to have a word with Rachel and tell her what was happening.

Rachel sighed after he had finished explaining it all. 'I thought as much. As soon as Julie came to tell me that Andrew had fallen over, I feared the worst.'

'How come he was allowed to go to the bathroom on his own?' Will asked, lounging against the door frame as weariness suddenly caught up with him. 'I thought you didn't allow the kids to wander about on their own when they were first on crutches.'

'We don't. Unfortunately, Andrew slipped out when we weren't looking.' Rachel sighed. 'We're short-staffed at the moment and there's only been the two of us on duty all afternoon. Andrew hates being accompanied to the bathroom and took advantage of the fact that we were busy with one of the other children. The end result is you having to redo all your good work, Will. Sorry!'

'These things happen,' he said lightly, knowing it wasn't Rachel's fault. Everyone was working flat out at the present time to make up for the shortage of staff.

'Especially when you're trying to do the work of ten people!' She grinned at him. 'Same old story throughout the hospital. I heard that you'd been called in several nights this week.'

'I don't know why I bother going home, to be honest.' He laughed ruefully. 'I'd be better off camping out in my office—that way I might get a couple of hours' sleep.'

'There is being dedicated and being dedicated,' Rachel retorted. 'Even I have to accept that I need to get away from this place once in a while.'

'I'm sure you're right,' Will agreed. 'Lisa was saying much the same thing earlier, funnily enough. She was trying to persuade me to take some time off,' he explained when Rachel looked at him quizzically.

'She was right, too, because the pressure does start to get to you. You spend most of your time struggling to keep on top of the job so that when you do have any time off then you end up too exhausted to enjoy it. My days off are usually spent sleeping!'

'How would you fancy doing something a bit more exciting for a change?' Will said hesitantly. He hurried on, not wanting to give himself time to think better of what he was doing. Hadn't he decided that he needed to think about his social life so why not take the opportunity to put his plans into action? He liked Rachel and had always got on extremely well with her so what harm could there be in asking her out?

'What do you have in mind?' she asked, grinning at him. 'I warn you that I'm not into extreme sports so hang-gliding is out and so is bungee-jumping!'

'And here I was thinking that you were a woman who loved taking risks.' He laughed when Rachel rolled her eyes. 'OK, then, how about the cinema one evening? That should be nice and safe. It's been ages since I saw a film and it would be great if you would come with me.'

'I'd love to, Will, so long as I'm not stepping on any toes.'

'Sorry?'

'You and Lisa.' She shrugged when he looked blankly at her. 'I've never been exactly sure what the situation is regarding you two.'

'We're just friends,' he assured her, although the words almost stuck in his throat. Maybe it was foolish to long to be more than Lisa's friend but he couldn't help it, just as he couldn't ignore the truth. Lisa regarded *him* as her best friend. Period. She certainly didn't imagine them having any other kind of a relationship.

'In that case, I'd love to come to the cinema with you, Will. Now all we have to decide is when, and *that* could be the really tricky bit. Do you think we're really going to be able to get some time off together?'

'I'll wangle it somehow. So, when are you next off duty of an evening?' he said, quashing any reservations he had. He was only asking Rachel out on a date so why get all het up about it?

'Tomorrow, as it happens. I've got the whole day off

and—barring flood, fire and pestilence breaking out in Dalverston—I fully intend not to set foot inside this place. We could go tomorrow night, if you're free?'

'I'll make sure I am.' Will smiled, not wanting Rachel to guess how unsure he was about this. He could tell himself a dozen times that he wasn't doing anything wrong but he couldn't help feeling worried.

'I'm not sure what time the evening performance starts at the Ritz so I'll check it out and phone you at home, if that's all right with you? We could go for a pizza after the film if you like.'

'Fine,' she agreed, then looked round when Andrew's parents appeared to have a word with her.

Will bade them all goodbye and left, but the whole time he was riding down in the lift he kept wondering if he had done the right thing. He liked Rachel and he wouldn't want her to think that he was using her. He also wouldn't like to upset Lisa…

He sighed when it struck him how ridiculous that idea was. Why should Lisa care because he had asked Rachel out? Lisa had her own future to think about and plan for. He may as well face the fact that he didn't feature in it.

It was almost lunchtime next day before Daniel Kennedy's lab results came back. Lisa took the printout into the office and sat down at the desk to read it. She'd been having trouble concentrating all morning, mainly because Will had behaved so strangely the night before.

It had been almost nine before he had arrived home and he had been unusually quiet for the rest of the evening. Lisa had gone to bed at half past ten, but he had stayed up, watching television. She had got up in the early hours of the morning for a drink of water and been surprised when she had realised the television had still been switched on.

She had no idea what time Will had finally gone to bed but it must have been very late. She'd left for work before he had got up so she hadn't spoken to him yet that day. However, she couldn't shake off the feeling that he had something on his mind.

Had it anything to do with this woman he was seeing?

She sighed as she picked up the lab report. It was no business of hers what was going on, as he had made it abundantly clear. He certainly hadn't confided in her about his feelings for this woman, whoever she was. Will obviously wanted to keep their relationship private and she had to respect that.

Lisa quickly read through the lab report, feeling her heart sink when she discovered that the bacterium had been identified as a strain of methicillin-resistant *Staphylococcus aureus*, or MRSA as it was commonly called. It was a serious infection which could cause many dangerous complications such as endocarditis—inflammation of the lining of the heart—and bone, liver and lung infection.

As its name implied, this particular type of bacterium was resistant to methicillin, one of the most frequently used antibiotics, and it could cause havoc if it spread throughout the IC unit. All the children would need to be tested to see if they had been infected by it and Daniel would need to be isolated. It was going to cause an awful lot of headaches.

Lisa went into the unit and told Angela what had happened. They both agreed that Roger Hopkins would need to be informed because they would be unable to accept any more patients into the unit until they knew just how widespread the infection was. MRSA spread through patient contact, respiratory droplets and food, and it was a major problem in many hospitals throughout the world.

Fortunately, Daniel was infected by a strain that could be treated with vancomycin. Lisa wrote him up for the drugs then explained to his parents about the lab results and why they would need to move Daniel to the isolation room. They were naturally worried and she did her best to reassure them, but it wasn't easy to calm their fears when it would have been wrong to play down the seriousness of the child's condition.

It was almost two before everything was organised. Daniel was safely ensconced in the side room and Angela and Jackie Meredith, the staff nurse on the unit, were busily taking bloods to send to the lab. There were seven children in the unit and each would need to be tested.

The infection control team had arrived and were testing the equipment that was used in the unit for traces of MRSA. The bacterium could inhabit the breathing apparatus and intravenous lines that were used on the children so it was vital that they made sure there were no signs of it. Other members of the team were carrying out tests in the operating theatre where Daniel had had his surgery, which meant that all elective paediatric surgery had been cancelled. Until they could be sure that the bacteria hadn't colonised any of the equipment, only emergency surgery would be performed, and that in one of the other theatres.

The staff canteen was almost empty by the time Lisa arrived for a late lunch. Most of the hot food had gone and she was too hungry to wait until there was any more ready. She put a plate of tuna sandwiches on her tray then added a jam doughnut and a bottle of mineral water and went to the till to pay.

She was just about to go and sit down when Will came in and she saw him hesitate when he spotted her. For a moment she honestly thought he was going to turn right around again and leave, and the thought made her heart suddenly ache. Since when had Will felt it necessary to avoid her?

* * *

Will summoned a smile as he let the canteen door slam shut behind him. He knew it was silly but he would have given anything to avoid having to talk to Lisa at that moment. He still wasn't comfortable with the idea of asking Rachel to go out with him, even though there was no reason why he should feel bad about it. It wasn't as though he was letting Lisa down by taking another woman out, for heaven's sake! However, it was hard to dismiss the guilty feelings that assailed him as he went over to speak to her.

'I see you've drawn the short straw for lunch as well,' he said, striving for lightness.

'Looks like it.' She gave him a cool little smile then carried her tray over to a nearby table and sat down with her back towards him.

Will frowned because he had the distinct impression that she had quite deliberately snubbed him. He quickly collected a plate of sandwiches and a cup of tea then went to join her, glancing pointedly at the empty chair.

'Mind if I sit here?'

'That's up to you.'

She ignored him as she started to peel away the film from her sandwiches. Will put his tray on the table and sat down. He shot her a wary look but she didn't even glance at him as she started to eat her lunch. He unwrapped his own sandwiches, wishing that he had some idea what was going on. Lisa was obviously annoyed with him, but what about?

His heart suddenly jolted and he put down the plate with a thud. Had she found out about him asking Rachel out?

The thought that she might be upset about him taking the other woman to the cinema made him feel all churned up inside. He couldn't help wondering why she didn't like the idea. Was it possible that Lisa was jealous, perhaps?

His mind seemed to go into overdrive at that point,

thoughts whizzing around so fast in his head that he felt positively giddy. It was far too much of an effort to pretend there was nothing wrong.

'Are you annoyed with me, Lisa?' he said hoarsely.

'Why should I be annoyed with you, Will? After all, if you suddenly decide that you don't want to talk to me, that's your business, isn't it?'

The bite in her voice brought him back to earth with a thump and he stared at her in dismay. 'What do you mean?'

'Oh, *please*! Do you think I'm stupid or something?' She tossed her sandwich onto the plate and glared at him. 'It was blatantly obvious that you weren't exactly thrilled to see me in here when you arrived. Given the chance, you would have turned tail and run! I don't know what I'm supposed to have done, Will, but if there is a problem then I would much prefer it if you came right out and said so.'

And he could just imagine her reaction if he did, he thought grimly. How would she react if he told her that the only problem he had at the moment was the thought of her leaving him? A confession like that would naturally lead to more questions, ones he wasn't sure that he could answer. How did he *really* feel about Lisa? He knew it was more than friendship, but was it the sort of all-consuming love that he had always dreamed of finding?

His parents had a wonderfully happy marriage and he had hoped that one day he might follow suit. The problem was he had never imagined that Lisa would be the woman he had been waiting for all these years. The idea was still too new and shocking for him to feel comfortable with it. His role had been that of friend and advisor for so long that it was hard to make the transition, especially when it would cause so many problems. Lisa was on the brink of marrying Cameron so how could he upset all her plans by admitting that he *thought* he was in love with her?

It could mark the end of their friendship because once she realised that his feelings for her were deeper than she had believed them to be then it would make her feel uncomfortable. He could just about live with the thought of her leaving if he knew that he wouldn't lose her friendship as well.

'Mmm, we are touchy today,' he said, grinning at her and praying that she couldn't tell how much it cost him to lie. 'I wasn't trying to avoid you, Lisa. I'd just remembered that I was supposed to give Ray a message. I couldn't decide whether I should go back and find him, or leave it until after I'd had something to eat.'

'Oh! I see.'

It was all Will could do not to grovel when he heard how wretched she sounded. It was obvious that she was giving herself a hard time for having accused him of trying to avoid her, and it made him feel even more guilty. He rushed to reassure her.

'Sorry if I seemed a bit off with you. It wasn't intentional. Good job we know one another so well, isn't it?' He smiled at her and was rewarded when she gave him a tentative smile in return.

'It is. And I'm sorry, too, for being so touchy.' She pulled a piece of crust off her sandwich and sighed. 'It's been one of those mornings, shall we say?'

'Tell me about it,' he said lightly. 'I've had to cancel three ops because of this outbreak of MRSA. The worst thing is that all the children were admitted yesterday so they would be ready to go to Theatre this morning. There's a lot of angry parents wanting to know why this has happened.'

'It's a real problem, isn't it?' she agreed. 'Hopefully, the infection control team will get it sorted out pretty quickly and give us the all-clear.'

'If it's got into any of the equipment then it could take

some time,' he warned. 'You know how hard it is to shift the bacterium once it gets a hold.'

'I know. I feel so bad about poor little Daniel Kennedy. He's going to need antibiotic treatment for at least two weeks—probably longer, in fact. MRSA can have a long-term effect so it's quite normal to have a patient on antibiotics for months after they've suffered a severe infection like this.'

'It's one of the biggest problems of having over-prescribed antibiotics in the past,' Will agreed. 'If more care had been taken about how often they were prescribed then the bacterium wouldn't have mutated this way. In Japan there is a strain of *Staph* which is partly resistant to vancomycin. We won't have anything left to treat it with soon.'

'It doesn't bear thinking about. I feel so guilty that I didn't start treating Daniel for it sooner. I just hope that it hasn't spread to any of the other children.'

'Hey, you weren't to know!' He frowned when he saw how dejected she looked. 'Come on, Lisa, you know very well that you did everything you could.'

'Mmm.'

'Never mind "Mmm"! You did and that's the end of it. OK?'

'Yes, sir!' She grinned when he rolled his eyes. 'Not that I'm implying you were pulling rank on me, of course.'

'Heaven forbid!' He shook his head when she laughed. 'Anyway, I wasn't trying to do that so sorry if it came across that way.'

'Apology accepted on one condition.'

'Which is?'

'That you treat me to a lovely soppy video this evening. I feel like doing something to take my mind off work so how about renting that new film that everyone's been talking about?'

She smiled at him and Will felt his heart turn over when he saw the warmth and laughter in her hazel eyes. 'And as an added inducement because I know romantic comedies are not really your thing, I'll treat us to a pizza *and* allow you to choose the toppings. Is it a deal?'

Lisa picked up her cup as she waited for him to answer. Not that she had any doubt he would agree, of course. Even though Will preferred adventure films to comedies he would go along with her choice. He was always so considerate in the way he treated her.

That thought made her frown because it made her see just how considerate he really was. He always let her choose which video they rented and what kind of take-away meals they ordered. He claimed that he didn't mind one way or the other, but all of a sudden she realised he had said that simply because he had wanted her to have what *she'd* wanted. Will always put her first in everything he did.

The thought made her feel all warm and tingly and she abruptly put down her cup. It shocked her to suddenly realise how spoilt she had been in the past few years. No man could have looked after her as well as Will had done. How could James hope to live up to him?

The thought made her mind spin so it was a moment before she realised Will had said something.

'Sorry, I didn't catch that,' she said, hoping that he couldn't tell how disturbed she felt. Maybe she shouldn't measure the two men against each other, but she couldn't help it and there was no doubt at all that Will had come out on top.

'I said that I'm going out tonight, Lisa, so I'll have to take a rain check on your offer of a pizza,' he repeated obligingly.

'Out?' She stared at him in bewilderment because it was

the last thing she had expected him to say. She couldn't remember the last time Will had been out of an evening.

'Yes.' He cleared his throat then hurried on. 'I'm taking Rachel to the cinema then we're going for something to eat afterwards.'

'Rachel?' she repeated, struggling to follow what he was saying.

'Rachel Hart—from Children's Medical,' he explained shortly. He picked up his cup then put it down again and sighed. 'Look, I can always cancel if you have your heart set on seeing that video. I'm sure Rachel won't mind if we make it another night.'

'Of course you mustn't cancel your date!' she said quickly. She picked up her cup and made herself drink a little of the tea, but it was an effort to swallow the tepid liquid when her stomach was churning.

Was Rachel the woman whom Will had been seeing? It had been one thing to speculate about some unknown female, but it was quite another to actually have a name and a face to go with it. She knew Rachel and liked her both as a person and as a wonderful nurse, but...

But—what?

What possible objection could she have? Rachel was lovely. Everyone who worked with her said the same thing, that she was one of the nicest people they had ever met. If she'd had to choose someone for Will then Rachel would have been an ideal candidate, in fact. Nevertheless, Lisa couldn't deny that the thought of him and Rachel seeing each other made her feel so queasy that it was an effort to pretend everything was fine.

It was far too much of an effort, in fact, and she hurriedly put down her cup. Pushing back the cuff of her white coat, she made a great show of checking her watch. 'Is that the time? I'll have to run.'

'What about your lunch?' Will said, frowning as he looked at her half-eaten sandwich.

'I'll take it with me.' She quickly rewrapped the sandwich in cling film and shoved it into her coat pocket.

'I've some parents coming to see me and I don't want to keep them waiting,' she ad-libbed.

She hated having to lie to him but the thought of him guessing how devastated she felt was infinitely worse. She should be pleased that Will had found someone as lovely as Rachel to share his life but she couldn't help feeling as though the bottom had dropped out of her world. It was an effort to summon a smile as she picked up her tray.

'There's going to be enough problems as it is once everyone finds out about Daniel Kennedy.'

'I doubt the infection will have spread to the other kids,' Will assured her. 'You've taken immediate steps to isolate him and the nursing staff on the IC unit are very much aware of the dangers of cross-infection. Angela continually drums it into them and the level of hygiene there couldn't be better.'

'Oh, I know! But the parents are bound to be worried when they find out what has happened,' she said quickly, not wanting him to think that she was criticising the staff in any way.

She edged away from the table, praying that she could hide her feelings for as long as it took to make her escape. Will was seeing Rachel. Would she ever get used to the idea?

'I suppose so. Who's coming to see you?' he asked, biting into his sandwich.

'Oh, um, Chloë Trent's parents,' she fibbed, feeling even worse. She'd never lied to Will before, had never had to because she had always felt that she could tell him anything.

It hurt so much to know how everything had changed. 'Anyway, I must dash. I'll catch you later, I expect.'

'I doubt it. I've got a meeting with Roger Hopkins and Morgan Grey to work out what we are going to do if the main paediatric theatre is out of action for any length of time. After that, I'm planning on taking the rest of the day off.' He grinned up at her. 'I shall be a gentleman of leisure this afternoon, so there!'

'Lucky for some!' she retorted, doing her best to respond the way Will would expect her to. 'Think about me slaving away while you're swanning about, won't you?'

'Oh, I shall, Lisa. I shall.'

There was something in his voice when he said that which made her breath catch, but she knew how foolish it would be to imagine it meant anything.

Will had been teasing her, she told herself sternly as she left the canteen. He hadn't been trying to imply that she was never far from his thoughts. They were simply friends— good friends, admittedly, but nothing more than that. He certainly didn't think about her the same way as he thought about Rachel.

Tears welled into her eyes all of a sudden but she dashed them away. She had no right to feel miserable because Will had found happiness at last. She should be pleased for him and for Rachel, too. Everyone needed someone to love them. Will needed Rachel and she needed James.

Her mind stalled on that thought. No matter how hard she tried, she simply couldn't picture the future she and James would have together. All she could think about was that Will wouldn't be there with her to share it, and it seemed wrong.

What kind of a future did she have to look forward to without her dearest friend?

CHAPTER SIX

WILL left the hospital shortly before three after discussing the current crisis with Roger Hopkins, the hospital's manager, and Morgan Grey, the head of surgery.

They had all agreed there was little they could do until the infection control team had finished their investigations, which would probably be the following morning at the earliest. However, the news so far had been very encouraging. It appeared they had found no trace of the MRSA bacterium in any of the equipment they had tested.

It could turn out that Daniel himself was the source of the infection and not the equipment that had been used during his surgery or his subsequent stay in the intensive care unit. Nevertheless, Theatre Three—the dedicated paediatric theatre—was to be given a thorough overhaul by the cleansing department and all the equipment that was used there would be either sterilised or discarded. It was a costly exercise but at least they had the comfort of knowing they were doing all they could to contain the outbreak.

Will drove out of the gates and turned onto the bypass, wondering how to fill in the afternoon. It was such a rare event for him to have any time off during the day that he wasn't what to do with it. In the end, he decided to go back to the flat and tidy up then go for a run. It had been ages since he'd had the time to go jogging and the exercise would do him good.

It didn't take him long to tidy up. With both him and Lisa working such long hours they spent very little time at home and, consequently, there wasn't much to do. He vacuumed the sitting room and put some washing into the machine then settled down to read the paper, promising himself that he would go for his run as soon as he had finished it.

He woke up a couple of hours later, feeling decidedly out of sorts for having dozed off in the middle of the day. So much for having time off, he thought ruefully as he got up from the sofa. He'd wasted most of it by sleeping, but at least he still had time for a run. He'd arranged to collect Rachel at seven but there would be plenty of time to shower and change when he got back.

He quickly changed into his running gear and set off. It had been so long since he had done any real physical exercise that he was puffing before he got to the end of the road. He gritted his teeth and carried on, but it was a relief when he arrived back home an hour later. He stripped off his shorts and top and headed for the shower. It had just turned six and he needed to hurry up if he didn't want to be late collecting Rachel.

He quickly showered then dressed, hesitating when it came to a decision about what he should wear. Normally he grabbed the first shirt and tie that came to hand but that night he stood in front of the mirror and tried first one tie then another to see how well they matched.

He sighed because both ties looked much the same to him. If only Lisa were there, he thought wistfully, she could have helped him choose the right one to wear that night for his date.

A searing pain lanced through him and he took a deep breath. What was the point of lying to himself? It was Lisa he really wanted to be taking out on a date, Lisa he wanted in his life tonight and every night to come—nobody else. He could tell himself a million times that he was doing the right thing by getting on with his life but it wouldn't change how he felt. Was it really fair to Rachel to start up a relationship when nothing could ever come of it?

He left the bedroom and strode along the hall, intending to phone Rachel and make some excuse to cancel their arrangement. He was just about to pick up the receiver when the front door opened and Lisa appeared. She stopped dead when she saw him and Will saw the oddest expression cross her face.

He felt a tingling sensation start at his toes and work its way up his body. Why on earth was Lisa staring at him that way?

Lisa felt a numbing pain grip her heart as she looked at Will. She couldn't remember when she had *ever* seen him looking so smart! Her eyes skimmed over the pale grey shirt and toning, darker grey tie he was wearing and the pain steadily grew worse.

He had obviously made an effort that evening and it was the reason why he had gone to so much trouble that hurt so bitterly. Will had wanted to look good for Rachel because her opinion mattered to him. If Lisa had needed proof of how he felt about the other woman, now she had it.

'It doesn't go, does it?'

She jumped when he spoke and raised startled eyes to his face. 'I'm sorry?'

'This tie. It doesn't go with the shirt.' He cast a rueful glance down. 'I'm hopeless at matching things up. I can't seem to tell what goes with what.'

'It's fine, Will, really it is.'

She fixed a smile to her mouth, praying that he couldn't tell how much it had upset her to acknowledge how deep his feelings for Rachel really were. 'I was just thinking how smart you look, actually. I hope Rachel will appreciate the effort you've made for her sake.'

She tried to inject a teasing note into her voice but it wasn't wholly successful and she saw him frown.

'You don't think I've gone over the top, do you? I don't want to give Rachel the wrong idea.'

She frowned when she heard the anxiety in his voice. 'What do you mean exactly by the wrong idea?'

'Well, it's just a night out.' He shrugged but she could tell how uncomfortable he was feeling. 'I wouldn't like Rachel to think I was coming on too strong or anything.'

'Don't be silly!' It was an effort to hold her smile when she saw how worried he looked. It was obvious that he must be deeply attracted to Rachel if he was so concerned about making the right impression.

'Of course Rachel won't think that you're coming on too strong, Will. She'll be flattered that you've made the effort to dress up and that's all.'

'Well, if you say so...' he began.

'I do.' Suddenly Lisa couldn't bear to discuss it any further. She shrugged off her coat and hung it on a peg then started towards the kitchen.

'I'm starving,' she said, deliberately changing the subject. 'I hope there's some food in the fridge. It's been ages since we went shopping.'

'There's some chops in the freezer and there should be some salad left, although I should have checked what we had in this afternoon. Let's have a look and if there's nothing you fancy, I can drive down to the shops and pick up some bits and pieces before I go out.'

Will moved away from the phone at the same moment as she tried to pass him, and they collided. Lisa's breath left her body in a small gasp when she found her breasts crushed against the hard wall of his chest. All she had on was a thin cotton blouse and Will was just wearing a shirt. It felt as though there was nothing separating their bare flesh...

'Sorry! Ladies first.' He stepped aside and bowed but there was a tautness about him that belied his joking tone.

Lisa summoned a smile but her legs felt as though they were stuffed with cotton wool as she led the way down the hall. Had Will felt it, too? she wondered shakily. Felt the sudden flare of sexual awareness which had passed between them? Or was it only she who had felt it, she who had been so aware of him that it had taken every scrap of self-control she possessed not to twine her arms around his neck and draw his head down so that she could kiss him…?

'Yep. There's some salad left, as I thought, plus half a dozen eggs as well if you don't fancy the chops.'

She took a deep breath when Will glanced round because it would be unforgivable to let him guess what she'd been thinking. How would Will feel if he discovered that she was having thoughts like that about him? Would he be shocked, embarrassed or disgusted even? He had been Gareth's best friend as well as hers and he might very well believe that it was wrong of her to harbour such feelings.

'I'll make myself an omelette, then.' It was an effort to keep the ache out of her voice but she did her best. 'I don't think I can be bothered to wait for the chops to defrost.'

'At least you won't starve and that's the main thing,' he said lightly, closing the fridge door. He glanced at his watch and sighed. 'I'd better get a move on otherwise I'm going to be late.'

'Yes, of course. Have a nice time and say hello to Rachel for me,' she said quickly, doing her best to behave as though everything was fine.

'Will do.' He paused in the doorway and Lisa saw an expression of indecision cross his face. 'Sure you'll be all right on your own, Lisa? I'm certain Rachel wouldn't mind if you came along.'

'Thanks but as you told me yourself two's company and three is one too many.'

It was an effort to smile but not for the life of her would she let him see how much it hurt to think about him and Rachel spending the evening together. 'I intend to have something to eat then put my feet up for the rest of evening.'

'Why don't you invite James round?'

Lisa frowned when she heard how flat his voice had sounded all of a sudden. She shot him a wary look but he just smiled at her.

'I should have said this before but I don't mind if you invite him to stay over, Lisa. Don't feel awkward about it, will you?'

'I won't. Thanks, Will.' She bit her lip but she knew that she had to return the favour even though the words seemed to stick in her throat. 'The same goes for Rachel. If you want to ask her to stay the night, it's fine with me.'

'Thanks. I'll bear it in mind.'

He gave her another quick smile then left and a few minutes later Lisa heard the front door closing. She opened the fridge and took out the carton of eggs then found a pan and set it on the stove before she realised that she no longer felt hungry. Maybe she would have a bath before she made herself something to eat.

She left the kitchen and went to her room, trying not to think about what had happened. Maybe she should have told Will that James was in Leeds at the moment. He was in the middle of a very important trial and had told her the other night at dinner that he wouldn't be able to see her until Christmas Eve when she went to the cottage.

James had phoned and left a message on her mobile phone to say how much he was looking forward to seeing her again. She knew that she should try to phone him back, but she simply couldn't face the thought of him asking her if she had made up her mind yet about what she was going to do when she was still so unsure about everything. Maybe she should have explained all that to Will while she'd had the chance?

She sighed because what difference would it have made if she had told Will that? Why should he care what she did? He had his own life to think about and he couldn't keep worrying about her all the time.

It was a strangely depressing thought and she tried not to dwell on it as she slipped out of her clothes. Will's old towelling robe was still draped over the back of the chair where she had left it so she put it on and went into the bathroom. Turning on the taps, she filled the tub then sighed when she realised there were no dry towels left. Will must have used the last one when he'd had his shower.

She took the damp towel off the rail, intending to dry it on the radiator while she soaked in the bath. She shook it out then paused when she caught the tangy scent of the soap Will always used coming off the damp cotton.

All of a sudden it struck her just how much she was going to miss sharing the everyday intimacies that were all part and parcel of them living together. It would be Rachel who dried herself on a towel that smelled of him in the future, Rachel who would wear his robe, Rachel who would share everything with him and not her.

She stared at her reflection in the steamy mirror over the basin and it was impossible to ignore the pain in her eyes. She simply couldn't bear to think of losing him to Rachel, or any other woman.

The evening was turning into a disaster. It hadn't been so bad while he and Rachel had been watching the film because it had meant that he'd been spared the task of having to make conversation. But once they left the cinema, Will found it increasingly hard to keep up the pretence that he was enjoying himself.

He kept thinking about Lisa back at the flat, and wondering if she had done as he'd suggested and invited Cameron round for the night. How was he going to feel if got home and found them there together?

The thought made him break out in a cold sweat and his damp palm slipped off the gear lever as he turned into the car park of the Indian restaurant where they had decided to eat after the film.

'Sorry,' he murmured as the car bucked in protest at such ham-fisted treatment.

He pulled up in a parking space, willing himself to calm down, but the thought of Lisa and Cameron in bed together made him feel as though a red-hot knife was being twisted in his guts. *Nothing* had ever felt this painful before!

'Not to worry.' Rachel turned to look at him and he heard her sigh. 'What's wrong, Will? And before you tell me that everything is fine, I have to say it doesn't look like it from where I'm sitting. You've hardly said a word all night.'

'I'm a bit tired, that's all. Take no notice.' He adopted a deliberately bright tone. 'Well, I don't know about you, but I'm starving. I believe the tikka marsala here is absolutely superb so I might try that. How about you? What do you fancy?'

'What I would really like is for you to tell me the truth.' Rachel put her hand on his arm when he went to open the car door. 'Why did you ask me out, Will?'

He sighed because he simply couldn't find it in his heart to lie to her. 'Because I felt it was time I got on with my life.'

'Well, at least you're honest! I'll say that for you.' She laughed softly and Will grimaced as he realised how that must have sounded.

'Sorry. That didn't come out the way I meant it to.'

He turned to her and smiled, wondering why he didn't feel anything when she smiled back. Rachel was very pretty and he could understand why many men would be attracted to her, yet he didn't feel even a flicker of interest.

His mind suddenly swooped back to those moments in the hall when he and Lisa had collided, and he had to bite back a groan. Feeling her small breasts crushed against his chest had made him long to sweep her into his arms and make mad, passionate love to her. How he had managed to resist the urge he would never know. If he hadn't moved away when he had, there was no doubt in his mind what would have happened.

All of a sudden he could picture *exactly* what would have happened. He could actually *see* himself carrying Lisa into his bedroom and laying her down on his bed. She'd been wearing one of those prim little blouses she favoured and his body spasmed with desire as he imagined undoing each tiny button until she was lying there in just her underwear...

'Tell me to mind my own business if you want to, but is it Lisa?'

Will blinked and all of a sudden he was back in the present with Rachel asking him a lot of awkward questions. 'I'm not sure I understand what you mean.'

'It's simple. Are you in love with Lisa?' Rachel shrugged when he didn't reply. 'I told you that I didn't want to step on anyone's toes when you asked me out, Will. So if you only did it to make Lisa jealous then I wish you'd tell me. I'll understand, really I will.'

'No, it wasn't like that,' he said quickly, his heart aching because jealousy was the last thing Lisa would feel with regard to him. 'Lisa is involved with someone else. He's asked her to marry him, in fact.'

'And how do you feel about the idea of her marrying this other guy?' Rachel asked gently.

'I'm pleased for her, of course,' he began, then stopped because he could tell that she didn't believe him. 'I hate the idea, if you want the truth. I know I shouldn't feel this way but I can't help it.'

'Because you love her?' Rachel sighed when he shrugged. 'I'm so sorry, Will. I know how it feels to love someone and lose them.'

Will shot her a questioning look. Maybe he should be focusing on his own feelings but it was easier not to think about himself at that moment. Was he in love with Lisa? Everything pointed towards it and yet the thought of loving her and losing her to another man was too much to bear.

'Do you want to tell me about it?' he asked gently.

'No.' She smiled sadly. 'Thanks, but there really is no point, Will. Suffice it to say that I understand how you feel. I also want you to know that I'll help any way I can, even if it's only by providing you with a cover story. Sometimes the only thing you can do is to save face and try not to embarrass yourself or the other person, isn't it?'

'Yes, you're right. And there is no way that I want to embarrass Lisa when she is getting her life back together.'

He leant over and kissed Rachel lightly on the cheek. 'Thanks for being so understanding, Rachel. I really appreciate it. Now, how about that meal I promised you?'

They let the subject drop and went into the restaurant. However, despite what Rachel had said, Will knew it would be wrong to ask her out again. He couldn't bear to think that he was using her, even though she had assured him that she didn't mind.

In the event it was quite a pleasant evening so that by the time he dropped her off at her home, he was feeling a little better about what had happened. His upbeat mood didn't last, unfortunately. The closer he got to home, the more depressed he felt about what might greet him.

It was a relief when the hospital beeped to tell him that he was needed. Ray was the designated on-call surgeon that night but he hadn't responded when the switchboard operator had tried to contact him.

Will assured the woman that he didn't mind covering for Ray. He turned the car round and headed back along the bypass, feeling as though he had been given a reprieve. At least now he wouldn't know whether or not Cameron had spent the night with Lisa. It was a small comfort at least.

'Will you be taking him back to Theatre this afternoon?'

Lisa took the chart off the end of the bed and handed it to Dave Carson. It was two minutes past six in the morning and she had only just come on duty when Dave had arrived. The anaesthetist wanted to check on a child who had been admitted to the unit during the night and was scheduled for further surgery later that day.

Seven-year-old Liam Donnelly had been rushed to the hospital after police had been called to his home. Neighbours had alerted them after they had heard the boy screaming. It appeared that the boy's stepfather had beaten him for wetting his bed.

The child had suffered several fractures along with a range of other injuries including a ruptured spleen and was in a critical condition. It had been deemed too risky to transfer him to Manchester, the nearest paediatric intensive care unit, so the decision had been made to admit him to Dalverston despite the current MRSA scare.

Lisa knew that it must have been difficult to weigh up the pros and cons and couldn't help wondering who had made the final decision. She'd not had time to read the child's case notes which would have provided the answer.

'Who decided to send him to us instead of transferring him to Manchester?' she asked as Dave handed back the child's notes.

'Will. He operated on him and it was his decision to send him here.' Dave shook his head as he looked at the boy. 'It was touch and go whether the poor kid would make it, apparently. Will obviously decided that it would be too big of a risk to move him.'

'I didn't realise Will had been called in,' Lisa exclaimed, then blushed when Dave shot her a questioning look. It was obvious the anaesthetist must have heard the relief in her voice.

She busied herself with putting the boy's notes back in the holder. Discovering that Will's bed hadn't been slept in when she had got up that morning had caused her more than a little heartache. It hadn't taken her long to reach the conclusion that he must have spent the night with Rachel. Finding out that he had been right here in the hospital made her feel as though a weight had been lifted off her shoulders all of a sudden.

'Why do I get the impression that it was good news to hear that Will had been here, working his socks off? You're not developing sadistic tendencies like the rest of us, I hope, Lisa?'

'I was just worried what had happened to him when I discovered that his bed hadn't been slept in,' she said lightly, hoping that Dave would take what she said at face value.

'You mean he didn't go home after he finished here?' Dave looked momentarily puzzled before he suddenly grinned. 'Ah, I see! Wait till I see Will. The sly old dog!'

'What do you mean?' Lisa asked, frowning.

'Will left here just after two. Mike Carruthers was the on-call anaesthetist last night and he happened to mention what time they'd finished when I passed him in the foyer on my way in. Will would have had plenty of time to go home to bed but he obviously had other plans.' Dave winked at her. 'Give you two guesses where he spent the night.'

'You mean he stayed at Rachel's?' she said, her heart sinking once more.

'Rachel? Do you mean Rachel Hart?' Dave laughed when she nodded. 'Brilliant! I've been dying to find out who he's been seeing. Wait till I tell Madge. She'll be tickled pink when she hears that it's Rachel he's been dating!

'Anyway, I'll come back later to see how Liam is doing. I'm not happy about him having another general anaesthetic at the moment, so we might need to leave pinning his femur for a day or so. The poor kid has had the stuffing knocked out of him all right. Let's hope the police lock up the step-father and throw away the key.'

Dave didn't give her a chance to say anything else as he hurried away, leaving Lisa miserably aware that she might have broken a confidence. She had no idea how Will would feel when he found out that she'd been the one to tell Dave about Rachel.

She went to the office to read through the notes Sanjay had left for her. He was always very thorough so it was a long report about what had gone on during the night. She tried her best to concentrate but her mind kept skipping about all the time, always coming back to the same problem of what she was going to do.

Will must be serious about Rachel if he'd spent the night with her because he wasn't the kind of man who would go in for one-night stands. In all the time she had known him, in fact, she couldn't remember him ever having an affair.

She frowned because that thought struck her as odd. Will was a very attractive man in the prime of his life and there must be a lot of women who would be thrilled to go out with him. Yet since Gareth had died, he hadn't even been out on a date. Why? Because he hadn't wanted to get involved with a woman when so much of his time had been taken up by her?

She sighed because it hurt to know how much he had given up for her sake. It made her see that the only way she could repay him for all that he had done was by giving him the space to get on with his life. Now that he had found Rachel and they were obviously making a commitment to one another then it was time she moved on. Maybe it would be best for everyone if she accepted James's proposal.

The telephone rang and Lisa jumped. She snatched up the receiver, wondering why she felt so relieved about not having to make a decision right at that moment. The sooner she made up her mind the better yet she couldn't quite bring herself to make the final decision to marry James.

Maybe it wouldn't hurt to put it off until after Christmas. Another week or so wouldn't make that much difference.

CHAPTER SEVEN

IT WAS mid-morning before Will realised there was something going on. He had been vaguely aware of an undercurrent in Theatre but had been far too busy to worry about it.

The infection control team had cleared all the theatres now and he was trying to catch up with some of the elective surgery which had been postponed. It had been rather like working on a conveyor belt as one patient after another had been wheeled in. Now when he looked up and caught Madge Riley and Dave Carson staring at him he sighed.

'OK, so what's going on? You two are like a couple of kids on Hallowe'en. I keep expecting you to shout "Trick or treat?"'

'Why should you imagine there's anything going on?' Madge said loftily. She quickly collected the swabs he had used and set them aside on the trolley to be counted then went to the corner of the room where the stereo was set up. 'How about a little mood music to soothe us all?'

Will raised his eyes. 'I didn't need soothing until you two started playing up.'

'Tut-tut, Mr Saunders. It's not like you to be so snappy.' Madge poked a gloved finger at the power button and switched on the machine. 'Anyhow, this should help to calm you down.'

Will decided that the best thing to do was to ignore them and bent over the operating table again. Five-year-old Katie Tomkins was having a myringotomy, a procedure in which an incision was made in the eardrum and a small tube—called a grommet—was inserted.

Katie had a history of ear infections which had resulted in glue ear, a condition in which the middle ear cavity became blocked with sticky secretions. This had led to a loss of hearing which had been picked up when the little girl had been given a routine hearing test at school.

The grommets, which Will was in the process of inserting, would equalise the pressure on both sides of the eardrums and allow the mucus to drain down the Eustachian tube. The grommets would then fall out of their own accord in six to twelve months' time.

It was the kind of routine surgery which he had performed more times than he could count, but it would make such a huge difference to Katie's life to be able to hear clearly that it was very worthwhile.

He carefully inserted the tiny tube into the child's right ear then frowned when he realised which song was playing in the background. Glancing up, he shot a questioning look at Madge who had returned to her customary place at his side.

'You must have dug this one up from the bottom of the pile. I can't remember when I last heard this song. Enjoying a little nostalgia trip this morning, are we, Sister?'

'Oh, I just thought it was highly appropriate in the circumstances.' Madge's eyes twinkled at him over the top of her mask.

'What circumstances?' he asked blankly, wondering what she was getting at.

'Your little *liaison* last night, of course,' Dave chipped in. He hummed a few bars of the melody then chuckled. 'So, was it an enchanted evening, then, Will? And before you try to deny what you were up to, I have it on very good authority that you didn't go home last night. That naturally

led me to conclude that you must have spent the night somewhere else. Am I right?'

'Oh, you're certainly right.' Will's tone was clipped because it hurt to know that Lisa had been gossiping about
him. It had to be Lisa who had told Dave that he hadn't
gone home—who else? Yet what would she think if she
found out how wrong she had been about where he *had*
stayed?

He cut off that thought, knowing it was pointless to hope
that she would be pleased to learn that he had spent the
night on the sofa in his office and not in Rachel's bed. He
simply hadn't been able to face the thought of going back
to the flat and discovering that Cameron was staying there
so had taken the easy way out.

In the event he had slept well enough, but the thought
that people were now adding two and two and coming up
with an answer that bore no resemblance to the truth, thanks
to Lisa, stuck in his throat. How could she have started such
an unsavoury rumour about him?

'I slept in my office last night and before you say anything, my secretary will vouch for the fact.' He treated Dave
to a frosty look. 'I nearly frightened the life out of her when
she walked in this morning and found me. So, whatever
fanciful notions you've got into your head, I suggest you
forget them.'

'Right. Um…sorry.' Dave sounded sheepish but Will
wasn't feeling kind enough to worry about the other man's
feelings. In his heart he knew that Dave and Madge hadn't
meant anything by their teasing but it didn't help.

He finished the operation in silence, steadfastly ignoring
the lilting music issuing from the stereo. In no way could
he describe his evening as having been *enchanted* although
he couldn't vouch for what Lisa's evening had been like, of

course. Had it been wonderful for her to have Cameron sharing her bed?

The thought made him want to throw up but he wasn't a man given to such extreme behaviour and he refused to indulge in it now. He thanked Madge and Dave in his usual courteous fashion then went through to change into fresh scrubs. He had another three operations scheduled before lunch, but all of a sudden he realised that he needed a few minutes' breathing space before he started on the next one.

'I'm taking a break,' he explained tersely as Dave followed him out. 'You may as well do the same. Tell the others that I'll expect them back here in fifteen minutes time, will you?'

'Sure,' Dave agreed readily. 'About what just happened, Will—'

'Forget it.' Will didn't give him the chance to apologise purely because he didn't want to have to deal with how it made him feel to think about Lisa gossiping about him.

Stripping off his gown, he left the theatre and made for the stairs, taking them two at a time as he ran up to the canteen, two floors above. His legs were a little stiff from yesterday's jogging session but he ignored the aching muscles. All he needed was a cup of coffee then he would be back on track.

Elbowing the canteen door open, he joined the queue at the counter and asked for a large cup of black coffee when it was his turn. The place was packed with staff having their morning breaks and the thought of having to share a table and make polite conversation was the last thing he felt like doing.

He paid for his drink then headed out of the canteen and made for the terrace instead. It was bitterly cold outside and he really wasn't dressed for such weather, but he wanted to be on his own. He needed to get his head round the idea that Lisa didn't even care enough about him not to start spreading rumours.

His vision blurred and he quickly raised the cup to his mouth and swallowed some of the fortifying liquid. He had to get a grip on himself and he had to do it sooner rather than later. He could either deal with what was happening or he could let it completely ruin his life…

Only it was already ruined because Lisa was leaving him for another man.

'So there you are. I've been looking *everywhere* for you, Will!'

He swung round when he recognised Lisa's voice, feeling his heart fill with sudden warmth when he saw the concern on her face. Had she been worried when she hadn't been able to find him? he wondered. And was it a sign that she truly cared about him, perhaps?

The thought was so mind-blowingly marvellous that it was all he could do to stop himself sweeping her into his arms and telling her how he felt.

'I owe you an apology, Will. I've done something awful and I'll understand if you're angry with me.' She took a deep breath then hurried on before he could say anything, the words tumbling over each other in her haste to get them out.

'I told Dave about you and Rachel. I didn't mean to. I swear. It just sort of…well, slipped out. I'm really, really sorry, Will. Can you ever forgive me?'

Lisa bit her lip but the grim expression on Will's face filled her with dread. It was obvious that he was angry with her and who could blame him? Rumours like the one she had unwittingly started could spread through the hospital at the speed of light. He must be furious with her for having put him and Rachel in such a difficult position.

'Will, say something!' she pleaded when he remained silent. 'Even if it's only to shout at me. I never, *ever* meant to cause you and Rachel any embarrassment. I swear!'

'It doesn't matter.' He drained his coffee-cup then strode towards the door, pausing when she failed to move out of his way.

'I can't let you go like this! I can tell you're upset and it's all my fault.' She put her hand on his arm when he went to step around her and gasped when she discovered how icy cold his skin felt. 'You're freezing! You shouldn't be out here in those clothes. You'll catch your death.'

Her gaze swept down his body then back up again but somehow it seemed to have absorbed a surprising amount of detail from that single glance. Lisa felt little bubbles of awareness fizz along her veins as she recalled how the green scrub suit had moulded itself to his body. There was quite a strong breeze blowing across the terrace and it had plastered the thin cotton fabric against his muscular chest and thighs. Quite frankly, Will might have been standing there stark naked for all the good the clothing was doing!

'I'm fine. I appreciate your concern but there is no need to worry about me, Lisa, I assure you.'

The flat note in his voice slowly got through to her and she raised worried eyes to his face. It wasn't like Will to be so unforgiving. Normally, he was the first person to want to resolve an issue, the one who played peacemaker whenever there was a dispute. It made her wonder if it was just her unthinking remark that had upset him or something else she had done. All of a sudden it seemed important that she should find out the truth.

'Will, what's wrong?'

'I'm sorry, but I have to get back,' he said, brusquely interrupting her. He stepped aside so that she was forced to release him and opened the door to go back inside.

'I really am sorry, Will,' she said softly, hating the thought that he was still angry with her. On the few occasions they had disagreed in the past they had quickly resolved their differences, but this was different. This didn't just involve him and her but Rachel as well. Was Will unable to forgive her because she had upset the woman he loved?

The thought was so painful that tears stung Lisa's eyes but she blinked them away. She was a grown woman, not a child, and if she had done something wrong then she had to admit it. There was no way that she would let him think that she was trying to play on his sympathy.

She stood up straighter when he glanced back, but it was one of the hardest things she'd ever had to do, to face the fact that he was more concerned about Rachel's feelings than he was about hers.

'I shall apologise to Rachel as well when I see her. The last thing I want is to cause trouble between you two. I wouldn't like her to think that you were the one to start everyone gossiping.'

'You don't need to worry about that,' he said tersely. 'Rachel will understand.'

'Of course.' She summoned a smile but she couldn't deny how foolish she felt. 'Obviously Rachel won't think it's your fault. She must know that you would never discuss your relationship. Just tell her that I'm sorry, though, will you?'

'Yes.'

He didn't say anything more before he hurried back inside. Lisa followed more slowly, shivering as she stepped back into the warmth. She hadn't realised just how cold she had grown through standing outside.

She went to the canteen and bought herself a cup of hot chocolate, hoping it would warm her up. Most of the staff had finished their breaks by now so she managed to find an empty table and sat down. She wrapped her hands around the steaming mug but icy shivers kept on passing through her system.

She sighed because the chill owed itself less to the outside temperature than to the frosty reception Will had afforded her. Having him treat her so coolly would take a lot of getting used to, but she had to accept that the situation had changed dramatically in the past few days. Rachel was the one he cared about now and there was little room left in his life for her. The sooner she accepted that, the easier it would be.

Her hands shook as she picked up the cup because she knew how difficult it would be to follow that advice. Accepting that Will was in love with another woman wasn't going to be an easy thing to do.

Daniel Kennedy's parents were waiting to see her when Lisa got back from her break. Daniel had shown some small signs of improvement during the night but he was still very ill and she knew how worried they must be. She took them into the relatives' room, smiling when Angela arrived a few seconds later with cups of tea for everyone.

'Thanks. Will you stay?' she asked the ward sister, knowing that it would help the parents to hear Angela's views on the progress their son was making. At a time like this, parents needed every bit of reassurance they could get. She turned to the couple as Angela drew up a chair.

'First of all I wanted to tell you that we are extremely pleased with the way Daniel has responded to the new antibiotic treatment. It's very encouraging.'

'So you do think he's responding then, Dr Bennett?' Jane Kennedy said hopefully.

'Oh, yes. I know it's difficult for you to tell how he is

doing, but we are able to assess Daniel's condition far more accurately and he is definitely improving.' Lisa turned to Angela. 'You agree, don't you, Sister?'

She waited while Angela briefly outlined the small improvements which had been noted in Daniel's condition, things like a drop in his temperature and his blood pressure rising.

'And that's good, is it, Doctor? They are positive signs that he is on the mend?'

'Indeed they are.' Lisa smiled reassuringly at Brian Kennedy, the boy's father. 'Obviously, Daniel has a long way to go before he gets better, but he is heading in the right direction at last.'

'I don't understand how he got this infection,' Jane put in. 'I spoke to my sister last night and she said that he must have caught it here in the hospital, but surely that can't be right?'

'It's one possibility,' Lisa conceded. 'MRSA is a problem in a lot of hospitals, although I'm happy to say that there hasn't been an outbreak at Dalverston General for a number of years. We have a very strict infection control policy here and that has helped to prevent an outbreak.'

'Then if Daniel hasn't caught this disease in here, how has he caught it?' Brian asked, frowning.

'MRSA isn't a disease but a strain of bacterium,' she explained. 'Basically, everyone has *Staphylococcus aureus* bacteria on their skin. The bacteria can also be found everywhere in the environment but for healthy people they don't cause a problem. It's only if you cut yourself or maybe get bitten by an insect—anything that breaks the skin, in fact—that you might suffer a minor infection as a result of *Staph*.'

'But if these bacteria aren't really dangerous, why are they making Daniel so ill?' Jane asked worriedly.

'Most *Staph* infections aren't dangerous because they can be treated with simple antibiotics,' she clarified. 'However, the strain which is causing Daniel to be so ill no longer responds to those antibiotics. The bacteria have become resistant to them and consequently cause more of a problem.'

'Why has it happened, though, Dr Bennett?' Brian put in.

'I'm afraid it's all due to the way antibiotics have been over-prescribed in the past. Many bacteria have altered their structure and are now resistant to the more widely used antibiotics. Unfortunately, it means there are only a few antibiotics left which we can use to treat MRSA.'

'But Daniel is responding to the new treatment, isn't he?' Jane said quickly.

'He is. I've prescribed vancomycin for him and it seems to be working, although I must warn you that he will need to be on antibiotics for some time. We need to be sure that the bacterium won't cause him any problems in the future.'

She gave the parents a moment to digest all that then stood up. 'Now shall we go and see how Daniel is doing? I know it's a bit of a chore, having to put on a gown and a mask every time you visit him, but it's vital that we stop the infection spreading to the other children.'

'How does it spread?' Brian asked curiously, following her from the room. 'Is it a bit like a cold germ?'

'Yes, it is. It can be passed on through respiratory droplets as well as carried on your hands or in the equipment we use.' Lisa paused outside the side room to where Daniel had been moved.

'That's why Sister is so keen on people washing their hands and pays such close attention to making sure that everything is sterilised after use. The standards of hygiene here in the intensive care unit are some of the highest I've ever come across.'

'That's what I told my sister,' Jane said firmly, taking a

gown from the pile outside the door. 'I told her that Daniel couldn't be in better hands and I meant it. He's lucky to have you looking after him, Dr Bennett, and very lucky it was that wonderful surgeon who operated on him. I doubt Daniel would still be with us if it weren't for him.'

Lisa smiled but it was hard not to let her feelings show as she listened to the woman praising Will. He *was* wonderful and not only in his work but in all sorts of ways. She couldn't help wishing that she had realised it sooner and acted upon it. Then he might not have needed Rachel in his life.

She bit back a sigh as she led the way into the room because that was just wishful thinking.

Will was glad when lunchtime arrived. Normally, he enjoyed his job to such an extent that he could block out everything else while he was working. However, that day he had needed to make a concerted effort to stay focused. Every time he had relaxed his guard, his mind had skipped back to what had happened on the terrace.

He knew that he had been less than gracious when Lisa had tried to apologise to him. Maybe she had been wrong to tell Dave about him seeing Rachel but surely he should have accepted her apology in the spirit it had been offered?

The thought that he had upset her by his brusqueness didn't sit easily with him. He realised that he would have to find her and clear up the misunderstanding. After all, it wasn't her fault that she had been more concerned about making amends than worried when she hadn't been able to find him.

He sighed because he had never considered himself to be an overly sensitive person before. Since when had he started getting all prickly because people didn't say or do what he wanted them to? He couldn't make Lisa feel things she didn't feel and he had to accept that and not go ruining their friendship. The last thing he wanted was to spoil that when it was all they had left.

He left Theatre and headed for the changing-room, pausing when he spotted Ray leaving Theatre Two. Ray had been late arriving that morning so Will decided that he may as well take the opportunity to have a word with him about his time-keeping. And while he was doing so he would find out what had happened the previous night, when Ray had been unavailable when the switchboard had tried to page him. Taking his turn on call was all part of the job, as Will intended to make clear.

'What happened to you this morning?' he asked without any preamble as Ray joined him. 'Everyone was waiting in Theatre for you to turn up, with the patient already prepped.'

'I overslept. Sorry,' Ray said lightly.

He hadn't sounded as though he'd meant it and Will frowned as he led the way into the changing-room. He didn't want to start making an issue of this but he was becoming increasingly concerned about the younger doctor's attitude.

'Please, make sure it doesn't happen again,' he said firmly. 'It causes no end of problems if we get behind with the lists. And while we're on the subject of you turning up, what went wrong last night? The switchboard told me that you hadn't answered your beeper.'

'Was I paged?' Ray queried, looking surprised.

Will could tell that he was lying, however, and it annoyed him to know that the man was prepared to lie rather than admit that he had chosen not to respond to the call. It was the kind of behaviour he wouldn't tolerate and he needed to make that perfectly clear.

'Yes, you were. There was an emergency admission, a young boy who had been badly beaten by his stepfather and suffered some very nasty injuries. If I hadn't been able to attend, the general surgical team would have had to deal with the case and, frankly, that isn't acceptable. I expect all the members of this team to pull their weight.'

'You're making it sound as though I *deliberately* didn't respond to the call.' Ray laughed as he opened his locker door. 'I didn't get it, Will, and that's the honest truth. My girlfriend drove up from London last night and decided that she didn't want our evening being interrupted. She switched off my beeper and I didn't discover what she had done until this morning.'

'Then may I suggest that you have a word with her and tell her not to do it again? Whoever is the designated on-call surgeon has to be available at all times.'

'Don't I know it!' Ray sighed as he took a bottle of shampoo out of his locker. 'One of the reasons why I decided to leave my last post was because I was fed up being at everyone's beck and call all the time. Every time I went anywhere there would be a phone call, asking me to go back to work. I had no personal life.'

'It's one of the hazards of the job,' Will said unsympathetically, because Ray should have known what he was letting himself in for when he had accepted the job at Dalverston. He'd been at pains during the interviews to make it clear that they had a very demanding workload but, obviously, Ray hadn't taken what he had said to heart.

'And maybe I'm just starting to realise that it's not something I'm prepared to put up with for very much longer.' Ray slammed his locker and headed for the showers, looking far from pleased about the reprimand.

Will didn't say anything because he could tell there would be no point. Ray was obviously having second thoughts about working at Dalverston and he doubted if there was anything he could say to make him change his mind.

He sighed as he followed the younger man to the showers. It looked as though they might have another vacancy in a few weeks' time. It would put all the pressure back on him, but that might not be a bad thing. The harder he worked the less time he would have to think about Lisa's imminent departure. He could immerse himself in his work until he had come to terms with it.

He grimaced. If he worked twenty-four hour days for the next umpteen years he would never get used to being without her! Still, at some point he would have to accept the inevitable. He also needed to apologise for the churlish way he had behaved that morning. It would be a shame to spoil what little time they had left together.

Will went straight to the IC unit after he had changed but there was no sign of Lisa when he got there. Angela was in her office so he knocked on the door but she had no idea where Lisa had gone to.

He went upstairs to the canteen in case she'd gone for lunch but once again he drew a blank. He headed back down the stairs, wondering where she had got to. She was always so conscientious about telling the staff her whereabouts that he couldn't understand why she hadn't mentioned where she was going that day.

He reached the floor where the children's wards were situated and hesitated, wondering if he should tell Rachel what had happened. Although he was fairly sure that Dave and Madge wouldn't gossip there was always a chance the story might get out and it seemed only fair to warn her.

He sighed as he made his way to Children's Medical because he couldn't help feeling guilty about Rachel. Asking her out last night had been a mistake and he wouldn't do it again. He would hate to think that she might end up the subject of any unsavoury gossip because of him.

He rounded a bend in the corridor and came to an abrupt

halt when he saw Lisa and Rachel deep in conversation outside the office. It was obvious they were discussing something important and his heart plummeted as he found himself wondering what they were talking about. What if Rachel told Lisa how he felt about her? What would she think if she found out that he was in love with her?

His mind spun but there was no way he could avoid the truth any longer. He *was* in love with Lisa.

Will took a deep breath but it wasn't easy to decide what to do. Should he stay and try to limit the amount of damage that might be caused by such a revelation or should he simply turn tail and run? It was hard to decide, and before he could make up his mind, Lisa glanced round and saw him.

Will felt his heart sink when he saw the shock on her face. Rachel must have told her! It was the only possible explanation for why Lisa was looking at him that way.

He swallowed a groan of dismay. Now what was he going to do?

CHAPTER EIGHT

'YOU two look very serious. What are you up to?'

Lisa hurriedly smoothed her features into a suitable expression as Will came to join them. Discovering that Will *hadn't* spent the night at Rachel's house had come as a shock. On the one hand she was deeply relieved because the thought of him and Rachel spending the night together was so painful, but on the other hand she knew that she shouldn't feel this way at all.

Will was a free agent and she had no right to feel hurt or betrayed if he slept with another woman! And yet if she'd had to stand up in a court of law and swear that she had felt neither of those things, she couldn't have done so. It was an effort to behave as though there was nothing wrong when he shot her a searching look.

'We were talking about you as it happens.' Rachel answered the question, mercifully sparing Lisa from having to do so.

'I don't know if I like the sound of that,' he said lightly, but Lisa could hear an undercurrent in his voice and frowned.

Why did Will sound so nervous all of a sudden? Was he afraid that she might have said something to upset Rachel? Bearing in mind their earlier frosty confrontation, it seemed likely and her heart ached because it seemed to mark the deterioration of their friendship.

'I was just telling Lisa what a lovely time we had last night.' Rachel grinned at him. 'There's no need to look so worried because I wasn't trying to get her to tell me all your darkest secrets! Anyway, she's far too discreet to do that.'

'I'm sure she is.'

Once again Lisa heard the edge in his voice only this time she understood what had caused it. She'd been far from discreet that morning when she had told Dave about him seeing Rachel. She rushed to explain what she was doing there. Will was obviously dubious about her motives and the sooner she set him straight the better it would be.

'I came to apologise to Rachel for what happened this morning. As I've just explained to her, I never intended to start any rumours about you two.'

'And for the hundredth time, Lisa, it doesn't matter!' Rachel patted her arm. 'Don't go giving yourself a hard time because there is no need—is there, Will?'

'Of course not.' Will turned to her and smiled. 'I know what Dave can be like. He's the proverbial dog with a bone when he starts digging for information.'

Lisa felt her eyes prickle with tears because it was such a relief to know that Will had forgiven her. She smiled up at him, unable to hide how happy she felt. 'Thanks. I was afraid that you would never forgive me for letting slip that you and Rachel were seeing each other,' she admitted huskily.

'Don't be daft! It would take more than that to ruin our friendship.' He looped an arm around her shoulders and gave her a quick hug then just as quickly let her go again.

'Well, I'm glad that's all sorted out.' Rachel beamed at them both. 'I'd hate to think you two had fallen out because of me.'

'There's no chance of that happening,' Will said firmly, and Lisa laughed.

'Ditto. Anyway, thanks for being so understanding,

Rachel. I promise that I shall be wary when Dave comes fishing for information in the future.'

'Oh, don't worry about it,' Rachel said cheerfully. 'There's a lot worse things that can happen to you than being the subject of a bit of idle gossip. Anyway, now that we're all friends again why don't we make up a foursome one night?'

'A foursome?' Lisa repeated uncertainly.

'Yes. You and your fiancé and Will and me.' Rachel lowered her voice confidingly. 'Will told me your news, Lisa. I hope you don't mind. I'm really thrilled for you.'

'Thanks, but I'm afraid congratulations are a little premature as yet.'

Lisa managed to hold her smile but it was hard to hide her dismay at the thought of Will discussing her with the other woman. Had he been so relieved at the thought that she would soon be off his hands that he hadn't been able to stop himself sharing the good news, perhaps?

'I haven't actually agreed to marry James yet so I don't think it would be right to claim him as my fiancé,' she said firmly, trying to blot out that painful thought.

'Oh, I see. I hadn't realised that.'

Lisa saw the oddest expression cross Rachel's face. She had no idea why the other woman should look so smug all of a sudden. She was just about to ask her what was wrong when Rachel turned to Will.

'You should have explained that Lisa and her boyfriend aren't officially engaged,' Rachel chided him. 'Here was I thinking the wedding was a foregone conclusion, but obviously it's not.'

'It never occurred to me,' he said flatly.

Lisa shot him a wary look when she heard the dullness in his voice and felt her heart leap when she discovered that he was looking at her. There was something in his eyes, a sort of yearning that shocked her so much that she found it impossible to look away. It was only when Rachel spoke that she managed to break eye contact and even then she could feel tremors of awareness passing through her. Why had Will been looking at *her* with such longing when it was Rachel he loved?

'Typical man, to get the facts wrong,' Rachel observed cheerfully, seemingly oblivious to what had happened. 'However, I shall forgive you on condition that you agree to take me to the staff Christmas party on Saturday. It's going to be a very up-market affair this year—black tie for the men and as much glitz and glamour as we women can supply. It will be fun to get dressed up for a change, won't it?'

'I'm not sure if I'll be free—' Will began, but Rachel didn't let him finish.

'Oh, you can't say no! I have my heart set on going.' She suddenly turned to Lisa and gasped. 'I've just had *the* most marvellous idea! Why don't you come too and bring your boyfriend? It would be the perfect opportunity to introduce him to all your friends.'

'I'm afraid that won't be possible,' Lisa said hurriedly, glad to have the perfect excuse to avoid going to the party. Although it was kind of Rachel to invite her, she couldn't cope with the thought of seeing Will and Rachel together as a couple. 'James is in Leeds at the moment. He's in the middle of a trial and needs to stay there in case anything crops up.'

'Then you must come with us. Mustn't she, Will?' Rachel didn't give him a chance to answer as she hurried on. 'That's all settled, then. It will be fun, won't it—the three of us going together?'

'Oh, but I couldn't,' Lisa protested, her heart sinking at the thought of being forced to spend the evening with them.

It would have been bad enough if she'd had James with her but infinitely worse if she had to go on her own. 'It's really kind of you, Rachel, and I appreciate it, but you and Will don't want me there. I'll only be in the way.'

'Rubbish! We won't take no for an answer so there is no point arguing.' Rachel glanced round as the office phone rang. 'I'd better get that. I'll see you both later.'

She hurried into the office and closed the door. Lisa bit her lip when she saw the grim expression on Will's face. It was obvious that he was less than pleased about Rachel inviting her to go with them to the party so she hurried to reassure him. She certainly didn't want them falling out again after what had happened already that day.

'I'll make some excuse not to go, Will. It's kind of Rachel to invite me, but I don't want to play gooseberry.'

'It isn't a problem,' he said gruffly.

'But you don't really want me there,' she insisted. 'You'll have a lot more fun if it's just the two of you.'

She fixed a smile firmly into place but it felt as though her heart was in danger of breaking. 'After all, this is your first Christmas together and you'll want it to be really special.'

'And it's also *our* last Christmas together, Lisa, so how about making it special for that reason?' Reaching out, he caught hold of her hands and Lisa shivered when she felt his fingers gripping hers. Maybe it was silly but it felt as though he was trying to tell her something that he was unable to put into words.

'I'm sorry I was so short with you this morning when you tried to apologise,' he said, his deep voice grating in a way that sent a spasm rippling through her.

'It's all right,' she said a little breathlessly, because it seemed to be incredibly difficult to get any air into her lungs all of a sudden.

'I know you wouldn't deliberately spread rumours about me, Lisa. Gossiping about your friends isn't something you'd do.'

'No, it isn't.' It was hard to think when he was staring at her so intently. She had the strangest feeling that her answer was vitally important to him.

'And that's what we are, isn't it, Lisa—friends?'

'Of course.'

She gave a tinkly laugh, wishing that she knew where this was leading. Her heart gave a sickening jolt when it struck her that maybe he was asking for her blessing. Did Will want her to tell him that she was happy because he had found love with Rachel and that she released him from his obligation to Gareth?

It made such perfect sense that she wondered how she hadn't seen it coming. Will's innate sense of duty wouldn't let him shirk his responsibilities and it was up to her to tell him that he was free to get on with his life.

'Your friendship has meant such a lot to me, Will. I doubt I would have got over Gareth's death if you hadn't been there for me, but now it's time we both moved on, isn't it?' She smiled up at him but inside her heart was weeping because this was the most painful thing she'd ever had to do.

'Now that I've met James and you've found Rachel, the situation is bound to change. I hope that we can always remain friends, though. I'd like to think that we'll be able to meet up in years to come and reminisce about the old days.'

She reached up and kissed him lightly on the cheek and it took every scrap of courage she possessed to smile at him when she felt like crying her eyes out because of what she was losing. In that moment she knew that nobody could ever replace Will in her affections, not even James. He was just too special.

'I hope that you and Rachel will be really happy together because it's what you deserve. You are a very special man, Will Saunders. The best friend anyone could ever have.'

Will could feel a burning pain twist around his heart when he heard Lisa say that. Maybe it had been foolish to hope for something more but he was only flesh and blood. He had come so close to telling her how he really felt but now he could see what a mistake that would have been. Lisa thought of him purely as her friend and he had to be content with that because there wasn't anything else.

'It means a lot to hear you say that,' he said huskily.

He gave her hands a final squeeze then let her go because it was too big a test of his self-control to continue holding them. Glancing along the corridor, he gave himself a moment to collect himself before he turned to her again, but it was an effort to behave as though everything was fine when it was a long way from being that.

'How's Liam Donnelly doing? Dave said that he wasn't happy about him having another general anaesthetic so we've rescheduled his op for Friday.'

'So-so.' Lisa grimaced. 'I'm glad you didn't transfer him to Manchester because I don't think he would have survived the journey. We're having problems stabilising him, I'm afraid.'

'He took a real hammering,' Will said darkly, thinking about the state the boy had been in when he had seen him last night. 'Has his mother been in to visit him yet?'

'No. There's been no sign of her. There hasn't even been a phone call, in fact.'

Lisa sighed and he saw her hazel eyes fill with sadness. 'How can any mother let that happen to her child, Will? It's something I shall never understand even though this isn't the first time I've come across a situation like this. I would fight tooth and nail to protect my children.'

'I'm sure you would. I'm also sure that you wouldn't get involved with a man who would present a threat to them either,' he said bluntly.

'I hope so, too, but it isn't always easy to foretell how a person will act. Maybe Liam's stepfather seemed nice enough at first and only changed after his mother married him,' she suggested.

'It's possible, I suppose.' He frowned because that idea had touched a nerve. He couldn't help worrying about how well Lisa knew James Cameron. Granted, they had been seeing each other for a couple of months now, but was that really long enough to get to know someone properly?

'I'd better get back before they send out a search party to look for me,' Lisa declared, checking her watch.

Will tried to quieten his concerns by reminding himself that she was unlikely to fall in love with a man who would treat her badly, although maybe it wouldn't hurt to make a few discreet enquiries about Cameron. It shouldn't be *that* difficult to find people who knew him.

He swallowed a sigh because he knew in his heart that he mustn't interfere. Lisa was old enough to look after herself and he had to accept that she knew what she was doing, even though it wasn't going to be easy to stop worrying about her. His life had revolved around making sure that she was safe and happy for so long that it was going to be a hard habit to break.

'I'd better get a move on, too.' He quickly checked his own watch because there was no point getting caught up on the thought of how difficult it would be to adjust to not having her around. 'I've just given Ray a dressing-down for being late so I'd better try to set a good example.'

'It must be hard work, being above reproach all the time, Mr Saunders,' she teased.

'Believe me, it is!' He rolled his eyes when she laughed, trying not to dwell on how lovely she looked. Even though she was only wearing work clothes, she still managed to look fantastic.

It made him wonder what she would look like on the night of the Christmas party, all dressed up for the occasion. All of a sudden he realised that he wanted to go to the party with her and spend what would probably be their last evening together. It seemed only fitting that it should be special, memorable.

'You will come to the Christmas party, I hope,' he said before he could think better of it. 'It might be the last chance we have to spend an evening together. You'll be moving out of the flat soon and, after that you'll be too busy planning the wedding.'

'I haven't accepted James's proposal yet,' she reminded him, and he frowned when he heard the quaver in her voice.

'But you're going to, aren't you, Lisa?' he said quickly, hoping that his urgency didn't show. Had she decided that Cameron wasn't the right man for her after all? His foolish heart raced at the thought.

'I expect so.' She gave him a brilliant smile. 'After all, James is quite a catch, isn't he? A woman would need to be mad to turn him down.'

'She would indeed.' Somehow he managed to return her smile as his hopes were dashed again. Lisa was going to marry Cameron and he had to accept that and not keep hoping it wouldn't happen.

'In that case, you definitely must come to the party,' he said, adopting a deliberately cheerful tone which was completely at odds with the way he was feeling. 'Look on it as a last fling before you settle down to being a respectable, engaged woman!'

She laughed at that. 'Implying that I'm not respectable at the moment? Thank you very much. And I thought you were supposed to be my friend! Anyway, I'll think about it. But now I have a job to do so I'll see you later.'

She gave him a last smile then hurried away. Will waited until she had rounded the corner before he started to follow her. He stopped when Rachel poked her head out of the office door.

'Before you go, Will, I think I owe you an apology.'

'What for?' he asked uncertainly.

'For putting you on the spot like that about the Christmas party.' Rachel grimaced. 'I just thought that if we all went together then you'd have a chance to get to know Lisa's boyfriend. I know how you worry about her and thought it might help. I had no idea he would be away on the night and it felt mean to take back the invitation when Lisa told me. Sorry!'

'It doesn't matter,' he assured her. 'It was kind of you to try to help.'

'I'll understand if you don't want to go, though.' Rachel looked wistful all of a sudden. 'It's been ages since I went to the Christmas party and it would have been fun to go this year.'

'Then I'll get tickets for all three of us,' he said firmly, hating to disappoint her.

'So Lisa has decided to go after all?'

'Yes.' Will frowned when he heard the satisfaction in Rachel's voice. He shot her a wary look but she simply smiled at him. 'I managed to persuade her in the end. Anyway, I'll sort out all the arrangements and get back to you. OK?'

'Fine,' Rachel agreed, going back into her office and closing the door.

Will hesitated, wondering why he had the feeling that he was missing something. He gave himself a brisk mental shake. Rachel was far too open to be planning anything.

He quickly made his way to his office to check if there had been any messages for him. His secretary had a mountain of letters that needed his signature so he did them while he had the chance. He'd just reached the bottom of the pile when there was a knock on the door and Ray appeared, carrying an envelope with his name written on it.

'I've brought you this, Will. It's my letter of resignation. I've decided that I may as well cut my losses and move on.'

'I'm sorry to hear that, Ray. Are you sure you won't reconsider?'

'No. I should have made the decision months ago.' Ray shrugged. 'I'm just not cut out for sainthood, unlike you, Will. I need some fun in my life and I'm not going to achieve that if I carry on doing this job. I've been in touch with that friend I told you about and he's going to arrange an interview for me with his firm. Hopefully, this will be the last Christmas I ever spend working nights!'

Will sighed as Ray left. Losing Ray would put them under a lot of pressure. He could only hope that Ray would fulfil his duties until he had finished working out his notice, but if the man's past performance was anything to go by he wouldn't hold his breath. Maybe he should forget about going to the Christmas party because it could turn out that he would be needed to cover for Ray again as he had last night.

He picked up the phone to ring Rachel and explain that he had changed his mind about going to the party then paused. If he cancelled their arrangements, he wouldn't be able to spend the evening with Lisa, would he?

He gently replaced the receiver in its rest. Maybe he was

making a mistake but he needed this one, last memory to hold onto in the future.

'Are you going to the Christmas party, Lisa?'

Lisa looked up as Angela came into the office and plonked a pile of dressings on the desk. It was almost time for them to go home, but she was making a last-ditch attempt to catch up with some paperwork. There had been one crisis after another that afternoon so that she'd barely had time to draw breath.

Liam Donnelly had given them all a scare when he had stopped breathing. It had taken them ages to get him back and he was being closely monitored. Shock and blood loss had caused most of the damage and Lisa desperately wished the boy's mother would visit him because it might help if Liam knew she was there.

She'd only just gone back to the office when Ben Carlisle, their young houseman, had come to fetch her because Chloë Trent had had a seizure. It wasn't uncommon for a child to have fits after a serious head injury but it was still worrying and terrifying for her parents, who had been at her bedside when it had happened.

Lisa had got one of the nurses to take them into the relatives' room while she'd dealt with Chloë, administering anti-convulsant drugs to control the attack. The child would need to stay on the drugs until they were sure that she wouldn't suffer another episode.

Calming down the child's worried parents had been a major task and it had taken her some time to convince them Chloë wasn't about to die. She had explained that the fits would hopefully stop as Chloë improved, but she hadn't been able to promise that the child would never have another one. Mandy and Alan Trent had been naturally distraught and when she had left them, they had been blaming themselves for the accident. All in all it had been a hectic day and she sighed as she tossed her pen onto the blotter.

'Yes, I'm going if I'm not worn to a frazzle beforehand. What a day it's been!'

'I know. It's been mad even by our standards,' Angela declared cheerfully. 'Still, at least the party is something to look forward to, a bit of a break from the usual grind. Who are you going with, by the way?'

'Will,' she replied automatically.

'Oh, good. I'm glad he's going. He works far too hard and needs to take some time for himself.' Angela stacked the dressings into a cardboard box then looked at her. 'At least he has you around to make sure that he doesn't overdo things, Lisa. Knowing Will, he would work every hour that God sends unless someone was there to call a halt. That man is just too conscientious for his own good!'

'He is. I only hope that Rachel will keep tabs on him when I move out of the flat and stop him doing too much,' she observed worriedly.

'Sorry. I'm not with you.' Angela abandoned her dressings and stared at her. 'What do you mean, you're moving out of the flat. And who is Rachel?'

'Oops, me and my big mouth again!' Lisa clapped a hand to her mouth in dismay. However, there was no point not telling Angela the rest of the story when she had let so much slip.

'Will is going out with Rachel Hart from Children's Medical,' she explained. 'Although I'd appreciate it if you didn't tell anyone, Angela. They don't want the news spreading around at the moment.'

'My lips are sealed,' Angela promised, but she looked puzzled. 'So the reason you are moving out of the flat is because Will is seeing Rachel? Have I got it right?'

'Yes and no.' Lisa sighed because it was obvious that

Angela had no idea what she meant. 'I'm not moving out because of Rachel but because I decided it was time I gave Will some breathing space.'

'Do I take it that something happened to prompt this sudden decision?' Angela queried.

'The man I've been seeing asked me to marry him,' Lisa explained. 'It seemed like the right time to make the move, basically.'

'I see. Obviously, I'm way out of touch because I had no idea that you were dating anyone, let alone that it was serious.' Angela was having difficulty hiding her surprise. 'Mind you, the same goes for Will. I just assumed that you and Will were a couple.'

'No, we're just friends. That's all we've ever been.'

It was an effort to pretend everything was fine when it felt as though her heart was breaking. It was a relief when Angela excused herself and left, although Lisa couldn't help wondering how many other people had assumed that she and Will were an item.

To an outsider their relationship must appear to be far more than it really was. They lived together so people had naturally assumed they were a couple. It made her realise what a shock it was going to be for everyone if she married James and Will married Rachel.

She took a deep breath but there was no point trying to avoid the truth. She might marry James and Will might marry Rachel. She should be happy that everything was working out so well for them both. However, it was hard to feel happy when it meant that Will would be sharing his life with another woman.

CHAPTER NINE

THE days flew past so that Will found himself wishing on more than one occasion that he could find a way to make time stand still. He was very aware that every day that passed brought him one day closer to Christmas.

Normally he looked forward to Christmas and enjoyed all the hustle and bustle, the chance it gave him to catch up with his family. However, this year all he could think about was Lisa spending Christmas with Cameron. If anything was guaranteed to make him wish that Christmas would never arrive, it had to be that!

He worked harder than ever in an effort not to think about it, staying late in his office to catch up with paperwork and putting in extra hours in Theatre while he whittled away the waiting list. It was only when Dave dryly asked him if he was aiming to get himself into the record books for the most number of operations performed in the shortest length of time that Will realised he had to call a halt. He had to stop hiding behind his work and face what was happening. Lisa was going to marry Cameron. End of story.

He picked up the tickets for the staff Christmas party on the morning of the event. He'd been lucky to get them because as soon as people had heard that the party was to be a special occasion and not just the yearly run-of-the-mill event, there had been a rush to buy tickets.

Will went back to his office and phoned Rachel to tell her that he would collect her at seven that evening. He was just about to hang up when she reminded him that it was black tie for the men.

125

He sighed as he put the receiver back on its rest. He didn't even possess a bow-tie let alone a dinner suit to go with it, which meant he would have to go out and buy one. For a moment he found himself wishing that he'd never agreed to go to the party before he reminded himself of all the benefits he would gain from the evening. Spending this last night with Lisa would make it all worthwhile.

Four hours later he arrived home, laden with parcels. Fortunately, he'd been so far ahead with everything that he had been able to give himself the afternoon off and had spent it in Manchester, shopping.

Amazingly, he'd managed to find a dinner suit which fitted him in the first shop he had visited and had had equal success finding a shirt and tie plus a smart pair of black shoes. It had left him with enough time to do his Christmas shopping so he had bought presents for his family—a cashmere jumper for his mother and a new golf bag for his father, gift vouchers for his sister and her husband because they would appreciate being able to choose what they wanted for their new house.

He'd added a few other bits and pieces, like a silk scarf for his secretary, luxury chocolates for the theatre staff and some toys to go in Santa's sack when presents were handed out to the children on Christmas morning. He'd decided to buy Rachel some perfume because he appreciated her kindness and he was hoping that she would like the one he had chosen. Lisa's present had been the last thing he'd bought, although he still wasn't sure whether or not he should give it to her.

He took the parcels into his bedroom and dumped them on the bed. Digging into his pocket, he pulled out a slim leather box and opened it. As soon as he had seen the necklace in the jeweller's window he'd known it would be perfect for Lisa. The delicate, gold filigree chain was set with tiny seed pearls and diamonds and would look stunning on her. The only problem was that he wasn't sure how she would feel about him giving her such an expensive present when they normally exchanged much more modest gifts. Would she be embarrassed to receive it from him?

He sighed as he closed the box lid and slid it into a drawer. If only he could give her the present *and* tell her how he felt, but he couldn't do that. He had to keep his own counsel and if giving her an expensive gift was out of the question then he had to be sensible about it. He could always buy her something else if he changed his mind, but right now he needed to start getting ready.

He took a deep breath but he couldn't deny that he was suddenly excited about the coming evening. Obviously, he had to pay as much attention to Rachel as he did to Lisa because Rachel was supposed to be his partner tonight. However, the thought of dancing with Lisa and holding her in his arms made his insides churn with anticipation. He intended to make this night one he would always remember!

Lisa was about to leave work that night when Liam Donnelly's mother turned up. It had been extremely busy in the intensive care unit for the past few days because Ben had been off sick with flu. Lisa had filled in for him a couple of evenings, staying on until Sanjay had come on duty.

It had been a relief not to have to spend too much time at home, if she was honest, although Will had also seemed to have been extremely busy. She'd seen him only briefly in passing and had not really had time to speak to him for several days. A couple of times she'd wondered if he had been avoiding her but as she couldn't think of any reason why he would want to do so, she had dismissed the idea.

When Ben had gone off sick she had toyed with the idea of telling Will that she wouldn't be able to go to the

Christmas party, but something had held her back. Maybe it would be difficult to watch him and Rachel enjoying themselves together, but the thought of spending this last evening with him was too tempting to resist. Once she went to the cottage with James everything would change. Whilst she knew that she should be happy at the thought of her new life, she couldn't deny that she felt sad about what she was losing.

When Angela came to tell her that Liam's mother wanted to see her, Lisa found it hard to hide her annoyance. Liam had been in the unit for several days now and it was the first time the woman had been in to see him. She found it difficult to comprehend how anyone could be so callous and uncaring about her own child.

'I expect you're wondering why I haven't been to see Liam, aren't you, Doctor?' Sarah Donnelly sank onto the chair and looked pleadingly at Lisa. She was a smartly dressed woman in her early thirties. However, the lines of strain on her face were clear to see. 'You must think I don't care what's happened to him, but I do!'

'It isn't my place to pass judgement,' Lisa said coolly, sitting down behind the desk.

'Maybe not, but you're only human. You're bound to have wondered why I haven't been in touch.' Sarah Donnelly ran a trembling hand over her hair. 'John wouldn't let me come here, you see. He said that I had to choose between him and Liam and that if I came to visit him then we'd be finished. I...I waited until he'd gone out then phoned for a taxi to bring me here, but I'll have to get back soon.'

'Are you saying that Liam's stepfather forbade you to visit him?' It was hard to keep the incredulity out of her voice and she saw Sarah Donnelly's face crumple.

'He's so jealous of Liam! He says that I care more about

Liam than I do about him. I've tried everything I can think of to reassure him but it makes no difference what I say.'

'But surely your first duty has to be to your son?' Lisa pointed out. 'Liam is only seven and he needs you to look after him.'

'But what will I do if John leaves me? How will I manage then?' Sarah took a tissue from her bag and blew her nose. 'I've been on my own before, Dr Bennett. Liam's father walked out on us when Liam was a baby and I remember how hard it was to manage. John didn't mean to hurt Liam, I swear. He just got carried away.'

'To the extent that Liam might have died as a result of the beating he gave him?' Lisa shook her head. 'I'm sorry but no amount of financial security is worth putting a child through that for.'

She stood up, knowing that she was in danger of saying too much. It wasn't her place to sit in judgement, although she intended to tell the social worker in charge of the case everything that Sarah Donnelly had told her.

She sighed because it was Liam who would end up getting hurt if the social services department decided to take him into care. How could a seven-year-old be expected to understand that his mother didn't love him enough to put his welfare first?

'I'll take you through to see Liam now,' she said shortly. 'He's still very ill, but I'm sure it will help him if he knows you're here.'

'I can't stay long,' Sarah said, anxiously checking her watch. 'John will be home soon and I don't want him finding out that I've been here.'

'I can't force you to stay, Mrs Donnelly. But I strongly urge you to think long and hard about where your responsibilities really lie.'

Lisa didn't say anything else as she took the woman into

the ward and handed her over to the staff nurse on duty. She left straight after that and caught the bus home. The meeting had left a bad taste in her mouth so that it was hard to summon any enthusiasm for the coming evening. Could she really cope with watching Will and Rachel together?

She frowned as she got off the bus and walked the rest of the way home. Why was it so difficult to accept that Will and Rachel were together? She liked Rachel and knew that Rachel would try to make Will happy so what was the problem?

Lisa's hand froze in the act of unlocking the front door. She took a deep breath but all of a sudden her heart was pounding. Was it possible that she loved Will not just as a friend but as a man?

Will was attempting to fasten his bow-tie when he heard Lisa's key in the lock. He sighed as he pulled one end of the black silk and the bow promptly unfurled itself.

He should never have let that salesman talk him out of buying a ready-made bow-tie because it would have been a lot easier than this. Maybe Lisa would help him? She certainly couldn't make a worse job of it then he was doing!

He went out to the hall and frowned when he realised that she still hadn't come in. Striding to the door, he whipped it open and looked at her in surprise. 'What are you doing, standing out there?'

'I...um...the lock seems to be jammed,' she murmured.

'Really?' Will frowned because he'd had no trouble getting in when he'd arrived home. 'Here, give me your key and I'll try it. Maybe your key's a bit worn and you need to get another one cut.' He went to take it off her then stopped when she shook her head.

'No, it's fine. Don't worry. It's probably me just being stupid.'

She went to hurry past him but it was obvious that some-thing had upset her. Without stopping to think, Will put his hand on her arm and drew her to a halt.

'What's happened, Lisa? I can tell you're upset.'

'I'm fine,' she denied quickly, but he could tell it was a lie.

'You're not fine at all,' he said firmly. 'I want to know what's wrong, so tell me.'

'L-Liam Donnelly's mother came to visit him,' she said huskily, avoiding his eyes. 'She told me that his stepfather had forbidden her to see the boy because he's jealous of him. I suppose it just upset me a bit.'

'No wonder!' Will sighed as he reached out and hugged her.

'Don't!' she snapped, shrugging him off.

'Sorry.' He let his arm fall to his side and looked at her in dismay. He couldn't have counted the number of times he must have hugged her in the past and not once had she objected before.

'No, it's me who should apologise, Will. I'm sorry.' She gave him an apologetic smile but he could see the troubled light in her hazel eyes. 'I just didn't want you crushing your shirt when you're looking so smart this evening.'

'I'd look better if I managed to sort out this wretched tie,' he replied lightly, although he knew for a fact that it had been an excuse. Lisa didn't want him to hug her because it made her feel uncomfortable to have any man apart from Cameron showing her affection. It was an effort to hide how much that thought hurt.

'I don't suppose you're any good at bow-ties, are you?'

'I've never tried to tie one, but I'll give it a go if you want me to,' she offered immediately.

'Great! Come and read the instructions first. I'm not say-ing they'll help but one can only hope.'

He led the way into his bedroom and sat down on the dressing-table stool while she read through the instructions that had come with the tie. His heart filled with tenderness when he saw the tip of her tongue peeping between her lips as she struggled to make sense of them. Her soft brown hair had started to come free from its pins and he felt a little fizzing start in the pit of his stomach when he saw how the silky tendrils had curled around her face.

Did she have any idea how adorable she looked? he wondered. Could she sense how much he wanted to take her in his arms and hold her?

He sighed softly because letting her know how he felt was out of the question, especially after the way she had reacted when he had tried to hug her. However, it wasn't easy to keep a rein on his emotions when he loved her so much.

'It's as clear as mud,' she announced at last, looking up. 'Does this mean that you wrap the right side over the left first, and which is the right side exactly? If I'm facing you then my right is your left.'

'You're asking *me* a question like that?' Will groaned, hamming things up for all he was worth because he was terrified that she would guess how he was feeling. 'You're talking to the man who hasn't a single drop of sartorial elegance in his entire body! I shall leave you to decide which way it works and I promise that I won't say a word if it ends up in a mess.'

'I'll hold you to that, Will Saunders, so be warned!' She laughed and he was relieved to see that she looked far less strained all of a sudden. 'OK, then, we'll give it a go. If you're game, so am I. Now, sit up straight.'

'Yes, ma'am!'

He sat up, trying not to smile when he saw the concentration on her face as she stood in front of him. Lisa gave everything her full attention, whether it was working out the best treatment for a seriously ill child or tying a bow-tie. It was no wonder that he loved her so much.

'You'd better fasten your top button first,' she scolded. 'If I do manage to tie this, I don't want you fiddling with it afterwards and ruining all my hard work.'

'Would I do such a thing?' he replied, rolling his eyes.

He quickly fastened the neck of his shirt and grimaced as he felt the starched collar rubbing his skin. 'I hate shirts like this. They make me feel as though I'm trussed up like a Christmas turkey.'

'You have to suffer if you want to look smart,' she declared unsympathetically, sliding the length of black silk around his neck.

Will felt a spasm shoot through him as he felt her fingers brush the back of his neck. He took a deep breath but every cell in his body suddenly seemed to be on red alert. Lisa was standing so close to him now that he could smell the scent of her hair and feel the warmth of her skin. He had an overwhelming urge to put his arms around her and hold her, keep her there and never let her go, only he didn't have the right to do that. Cameron was the only man who was allowed to hold her now.

A knifing pain shot through him at the thought of the other man holding her in his arms as he longed to do. It was an effort not to show he was upset when she looked up.

'Now, from what the instructions seem to say you have to pass this end over that one then loop it through here like this…'

Once again the tip of her tongue peeped between her lips. Will, unsuccessfully, tried to swallow his groan. Why hadn't he realised how stressful this was going to be? It was the sort of test no red-blooded male could ever hope to pass.

'Are you all right?' She stopped and looked at him in concern. 'I've not pulled the tie too tight, have I?'

'No, it's fine. I've just got a bit of a tickle in my throat and I was trying not to cough,' he fudged, using the first excuse that came to mind. He cleared his throat in the hope that it would give a bit more credence to the lie and saw her frown.

'I hope you're not sickening for something. Ben has been off with flu for the past few days. Evidently, there's a lot of staff off sick with it at the moment. Do you have a temperature?'

Lisa laid her hand on his forehead and Will almost choked for real this time. It felt as though an electric current had passed through his system. He could feel his heart racing, his pulse pounding, his blood pressure soaring. And as for the rest of him… Well!

He willed himself to calm down but the throbbing in the lower part of his body refused to obey. He took a deep breath, praying for enough will-power to help him through this moment. How would Lisa feel if she realised that he was sexually aroused because she'd taken his temperature?

'You do feel rather warm.' She lowered worried hazel eyes to his. 'How do you feel, Will? Do you think you're sickening for something?'

'I'm fine,' he said hastily. 'If I feel hot it's because I've been struggling with this pesky tie and got myself into a real lather about it.'

'Well, don't worry about it. I'm sure we can sort it out between us.' She treated him to a reassuring smile then turned her attention to the task at hand.

Will let out a heartfelt sigh of relief at having escaped detection. He shifted slightly, praying that the loosely cut trousers would hide the evidence of his arousal. He *couldn't* and *wouldn't* embarrass Lisa by letting her see how much he wanted her.

'I'm going to start this again right from the beginning,' she declared, unfastening the tie. 'It can't be *that* difficult to tie this wretched thing. Now, hold still while I give it another go.'

She bent towards him again and sighed. 'I just can't seem to get close enough to see what I'm doing properly.'

'Is this better?'

Will parted his legs so that she could stand between them then immediately realised his mistake when his body instantly responded again to the intimacy of their position. He tried breathing deeply but there was no way that an extra supply of oxygen was going to have any effect when Lisa was standing so close that they might have been making love…

He shot to his feet, uncaring about what she thought as he brushed past her. He wanted her so much that it was pure torture not to be able to do anything about it.

'Will, what's wrong?' she asked uncertainly, and his heart almost came to a halt when he heard the alarm in her voice. The thought of her shock and dismay if he told her the truth was more than he could bear. Lisa thought of him as her friend so how on earth could he explain that he ached to be her lover?

'A touch of cramp, that's all,' he lied, turning away so that she couldn't see his face. He hated having to lie to her but what choice did he have? He couldn't ruin their friendship by telling her the truth.

He summoned a smile as he glanced round, feeling his insides knot with longing as he looked at her, standing there. He wanted to sweep her into his arms and make mad, passionate love to her, then make love to her all over again only slowly and tenderly this time. She was his whole world

but he loved her too much to hurt her by telling her that.
All he could do was be glad that she had found happiness
at last, even if it wasn't with him.

'Anyway, it's late and you need to get ready. I'll give it
another shot myself.'

'If you're sure…?' She shrugged when he nodded. 'OK.
But I'll try again after I'm dressed if you still haven't managed to do it.'

She picked up her bag from his bed and suddenly spotted
the parcels which he'd left there. 'Looks as though you've
done your Christmas shopping.'

'I thought I'd get it over and done with while I had the
chance.'

He went to the dressing-table and picked up his cuff-
links, watching her in the mirror as she studied the heap of
brightly wrapped gifts. A tender smile curved his mouth
because Lisa took an almost childish delight in giving and
receiving presents at Christmas.

'No peeking!' he warned. 'It won't do you any good because your present isn't there. I've hidden it.'

'Meanie!' she accused. 'Fancy making me wait until
Christmas Day to see what you've bought me.'

'I won't see you on Christmas Day, remember? You can
have your present on Christmas Eve.'

It was an effort to hold his smile as the full enormity of
what was happening hit him afresh. Lisa wouldn't be with
him on Christmas Day. She would be with Cameron after
having spent the night with him. How could he bear to think
about Cameron making love to her when he wanted to be
the one to do so?

All of a sudden Will knew that he had to tell her how he
felt and stop her leaving him. He couldn't go on if Lisa
wasn't with him. Life would have no meaning without her

there beside him. He swung round then jumped when the phone beside his bed suddenly rang.

Lisa reached for the receiver and listened for a moment. 'He's right here. Hold on.' She offered him the phone. 'It's Rachel for you. I'll go and get ready while you talk to her.'

Will took the receiver but it was several moments before he managed to lift it to his ear. Even then his hand was trembling so much that it was difficult to hold it steady, harder still to respond to what Rachel was telling him.

He hung up, wondering what to do. Rachel had phoned to tell him that she couldn't go to the party because her niece was ill and she wanted to stay with her. It meant that he and Lisa would have to go on their own, but might it not be better in the circumstances to cancel their plans?

He had come so close to telling Lisa the truth about how he felt just now and he knew what an awful mistake that would have been. It would have ruined their friendship because Lisa would have been too embarrassed by such a revelation to let it continue.

If they went to the party, could he trust himself not to make the same mistake again? Could he be certain that he would be able to keep control of his emotions? And yet if they didn't go, how could he cope in the coming years when he desperately needed this one last, wonderful memory to see him through all the lonely times ahead?

CHAPTER TEN

LISA stood in front of the mirror and studied herself critically. She'd spent ages looking for a dress for the party on her last day off and she still wasn't sure if the one she had chosen was right for the occasion. It was certainly far more sophisticated than anything she'd ever worn before.

Her eyes skimmed assessingly over the rich, burgundy-red velvet. The dress was simply cut with long sleeves and a high neckline. The narrow-fitting skirt ended just below her calves so that from the front the dress looked extremely demure. It was only when she turned and glimpsed the back in the mirror that she realised how daring it really was.

The entire back of the dress consisted of a network of interlaced satin straps which extended from her nape to her waist. She could see the pearly sheen of her bare skin through the straps and frowned. Was it *too* sophisticated perhaps and not really her? What would Will think? Would he like it?

She turned to face the mirror again and picked up her hairbrush, trying to calm the rush of adrenaline that had surged through her. The whole time she'd been getting ready she had refused to think about what had happened earlier, but it was impossible to blot it out now.

Was she in love with Will? Or did she simply love him as a friend?

She had no idea what the answer was and it scared her to think that she couldn't make up her mind about something so important. If she was in love with Will then how could she marry James? Yet how could she *not* marry James when it might mean that Will would continue to feel responsible for her?

She sighed because whatever decision she reached would affect somebody. She hated to think that she might hurt James if she decided not to marry him, and she certainly wouldn't be able to live with herself if Will ended up getting hurt. She had to decide what would be the right thing to do for everyone concerned.

She finished brushing her hair and picked up the tiny velvet evening bag lying on the end of her bed. It was barely big enough to hold her comb and a lipstick, but it was such a perfect match for the dress that she hadn't been able to resist it. She'd even bought new shoes for the occasion—strappy evening sandals with wickedly high heels which she probably wouldn't wear again. However, she'd wanted to look her best tonight, even though Will would be far more interested in what Rachel was wearing.

It was a rather deflating thought but she tried not to think about it as she went to find him. He was looking out of the sitting-room window and didn't appear to have noticed her coming into the room. Lisa paused in the doorway, thinking how handsome he looked in the formal evening clothes. The tailored, black jacket emphasised the width of his shoulders while the starched, white evening shirt was the perfect foil for his dark hair. He'd even managed to fasten his bow-tie, although she couldn't help smiling when she noticed that it was just a little bit crooked at one side.

A wave of tenderness washed over her because if Will had looked too perfect, it wouldn't have felt right. Will wasn't the kind of man who spent time worrying about his appearance. He was always far too concerned about other people to think about himself. Rachel was so very lucky that he had fallen in love with her.

He must have sensed she was standing there because he

suddenly turned. Lisa drove that painful thought from her head when she saw his eyes widen. She gave him a tentative smile but she couldn't deny that her nerves were humming with tension as she waited to hear his verdict. Would Will think that she looked beautiful that night, perhaps?

'You look wonderful, Lisa. That dress is just perfect.' He crossed the room and she felt her pulse race when she saw the admiration on his face.

'You think it's all right, then?' she asked, loving the way his eyes crinkled at the corners when he smiled at her.

'Rather more than "all right"! You look fantastic.'

'You don't look too bad yourself,' she replied, struggling to keep control of her pulse before it beat itself to death. Maybe it was silly to set so much store by Will's opinion, but she couldn't seem to help it.

'Thank you kindly. But what about the tie? Is it OK?' He started to twitch one end of the bow-tie but Lisa quickly swatted his hand away.

'Leave it alone! It looks fine and you'll only end up making a mess of it if you start fiddling with it again.'

'So long as you're sure I don't look a complete idiot,' he began, but she shook her head.

'You look wonderful, Will. Honestly. You scrub up a lot better than I thought you would!'

'That's a backhander if ever I heard one,' he declared, laughing at her.

'If you will go fishing for compliments, you should expect to get knocked back,' she retorted, although she couldn't deny that her heart was racing like crazy. Maybe it was her imagination but there seemed to be a definite tension in the air all of a sudden. Will seemed as aware of her as she was of him and it was hard not to let it affect her.

She took a steadying breath as she turned towards the

door, deeming it safer not to dwell on the reason why it was happening. 'Anyway, enough of these compliments. We'd better get a move on or Rachel will be wondering where we've got to.'

'Rachel isn't coming, I'm afraid.'

Lisa swung round. 'She's not coming? But why on earth not?' Her heart suddenly sank as a thought occurred to her and she looked at him in dismay. 'It hasn't anything to do with me, has it?'

'No, of course not!' he denied immediately. However, Lisa wasn't convinced.

'Are you sure? Look, Will, I would far rather you told me the truth. If Rachel has had second thoughts about me going with you then just say so. I don't want to spoil the evening for you both.'

'It has nothing whatsoever to do with you,' he said firmly. 'Rachel isn't going because her niece is ill. Rachel is the girl's guardian and, naturally, she wants to stay at home and look after her.'

'Oh, I see. What a shame that she's going to miss the party, although I expect I'd feel the same in her place.'

Lisa felt a wave of disappointment wash over her because there was no way that she could expect Will to take her to the party now. He'd only offered to do so because Rachel had asked her to go. 'It seems we've got all dressed up for nothing, doesn't it?'

'We're still going, Lisa.' He frowned when she looked at him in surprise. 'That's if you still want to go?'

'I do, but are you sure that you want to go now that Rachel won't be there?' she said slowly. 'It won't be the same without her.'

'Of course not, but it would be a shame for all of us to miss the party.' He smiled but Lisa had seen the sadness in his eyes and bit back a sigh. It was obvious that Will was disappointed that Rachel wasn't able to go with him but, typically, he didn't want to spoil the evening for her.

'After all, this night was supposed to be special for a number of reasons, Lisa. It's probably the last chance we'll have to spend much time together so let's go and enjoy ourselves.'

'Why not? It sounds like a good idea to me.' Lisa summoned a smile because she didn't want him to know how much it had hurt to be reminded that they would be going their separate ways soon.

'Then what are we waiting for?' He stepped aside and bowed low. 'Cinderella *shall* go to the ball!'

Lisa laughed but her heart was heavy as they left the flat and drove to the hospital. There were just two days left before she was due to go to the cottage. Maybe she should be looking forward to it and making plans for the future, but all she seemed able to think about was how much she was going to miss Will. Leaving him for any reason wasn't going to be easy.

The party was being held in the hospital's gymnasium and the staff social committee had worked miracles, transforming it for the occasion. All the equipment that was normally used in there by the physiotherapy team had been cleared away and the whole room had been decorated with boughs of greenery from which were hung red and gold streamers.

Tables had been brought down from the canteen and draped with sheets, and there were red and green candles in wine bottles on every one. Lisa was amazed by the transformation and said so as Will handed over their tickets at the door and escorted her inside.

'It's fantastic! I never imagined the place could look this good.'

'It's certainly different to how it looked yesterday when

I came to see how young Andrew Brown was getting on with his physio.' He sniffed appreciatively. 'It even smells different. There's none of that liniment aroma which is usually the first thing you notice when you come in here.'

'That's because of all the greenery,' she said, glancing up as they passed under an archway of spruce placed just inside the main doors.

Will looked up and grinned when he saw a large bunch of mistletoe strategically placed above the entrance. 'Somebody has obviously caught the Christmas spirit.'

Lisa laughed. She was about to move on when he caught hold of her hands and turned her to face him. 'Happy Christmas, Lisa,' he said softly.

Lisa felt her breath catch as his mouth found hers. The kiss lasted no longer than a couple of seconds but she was trembling when he let her go. She pressed her hand to her mouth as Will moved on to let the next people in the queue take their turn under the mistletoe but she was deeply shaken by what had happened.

She felt her heart start to race as she stared after him. If Will loved Rachel then why had he kissed *her* with such passion?

He should never have done that!

Will could feel himself breaking out into a cold sweat as he crossed the room. Lisa was still standing by the door and he longed to look back at her yet dreaded what he would see. Had she realised that kiss had been far more than the token she would have expected from him?

He ground his teeth in frustration because there was nothing he could do about it now. He should have kept a tighter rein on himself but the moment he'd felt her soft mouth under his it had been impossible to control his emotions. It was a relief when Dave Carson came hurrying over because it meant that he didn't have to deal with what he had done right then. However, there was no way that he could forget about it when it might have all sorts of repercussions.

'We've got ourselves a table in the corner,' Dave informed him, pointing across the room.

Will summoned a smile when he saw Madge waving to him. 'At least we'll have somewhere to sit down. The place is really packed tonight.'

'Every ticket has been sold, apparently. That's why Jilly and I decided to get here early and grab some seats. Right, I was just on my way to the bar so what are you having?' Dave frowned as he looked towards the crowd of people who were filing into the room. 'Where's Rachel got to? I can't see her anywhere.'

'She couldn't come,' Will explained tersely because Lisa had joined them.

His heart sank as he watched her greeting Dave then make her way across the room to where the rest of their party was sitting. It was obvious that she had deliberately avoided looking at him and he could only draw his own conclusion from it. It was an effort to respond when Dave asked him why Rachel hadn't come.

'Her niece is ill and she wanted to stay at home with her,' he explained, struggling to control his panic. Had Lisa worked out why he had kissed her like that? Had she realised that he was in love with her? The thought made him feel light-headed with fear because he had no idea how she might react to the revelation.

'That's a shame,' Dave said sympathetically. 'Still, at least you've got the whole of Christmas to make up for her not being here tonight. Lucky you to have managed to get both Christmas Day *and* Boxing Day off!'

'There has to be some perks for being the head of the department,' Will observed dryly, doing his best to behave as though nothing was wrong. 'There's certainly a lot of disadvantages that go with the job.'

'Like having to keep an eye on our newest recruits, for instance,' Dave said acerbically.

Will frowned. 'Do you mean Ray? What's he done now?'

'It's what he hasn't done which is more to the point. He never turned up again this afternoon. We were all ready in Theatre, waiting for him, and he just didn't show up.' Dave sounded grim. 'I could throttle him, to be honest. There's nothing worse than having to tell a kid's parents their child's operation isn't going ahead after they've psyched themselves up for it. It's really stressful for them.'

'It is and I can understand why you're annoyed,' Will agreed, sighing. 'I'll have a word with Ray, although I'm afraid it will be a waste of time. He's handed in his resignation,' he explained when Dave looked at him quizzically. 'He's after a job with a pharmaceutical company so I don't imagine he's overly concerned about blotting his copybook here.'

'Good riddance is all I can say. We can do without staff like him, although it does mean that you're going to be pushed until we can find a replacement.' Dave clapped him on the shoulder. 'Right, enough of all that. We're here to enjoy ourselves not talk shop all night. What are you drinking?'

Will gave his order then went to join the others. Madge greeted him warmly, patting the chair next to her in an invitation to sit down.

'Thanks.'

Will smiled around the table but he was very aware that Lisa was still ignoring him. Had she worked it out yet and realised what had been behind that kiss? he wondered. The thought that he might have ruined their friendship made him feel quite ill so that it was an effort to respond to Madge's questions about Rachel's whereabouts.

'She wanted to stay at home with her niece. Apparently the girl isn't feeling well and Rachel didn't like to leave her on her own,' he explained once again.

'It's a shame she couldn't come,' Madge said sympathetically. 'Rachel is such a love. There's not many women who would put their lives on hold to bring up their sister's child, like she's done. Still, it looks as though things might change for the better for her in the not too distant future.'

Madge winked at him then turned to speak to Dave's wife, Jilly. Will sighed because he couldn't help feeling guilty about letting everyone think that he and Rachel were an item.

His gaze moved to Lisa and he felt a sharp pain pierce his heart. If only he could tell Lisa the truth, it wouldn't matter what anyone else thought!

Lisa knew that Will was watching her. She could feel his eyes on her in a way that shouldn't have been possible. Nobody could actually *feel* a look yet she could feel him watching her.

She knew to the split second when he looked away as Dave arrived with their drinks, and breathed a sigh of relief. She had to put what had happened into context and not start making too much of it.

So Will had kissed her under the mistletoe. Big deal! It was what thousands of people did each Christmas and it didn't mean anything. And yet it felt like a big deal to her. Even now she could feel the tingling imprint his lips had left on hers and had to bite back a moan of dismay because, try as she may, she couldn't simply dismiss that kiss.

'Lisa?'

She jumped when Will leant across the table and set a

glass in front of her. 'Thanks.' She lifted the glass to her mouth, hoping the alcohol would steady her nerves. She had to calm down and not let him see how confused she felt but it wasn't easy to pretend that nothing had happened.

'I hope it's OK,' Will said, picking up his own glass of lemonade and looking at her over the rim. 'I wasn't sure what you wanted but I know you prefer white wine to red so I told Dave to get you that.'

'It's fine,' she assured him.

She took another sip of the wine then put the glass on the table because her hand was shaking so hard that she was in danger of spilling it. That comment had touched a nerve because it had brought it home to her just how well Will knew her.

He didn't need to consult her to know that she preferred white wine to red. It was the same for her because she knew his tastes just as well. They could have appeared on one of those television game shows as the perfect couple and answered questions about each other, but their relationship had always been that of friends, not lovers. But if that was true then why had he kissed her that way? It didn't make sense.

It was an effort to concentrate as the conversation flowed around the table when that thought kept playing in the background all the time. Lisa did her best to join in but it was a relief when the music started. Dave whisked Jilly to her feet, ignoring her protests that she didn't think her feet could stand him trampling all over them.

'It's all part and parcel of being married, my love.' He leered at her. 'You have to put up with a bit of pain occasionally to stop you overdosing on the pleasure of being my wife!'

Everyone laughed when Jilly groaned as Dave swept her onto the dance floor. Madge had got up to dance with her husband, Harold, and Angela was trying to persuade her fiancé to get up as well. Lisa knew that Will would ask her to dance any minute and quickly stood up.

'I'm just popping to the loo,' she explained to nobody in particular, and beat a hasty retreat.

She made her way through the gyrating couples and took refuge in the ladies' lavatories. There was nobody else there so she went to the mirror and renewed her lipstick, even though it didn't need freshening up. She was simply putting off the moment when she would have to go back to the party and dance with Will. How would it feel to have him holding her in his arms?

A shudder ran through her because she could imagine only too easily how it would be. His skin would be warm to the touch and the heat from it would warm her, too. His hand would be pressed against the small of her back as he guided her round the floor, his fingers lightly brushing her bare skin through the interlaced straps.

Lisa's breathing quickened as the scene unfolded in her mind's eye. He would smell of soap and shampoo—nothing fancy or expensive—just that wonderfully clean scent that was purely Will's own. Halfway round the dance floor he would look down at her and smile, and his eyes would fill with tenderness because he cared about her so much.

Will was her friend, her rock, her port in a storm, and everything he had ever done had been aimed at making her happy. He had given her so much over the years and he had done it willingly and with love, and it was *that* which made it so easy to get confused. Will loved her as his best friend, as Gareth's fiancé, but he didn't love her as a man loved a woman. He couldn't.

Lisa stared at herself in the mirror as the pictures inside her head slowly faded. Will could never love her the way he loved Rachel. It made her see how foolish it would be to imagine that kiss had meant anything.

*   *   *

Where *was* Lisa?

Will checked his watch once more. It had been a good twenty minutes since Lisa had disappeared. Dave and Jilly were still dancing but Madge and her husband had abandoned their attempts, claiming that they couldn't keep up with the beat.

Angela and her fiancé, Graham, were deep in conversation with a couple at the next table which left him feeling rather conspicuous, sitting there on his own. However, that wasn't the reason why he was so edgy. He couldn't shake off the feeling that Lisa's lengthy absence had something to do with that kiss he'd given her. For the umpteenth time Will wished that he had never given in to the urge.

She suddenly appeared and his heart jolted nervously as he watched her crossing the room. The music suddenly came to an end and the DJ announced that the next dance would be a Scottish reel. Madge gave a whoop of delight as she grabbed his hand and pulled him to his feet.

'This is my kind of music! Come along, now. Let's form a circle.'

Before Will knew what was happening he found himself on the dance floor. Dave and Jilly joined them then Angela and her fiancé gave in to Madge's imperious summons to get up. People were forming circles all round the room, laughing as they tried to persuade others to join them.

Will saw Lisa shake her head when Morgan Grey tried to get her to join his group. Morgan was with his wife, Katrina, and several of the staff from the surgical team, but Lisa resisted their pleas to make up their numbers. She carried on past, heading for their table, and she might have made it if Madge hadn't spotted her.

'Over here, Lisa! Hurry up, the music's going to start at any moment.'

Will saw an expression of indecision cross Lisa's face. He realised that he was actually holding his breath as he waited for her to make up her mind. The thought that he might have ruined her evening by his lack of self-control was hard to swallow. He'd wanted tonight to be special for both of them, a time they could both look back on with pleasure, not regret.

Holding out his hand, he looked Lisa straight in the eyes, knowing that he had never done anything as difficult before in his entire life. Making himself look at her purely as a friend wasn't easy when he loved her so much, but it was the only way he could think of to make things right between them again.

'Come on now. No excuses,' he exhorted. 'If I have to suffer then you can, too!'

'Thanks a lot!' She gave a soft little laugh but Will could hear the strain it held. His heart ached because the last thing he'd wanted had been to upset her.

'That's what friends are for, isn't it?' It was an effort to keep the ache out of his voice when his heart seemed to be breaking, but it was Lisa who mattered most, her feelings that were his main concern. 'To share things with?'

'Is that a fact? Then remind me to be more choosy about who I pick for a friend in future, Will Saunders,' she retorted. She rolled her eyes when he fixed a pleading expression to his face. 'Oh, all right, then. But I'm doing this purely out of friendship, you understand?'

'Oh, I do. And I appreciate it.'

Somehow Will managed to smile as she dropped her bag on the table and came to join them. Hearing her state that friendship was all she felt for him had made his heart ache, but there was no way that he would ruin things again by letting her see how he felt.

He gave her hand a quick squeeze as she took her place beside him in the circle. 'Friends it is!'

The music started before she could reply and Will was glad. There was only so much he could take but he would learn to deal with the situation in time. So long as Lisa was happy then he could be happy, too, although it wasn't going to happen overnight. He would just have to content himself with the thought that things usually worked out in the end, even though there didn't seem to be even a glimmer of light at the end of this particularly long and dark tunnel. Maybe in a hundred years' time he would start to feel better.

He led her forward at Madge's prompting, taking her hands and whirling her round. The others were clapping in time to the music, laughing and shouting encouragement as they watched him twirling Lisa around until they were both breathless and it was someone else's turn.

They moved to the side while Dave spun Jilly round with much enthusiasm and very little grace. Will laughed and clapped and did everything possible to make it appear as though he was having a wonderful time, but he knew it was all an act.

He glanced at Lisa, standing beside him, and knew that he would remember how she looked at that moment for the rest of his life. She looked so young and lovely, so happy compared to how she had looked once upon a time.

He had achieved what he had set out to do and he had to draw comfort from that so that he could cope when she left him. Maybe she wouldn't move out of the flat for a while, but Christmas Eve would mark the end of their relationship. Once she slept with Cameron it would be the start of a commitment which he hoped and prayed would last all her life. She wouldn't need him any more after that.

Tears misted his eyes and the whirling dancers became a blur. He was going to miss her so much.

CHAPTER ELEVEN

IT HAD been a wonderful evening.

As everyone gathered on the dance floor to sing 'Auld Lang Syne' as the party drew to a close, Lisa knew that she was glad she had come. It had been fun spending time with people she liked, but the best thing of all had been spending this time with Will. He had gone out of his way to make the night special for her, dancing every dance with her until she'd had to beg him to let her sit down. She would remember this night all her life and look back on it with pleasure.

'I am absolutely *shattered*. How about you?'

She glanced round as Will came to join her. 'Completely exhausted, if you want the truth. My poor feet are *throbbing* from dancing in these high heels.'

'It could have been worse,' he told her with a grin. 'Dave might have asked you to dance and pity help your poor feet then!'

Lisa laughed sympathetically as she watched Jilly limping onto the dance floor. 'It doesn't bear thinking about! Poor Jilly's feet must be black and blue. It must be love if she's prepared to put up with Dave trampling all over them is all I can say.'

'Must be,' he agreed.

Lisa shot him a frowning look when she heard the dullness in his voice. He'd turned to speak to Angela and had no idea that she was watching him. Lisa felt her heart ache when she saw how sad he looked as Angela moved away

Will had put up a good show of enjoying himself tonight but he must have missed not having Rachel there with him.

She summoned a smile when he turned, hoping that he couldn't tell how much it hurt to know that she could never match Rachel in his affections. Rachel was the woman he loved while she was just his friend so Will was bound to feel differently about her. However, it wasn't easy to accept that she was second best.

'I've offered Angela and her fiancé a lift home—I hope you don't mind, Lisa. They've tried phoning for a taxi but they're all booked up.'

'Of course I don't mind,' she assured him. 'Angela lives in those new houses by the park, doesn't she? I remember her mentioning something about them moving in a couple of months ago.'

'That's right. We have to go that way so it's no problem to drop them off. It's a nice spot to live. You've got the park on your doorstep and the river is only a short walk away. Perfect for kids.'

Lisa nodded because she didn't trust herself to speak. Was Will thinking about starting a family, perhaps? If he and Rachel got married it would be the next, logical step, and yet the thought of him and Rachel having children together almost broke her heart. It was a relief when the DJ put 'Auld Lang Syne' on the deck.

Lisa linked arms with Will on her left and Harold on her right as everyone began to sing. She felt her eyes prickle with tears as she realised how apt the words were. Next Christmas she and Will would be merely old friends. They would be leading separate lives by then and she doubted if they would see very much of each other outside working hours.

The circle started to move and she felt Will grip her hand as everyone surged forward. A lump came to her throat because even now he was looking after her. Will was such a special person that it was no wonder she couldn't imagine living without him.

A great cheer erupted when the music came to an end. People were laughing and kissing each other. Harold gave her a noisy kiss on the cheek then Dave swept her into an exuberant bear hug and swung her round. Lisa was laughing when Dave set her back on the ground but she felt the laughter die in her throat when she found herself facing Will.

'Happy Christmas, Lisa—again.'

His lips were cool when they touched her cheek. Lisa felt her heart ache because it simply proved how right she'd been to decide that all Will felt for her was friendship. He couldn't possibly have behaved so indifferently towards her if he'd felt more than that.

'Happy Christmas,' she parroted, turning away before he could see the despair on her face.

It was a relief when the party broke up a few minutes later and everyone began to leave. Lisa walked on ahead with Angela, doing her best to pretend that everything was fine. Will was talking to Graham and just the sound of his voice in the background seemed to exacerbate her sadness. Two more days and that would be it. Once she went to the cottage with James then everything would change. Maybe she and Will could remain friends but it wouldn't be the same. He would no longer be at the centre of her life, neither would she be at the centre of his.

The thought plagued her all the way home. Fortunately the others made up for her silence as they discussed what had gone on at the party. They dropped off Angela and Graham outside their house then carried on home. Will drew up outside the flats and Lisa steeled herself not to show how upset she felt when he turned to her.

'I'll leave you here, if you don't mind, Lisa. You have got your key?'

'No, I never thought to bring it.' She frowned as he hunted through his pockets and handed her his keyring. 'But where are you going at this time of the night?'

'I thought I'd call round to see Rachel. I know it's late but I'm sure she'd enjoy hearing all about the party.'

'Oh, I see. Of course. Sorry, I didn't mean to be nosy.'

She quickly got out of the car, praying that he couldn't tell how devastated she felt. Will was bound to want to see Rachel. He must be longing to spend some time with the woman he loved yet the thought was like salt being rubbed into a raw wound.

'I won't be back tonight so make sure you lock the door,' he warned.

'Of course. Don't worry about me.' Somehow she managed to smile as she turned to close the car door.

Will leant across the passenger seat and Lisa felt her heart ache when she saw the concern in his eyes. When Will looked at her like that she could almost pretend that everything was back to normal, but it never would be now. She was no longer the most important person in Will's life. It was Rachel who could claim that honour. Even though she knew it was unfair, she couldn't help feeling hurt.

'I can't help worrying about you, Lisa,' he said softly, his eyes searching her face. 'It's not easy to break old habits.'

'I'll be fine, Will. Really.'

She smiled again, wondering how it was possible to say one thing and feel something entirely different. She wasn't fine at all. The thought of Will spending the night at Rachel's house, sleeping with Rachel in her bed, made her feel so sick that she could have wept.

It was only pride that stopped her making a fool of herself, pride and the fact that she would never forgive herself if she spoiled things for him. Will deserved every bit of happiness he could find and if Rachel was the one person who could make him happy then she wouldn't do anything to ruin things for him.

'Give Rachel my love and tell her that she missed a great evening. I'll see you whenever.'

She closed the car door and hurried inside. She ran upstairs to the flat and went straight to the sitting-room window and watched as Will drove away.

Tears welled from her eyes and this time she didn't try to stop them because there was nobody to see if she cried and nobody to care. She was on her own now and Will wasn't there.

Will drove straight back to the hospital and went to his office. He let himself in and switched on the lamp on the desk. Telling Lisa that he was going to Rachel's had been a lie and although he didn't feel good about it, he'd had no choice. He simply hadn't been able to stand the thought of going back to the flat and pretending that everything was wonderful when it was a long way from being that.

Lisa had been hurt by the way he had kissed her so coolly after they'd sung 'Auld Lang Syne', but what else could he have done? If he had kissed her the way he had longed to do she would have been shocked. It had been safer to feign indifference rather than show any real emotion.

He cursed roundly, giving vent to his frustration in a rare outburst which would have surprised the people who knew him. He'd never had any problem controlling his temper in the past but he was having difficulty doing so now. He wanted to shout and smash things in the hope that it would ease this agony he felt. He loved Lisa and it wasn't fair that he could never tell her that!

He sighed as he went to the window and opened the blind. When had anyone said that life should be fair? He could rail against fate all he liked but it wouldn't change things. Lisa was going to marry another man and at some point he would have to accept that. Yet as he stood there, looking out over the sleeping town, it felt as though he was staring into a black pit of despair.

He had no idea how he was going to get through the next two days, let alone the weeks until Lisa moved out of the flat. How could he bear to see her each day and know that it was Cameron's arms which had been around her on Christmas Eve, Cameron who had helped her rediscover the joys of being a woman?

He was only flesh and blood and the thought of another man making love to her, when he ached to be the one, was too much to bear. After Christmas he would have to find somewhere else to stay until she moved out of the flat. There were a number of small hotels in Dalverston and it shouldn't be difficult to find temporary accommodation. So long as Lisa never found out how he really felt about her, he could put up with any inconvenience.

Will closed the blind then went and lay down on the sofa. He would spend the next two nights in his office and keep out of the way until Lisa had left for the cottage. After that, he would make other arrangements and try to get his life back together, but filling the gap she left wouldn't be easy. No woman could ever replace Lisa in his affections.

The next two days were a nightmare. Lisa did her best but it wasn't easy to deal with the situation. Will had been staying at Rachel's since the party and he'd only been home to collect some clothes.

She'd been out shopping at the time and he had left her a note, telling her what he'd done. She had seen him only briefly in work when he'd visited the ward. He had been polite and friendly on each occasion but distant, and she hated having him cut her out of his life this way.

She busied herself with her work in the hope that it would take her mind off what was happening, but it wasn't easy to handle the shift in their relationship. It didn't help that she was growing increasingly nervous about spending Christmas with James.

He had phoned to give her directions to the cottage and apologised for not being able to drive her there himself. The trial was dragging on and the judge had decreed that they would need to work on Christmas Eve. It would be too late by the time James left Leeds to collect her and drive them both to the cottage, so he had decided to go straight there.

Lisa assured him that she would find her own way there by train, but she couldn't deny how worried she felt after she hung up. She still wasn't sure that marrying James was the right thing to do. She liked him and they got on well together, but was that really enough?

She tried to recall how she had felt about Gareth but, surprisingly, she could barely remember the heady excitement of falling in love for the first time. What she had felt for Gareth now seemed rather shallow and insubstantial.

He had been great fun and she had enjoyed being with him. He had been kind and caring as well, and had helped her get over her mother's death. It had been a very difficult period in her life and having Gareth there had helped her through it. But had she *really* loved him or had she simply needed the comfort of believing that she was in love?

The idea plagued her so it was a relief to go into work and not have to think about her own problems. Daniel Kennedy was making excellent progress and, although he was still confined to a side room, his infection was under control. Lisa was quietly confident that he would pull through.

Chloë Trent hadn't had any more fits and they were able to raise her level of consciousness. They had deliberately kept her sedated and it was a very tense time as they reduced the amount of drugs she was receiving. When she opened her eyes and asked for her mummy, everyone breathed a sigh of relief, and Mandy and Alan Trent were ecstatic.

The child who was still giving them the most cause for concern was Liam Donnelly. They had continued having problems stabilising him and Lisa knew that they urgently needed to do something about it. Physically, he should have been recovering by this stage but he lapsed in and out of consciousness. It was as though the boy had lost the will to live.

She had a word with Sanjay and they decided that they needed to persuade the boy's mother to visit him again. Sarah hadn't been back to the unit and the social worker in charge of the case had been unable to contact her.

Lisa decided to phone the woman herself and try to make Sarah see how important it was that she visit Liam. She put through a call but all she got was an answering-machine and she was forced to leave a message, asking Sarah to get in touch. The thought that poor little Liam might not pull through lay heavily on her heart but there was little else she could do.

The morning of Christmas Eve arrived at last and Lisa awoke to find that it was snowing. She'd managed to get the afternoon off and was planning on going straight to the station as soon as she left work.

She showered then packed an overnight bag, trying to remember everything she would need. James had told her he was expecting some friends for drinks on Boxing Day so she hunted through her wardrobe for something suitable to wear.

Her hand hovered over the burgundy velvet dress she had worn to the staff party before it moved on. She took a black crêpe dress off the rail instead and packed it in the case, feeling a lump come to her throat. She couldn't bear to wear the red dress ever again because it would remind her of Will.

She locked the case and left it in the hall so she wouldn't forget it when she set off for work. She put on a warm, apricot lambswool sweater and grey flannel trousers then added boots and her winter coat and set off. The path leading to the street had been swept by the caretaker but once she got out on the pavement she had difficulty keeping her footing. The snow was quite thick in places and several of the roads were blocked.

When the bus finally arrived it was packed with commuters. People had obviously decided to give themselves extra time to get to work because of the snowy conditions and every seat was taken. Lisa had to strap-hang all the way to the hospital, with the overnight bag banging against her shins every time anyone wanted to get on or off.

She was glad when it was her turn to alight, although she couldn't help sighing as she walked up the drive and thought about the journey planned for that afternoon. Heaven only knew how long it would take her to get to the cottage if the weather was as bad as this in Derbyshire. She had to change trains and James had warned her the service could be a little erratic at times.

'What a day!' Angela had followed her inside and Lisa saw her shiver appreciatively as they stepped into the warmth of the hospital's foyer.

'Oh, does that feel good! Our central heating isn't working and it's absolutely freezing at home. I've left Graham frantically phoning around all the plumbers in the town to find one who will come out and fix it.'

'Typical that it should happen today of all days, isn't it?' Lisa said sympathetically. She pressed the button for the lift then put her case on the floor because her arm was aching from carrying it.

'Where are you off to, then?' Angela asked, glancing at the case.

'Derbyshire. I'm spending Christmas with a friend,' she explained.

'Not friend as in *boyfriend*, by any chance?' Angela asked her, grinning.

'I suppose you could put it that way,' she agreed uncomfortably. She knew it was silly but she couldn't help feeling embarrassed at the thought of everyone knowing that she would be spending Christmas with James, and all that it implied.

'Then I hope you have a wonderful time, Lisa. You deserve it because you work so hard.'

Angela grimaced. 'Mind you I could say that about most of the staff here. Everyone seems to put in one hundred and ten per cent effort. I hope your boyfriend realises what he's letting himself in for when you get married. If he's hoping to have a wife who will be waiting at home with his pipe and slippers then he's in for a shock!'

Lisa laughed but the comment had touched a nerve. It wasn't the first time that she'd wondered how James would react to her working such long hours. It was all part of the job and she accepted that, but would James be happy about it or would he expect her to give up her job and spend more time with him?

The idea worried her because it made her see that she hadn't given enough thought to the problems they might encounter if she agreed to marry him. It would be unfair to

James to spend so much time at work but it would be equally unfair to expect her to give up a job she loved. Maybe she needed to talk through all the problems with him before she made a final commitment, but going to the cottage *was* a final commitment. How could she refuse to marry him if she spent Christmas with him?

By the time they reached the intensive care unit Lisa's head was throbbing from trying to decide what to do. She took her case into the staffroom then went into the unit. Angela was busy taking the night staff's report so Lisa went to check on the children, stopping off at Daniel Kennedy's room first.

She slid a gown over her clothes and went in, smiling when she discovered that Daniel was awake. The boy should have been moved to a ward by now but they'd had to keep him in the intensive care unit to avoid the risk of spreading the infection. Lisa knew that he was growing increasingly bored with spending so much time on his own and made a point of popping in to see him whenever she could.

'And how are you this morning, young man?' she asked, going over to his bed.

'OK, I suppose.' He sighed as she checked his notes. 'When can I go to the ward with the other children, Dr Bennett?'

'I'm not sure yet. It all depends on how quickly we clear up these nasty bugs.' She smiled sympathetically. 'Are you feeling fed up because you're stuck in here all on your own?'

'Uh-huh. I've nobody to talk to when Mum and Dad have to go home to look after my little sister.' He suddenly brightened. 'Mr Saunders came to see me last night and he read me a story. That was fun. Will he come back again tonight, do you think?'

'I'm not sure,' Lisa said, trying to hide her surprise. What on earth had Will been doing here during the night? Unless Daniel had become confused about the time, of course.

'What time did Mr Saunders come to see you, Daniel?' she asked casually, not wanting the child to think there was anything unusual about Will's visit.

'I don't know.' Daniel screwed up his face as he considered the question. 'I heard the big clock on the church chiming three times after he left, though.'

'Did you indeed! It must have been very late, then.'

She smiled as she replaced the boy's notes in the holder but it was hard to hide her surprise. Daniel couldn't have been confused about the time because she'd been in the unit all the previous afternoon and there had been no sign of Will then.

What had he been up to, coming into work and reading the boy a story at three o'clock in the morning?

It was a puzzle and one which she found herself thinking about frequently for the rest of the morning. She was due to leave work at two so she decided not to take her lunch-break. Sanjay had agreed to cover for her but it would still leave them very short-staffed and she felt guilty about it. She decided that she would try to get through as much work as possible and just have a sandwich on the train.

By two o'clock Lisa had worked her way through a mound of paperwork and was ready to leave. She got up then paused as a thought struck her. Picking up the phone, she dialled Sarah Donnelly's number and left another message on the answering-machine. Maybe it would have no more effect than the last one had done but she couldn't bear to think of poor Liam lying in hospital with nobody to visit him over Christmas.

She went into the ward and wished everyone a happy Christmas then collected her coat and bag from the staff-room. It was still snowing when she reached the foyer and

she found herself wondering if it really was a good idea to
set off on a journey in such conditions. Maybe she should
phone James and tell him that the weather was too bad for
her to make the trip.

She sighed because she knew that she was looking for an
excuse not to go. And yet if she didn't go, what would she
do? Sit at home thinking about Will spending Christmas
with Rachel? Surely it was time that she got on with her
life as Will was doing?

Maybe she wasn't head over heels in love with James but
they could have a good marriage if she worked at it. Love
wasn't the be-all and end-all of a successful relationship.
Look how wonderful her friendship with Will had been. If
she could find a fraction of the happiness with James that
she had found with Will then their marriage would work
out perfectly fine.

She picked up her case and opened the door and if there
were tears in her eyes, she refused to wonder why. She
wasn't leaving Will, she was going to meet James. She
should be happy about it, not sad.

Will found that he was constantly watching the clock as the
morning wore on. With it being Christmas Eve there was
no elective surgery scheduled that day and time was hanging
rather heavily. He did his ward rounds, putting up a good
show of being full of Christmas spirit as he chatted to the
children and their parents.

Andrew Brown—the boy with the displaced epiphysis—
was very excited about the coming visit of Santa Claus
planned for the following morning. Will teased him about
it.

'I thought you told me that you didn't believe in Father
Christmas so what's happened? Have you changed your
mind?'

'Course not!' Andrew declared, his ears turning pink. 'But you have to pretend for the sake of the little ones, don't you? I mean, *they* still believe in him and it wouldn't be fair to spoil their fun.'

'Of course not,' Will replied gravely, exchanging an amused look with Andrew's mother. 'So, what are you hoping that Santa will bring you this year?'

'A snowboard,' Andrew said promptly. 'My best friend goes to the new snowdrome and he says it's wicked!'

'Good job we got that leg sorted out, then, isn't it?' Will declared. 'You'll be able to have snowboarding lessons once everything is properly healed up.'

'It won't cause any damage to Andrew's leg if he goes snowboarding, will it, Mr Saunders?' Mrs Brown put in quickly. 'I'd hate to think that he might injure himself again.'

'There's no need to worry about that,' Will assured her. 'The metal pins will keep the epiphysis in place and I doubt if even Andrew will be able to dislodge them this time.'

He clapped the boy on the shoulder and smiled at him. 'You leave Santa a letter tonight and tell him that you can have a snowboard with my blessing!'

He moved on as Andrew and his mother laughed. The ward was packed with visitors that day as parents arrived to see their children and make arrangements to bring in their presents the following day. The staff had done a wonderful job of decorating the ward with balloons and streamers. There was even a huge Christmas tree set up by the door and Will paused to admire it.

He sighed as he studied the glittering baubles and tinsel that adorned it. Normally he and Lisa bought a tree for the flat, but this year they hadn't bothered. She hadn't mentioned getting one and he hadn't seen any point, although undoubtedly Cameron would have arranged to have a tree and all the trimmings at the cottage. Cameron would want everything to be perfect, a celebration of their coming union.

The thought was so mind-numbingly painful that he had to take a deep breath. The thought of Lisa and Cameron spending the holiday planning for their future made him want to throw up. It was an effort to respond when one of the nurses came over to wish him a happy Christmas because Will knew that he was within a hair's breadth of losing control.

He quickly left the ward and made his way to his office, struggling to hide his impatience when Dave hailed him. He sincerely hoped he wasn't going to be presented with a major problem because he didn't feel up to dealing with it. All he could think about was Lisa and her coming trip to Derbyshire.

'Is something wrong?' he asked as Dave hurried over to him.

'Jilly's just phoned. She's stuck in snow the other side of Cartmel. She's tried phoning the breakdown service but they've been inundated with calls and don't know what time they'll be able to get out to her,' Dave explained worriedly. 'I want to go and fetch her but Roger Hopkins said to have a word with you first to make sure it was OK. Tim Jackson will cover for me but it could be half an hour before he gets here and I'd like to leave straight away.'

'It's fine by me.' Will assured him. 'Even if we have an emergency admission it would take some time before we got the patient to Theatre and Tim should have arrived by then.' He frowned. 'I didn't realise the snow was that bad.'

'Didn't you have any trouble getting here?' Dave sounded puzzled. 'It took me ages just to get the car off our drive and the roads were a nightmare. It took me twice as long as it normally does.'

'I stayed the night in my office so I didn't need to drive here this morning,' Will said shortly.

'I didn't know you'd been called out,' Dave exclaimed.

'I wasn't.'

'Then what on earth were you doing, sleeping in your office?' Dave sighed. 'Tell me to mind my own business if you want to, Will, but what exactly is going on? You've not been yourself for days now. Is it Rachel?'

'No, it has nothing whatsoever to do with Rachel.'

Suddenly Will didn't have the heart to lie. His feelings for Lisa were eating him up and he needed to tell somebody how he felt or he would go mad. 'Rachel was just a smoke-screen. It's Lisa I'm crazy about.'

Dave whistled. 'Well, you had me fooled all right. Although thinking about how you and Lisa looked the other night at the party, I don't know why I should be surprised. It was obvious there was something between you two. Even Jilly noticed it.'

'Lisa and I are just friends,' he denied tersely. 'At least that's the way she thinks about me.'

'And you're sure about that, are you?' Dave shrugged when he nodded. 'Well, I suppose you should know, Will. But Lisa didn't give the impression that she was totally indifferent to you the other night.'

'Then why is she going to spend Christmas with this guy? If Lisa felt anything for me, it's the last thing she'd do!' he exploded.

'Maybe she's doing it for the same reason that you let everyone think that Rachel was the woman you were interested in.'

Dave clapped him on the shoulder and grinned. 'Take it from me, Will, it's never easy to tell what is going on in a woman's mind. They don't think like we do, although I've a pretty good idea what Jilly will be thinking if I don't go and fetch her soon. I might just find myself wearing the Christmas pudding rather than eating it!'

Will laughed as Dave hurried away but it was hard to contain the excitement that was pouring through his veins all of a sudden. Was it possible that Dave was right?

His mind spun as he tried to deal with the idea, but it was simply too much to take in. He realised that he needed to see Lisa and find out the truth once and for all. He would never forgive himself if he lost her because he was too much of a coward to tell her the truth. He would tell her that he loved her and see what she said then.

Will went straight to the intensive care unit but there was no sign of Lisa when he got there. Angela was on the phone and Jackie Meredith was talking to Sanjay and Daniel Kennedy's parents. The rest of the staff must have gone for their breaks because there was nobody else around.

Will waited impatiently but he was getting a bad feeling all of a sudden. What was Sanjay doing here at this time of the day when he normally worked nights? Was he covering for Lisa? By the time Angela came out of the office he had worked himself into a real state and it was impossible to disguise the urgency in his voice.

'Where's Lisa? I need to speak to her.'

'I'm afraid she's already left,' Angela told him, frowning. 'Is something wrong, Will?'

'What time did she leave?' he demanded, ignoring the question.

'Just after two. She told me that she was catching the two-thirty to Bakewell,' Angela explained in bewilderment.

'You mean she's travelling by train and not by car?' he clarified.

'Apparently. Look, Will, if something has happened I wish you'd tell me…. Will? Will!'

Will didn't stop as he turned and raced along the corridor

It was fifteen minutes past two already but there was still a chance that he could catch Lisa if the train was late.

He took the stairs two at a time, ignoring the startled looks from the people he passed. There was no time to spare. He had to stop Lisa getting on that train. He had to tell her that he loved her before it was too late!

He reached the foyer, thanking heaven that he had his car keys in his pocket so didn't have to waste time going to his office to fetch them. His coat was upstairs but that didn't matter. He could put up with the cold and any discomfort if it meant he had a chance to stop Lisa making the biggest mistake of her life. Cameron couldn't love her as much as he did! He had to make her understand that.

He was actually opening the door when he heard his pager beeping and automatically stopped. He dug it out of his pocket and checked the display, feeling his heart sink when he saw that it was A and E trying to reach him. He couldn't ignore it and yet if he responded he wouldn't be able to stop Lisa getting on the train.

What should he do? Should he put Lisa and this last chance of happiness first? But if he did that, could he live with himself if a child died because he had failed to do his job? Whatever he decided, someone was going to lose out.

CHAPTER TWELVE

THE train had been delayed because of snow on the tracks. Lisa waited in the station café, hoping that it wouldn't be too long before it arrived. The more time that elapsed the more nervous she was becoming.

Was she doing the right thing? Should she marry James when she didn't love him? But if she didn't marry him, what was she going to do? How would she cope when Will married Rachel?

Tears stung her eyes and she picked up the cup of tea she'd bought from the buffet and forced herself to drink a little of the tepid liquid. She had to calm down and think things through calmly and rationally. That was what Will always made her do and it had worked in the past, but, then, nothing had seemed difficult with Will there to help her. How could she bear to live the rest of her life without him?

'Lisa! What a surprise to see you here.'

She looked up when she recognised Rachel's voice, feeling her heart sink because the last thing she needed at the moment was to have to make polite conversation. 'Hello, Rachel. How are you?'

'Fine, although I'll feel a lot better once the train arrives.' Rachel sighed as she sat down. 'I was supposed to be going to Manchester to do some shopping and the train's been delayed because of the snow. I knew I shouldn't have left everything until the last minute!'

'It's typical, isn't it?' Lisa smiled sympathetically. 'You should have got Will to take you there by car the other day. It would have been easier.'

'Nice idea but I've not seen him for ages, I'm afraid,' Rachel remarked, pulling off her woollen mittens.

'But I thought he'd been staying at your house since the staff party?'

Lisa could feel her heart starting to race all of a sudden. She saw Rachel grimace and frowned. What was going on? Why had Will told her he was staying with Rachel when it hadn't been true?

'Oops, I think I may have just put my foot in it,' Rachel admitted ruefully. 'I don't know what Will has told you, Lisa, but he hasn't been staying with me.'

'But I don't understand. Why would he lie to me?' she exclaimed.

'Maybe you should ask him that,' Rachel said carefully. She shrugged when Lisa looked at her. 'I'm sorry, Lisa, but it wouldn't be right for me to break a confidence. Will must have had his reasons for telling you he was staying with me but that is something you need to discuss with him. It's about time you two sorted this out.'

'Sorted what out? Look, Rachel, I'm not asking you to betray a confidence. I just don't understand what is going on. You say that you haven't seen Will in days and yet I thought you two were serious about each other?'

'Will and I have been out for one date,' Rachel told her gently. 'There's no question of us being serious about each other. Will knows that as well as I do.'

'Then why did he lead me to believe that you two were an item?' She shook her head because she couldn't seem to understand what Rachel was telling her. 'None of this makes sense.'

'Doesn't it? It does if you try hard enough to work it out, Lisa. Will is the most honest and open guy I've ever met so why would he lie to you about me? Why would he want you to think that we had something going for us? It's really obvious if you think about it.'

Rachel looked up as a voice came over the loudspeaker and announced that the Manchester train would be leaving from platform two in five minutes' time. 'That's my train. I'd better go. I'm meeting my niece and she'll be wondering what's happened to me.'

'She's feeling better, then?' she queried, her head reeling from trying to work out what Rachel had meant. 'Will told me that she wasn't well the night of the party.'

'Beth's fine, thank you.' Rachel sighed as she got up. 'I may as well come clean and confess that there was nothing wrong with her the other night. I just wanted to give you and Will the opportunity to talk to one another. Obviously, you didn't do that but it still isn't too late. Think about it. Have a great Christmas, Lisa.'

'You, too,' Lisa responded automatically. She picked up her cup then put it down again as she thought about what Rachel had said to her. It all seemed to come back to the same question of why Will would lie to her about his re-lationship. Why had he led her to believe that he was in love with Rachel when it patently wasn't true?

Because he had thought it better to lie rather than admit that he was in love with her?

Her breath caught because all of a sudden everything made sense. Will would lie if he thought it was for her own good. He wouldn't be happy about it but he would do it if it meant that she wouldn't get hurt. He had been acting very strangely ever since she'd told him about James's proposal, in fact, and the more she thought about it, the clearer it all became.

Will had lied rather than tell her how he really felt about her. He had only ever wanted her to be happy and if he believed that she would be happy marrying James then he would make sure that nothing stood in her way.

Lisa smiled as a feeling of intense joy flooded through her. She couldn't be happy without Will because she loved him, and she loved him not just as a friend but as a man. She'd sensed it was so a week ago but had deliberately closed her mind to the idea.

It had been too difficult to deal with it when she'd believed that Will had been in love with Rachel. Now there was no reason to shy away from the truth: she loved Will with all her heart and nothing was going to stop her telling him that. Whether he would admit how he felt was something she would have to face when the time came, but she was no longer prepared to lie to him or to herself.

The announcer's voice came over the loudspeaker again to say that the Bakewell train would be arriving shortly. Lisa stood up. There was one thing she needed to do first before she did anything else.

The snow had caused a pile-up on the bypass and three children had been injured on their way to a matinée performance of the yearly pantomime at the local repertory theatre. Will took the most seriously injured, a little girl with a very nasty head injury, into Theatre and set to work.

Surprisingly, Ray had been on time that day and he was in Theatre Two, pinning and plating a badly broken arm. It was a bad injury and Will had been in two minds about letting Ray do it. However, he had decided in the end that, as he couldn't be in two places at once, he had to trust him.

Morgan Grey was operating on the driver of one of the vehicles involved in the collision. Will knew it would be touch and go whether the young woman survived. The child he was operating on was apparently her daughter and he could only pray that the little girl wouldn't be left without

a mother at Christmas. It all added to his feeling of desolation. Lisa would have caught the train by now and he was
too late to stop her.

He worked steadily, removing the splinters of bone that
had been pushed inwards by the blow to the child's skull.
Although the little girl had been sitting in the rear of the
car she hadn't been wearing a seat belt. She had been cat-
apulted forward by the force of the collision and had hit her
head on the dashboard. There was extensive bleeding from
the blood vessels in the meninges—the membranes covering
the brain—so he dealt with that then covered the wound.

The child would need antibiotics to prevent the risk of
infection and close monitoring until she recovered consciousness so he sent her to the IC unit. Sanjay was there
to sort everything out even if Lisa wasn't. Lisa must be
almost at the cottage by now.

It was an effort to hide how devastated that thought made
him feel as he thanked the staff and left Theatre. Ray had
finished before him and was on his way out of the changing
room.

'Everything OK?' Will asked politely, holding the door
open for the younger man.

'Fine. It was a bit like putting together a jigsaw puzzle
but I got there in the end.' Ray suddenly sighed. 'It made
me realise why I went in for surgery, to be honest. You
derive a great deal of satisfaction from doing a job like that.'

'It isn't too late to change your mind, Ray. I still have
your letter of resignation on my desk and I can hold onto it
for a while longer.' He clapped Ray on the shoulder. 'Why
don't you think about it over Christmas and then let me
know what you want to do?'

'I'll do that,' Ray said slowly. 'Thanks, Will. I haven't
exactly made a sparkling impression since I arrived here and
I appreciate you giving me another chance.

'Don't mention it.'

He let the door swing to as Ray hurried away but that last comment had touched a chord. If only he could have another chance to tell Lisa how he felt, he most certainly wouldn't waste it!

It was pointless wishing for the impossible so he tried to put it out of his mind as he showered and changed. It was gone five by the time he finally left. The car park was ankle deep in snow and it took him ages to start his car because it had been standing in the cold for the past two days.

He got it going at last and drove home. He turned off the engine and took a deep breath because he wasn't looking forward to going into the empty flat. The thought of spending the next two days there on his own, thinking about Lisa and Cameron at the cottage together, was almost more than he could stand. How could he bear to think about her and another man?

His heart felt like lead as he got out of the car and went inside. He unlocked the front door and stepped into the hall then froze. He could hear music playing and see that there were lights on in the sitting room. What the hell was going on?

Warily, he made his way along the hall and peered into the sitting room, stopping dead at the sight that met him. For a moment he wondered if he was dreaming as his eyes skimmed over the paper chains and streamers, the tinsel and balloons which adorned the room. His gaze finally alighted on the Christmas tree standing in front of the window and he swallowed. Where had all this come from?

'Will! I didn't hear you coming in. What perfect timing. I was just about to start decorating the tree and now you can help me.'

Will spun round and seriously thought he was going to pass out when he saw Lisa standing in the hall, smiling at him. What on earth was she doing here when she was supposed to be at the cottage with Cameron?

'What are you doing here?' he demanded hoarsely. 'Why aren't you at the cottage?'

'Because I wanted to spend Christmas here with you.'

She smiled at him and his heart began to race when he saw the expression in her eyes. Lisa was looking at him in a way that she had never looked at him before and he was almost afraid to believe what his brain was telling him. It was an effort to concentrate when she continued.

'Christmas is all about spending time with the people you love, and I love you, Will. I really do.'

Lisa felt a wave of tenderness wash over her as she saw the shock on Will's face. That announcement was bound to have come as a surprise to him but once he had time to think about what she'd said, he would be fine. She felt better than she'd felt in ages, in all honesty. She was suddenly able to think clearly and it was such a relief after the past two weeks of confusion.

'You love me?'

'Mmm, that's right. I know it's difficult to understand why I should after the way you lied to me about Rachel, but I'll forgive you. I'm sure you must have had your reasons,' she said gently.

'Who said I lied?' he asked tersely, running a trembling hand through his hair.

'Me.'

She took a slow step towards him, hiding her smile when he backed away. 'You lied rather than tell me how you feel, didn't you? You decided it would be easier if you let me think you were in love with Rachel and that way I'd marry James and live happily ever after.'

She shook her head as she took another step and this time

he didn't back up. 'Sorry, but that's not how it works, I'm afraid. I can't live happily unless you're there with me, Will.'

'I... You... Oh, hell!'

Reaching out, he yanked her into his arms and enveloped her in a bear hug. Lisa closed her eyes, feeling her heart fill with joy. Will loved her. He really did. Now all he had to do was tell her that then they could start getting on with their lives.

'I love you so much,' he grated. 'I was so scared when you told me about Cameron.'

His voice broke and she held him tighter, feeling her eyes fill with tears as she realised what he must have been going through in the past two weeks. 'I'm so sorry, my darling. I never meant to hurt you like that. I just didn't realise how I felt, you see.'

She reached up and framed his face between her hands. 'I love you, Will Saunders, and it's you I want to spend the rest of my life with if you'll have me.'

He didn't say anything as he bent and kissed her but there was a world of promise in the way his mouth took hers so gently and so tenderly, so lovingly. He drew back and looked deep into her eyes and Lisa felt her emotions spill over when she saw the depth of his love for her.

'I shall love and cherish you until the day I die, Lisa. You mean everything to me. I think I fell in love with you right from the beginning but I would never admit to myself how I felt because it wouldn't have been right.'

'You mean because of Gareth?' She sighed when he nodded. She pressed a kiss to the corner of his mouth then smiled at him. 'I loved Gareth very much, Will, but what I felt for him bears no resemblance to what I feel for you.'

'What do you mean?' he said uncertainly.

'That I met Gareth at a time in my life when I desperately

needed to love someone and be loved in return,' she explained gently. 'Losing my mother like that was very hard for me to deal with and Gareth helped me through it. I transferred all my feelings to him and that's why I was so devastated when he died and why I fell apart the way I did. Now I know that my feelings for him were nowhere near as deep as the ones I have for you.'

She reached up and kissed him on the mouth. She felt him shudder and smiled. 'Now, do you want to continue this conversation or shall we find another way to convince each other how we feel?'

He laughed softly. 'What did you have in mind, exactly?'

'Oh, I'm pretty sure you can guess what I'm thinking, Will. You always could read my mind.'

She laughed up at him then felt the laughter dying on her lips when she saw the way he was looking at her with such hunger, such need. Her heart was racing when he lifted her into his arms and carried her from the room. He took her into his bedroom and laid her down on the bed, and his eyes were full of so much tenderness and love that tears ran down her face.

'I love you, Lisa,' he whispered as he bent to brush his lips over hers. 'You are my whole world. The only thing I want from life is to make you happy.'

'And I'll be happy so long as I have you, Will.' She kissed him back, loving him with her eyes, wanting him to know how much he meant to her. 'You've been the best friend anyone could have had, but I'm greedy. I want more. I want you to be my lover as well as my friend.'

'Then, my lady, your wish shall be granted.'

He kissed her again only this time with so much passion that her heart melted. Wrapping her arms around his neck she gave herself up to the sheer joy and magic of being loved by him.

He drew back and smiled when she murmured a protest. 'I'm not going anywhere. I just want to get out of this coat.'

'Oh!' Lisa gasped, then laughed as she realised that he was still wearing his outdoor clothes.

He unzipped his coat and tossed it onto the chair then shed his jacket and tie. He sat down on the side of the bed and pulled her upright. 'Your turn now.'

Grasping the hem of her apricot sweater, he tugged it over her head and tossed it onto the chair. Lisa felt her heart race almost out of control when she saw the desire in his eyes as he looked at her sitting there in just a lacy bra.

Bending, he pressed his mouth to her breast and she cried out when she felt his tongue rasping against her nipple. She closed her eyes, struggling to contain the sudden flare of longing that flowed through her as he turned his attention to her other breast and lavished it with the same attention, but it was impossible to deal with the way it made her feel to have Will loving her this way.

She twined her arms around his neck and drew his head down to her, arching her back in ecstasy as he kissed her breasts again then reached behind her to unfasten the hook of her bra. Slowly, with the utmost delicacy, he drew the straps down her arms until the wisp of lace fell away and she was sitting before him naked from the waist up.

'You are so beautiful, Lisa,' he whispered, and she felt her heart spill over with love when she heard the awe in his voice.

'You're beautiful, too, Will,' she replied, reaching out to undo the buttons on his shirt. She undid one then two then found her hands had started to tremble so much that she couldn't deal with the third.

Will pressed a kiss to her mouth then unceremoniously dragged the shirt over his head and tossed it aside. 'Is this better?' he asked roughly, taking hold of her hands and placing them, palms down, against his warm, hair-roughened chest.

'Much,' Lisa whispered, her breath catching. She slid her hands experimentally over his chest then stopped and bit her lip. Being given this licence to touch him suddenly scared her because it made her see how close she had come to losing him. If she'd got on that train today, she wouldn't be here now. The thought was almost too much to bear.

'What's wrong, sweetheart? Tell me.'

His hand was so gentle as he tilted her face, his voice so full of love that tears welled from her eyes again. 'I was just thinking how close I came to losing you. If I'd got on the train…' She couldn't go on as emotion overwhelmed her.

Will drew her into his arms and cradled her against him and she could hear the ache in his voice.

'Don't even think about it! I was on my way to the station to beg you not to go when I had a call from A and E. I don't know how I made myself turn round and respond to it.'

'You were coming to find me?' she asked incredulously.

'Yes. I wanted to tell you the truth about how I felt, you see.' He sighed as he wiped away her tears. 'I had no idea if it would achieve anything but I couldn't bear to let you go without telling you that I loved you.'

'Oh, Will! We've been such idiots, haven't we? Both of us were trying not to hurt the other and yet that's what we almost ended up doing.'

'But it was "almost". We came to our senses in the end.'

'Yes, and thank heaven that we did. It would have been the biggest mistake of my life if I'd gone to the cottage.' She kissed him tenderly then smiled into his eyes. 'I phoned James and explained everything to him. He was very nice about it, too.'

'Mmm, if that's an attempt to convince me that Cameron deserves my sympathy, I'm not sure it's going to work. He's put me through hell in the last couple of weeks with that proposal of his!'

'Now, Will, it's not like you to be unkind.' She kissed him again and sighed. 'One of the things I love most about you is the concern you always show to other people.'

'What other things do you love?' he said, grinning at her in a way that made her heart race.

'Well, you're good-tempered and very easy to get on with. The fact that you just happen to be extremely handsome also goes in your favour.'

'So you think I'm handsome, do you? Good. What else?'

She rolled her eyes but there was something rather delicious about playing this game with him when she knew how it was going to end. 'You're good company and never boring. You know how to cook and—'

'Mmm, I think that's more than enough. We'll stop right there.' He pressed her back against the pillows and his eyes were filled with love as he looked down at her.

'You've convinced me that you are a woman of taste, Lisa. It would be a shame to waste any more time discussing my virtues when I have a much better idea how to utilise it.'

Lisa closed her eyes as he bent towards her. She gave a little sigh of contentment when she felt his lips find hers. Will was right because it would be a shame to waste the night talking when they could spend it loving each other.

He hadn't realised it was possible to be this happy!

Will smiled as he looked down at Lisa, lying beside him. She was fast asleep and for a moment he allowed himself the simple delight of watching her. Their love-making had been everything he could have dreamt it would be. Being able to show Lisa how he felt had been so marvellous that there weren't words to describe it. He knew that he would never forget how she had responded to him so sweetly and joyously.

Her eyelids suddenly flickered and he bent and kissed her gently on the mouth. 'Happy Christmas, sweetheart.'

'Happy Christmas to you, too,' she murmured sleepily. She dragged her hand through her tousled hair and yawned. 'What time is it?'

'Just gone eight.' He rolled her over so they were facing each other and kissed the tip of her nose. 'So how do you feel this morning? Do you still love me?'

'Mmm, I'm not sure…' She gasped when he tickled her ribs. 'OK, I give in! Yes, I love you. I love you heaps and heaps and then a whole lot more. Is that what you wanted to hear?'

'Yep. So long as you promise to start each day by telling me that you love me, I'll be satisfied,' he assured her.

'That's a very easy promise to make and stick to.' She kissed him lightly on the mouth then smiled at him. 'I don't think I shall ever grow tired of telling you that I love you, Will.'

'Me, too,' he whispered, pulling her close. He sighed as he nuzzled her hair. 'I'm so happy that it hurts, Lisa. I feel as though I want to shout it from the rooftops and tell everyone what's happened. I want the whole world to know that you're mine!'

'It's such a wonderful feeling, isn't it? And it's even better that it should have happened at Christmas. It makes it even more special in a funny sort of way.'

'It does.' He kissed her lightly on the lips then tossed back the quilt.

'Where are you going?' she demanded, leaning up on one elbow to watch him.

'I'm getting your present, of course.' He opened the dresser drawer and took out the box containing the necklace, feeling a lump come to his throat. He'd never believed he would actually give her this gift and it was unbearably poignant to be able to do so.

'Happy Christmas, darling,' he said softly, placing the box in her hands.

She opened the lid and he saw the delight on her face as she lifted out the necklace. 'Will, it's just gorgeous! I love it. Here, help me put it on.'

She turned so that he could fasten the clasp around her neck then slipped out of bed and went to the mirror to look at it. Will felt his body surge to life as he watched her standing there wearing nothing but the exquisite golden chain.

He got up and put his arms around her, dropping a kiss on the nape of her neck as he held her against him and let her see the effect she was having on him.

'I'm glad you like it. I wasn't sure if it would be right to give it to you, which is why I hid it away in the drawer.'

'Because you had no idea how I felt about you?' She turned in his arms and slid her arms around his waist. 'I love you, Will. I just wish I had a present like this for you. It would be a token of how I feel about you.'

'I don't need presents, Lisa,' he told her roughly. 'I don't need anything at all now that I have you. You are all I could ever want.'

There was no stopping the passion that claimed them once again. Will carried her back to bed and their love-making was just as wonderful as it had been the night before. They stayed in each other's arms a long time and might never have got up if the phone hadn't started ringing.

Will grimaced as he reached for the receiver. 'I hope this isn't a call to say I'm needed.'

He listened intently for a few minutes then sighed as he hung up. 'Do you want the good news first or the bad?'

'Mmm, the good, I think, although I honestly don't believe that anything really bad can happen on a wonderful day like this,' she declared, smiling at him with her heart in her eyes.

Will kissed her softly, loving her so much that it hurt. 'I know exactly what you mean and it really isn't anything terrible. But the good news first is that Sarah Donnelly came in to visit Liam last night and stayed. She told Sanjay that she'd left her husband. Apparently the police are going to prosecute him for what he did to the child. Sarah intends to find a place for her and Liam to live once he's well enough to leave hospital. Evidently, he's a lot better this morning so it just goes to show how powerful a force love is.'

'Oh, that's just brilliant news! I'm so pleased for him. Having his mum there with him will make all the difference.' Lisa smiled at him. 'OK, now to the bad bit. Come on, I can take it.'

'The little girl I operated on last night is giving them cause for concern,' he explained. 'Sanjay was very apologetic about it but he wants me to take another look at her.'

'Then you have to go,' she said firmly. She kissed him quickly then tossed back the quilt. 'I'll make some coffee while you shower.'

'I hate to leave you like this,' he began.

'Will, it doesn't matter!' She smiled at him and there was a world of love in her eyes. 'If you have to go into work, I understand. Your job is all part of the package that is Will Saunders and I wouldn't change a thing. Now, you go and do what you have to and I'll see what we've got for lunch. I'm afraid that turkey is off the menu, though. I remembered the tree but not much else!'

'I don't care what we eat so long as we're together,' he told her because it was true.

'In that case, you won't be disappointed with beans on toast,' she said, laughing at him.

Will watched her hurrying towards the kitchen then took a deep breath as the full enormity of what had happened suddenly hit him. It didn't matter how long he was gone because Lisa would be here, waiting for him, when he got back.

They would be spending Christmas at home this year. Together.

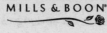

MILLS & BOON

Live the emotion

Medical
romance™

THE MIDWIFE'S CHRISTMAS MIRACLE
by Sarah Morgan

It was a miracle he'd found her – freezing cold and alone in the snow. With nowhere else to go, Miranda Harding finds herself spending a magical Christmas Day with her disturbingly attractive rescuer, Jake. Consultant Jake Blackwell gets a shock the next day, when Miranda appears as the new midwife in his O&G department…and it is startlingly obvious she is six months pregnant!

ONE NIGHT TO WED by Alison Roberts

Dr Felicity Slade has come to the small coastal town of Morriston for a quieter life – and to distance herself from gorgeous paramedic Angus McBride. When Angus turns up as part of a medical response team her feelings are thrown into confusion. It becomes clear to Angus that this is his last chance – his one night to prove that he is the right man for Felicity…

A VERY SPECIAL PROPOSAL by Josie Metcalfe

Privileged doctor Amy Willmot has never forgotten her crush on Zachary Bowman – the boy with the worst reputation in town… Returning home, she cannot believe her eyes when she is introduced to the new A&E doctor – it's Zach! Can Amy persuade Zach to look past their backgrounds, and convince him that love really can conquer all?

On sale 1st December 2006

Available at WHSmith, Tesco, ASDA, Borders, Eason, Sainsbury's and most bookshops

www.millsandboon.co.uk

MILLS & BOON®

1106/03b

Live the emotion

Medical romance™

THE SURGEON'S MEANT-TO-BE BRIDE
by Amy Andrews

Nurse Harriet Remy and her surgeon husband Guillaume thought they had the perfect marriage. Then Harriet's fertility came under threat and her subsequent desire for a baby came between them. After a year apart, Gill still adores his wife, and on a final overseas aid mission with her, decides this will also become a mission to save their marriage – and keep his wife by his side…for ever.

A FATHER BY CHRISTMAS by Meredith Webber

Neonatologist Sophie Fisher is bowled over by her new boss's strength and kindness. She hasn't yet told Gib that Thomas, the little boy in her care, is actually her nephew, and that she is trying to find his father. Gib is dedicated to his patients and not looking for love – though there is something about Sophie that is changing his mind. Then he makes a discovery about Thomas…

A MOTHER FOR HIS BABY by Leah Martyn

Dr Brady McNeal is hoping a new life for him and his tiny son will be just what they need, and the Mount Pryde Country Practice seems like a small slice of heaven – especially when he finds that he is working with GP Jo Rutherford. The attraction between Brady and Jo is undeniable. Soon Brady is wishing that Jo had a more permanent role in his life…

On sale 1st December 2006

Available at WHSmith, Tesco, ASDA, Borders, Eason, Sainsbury's and most bookshops

www.millsandboon.co.uk

All you could want for Christmas!

Meet handsome and seductive men under the mistletoe, escape to the world of Regency romance or simply relax by the fire with a heartwarming tale by one of our bestselling authors. These special stories will fill your holiday with Christmas sparkle!

On sale 6th October 2006

On sale 20th October 2006

*On sale
3rd November
2006*

On sale 17th November 2006

*On sale
1st December
2006*

*Available at
WHSmith, Asda,
Tesco and all
good bookshops*

www.millsandboon.co.uk

M&B

**Enjoy the
dazzling
glamour of
Vienna on the
eve of the First
World War…**

Rebellious Alex Faversham dreams of escaping her
stifling upper-class Victorian background. She yearns
to be like her long-lost Aunt Alicia, the beautiful black
sheep of the family who lives a glamorous life abroad.

Inspired, Alex is soon drawn to the city her aunt
calls home — Vienna. Its heady glitter and seemingly
everlasting round of balls and parties in the years before
WW1 is as alluring as she had imagined, and Alex finds
romance at last with Karl von Winkler, a hussar in the
Emperor's guard. But, like the Hapsburg Empire, her
fledgling love affair cannot last. Away from home and
on the brink of war, will Alex ever see England
or her family again?

On sale 3rd November 2006

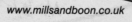